# The Path TO LOVING Him

# MEGHAN QUINN

# Prologue

## RYLAND

"I can see the vein in your forehead pulsing," Abel, my best friend, says as he lifts his stout to his lips. I watch his eyes stay fixated on me, in that examining way he does so well as he takes a pull. "Kind of scary, man."

I lean back in my chair and twist my glass of beer, staring down at the amber liquid.

MacKenzie, my niece, who I have custody of, is with my sister Aubree and her husband, Wyatt, at the farmhouse playing horsey. I know this because I've received several pictures from Aubree of Wyatt being combed, brushed, and saddled up. Seeing his grown ass with flowers in his hair and a collar around his neck is the only reason I haven't broken the glass in my hand.

"Not in the mood," I say as I take a large chug of my beer.

"I can sense that." He lifts one of my untouched fries from my plate and pops it in his mouth. "I have to say, your company this evening has been unmatched."

I eye him. "Do you think poking the bear is going to help?"

"I mean, when you first arrived, you stated you wouldn't be talking about your day. You huffed. You grumbled. And then you shoved your cheeseburger in your mouth without a word. I've continued to bother you with snide, sarcastic comments, and I feel like I'm right on the edge, almost getting you to tip over and tell me what's been bothering you." He waggles his brows. "I'm right, aren't I? You're ready to spill."

"Fuck you."

"A-ha!" He points at me with a large grin. "I knew it, you're ready." He sets his beer down and leans his arms on the table. Batting his lashes like a fucking moron, he says, "Go ahead, big boy, tell me what's going on."

I shake my head, annoyed with my best friend, but I also know he won't let this go. So I stare at my glass of beer as I say, "The newest school board member has decided that I shouldn't be involved in hiring my assistant coach."

Abel's expression morphs into confusion. "Wait, so as the head baseball coach for the high school, who has brought the team to a state championship win, who is *also* bringing interest from colleges all around the country, you won't be involved in hiring your own assistant? Tell me how that makes sense."

"It fucking doesn't," I grumble. "But this fucker who thinks he knows what's best for the program thinks I need to step away from the process since I'm already too involved in the program."

"Uh . . ." Abel blinks. "Because you're the fucking head coach."

"I know," I practically shout. People around us turn in our direction. Lowering my voice, I say, "It's all fucking politics at this point. The guy has no experience in managing a baseball team and what goes into it, nor does he even have a child in the school district."

"What?" Abel asks. "How the fuck was he elected to the school board?"

"Money," I say. "And boredom. The guy probably has nothing else better to do with his life than fuck with mine."

"Who is it?"

"David Ganbear," I answer. "Just moved into town. And somehow was able to infiltrate. Not sure how the fuck that happened but it did." I drag my hand over my face in frustration. "They had a bunch of interviews today, and from what I've heard, they think they found their person."

"Jesus," Abel says. "When you first got here and I saw your mood, I thought it was because you're often just irritated, but I'll hand it to you. You have the right to be angry." He tilts his drink in my direction as a nod, then takes another drink.

"Thank you?" I say in question, unsure if I should take that as a compliment or not.

"You're welcome." Abel smirks at me. "Now that you've shared, I think I have a solution for you."

"If it's to walk up to David Ganbear and introduce him to my fist, I've already considered the option, but given I need to think about Mac and how my actions affect her, I ended that thought rather quickly."

"Smart, but that's not what I was going to suggest."

I raise a brow. "If that's not your suggestion, then what is?"

"Easy," he says with a grin. "You need to take out that energy elsewhere. You need to hook up with someone."

I roll my eyes. "Jesus, Abel. You're a well-respected doctor in town, and you're suggesting frat boy-type behavior?"

"As your personal doctor who is concerned with the color of your balls, I'm simply prescribing a way to take care of yourself other than using your hand."

I shake my head. "And this is exactly why I should have gone out with Hayes instead. He would have sat here in silence with me, letting me stew."

Hayes Farrow is our other best friend and my sister Hattie's boyfriend. We used to be enemies, and when he started dating my sister, I thought I was going to murder him, but we resolved our differences, and even though I hate to admit it at times, I'm glad he's back in my life.

Abel presses his hand to his chest. "When you say things like that, it hurts."

"You deserve it when you offer stupid ideas."

"Finding someone to help you dispel this pent-up anger and

energy . . . that's stupid? Pretty sure if I asked anyone what you should do, given your situation and how . . . backed up you are, they'd suggest the same thing."

"Who's to say I'm that backed up?" I ask.

He folds his arms across his chest and stares me down. "You have not once looked at a woman since Cassidy passed and you took guardianship of Mac. Don't even tell me I'm wrong."

He's not.

He's absolutely right.

And my celibacy started months before that, when Cassidy got her cancer diagnosis with only months to live. I went into protective mode like I've always done. I set aside everything in my life, did the bare minimum to make sure my responsibilities were taken care of, and then put all my focus on my dying sister and her daughter.

And now with Mac being my number one responsibility, my needs, well, they've been put on the back burner.

"See, you have no response because you know I'm right." He nudges my shoulder. "Come on, let's go to the bar and see if we can find you someone. Aubree and Wyatt have Mac taken care of."

I shake my head. "I'm not about to just go do it with some townie. That shit would stay with me."

"Then let's see if we can find someone from out of town."

I roll my eyes. "In a small town? Yeah, good luck with that."

"Never know until we try," Abel says as he stands and tugs on my arm, pulling me up with him.

"What the hell are you doing?"

"Doing something I should have done a while ago."

# Chapter One

GABBY

"I can't even believe he wasn't there," I say to Bower as I pick at a bowl of nuts in front of me.

"He wasn't?"

"No," I say on a huff. "Couldn't even bother showing up. You would think he should be there, but nope. And I was so thrown off that I totally botched the entire thing."

"You probably think that, but I bet it went well."

"Trust me, Bower, it didn't." I slouch on my barstool and down the rest of my second vodka and lime. Yup, hitting up the hard stuff tonight.

After that embarrassment of an interview, I need it.

"What makes you think it didn't go well?"

"Well, to start, I tripped walking into the room, sending myself straight into the wall."

She snorts, just as expected, but follows it by saying, "I'm sorry. I don't mean to laugh."

"I ran into the wall so hard that I bent my finger back and nearly broke the stupid thing. It's really sore."

"Well, at least you didn't break it, as that would have made the interview even worse."

I toss a cashew in my mouth and wave down the bartender, asking for another drink. I plan on walking back to the inn with wobbly legs and a fuzzy head. Anything to help me forget today and the shot that I completely blew.

Ugh.

It's not very often that women get the chance to break into the field of men's sports. And this was it for me, an opportunity to start over—to procure a teaching job at the school and possibly assist the men's baseball team—but one trip into the wall sent that idea tumbling away faster than I could say "ouch."

And I needed this.

I needed it bad.

With my brother still in the minor leagues, I'm helping him pay his bills while he waits for that big break, and since there were budget cuts at my last school, this was an opportunity of a lifetime.

That meant sucking up my pride and returning to Almond Bay after leaving for three years. Did I grow up in the small coastal town? No. But did I move here when I found out that the high school had one of the best baseball programs in the state? Absolutely. I kept my distance, though.

I worked a job up north at a roadside pub with a flexible schedule so I could catch Bennett's games and also have time to earn my degree in teaching. I was easily the oldest graduate.

From the outfield, I watched Bennett play while I studied. We shared a studio apartment, and while I spent late nights at the bar, he worked on his dream of becoming a professional baseball player, a dream I know will come true. A dream that we have both sacrificed for.

But it's taking longer than we expected. I assumed he would have been called up by now, but he hasn't, and well, the money is drying up, hence this job.

Also why the vodka I'm drinking is what I used to drink in high school because it was all I could afford.

"Are you going to come back home tomorrow?"

"Yeah," I mumble. "Since the interview ran late, I didn't think it would be best to come home tonight. Thanks for the coupon for the free night at the inn. It came in clutch."

"That's what I'm here for, saving you money through online surveys."

Bower is the master at an online survey. She fills them out while watching shows at night and ends up with a whole bunch of free things. I don't have the patience . . . or the time for that matter.

"Also, you can always pick up some shifts at the Olive Garden. My dad said he'd take you on whenever you need it."

That's the last thing I want to do, but it looks like I might not have a choice after today's pitiful showing.

"Thanks." I sigh. "Might have to take you up on that." The bartender hands me another drink, and my mind starts to get that fuzzy feeling, just what I was looking for. I take a large gulp of my drink, and just as I set it down, the door to the bar opens, and a very familiar yet rugged face appears.

I feel every muscle in my body stiffen as a set of mossy-green eyes scan the bar . . . passing right over me.

Ryland Rowley.

"Holy shit," I say quietly into the phone.

"What?" Bower says as my eyes shamelessly scan Ryland, who seems to be encouraged by his friend behind him to keep walking forward.

He . . . he's even more attractive than I remember.

Broad shoulders, boulder-like biceps tugging on his shirt-sleeves, and pecs perfectly defined by the fabric pulling across them. His height towers over the patrons in the bar, while his dark stare gives the feeling he's not one to mess with. And his forearms are ripped and defined, all the way to his large hands. Hands that instinctively curl ever so slightly, almost like he's always gripping something . . . or ready to throw a punch. Well-worn jeans encase his long legs, and his tapered waist, along with the rest of his chest, gives the impression that he might not play baseball anymore, but that hasn't stopped him from continuing to make some gains in the gym.

I remember the first time I laid eyes on Ryland Rowley. I was . . . I was awestruck. He was fit, attractive, at times . . . mesmerizing, and he was my brother's coach. All of Bennett's other coaches have been much older, like they've seen their fair share of days out on the field. Ryland was a different breed. He was fresh and innovative but with a dark stare that could make you faint if he locked eyes with you.

And he treated Bennett differently. Not only did he teach him how to improve upon his already established talent but he also taught him how to be an adult. How to take responsibility on and off the field. And he gave Bennett the opportunity he needed to be seen by scouts, which led to him being drafted right out of high school.

Now that he's standing a few feet away, I'm still experiencing that awestruck feeling, but there's a mask over it this time.

A mask of indifference because he . . . he didn't show up.

"What's going on?" Bower shouts into the phone, pulling me out of my reverie.

"He just walked in."

"Who just walked in?" Bower asks.

Whispering now, I say, "Ryland."

"He just walked into the bar? Nooooo. Put me on FaceTime. I have something to say to him."

"I'm not putting you on—oh shit, he's coming over here." I straighten up, and for some reason, look around for something to hide behind.

"Perfect, this is your opportunity."

Coming up short, I consider putting my hand in front of my face. "My opportunity for what?"

"For telling him off."

"Have you lost your mind? I'm not telling him off." I spot my cocktail napkin and consider unfolding it and draping it over my head, but that might draw more attention.

"Why not? He deserves it."

Unable to deal with Bower as Ryland approaches, I say, "I . . . I have to go." I hang up the phone and cross one leg over the other just as Ryland approaches the chair next to me.

Be cool.

Act nonchalant.

Don't embarrass yourself.

Chin held high, I mentally prepare for him to recognize me and to ask me how Bennett is doing, in which my retort will be, great because of my coaching.

Is that telling him off?

Maybe I could be more snappy about it. I could channel my inner Bower.

Tell Ryland that Bennett's great because of my coaching, something you will never have the privilege of seeing.

That seems more like Bower.

God, why am I even trying to channel her?

Maybe because I'm slightly tipsy and irritated. Not a great combination.

Ryland and his friend move in and stop right in front of me. I lift my glass, and as Ryland makes eye contact with me, I take a sip of my drink.

He clears his throat, and I prepare my onslaught of distaste.

He ruffles his hair and says, "Uh, is anyone sitting here?" He points at the bar seat beside me as his friend sits down.

I swallow the liquid in my mouth and tilt my head to the side. "You're asking if the seat next to me is taken?"

His brow creases. "Yeah . . ."

I repeat, "You're asking me"—I point at my chest—"if the seat is taken?"

"Uh . . . yeah . . ." he draws out, looking more confused than ever, and that's when it hits me.

Oh my God.

He has no idea who I am.

Absolutely zero idea.

Which just makes this entire day . . . feel like it's coming full circle.

Yup. Like this moment is the cherry on top of the shit cake that is my day.

He not only didn't show up to the interview, but he doesn't know who I am, it's just so . . . insulting.

Turning away from him, I say, "No, it's all yours."

"Thanks," he says as he takes it and then turns toward his friend, where they bicker about what to get to drink.

Wow.

Just wow.

I pick up my phone and text Bower.

**Gabby:** *He has no idea who I am.*

Thankfully, she texts me right back.

**Bower:** *Are you sure?*

**Gabby:** *Positive. Zero recognition in his eyes. Took the seat next to mine and turned away from me. Completely clueless. Just goes to show how self-involved he is. Can't show up for an interview and now can't even recognize the sister to one of his best baseball players ever. Frankly, I'm embarrassed for him.*

**Bower:** *Are you? Or are you mad?*

**Gabby:** *Embarrassed.*

**Bower:** *Liar.*

**Gabby:** *Fine, yes, I might be a little mad. Irritated. Like this all has to be some sort of sick joke.*

**Bower:** *Maybe it is . . . which means you should probably get in on the joke.*

**Gabby:** *What the hell is that supposed to mean?*

**Bower:** *I don't know . . . make a move.*

**Gabby:** *What? Have you lost your mind?*

**Bower:** *Perhaps. But instead of being all bitter and angry and picking through cashews, maybe . . . maybe just have some fun before you leave.*

**Gabby:** *Are you suggesting I hook up with Ryland Rowley?*

**Bower:** *Yeah.*

**Gabby:** *Yup, you've lost your mind.*

**Bower:** *No, I haven't. Listen, you said it yourself, you didn't get the job. You're coming back home tomorrow. You'll probably never return to Almond Bay, so you might as well have some fun before you leave.*

*Gabby: I'm not doing that.*

*Bower: Not to mention, I can recall the many times you told me how hot the man was. How many lewd jokes we shared about you playing with his \*wiggles eyebrows\* baseball bat.*

*Gabby: I beg you not to repeat that ever again.*

*Bower: Oh, I forgot the balls too. \*clears throat\* Remember all the times you told me you wanted to play with HIS bat and balls?*

*Gabby: I truly dislike you at the moment.*

*Bower: Come on, just do it. You know you want to.*

*Gabby: Not happening.*

*Bower: Chicken.*

I grind my teeth together. Bower's getting on my nerves. She knows me way too damn well to know I hate that term . . . chicken. I hate it with everything in me. Because I am anything but a chicken. I took risks my entire life. I've worked tirelessly to keep Bennett and me together—*throughout foster care days and beyond*. Even if it meant the foster care parents got the government payments without keeping Bennett. I've kept us alive. Fed. That took guts.

Strength.

I am *not* a chicken.

*Gabby: Don't call me that. You know better.*

*Bower: I know, I'm sorry. But come on, Gabby. You've always told me how hot he is. You'll never see him again . . . ever. Might as well fulfill a fantasy for one night and then leave, head held high. Rock his world and leave him begging for so much more.*

I move my lips back and forth. Well, when she puts it like that . . .

# Chapter Two

RYLAND

I'm uncomfortable.

And the moment the bartender hands me my drink, I down it in one large gulp, the alcohol stinging all the way down my throat. When I set the glass down and turn toward Abel, I find him holding his drink halfway to his mouth, staring at me with a bewildered look.

"Do that again, and I'm not sure you're going to get it up to even have some fun."

I grab a napkin and wipe my mouth.

"Can you keep your fucking voice down?" I whisper.

"Sorry," he whispers back. "Didn't know you were so shy."

"I'm not shy. I just . . . I don't need people hearing my business."

"You don't want people knowing about the possible chance of a flaccid penis tonight?" he says in a controlled, low voice.

My eyes narrow at my friend. "There will be no flaccid penis."

"Ah, so we're expecting a full erection. How exciting."

"Jesus fuck," I mumble as I press my palm to my eye, trying to rub away the migraine that's forming from his idiotic plan.

I don't even know why I followed Abel here.

Pretty sure it wasn't me that followed and more like my dick that did the walking.

Because fuck, it's been a while.

A really long time and now that I'm already a few drinks in, I told Aubree I wasn't driving home tonight because I don't drink and drive, meaning she can take care of Mac while I can . . . well, I guess I have two choices. I can find someone to hook up with and get Abel off my case while simultaneously solving the issue of my pent-up tension. Or I can go home with Abel tonight, sleep on his couch, and regret going out the following morning.

"You look distressed. Should I get you another drink if you promise to drink it slowly?" Abel asks.

"Sure, and while you're at it, can you order me a new friend as well?"

He presses his hand to his chest. "You know, when you say things like that, it really hurts."

I roll my eyes just as there's a tap on my shoulder.

I turn on my barstool and come face to face with a woman.

Not just any woman though . . . the woman who I immediately saw when we walked into the bar.

Platinum-blond hair, freckles splattered across her nose, and rosy cheeks . . . and now that I'm seeing her up close, the prettiest pair of eyes I've ever fucking seen. One blue and one green, both highlighted by mascara-coated eyelashes.

Jesus.

Not to mention . . . curves.

From what I can see, amazing curves.

"You know, it's rude to sit next to someone and not introduce yourself," she says with a confidence I'm jealous of.

From under the bar counter, I feel Abel kick my leg, encouraging me to turn.

So I do.

"Sorry, I didn't intend to be rude."

"What did you intend, then?" she asks as she leans one elbow against the bar counter and rests her head against her hand.

Jesus, she's so hot.

Swallowing and attempting to find my cool, I say, "Find a place for my friend to sit because he has fragile legs."

She grins. "Well, in that case, I should praise you for being a good friend."

Abel slides my drink in front of me and pats me on the back. Then I feel him leave, just like that. He's not even going to feel out the situation with me. That means I'll never hear the end of it if this doesn't go the way he's planning.

I take my drink in my hand but don't sip it, not yet.

"I like to think that I am."

"Well, now that your friend seems to have rested his legs and is sneaking out of the bar, do you care to introduce yourself?"

I hold out my hand. "I'm Ryland."

"Ryland, nice to meet you." She takes my hand in hers, her tiny fingers wrapping around my large ones. "I'm Gabby."

When she lets go, she sips from her drink, only for her eyes to return to mine when she lowers her glass back to the bar.

"Gabby, it's nice to meet you as well." Feeling all kinds of nervous, I take a quick sip of my drink. "Are you in Almond Bay visiting anyone? Just move here?"

"No, actually," she answers confidently. "I was in town for business."

"Business?" I say. "What do you do?"

Her eyes glance to the side before a slow smile spreads across her lips. "I work for a travel company. I go around from small town to small town and scope out the scene, trying to find the latest and greatest nugget to write about."

"Wow, that's really interesting. I'm assuming you travel a lot."

She nods. "Yup, all over the country."

"How does Almond Bay rank? Did you find a nugget?"

"I did," she says as she lowers her hand to my thigh.

Fuck . . .

Okay. So she's interested. That's all I need to know to push forward.

I scoot a little closer so she doesn't have to reach as far. "Think you would come back again?"

"I plan on *coming* . . . back, for sure." She wets her lips with the tip of her tongue, and I'm fucking mesmerized just watching it.

"Are you leaving tomorrow?"

"Sadly, yes," she says as her thumb rubs against my thigh.

"That is sad." I try not to gulp in front of her from the way her hand on my thigh feels.

Like I said, it's been a really fucking long time for me.

"I didn't get to accomplish everything I wanted to while being here."

"No?" I ask. "What didn't you accomplish?"

"Well, you see, I'm staying at Five Six Seven Eight, the inn."

"Yup," I say, quite aware of the inn.

"And well, one of my responsibilities is to test everything out, including the bed." I gulp. I can't hold it back. It happens.

"Oh, uh . . . well, can't you test it out tonight when you sleep?"

Her hands float up to my chest as she moves in closer. "I don't like to test it just for sleep . . . Ryland."

Christ.

I see where this is going, so before she can say it, I cut in. "Do you need help testing it?"

An earth-shattering smirk crosses her lips. "I'd love to have you help me test it." And then just like that, she slides off her barstool and steps between my legs. "Want to go now?"

Hell, that was quick.

So quick that it almost feels too easy.

Like I'm missing something.

But I like the promise in her gaze because, fuck, I need this.

I lift my glass, keeping my eyes on her, and swig the rest of my drink for courage before setting it down. "I do," I answer.

"Good. But first, I need to make sure you're worth it."

And before I can ask her what she means, she slides her hand behind my neck and pulls me close. I have about one second to wet my lips before she presses her mouth to mine and kisses me.

The moment our lips meet, I feel a bolt of electricity fly through me, kicking up a part of me that I've stuffed away for what feels like so long. A dead, hollowed-out piece of me. A piece of me that's been broken, hurt, and damaged beyond recovery, yet with her lips on mine, it almost feels like it's healing. And that part of me breaks down a wall, allowing me to wrap my hand around her waist, pull her in even closer, and tilt her mouth up, giving us a better angle. I swipe my tongue across her lip, looking for access, and when she parts her lips, I take that as a sign and slide my tongue against hers.

She leans into me, using my chest to steady herself, and as her kiss grows deeper, she moans against my tongue.

Jesus, I need this.

So fucking bad.

I didn't know how much I needed this until she started kissing me.

But this . . . this is a drug, a high, something I can find myself becoming easily addicted to. She tastes like alcohol and promises. She kisses like it's her last. She grips me like she's holding on to me for safety.

I'm intoxicated.

I need more.

So much fucking more.

She lifts away, her beautiful fucking eyes blinking a few times as she stares back at me. She almost seems . . . stunned as well.

I feel the same way, so I step off my barstool, take her hand in mine, and say, "Let's get out of here."

⊏▭⊐

"What room?" I ask as we head up the back stairs of the inn. The last thing I wanted was to run into Ethel, the owner, because Lord fucking knows, word would get around town that I was fucking somebody at the Five Six Seven Eight. That's the last thing I need.

"Room at the end of the hallway on the left," Gabby says as I lead the way, her hand in mine.

We haven't said anything since we left the bar, not one single word. Not that we need to. I think we both know where this is headed. Both of us are buzzing. *Desperate.*

She pulls out her key when we reach her room, and I unlock the door. After pushing me through the threshold, she shuts the door behind us. When I turn to face her, her eyes roam my body right before she reaches for the hem of her blouse and pulls it up and over her head, revealing her ample breasts in a black lace bra.

Christ.

I reach over my head, tug on my shirt, and pull it off before dropping it to the floor.

And I let her fucking feast.

Those hungry eyes wash over my body, taking in every contour, every muscle, every inch of sinew I've built over time.

"Fuck," she murmurs right before she pulls me into her, causing me to press one hand against the door behind us and the other to her waist. Her hands fly up my chest, over my pecs to my neck where she grips me tightly and brings my mouth back to hers.

I fall into her embrace, into the way her mouth works mine. I'm desperate to hear her sounds to fill this unsatisfied need rolling through me.

As my mouth works hers, our tongues colliding, I drag my fingers up her side, just below her breast. She moans softly, brings her hand to mine, and lifts it to her breast, where she pulls down the cup of her bra. A surge of lust bursts through me as I take her heavy breast in my hand and drag my thumb over her hard nipple.

Her leg wraps around mine, and I take that moment to lower my hand that's propped up against the door and smooth it up and under her ass, only to lift her with one arm and press her against the door.

She groans into my mouth as her center presses against my rock-hard cock.

"Fuck, you're big," she says as she wiggles against me.

"Can you handle me?" I ask as I bring my lips down her jaw to her neck.

"That's not the question you should be asking," she says as she tilts her head to the side.

"What should I be asking?"

"You should be asking it the other way around . . . if you can handle me."

She takes that moment to release herself from my waist and drops down in front of me. Eye level with the fly over my zipper, she undoes my jeans, then yanks them down, along with my briefs, freeing my erection right in front of her.

I don't even have time to fucking gasp before her tongue swirls around the tip of my cock.

"Mother . . . fucker," I say as I brace my hand against the door in front of me. My other hand goes to her face, where I tilt it up just enough so I can see her eyes and her mouth work over my cock.

It feels so fucking good.

Too fucking good.

Like this is all some sort of fever dream.

She bobs her mouth over my length, sucking as she moves down, sucking even harder as she moves back up. Her grip at the base is fucking tight, and as she continues to suck and tease and do fucking good things, I can feel my body climb, my orgasm driving my need to go deeper. There's no way I'll fucking last if she keeps doing this.

No goddamn way.

So I say, "On your feet, Gabby."

She pulls her mouth away from my cock just long enough to say, "What?"

"On your feet."

Taking her hand, I help her up before shucking out of my shoes, socks, jeans, and briefs. Then I walk her over to her bed, feeling her eyes on me the entire time.

"I want you naked."

Her eyes light up as she reaches for the waist of her jeans and undoes them. She pushes them down to the floor along with her shoes and then stands there in a matching lingerie set, looking so goddamn hot that I can feel my balls tighten from the sight of her.

She pushes me on the bed so I'm sitting up with my feet firmly planted on the ground. Then she turns around and takes a seat on my lap, her thong-covered ass rubbing right up against my cock.

She anchors herself by placing her hand behind my neck and starts rocking over me.

"Jesus," I whisper as I push her hair to the side and start pressing kisses along her neck and behind her ear.

She moans as I grab her waist, my fingers pressing into her skin.

Indenting.

Making my mark.

"Touch me," she says as she spreads her legs. "Feel how wet I am, Ryland."

Experiencing another surge of desire, I drag my hand across her stomach, to the waistband of her thong, and slide two fingers under the delicate fabric and right between her legs.

I let one finger dip along her slit, and when I'm met with her arousal, I groan into her ear.

"Fuck, Gabby, you're ready for me."

"So ready," she says softly as I press my fingers to her clit, causing her legs to spread more.

"You want me here?" I ask, slowly stroking the sensitive nub.

"Badly," she says.

"Well, I want to fucking taste you." I swipe my tongue along my fingers.

I'm met with a fucking glorious taste, a taste I haven't experienced in far too long, and it does something to me.

Turns me into a goddamn animal because before I can stop myself, I pick her up and flip her to her back on the mattress.

"Need more," I say as I tear her thong off her body. Then I eye her bra and notice the front clasp. I quickly pop it open and let my eyes feast. "You're so fucking hot."

So goddamn hot.

She has curves, the kind of curves that I can grip on to and get lost in. With thicker hips, fuller breasts, and strong thighs, she's a goddamn dream—everything that turns me on.

Everything that makes me hard as fuck.

I hover above her and lower my head to her breasts, where I grip one and pull her nipple right into my mouth.

"Yes," she cries out as her hand filters through my hair. "Oh my God, yes, Ryland."

I fucking love it when a girl is responsive to her breasts being played with . . . especially their nipples. I've always been a tit man, obsessed with making a woman beg with need from playing with the hard pebbled nubs—sucking on them, plucking at them, and rolling them between my fingers.

And Gabby is no exception.

Her tits are sexy as fuck.

Round, more than a handful, with responsive nipples that seem to beg to be played with, so I bring the pebbled nub into my mouth and suck . . . hard.

I nibble.

I lick.

I suck again and again.

She writhes beneath me, her pelvis seeking out release by thrusting up into me. I let go of her breast and press my hand to her pelvis, keeping her still.

"My time," I say as I kiss my way across to her other breast. "I will do this on my fucking time."

Then I work her other nipple, causing her to moan.

To grunt in desperation.

To beg for more.

Her reaction fuels me to play with her longer, to edge her, because she's so responsive.

She's so soft.

So fucking warm.

And she smells amazing.

Tastes amazing.

Fuck, why have I waited so long to enjoy this?

I lap at her nipple, loving how her fingers thread through my hair and tug on the strands. Her heels dig into my back as they wrap around me. Her pelvis lifts, barely grazing my cock. It's just enough that a fire ignites within me, reminding me there is so much fucking more to do with her.

So I kiss between her breasts, down her stomach, and lower myself between her legs.

Without hesitation, she spreads and then pulls her knees toward her chest.

Jesus Christ.

I fucking love that.

Not a shy bone in her body.

I take in her bare, wet pussy, and with two fingers, I spread her before lowering my mouth. I press a kiss right to her arousal, and she sucks in a harsh breath before I languidly run my tongue along her slit. It's slow and methodic, letting the flat of my tongue do all the work.

"Oh fuck . . ." she groans as her tense body melts into the mattress. "Yes, Ryland."

The sound of my name coming from her husky voice makes me feel like a fucking king.

I bring my other hand to her pussy, and with two fingers, I press inside her while I continue to lap at her arousal.

"Yes . . . oh my God, yes. Play with me, Ryland. Fucking play with me."

Jesus.

Sweat breaks over my back from her pleas.

I want to make this woman come. Multiple times. I want her

writhing, screaming my name, and waking every goddamn person in this inn.

I want her coming on my face.

On my cock.

I want to see how much I can make this woman lose her goddamn mind.

So I run the tip of my tongue over her clit and watch as her eyes fly wide open, her jaw dropping in shock, a silent gasp barely passing her lips.

That's what I fucking want.

And more of it.

As I swipe at her clit, I add my fingers with every stroke. Scooping up inside her and playing with her G-spot, letting her see that I can please her in multiple ways.

And it seems to be working as her fists curl around the sheets beneath her and her chest heaves in anticipation of her orgasm.

Her nipples are hard, red from when I was playing with them.

The new beard burn across her chest marks her as mine for the night.

And the expression on her face, like she's about to meet fucking God.

It's everything I need at this moment as I move my tongue faster and stroke her with my fingers, picking up the pace and thrusting in and out of her over and over again.

"Yes . . . yes . . . fuck . . . please . . ." she cries out, her neck muscles tightening.

Her legs start to clamp around my head.

"Ryland . . . oh God. Ahhh, fuck!" She screams right before I feel her walls tighten, and she's coming all over my goddamn face. She uses my tongue as her personal fuck toy, rocking against it and searching out every last ounce of her orgasm until she's wiped.

"Oh my God," she whispers as she lowers her legs and catches her breath.

I take that moment to go back to my pants, grab my wallet,

and fish out a condom that Abel slipped in there before we got to the bar. I thought he was an idiot when he did it. Now, I'm a grateful motherfucker.

As I move back toward the bed, her gorgeous, heady eyes watch me the entire time, so I give her a show.

I tear the condom wrapper open with my teeth as I stare down at her, holding my cock with one hand at the base. I watch her eyes take me all in, her tongue wetting her lips as she stares at my length.

She's still hungry.

She still wants more.

Thank fuck.

I sheathe myself and then move closer to the bed.

"On your stomach," I say to her.

With a smirk, she flips around to her stomach, scoots toward the edge of the bed, then props her ass in the air.

Perfect.

Beautiful.

I run my hand over the globe of her ass, loving how thick her backside is. A fucking handful to grab on to is just what I love. I bring my cock up to her entrance and slowly start to enter her.

"Oh . . . yes," she says as I move in farther, having a hard goddamn time taking it slow because Jesus, this feels amazing.

She feels incredible.

Warm and perfect, wrapped around me, pulling me in.

"Christ, this cunt," I say as I push in deeper. "So good. So fucking good."

I run my hand up her back, and when I reach her shoulder blades, I push down on her, angling her even more so when I bottom out, I'm at such a delicious angle that it feels like she's tugging on my cock.

"You're so big," she says as I rock into her. "God, I can feel every inch of you."

"Good," I grumble as I thrust my hips down into her, the angle everything I fucking need. "Take this cock, Gabby. Make me come."

"Spank me," she says, surprising me so much that I pause my thrusts.

"You sure?" I ask.

"Positive," she says.

So I lift my hand and then slap her ass, the sound of it echoing through the room, followed by the most delicious moan I've ever heard.

I stare down at her ass, the red mark of my handprint painted across her fair skin.

The sight of it? Only one of the most addictive images in my head.

Because that's me, marking her.

That's my handprint.

Claiming her.

"Again," she begs.

But what she doesn't know is that she doesn't have to beg. No, my mouth is watering for more. So I spank her again, a touch harder this time, and motherfucker, it makes her tighten around my cock, nearly making my eyes roll in the back of my head.

"Fuck," I mumble as I take a breath. I'll come really fucking fast if she keeps doing that.

"Again, Ryland," she says, breathless.

I swallow, trying to gain control over the feelings pulsing through me.

"Again," she begs. "Please. I . . . I'm close."

Jesus Christ, this woman.

Grinding down on my teeth, I spank her again, and she contracts around my cock, squeezing me so goddamn tight.

"Fuck, Gabby . . . you're . . . you're going to make me come."

"Good. Now spank me harder."

Never in my goddamn life . . .

I lift my hand and spank the other cheek, leaving my handprint. Once again, she moans and contracts. So the next time I do it, I pulse inside her, causing her moans to grow louder and louder.

It makes me lose all control.

I snap, and before I know it, I'm spanking and thrusting. She's calling out my name, and I'm growling, seeking out my orgasm. Both of us go wild. The sound of our bodies slapping together fills the air.

She cries out.

I groan.

She clenches.

I thrust harder, bottoming out every goddamn time.

And it's so fucking good.

So fucking perfect.

So goddamn delicious that my balls tighten. In one quick burst, my cock swells, and I'm coming at the same time she does.

The room around me fades to black. I can hear her screaming out in pleasure, but it almost sounds muddled because of the roar of my own orgasm.

It is easily the most intense orgasm of my life.

As we both catch our breaths, I remove myself from her and flop on the bed, where I take a few seconds to let the life flow back into my body.

I stare at the ceiling as I feel her shift off the bed and go straight to the bathroom.

Christ . . . now that's a fucking one-night stand.

# Chapter Three

GABBY

## *Three days later . . .*

"You know, I never thought I was going to be the one who would have to come to you," Bower says as she stands outside my apartment, holding a can of whipped cream in one hand and a jar of maraschino cherries in the other.

I don't bother with the door. She can handle it as I make my way back to the couch where I've been rotting ever since I returned from Almond Bay. Since I don't work on Mondays, I decided to carry through my weekend depression for one more day.

And why do I have a weekend depression?

Um, because I experienced the best sex of my life, that's why.

How does that calculate depression?

Well, for one, I was hoping Ryland would turn out to be a dud so I could hold that against him.

That was not the case at all.

In fact, he was anything but a dud . . . not to be cheesy, but he was more like a stud.

That man knows how to fuck.

He knows how to fuck with no feelings but rather chase plea-sure, which has inadvertently put me into this state of depression because I know I won't have it again.

I flop back on the couch and curl my holey-sweatpants-covered legs up to my chest, holding them tightly.

"This is all your fault."

Bower takes a seat next to me and pops open the cherry jar. I take it from her and thank the heavens above that she grabbed the unstemmed cherries. I plop a few in my mouth and chew.

"What's my fault?" she asks before she sprays some whipped cream into her mouth.

"This feeling I have. It's your fault."

"And what feeling would that be?" I open my mouth, and she squirts some whipped cream against my tongue. I plop a cherry against it and chew before answering.

"This depressed feeling."

"Depressed?" she asks, confused. "Why the hell are you depressed? You had amazing sex. How is that depressing?"

"It's depressing because I now know what amazing sex is, and I know for a fact I will never have it again. I never should have even considered your asinine idea of making a move on Ryland Rowley. Now look at me, depressed and sad. Sometimes I can still feel him between my legs when I walk."

Bower smirks. "That's hot."

"Bower," I complain and nudge her with my foot. "You ruined me."

She shakes her head. "No, Ryland Rowley ruined you. I just encouraged you."

"Well, you shouldn't have." I set the cherries down and curl in on myself. "I can't stop thinking about it, and it's depressing. For one, I shouldn't be thinking about the jerk who didn't even remember who I was. Or the jerk who couldn't bother to show up to my interview. But because he made me come multiple times in one night, he's all I can think about, and he's all my body wants. Like . . . I feel needy, Bower."

She chuckles. "That's what a good dick will do to you. It will make you feel needy."

"Bower, I don't want to feel needy for a dick."

She continues to laugh. "Unfortunately, we have no control over it."

I groan and stare at the ceiling. "This is stupid. All of this is stupid. I really needed that job. I thought I had a chance, especially since my teaching abilities speak for themselves, let alone my coaching and how I was able to help my brother reach the minor leagues. It's just so . . . so . . ."

*Buzz. Buzz. Buzz.*

"Is that your phone?" Bower asks.

I glance at the coffee table where my phone vibrates against the hard wood, an Almond Bay number flashing across the screen.

I feel my breath steel in my chest as I reach for the phone.

"Who is it?" Bower asks.

"I don't know, but it's an Almond Bay number."

She nudges me with her foot.

"Well, answer it."

I swipe on my phone and put it on speaker. "Hello?"

"Hello, is this Miss Brinkman?"

"It is," I say, feeling my nerves dance in my stomach.

"Hello, Miss Brinkman. This is David Ganbear. How are you today?"

My mouth falls open as I squeeze my eyes shut, all hope riding on this phone call that I never expected to receive.

"I'm doing great. How are you?"

"Good, good. I'm calling you about the job you interviewed for on Friday." Bower shakes my foot quietly, her excitement making me giddy. Please don't let this be a rejection. "We thought you would be perfect for the position and want to offer you a teaching job as well as the assistant coaching position."

Holy shit.

Oh my God.

Is this a joke?

Please don't let it be a joke. I don't think my heart can handle it.

"Really?" I ask as Bower pumps her arms up and down, cheering silently.

"Yes, really. I'm going to have HR send over the paperwork along with the offer. Please take your time to think about—"

"I'll take it," I nearly shout.

David chuckles. "Are you sure? You don't want to think about it?"

"Nope," I say. "I'll take it."

"Well . . . that's great to hear. We're excited to have you on staff, especially as our new assistant baseball coach. We have a great program, but I think we need a bit of a feminine touch to take us to the next level."

"Thank you, Mr. Ganbear, this means a lot. Thanks for taking a chance on me."

"Of course. Look out for an email from HR. We shall see you in about two months when the school year starts. Oh, and if you need help finding a place to live, I know of a place in town near the school that might work great."

"That would be amazing. I know how hard it is to find housing in town, so any suggestions would be appreciated."

"I'll be sure to send it over. We're excited to have you."

"Thank you," I say before we both say bye, and I disconnect the call.

"Oh my God!" Bower squeals, then launches herself on me. "You got the job. You got the freaking job."

Tears well up in my eyes. This is the kind of break that Bennett and I need. Based on what Mr. Ganbear said during the interview, the salary alone will be more than enough. I'll be helping Bennett and getting my foot in the door of a male-dominated position.

"I can't believe it." I shake my head. "I really thought I messed it up."

"You didn't. You nailed it. Ugh, how satisfying." Bower pulls me into a hug. "I'm so proud of you."

"Thank you." When I back away, I say, "But that means I have to move."

"I know," she says with a sad smile. "But we knew that when you went for the interview, and we were willing to face that hardship for an opportunity like this. It's not like you're that far away. Three hours is drivable. This is what you need."

"I know." I smile, sitting back on the couch. "I can't believe it. This is amazing. Really freaking . . ." My mind starts connecting the dots, and I think about what this means. "Holy shit, Bower."

"What?" she asks.

"I got the job."

"I know." She smiles and takes my hands in hers, dancing them about. "We got the job."

"No." I grow serious. "I got the job."

She matches my energy as she nods. "Yes, you got the job."

"Don't you know what that means?"

Confused, she asks, "More opportunity?"

"No, Bower." I grip her shoulders. "It means I have to work with Ryland Rowley. The man who just rocked my world!"

"Ohhhh," she says, shrugging. "So?"

"So?" I ask, getting up from the couch. "All you have to say is so? Bower, this is not a shrug, 'so' moment. This is a *holy shit, we need to freak out* moment."

"I don't see why. So you had sex, who cares?"

I point at my chest. "I do. I care. I care a whole fucking lot. I told him . . . oh, Jesus." I grip my head, remembering that night. "I told him I was a travel blogger, or something like that, going from town to town writing about all the quirky places I stay."

"Why would you say that?" she asks with a snarl to her lip.

"Because I didn't think I was going to see him again," I say through clenched teeth. "I didn't think there was a chance in hell that I was going to get that job, so I thought, why not throw all caution to the wind, make up an alter ego, and run with it."

"Well, good job accomplishing that plan."

"Bower," I groan, pacing the living room of my tiny apartment. "This is serious. What the hell am I going to do? Should I call Mr. Ganbear back and tell him I regret to inform him that I actually can't take the job because I fucked his head coach and he thinks I'm a travel blogger?"

"Uh . . . no."

"Then what?" I ask, holding my hands out.

"Isn't it obvious?"

"Does this face look like someone who knows the obvious?" I ask, pointing at my face.

"Possibly."

"Bower," I groan. "Come on. This is serious."

"It's serious, but it's nothing to be worried about. Do you know why? Because you're going to walk into that school and on that baseball field like you own it, just like you owned Ryland Rowley the other night."

"I did not own him. He owned me."

She shakes her head. "Not how it works. A man can only own a woman in the bedroom if she allows it. Therefore, you owned him."

I go to argue but then think about it for a second. I mean, she's kind of right. I have to give him permission to own and control my body like he did . . . maybe I did own him. *And I let the man spank me. Spank. Me.*

"I can see it in your eyes. You owned him."

"I mean . . . maybe I did a little. He did come really hard and then had to lay on the bed a bit to catch his breath."

"See. You owned him. So take that power you harnessed and walk into Almond Bay unapologetically."

"Do you really think I can do that? I mean, I lied to him and slept with him. Don't you think it will be awkward?"

"Only if you make it." She crosses her legs. "This is an opportunity, Gabby, one that you need. Do not let it slip by you because you took one night for yourself and did something unapologetically. Also, when have you ever cared what people thought?"

"True," I say as I sit on the couch again. She takes my hand and looks me in the eyes.

"You go into Almond Bay and turn that town upside down. That includes Ryland Rowley."

"Yeah." I nod. "I can do this. I'm going to do this." Chin held high, I add, "Look out, Almond Bay, I'm coming."

"In more ways than one," Bower adds with a waggle of her brows.

"Oh my God," I say as I push my friend away. "Trust me, if there is one thing I know for sure, sex with Ryland Rowley is completely off the table. No one will be coming . . . for a while."

# Chapter Four

## RYLAND

"He what?" I shout at my principal, Herbert Jenkins.

Mustache twitching over his upper lip, bald head shining under the fluorescent lights of his office, he calmly says, "David hired your assistant coach." He tosses me a paper with a single name on it: Gabriel Brinkman.

I stare down at it and then back up at Herbert. "Who the fuck is Gabriel Brinkman?"

"Also our new math hire."

"How the hell was this even allowed? I don't know this fuck," I say, my anger getting the best of me. Thankfully, Herbert has known me long enough to understand that my unprofessionalism isn't because of him, but because of my irritation with the situation. "For all we know, this guy could be a real shit on the field. What are his qualifications even? Has he ever played baseball?"

"From what I learned, SHE earned her teaching degree in trigonometry so you won't have to take on as many classes as you have been. As for baseball, she helped her brother learn how to play."

I blink a few times, because not only am I surprised about the she part, but . . . helped her brother?

Helped?

That is such a broad term that I don't even know where to begin.

"She helped," I say. "And also . . . she's a she?"

"Is that going to be a problem, Rowley?" Herbert raises a singular brow.

"I mean . . . no. I'm all for women in sports, but I was just . . . I wasn't expecting it. Not to mention, you're talking about a bunch of horned-up teenagers here who think more with their dicks than their brains. Do we think that it's smart having a woman on staff?"

"Did that sentence really just come out of your mouth?" he asks.

I groan and drag my hand over my face. "I'm not saying it in a sexist way. I'm just . . . it's concerning. She's a woman."

"Yes, she is, and I think one of the main reasons David hired her is because he wants to break the boundaries for those you might be overlooking."

I sigh and lean back in my chair. "I get that, and being that I'm raising a girl on my own at the moment, I'm more than happy for a woman to get her chance. But did she get the job because she's a woman or because she's actually good at coaching? I don't have time to teach someone how to do their job, Herb. I need someone ready to help me and who can handle the boys on their own. I have enough going on with finding a house to buy, taking care of Mac, and navigating her feelings. I don't have time to babysit."

"From what David told me, you won't have to babysit. She seems to be very competent."

"Doubt it," I say on an irritated huff.

Herbert's chair squeaks as he leans forward and places his forearms on his desk. "It would behoove you to take this new hire seriously, Rowley. Unfortunately, David's calling the shots. He's the biggest donor to our school district. His money is why your baseball program is thriving."

"Fuck that, it's my coaching," I say. "We'd still be winning games if we showed up in ratty uniforms and biked our way to the baseball fields rather than taking fancy fucking buses."

"Yes, but you wouldn't have the best kids transferring to our school, either."

Eh, he's right about that.

"You need to suck it up and realize that even though you don't like this decision, you're going to have to live with it."

I slouch in my chair and massage my temples a few times, trying to see a way where this isn't my new reality.

"What could be so bad about it?" he asks.

I look up at him. "Uh, a lot. How about that she doesn't know what she's doing? That she's no help whatsoever? That she could be the worst hire that Almond Bay has ever seen, and I'm the one who will have to suffer through it because the man with the wallet feels so fucking self-righteous that he thinks he can make all the decisions without consulting one goddamn person?"

"Or . . . she could be really good and help improve your program."

I stand from my chair. "Herbert, you've known me for a long goddamn time. You've seen the lack of luck in my life. So where the fuck do you come off thinking that this hire is not going to come back to bite me in the ass?"

He rubs his hand over his scruffy jaw and chuckles. "When you put it like that . . ."

"Jesus, fuck," I say before stomping toward his door.

"For what it's worth," he calls out, "at least you won't have to teach trigonometry anymore. I know how much you hated it."

"Great, the one good thing happening in my life."

---

"Uncle Ry Ry!" Mac shouts when she spots me from her daycare playground. She sprints toward me, her pigtails that I struggled with this morning askew and swaying as she leaps into my arms and hugs me tightly.

I squeeze her back, taking a second to enjoy this moment with my niece because if I don't take these moments, I become fucking overwhelmed.

So fucking overwhelmed.

I never thought this was what my life would be like. I had big dreams—dreams that were carving a path I was confident I'd head down. I was going to play professional baseball. I'd live in a big city, away from Almond Bay and the frayed and tattered roots I've planted here. But those dreams washed away when I quit baseball, got my teaching degree, and started teaching and coaching in Almond Bay. And then that's when it all happened.

My eldest sister, Cassidy, lost her husband, leaving her as a young single mom. Given the lack of parents in our lives, I knew it was my time to step up again, so I did. I was there every second I could offer to Cassidy to help with the farm, with the store, with her dreams . . . and with Mac. We grew a sense of routine until that one dark day when Cassidy found out she had stage four breast cancer.

Life as we knew it shut down.

Nothing felt right.

Nothing felt fair.

And as I watched my sister slowly die, I knew that nothing would ever be the same.

*"Please, Ryland, please take care of her for me. Give her a beautiful and special life. Teach her everything I would teach her. Love her the way I would love her. And please keep my memory deep in her heart."*

It was the most painful and heartbreaking conversation I've ever had. I still remember the way she looked at me from her bed as she held my hand, asking me if I'd take care of her precious baby girl.

*Her world.*

*Who then became mine.*

I can still feel the lump in my throat as the heaviest weight was placed on my shoulders. But I made her that promise, and I will live every day preserving that promise.

Mac pulls away from our hug, and she looks at me with a scrunch to her face. "Why is your face all crinkly?"

Got to love kids.

"It's called getting old. We get crinkles."

She rolls her eyes cutely and presses the spot between my eyes. "No, right here. You look mad."

"Oh." I set her down and pick up her backpack from the ground, only for her to take my hand in hers, a feeling I'm not sure I will ever get used to. "Uh, I'm not mad."

"Seems like you're mad."

"I'm not." I try to force a smile. "I'm happy, see?"

She glances up at me, studies me for a moment, then says, "You have a nice smile."

Well, warm my cold, dead heart.

"Not as nice as yours," I say and squeeze her hand as we head to my truck. "You know, it's kind of a hot day, don't you think?"

"Very hot," she says as she makes a show of panting.

God, she reminds me so much of Cassidy that it hurts at times. From her cute, round face to her mannerisms to her sense of humor . . . it's insane. It's like her mother reincarnated, offering me comfort and a polarizing sadness at the same time.

"I'm glad you agree because I was thinking about getting some milkshakes. Want to join me?"

Her eyes light up as she looks at me. "Really?"

"Yeah, really."

"Yeah!" she cheers. "Can I get a strawberry milkshake?"

"You can get whatever flavor you want," I say.

"Yay." She jumps.

"I also brought Chewy Charles so he doesn't feel left out."

"And can the spiders come too?"

"Yes," I nearly sigh. "The spiders can come too."

Chewy Charles is her sacred horse stuffie who is her best friend. Recently, she got another horse stuffie from Uncle Wyatt,

my sister's husband. Naturally, she named the other horse Chewy
Chondra. Currently, Chewy Charles and Chewy Chondra are
fighting, which is why I didn't bring her. We don't need bad
blood while getting milkshakes.

And the spiders . . . well, those would be her fingers. She likes
to pretend her fingers are spiders, dancing them over every
diseased surface she can find. I don't tend to allow the spiders to
join us because they become disease-sucking sticks, and I'm not
into the whole sick-kid thing. But given the conversation I need to
have with her, I'm allowing spiders.

On the way to Provisions, Mac tells me about her day, how
Gregory took her marker that she was using, and she was not
happy about it, then he didn't even apologize. I make a mental
note to check out Gregory and give him the *don't fuck with my niece*
look. She also expressed her displeasure for not being picked for
one of the specials and how she'll never, ever be picked. The
specials in her classroom are chosen at random on Fridays, and
they range from being able to take the class stuffie home for the
weekend, to taking home the estimation jar, or the mystery bag.
They're all interactive activities and apparently very coveted.
She's been chosen for the estimation jar before, which just meant
we had to put a multiple of something in the jar, and the classroom tried to guess how many were in the jar just by looking
at it.

Initially, Mac wanted to put sand in the jar and count the
grains of sand, but I told her that maybe it was not the best idea.
It would be hard to count the grains, so she went with her
polished rocks instead.

When we arrive at Provisions, I help her out of her car seat
as she stuffs Chewy Charles in her shirt, letting just his head poke
out from the neckline. She saw a mom carrying a baby in one of
those pouch things, and ever since then, Mac believes she needs
to carry Chewy Charles the same way—minus the baby
apparatus.

When I shut the car door and she's ready to walk, she reaches
up and takes my hand. I glance down at her, and she looks up at

me with a gleeful smile on her face, the kind of smile that rips your goddamn heart out, because how?

How could this child be so goddamn happy?

She lost both of her parents, her mom, who she was incredibly close with, and now has to live with her uncle, who barely knows what the hell he's doing. Yet she's smiling.

She loves holding my hand.

She loves skipping while I walk.

And she loves just . . . being with me.

I don't get it. I'm not sure I ever will. *But fuck, am I thankful.*

When we reach the hostess station, I ignore the fact that the hostess is one of my students and motion for a table of two with my fingers. She walks us to a table in the back corner and then places menus in front of us.

"Your server will be with you soon."

"Can we get fries?" Mac asks as she dances her spider fingers across the menu. "I like dipping the fries in my shake."

"Yeah, we can get fries," I say, already thinking about how dinner is most likely going to be a no go when we get home. It's fine. It's okay to spoil Mac every once in a while, and she'd probably benefit from not having to eat whatever I decide to put on the table tonight.

Let's just say taking care of a child and figuring out healthy meals wildly accepted by said child has been a challenge.

"I love fries. Can we get waffle fries?"

"Sure, if that's what you want."

"Yay! I want the waffle fries. I like sticking my tongue in them."

"As we all do," I say as I lean back in my chair and watch my niece dance her fingers across the table with a horse sticking out the top of her shirt.

She's a weird kid.

I'd be the first to admit it.

She doesn't like the same things her friends like, and she sure as hell doesn't act the same. There are times I wonder . . . is she going to be okay? Do I need to get her help? Is it normal for her to convince me that wearing a T-shirt as pants is acceptable? Aubree told me shirts as pants do not work for many reasons, but . . . I don't know, she's a very convincing child.

"Hey, Mr. Rowley," someone says as they approach our table. It's one of my least favorite things about living in a small town. I glance to the right and see Kenna, another one of my students.

"Hey, Kenna."

She holds a pen and notepad in her hand. "What can I get you two?"

"Mac, would you like to order?"

Mac pats Chewy Charles on the head, then says, "Strawberry milkshake, please, and a lot of fries. Like all of the fries."

Kenna smirks as she writes down the order. "Do you want waffle fries?"

"Yes!" Mac shouts. "Waffle fries."

"Please." I remind her of her manners.

"Waffle fries, please," Mac says before her fingers dance over the salt and pepper shakers.

I look up at Kenna and say, "Chocolate shake, please."

"Sure thing, Mr. Rowley." She takes the menus from us and heads to the kitchen.

Now is the time to talk to her, when she's not distracted by her milkshake and fries and she can actually listen to what I need to say.

So I shift on my chair and clear my throat. "Mac, could I talk to you about something?"

"Sure," she says. "The spiders like the salt." Her fingers "lick" at some spilled salt on the table.

"Um, could the spiders sleep for a second while I talk to you?"

She lifts one brow at me. "They're not tired."

*Patience.*

That is what Mac has taught me over the past few months.

*Patience.*

I press my lips together. "Well, I need them to take a rest because I need to talk to you. It's important."

"Important?" she asks as she rests her hands in her lap, and those big, innocent eyes stare me down. "Am I in trouble?"

"No," I say quickly. "No, not at all. I just . . . I need to talk to you about something that I've been thinking about, and I want to know how you feel about it."

"Okay," she says simply despite the raging nerves I have inside me.

"Well." I place my hands on the table, palms down even though they're clammy. "I've been doing some thinking—"

"My elbow itches. Can I itch it?"

I press my lips together and nod.

Talking to a fucking four-year-old feels like talking to a goddamn ant.

"Yes, you can scratch your elbow."

She lifts her elbow and shows it to me. "Does it look green?"

"Green?" I ask.

"Yeah, Gregory was saying if your elbow is green and itches, it means you're a zombie. So am I a zombie? I don't want to be a zombie. Gregory said zombies only eat brains, and I don't want brains. I want fries and milkshakes."

I pinch the bridge of my nose. She needs to stop talking to fucking Gregory.

"Your elbow isn't green. No signs of being a zombie."

"Okay." She stares at the table. "If I were a zombie, I would have to eat your brain, Uncle Ry Ry."

"Well, it's a good thing you're not a zombie, then, right?"

"Yeah, good thing." She smiles back at me, those eyes of hers sparkling. "Because I bet your brain tastes yucky."

"I think any brain would taste yucky."

She quirks her head to the side. "Then why do zombies eat them?"

I drum my fingers on the table, losing a little bit of patience because, fuck, I just want to talk to her about this and get it over with.

"You know, I'm not sure, but we can look it up later because I really want to talk to you about something. Can you give me a few seconds, then we can do all the research on zombies?"

"Promise?" She points her finger at me.

"Promise." She nods at me like a fucking CEO in the board-room, offering me the chance to continue. "I wanted to talk to you about our living situation."

Her brow quirks up. "What does that mean?"

"Well, uh." Jesus, why am I nervous? "I was thinking with Aunt Aubree and Uncle Wyatt being married now they might want more room. And since they work on the farm, I thought it might be nice for them to have the house."

"What house?"

"Our house."

You know that fucking cat, the one that's supposed to be Zorro? What the hell is its name? Puss in Boots? Some shit like that. Well, you know how he takes his hat off and then offers those big glassy eyes?

That's Mac right now.

She's been watching that movie too much because she looks just like the damn feline, and I won't be able to survive this conversation if she keeps it up.

"Our house?" Her lip nearly shakes as she says it.

"Yeah." I clear my throat. "I found another house in town, closer to school, and right across the street from the park that you love. The park with the twirly slide. It has big windows and get this . . . it's purple."

Her eyes widen. "The house is purple?"

I nod. "Yup, purple."

"I like purple."

"I know. And it has a corner bedroom with a window seat where the sun comes into the window, a perfect spot for Chewy Charles to sleep while you're at school."

She tilts Chewy Charles's head and says, "Errrr?"

Knowing what has to be done, I direct my attention to the stuffie with the crooked nose peeking out of my niece's shirt and say, "That's right, Chewy Charles, a whole window seat just for you."

"I like that," Mac says in a Chewy Charles voice that is screechy and made for nightmares.

"I'm glad because your opinion matters too, Chewy Charles. I want to make sure we are all happy about moving to a new house."

Mac's little nose scrunches. "What about Aunt Aubree and Uncle Wyatt? Would they move too?"

I shake my head. "No, they'd stay in the farmhouse."

Her lips turn down. "What about my bed? And Chewy Chondra?"

"We'll take your bed with us and Chewy Chondra."

"What about my clothes?"

I see where this is going . . .

"MacKenzie, we'll take all your things with us. Anything you want, you can bring."

She thinks about that for a second. "Can I see the house?"

"Of course," I say just as our milkshakes and fries arrive. "We can go see it whenever you want."

She perks up. "I would like to see it today."

*Well, thank God for that.*

# Chapter Five

GABBY

"Did you like the pictures I sent?" I say into the phone as I rip open one of the few boxes I moved with.

"Yeah, it's nice," Bennett says. "Do you feel safe there?"

"It's Almond Bay, Bennett. What do you think?"

"I know," he says on a sigh. "It's one of the safest towns in the country. I swear only happiness is allowed to happen there."

He's not wrong.

When we lived close by, it felt like everyone was filled with joy when walking the streets. Sort of annoying when you're clawing at life just to hang on. But now that everything is looking up, I don't mind bouncing around with the rest of the jolly mother-fuckers.

"Very true."

"You can afford the place?" Bennett asks, concern in his voice.

"Yes. I worked out a deal with the landlord who's friends with David, the board member who hired me. It's part of the purchase deal."

"What purchase deal?"

"The owner of the house is selling, and part of the stipulation is that I can maintain the lease for at least a year. After that, it's up to the buyer to figure out what they want to do."

"Wait, hold on . . . so you'll be living with a stranger?"

I chuckle into the phone as I pull out my sheets from a box and set them on my bed. "No, it's the apartment above the detached garage. I told you that."

"Right," he says. "Guess I missed that. Okay, so what if this buyer is a prick?"

"I have an ironclad rental agreement. They can't be a prick. Plus, David seems to be on my side with this. I'm sure if something happened, he'd help me."

"And is this David guy interested in you?" Bennett asks, making me laugh.

"No, he's gay and has a partner of ten years. I think he just likes to be helpful. Also, he wants to change things up within the sports industry. Hence why I'm going to be the assistant coach."

"Have you talked to Coach Rowley?"

Technically, a month or so ago, yes.

Although, there wasn't a lot of talking.

More like a lot of thrusting.

And moaning.

And how much he liked sinking into my pussy.

And how I loved the way he would make me come.

And the sound of spanking filled the room, over and over again.

God, I can still feel it.

But talking about this job? Not so much.

"No, not yet. But I'm sure I'll talk to him soon. School doesn't start for a few more weeks. I moved because I wanted to get settled and establish myself before everything got too crazy. Plus, my lease was up, and this place was available, so it worked out. I'm picking up a few shifts at the old bar in the meantime. I should be making more than enough to help pay for some of your expenses."

He sighs heavily. "Gabby, I told you—"

"I know what you told me, Bennett, but you need help, and that's okay. That's what I'm here for. And when the season is over, you can stay with me. There's enough room here—"

"I'm not staying with you, Gabby. You need to live your life and stop putting it on hold for me."

"I'm not putting my life on hold. I'm just helping. Your dreams are important."

"And what about your dreams?" he asks. "How come I'm the one who gets to have dreams, and you don't?"

"I have dreams," I say defensively as I take a seat on my bed. "But yours are just bigger."

"That's bullshit. You matter just as much as I do. I hate seeing you scrounge up every last penny to help me. I want you to do something for you."

"I am," I reply. "This coaching position means a lot to me. It's a step toward what I want to do. A step in the right direction, and if the little bit of money I get from doing it helps pay for some of your food, then that's a plus." He sighs again, so I say, "And stop sighing. I want to do this. It's my responsibility to take care of you, so . . . just be nice and say thank you."

He pauses for a moment. "Thank you, Gabby."

"You're welcome."

"And you know, when I get called up and I sign a fat contract, the first thing I'm doing is taking care of you."

"I don't need you to. I just need you to enjoy every second of all the hard work you put into this."

"All the hard work *we* put into this."

I smile to myself. "Yes, we. And you know, if you happen to give your sister a shoutout during your first press conference, I won't be mad about it."

He laughs. "I think I can manage it."

I stand from the bed and take my sheets to the linen closet next to the bathroom. "Okay, well, I'm going to finish unpacking. I can't have things unorganized. Good luck tonight."

"Thank you," he says. "Love you, Gab."

"Love you, Benny Boo Boo."

46

"Don't call me that."

I laugh, and we both hang up. I toss my cell onto the bed and look around my quaint apartment. It's really nice. When I was told it was an apartment above a garage, I assumed it would be a studio apartment with a mini fridge and microwave as a kitchen. But it's a one-bedroom with a separate living and sleeping space, an en suite bathroom, a full kitchen with appliances, and a dinette with a window that overlooks the park across the street.

It's probably one of the nicest places I've ever stayed in, and it's such a good price. I have no doubt that if it wasn't for David hooking me up, I'd be living in a cardboard box down by the ocean.

Wanting to make this place my own, I take in the windows that need curtains, the couch that could use some throw pillows, and the coffee table that could stand a candle. So I grab my phone again and start a new note, writing down all the things I want to get for the apartment. I have very little saved up, but if I make a list, then I can probably get something once a week.

Once my list is complete, I take a break from unpacking and grab some food because my stomach is growling. I know if I order a pizza, I can make that last a few days for meals, so I grab my keys and head out of the apartment, making sure to lock up. As I make my way down the stairs on the side of the purple garage, two cars pull into the large driveway, causing me to halt.

The first person to step out is the real estate agent of the empty house. I can't remember his name . . . Doug maybe? I met him the other day while reviewing the lease agreement. There is an offer on the house, which means . . . maybe this will be my new landlord.

I slowly make my way down the stairs, keeping my eyes on the large black truck in the driveway, only for my stomach to nearly fall out of my ass when I see a very attractive and very familiar man step out of the driver's side.

Ryland Rowley?

No.

It can't be.

Please don't let it be him.

I squint, giving myself a better look, as if that would help me distort his image and convince myself that I'm not seeing Ryland Rowley, but nope . . . still him.

This can't be real, right?

Maybe . . . maybe he's, I don't know, looking at the house for another reason. Maybe he wants to check out the architecture and copy it for a house he's building.

Maybe he's the seller going in for one more snapshot memory.

I know it's wishful thinking, but I hold on to that thought as I watch him help a little girl out of the back of his truck.

Umm . . . who is that?

She has to be at least four, maybe five, and she has the cutest pigtails that swish side to side when she walks and . . . hold on . . . is that a horse sticking out of her shirt?

"It's so big," the little girl says.

"Do you like the purple?" Ryland asks in a voice he definitely didn't use when we were together that one night.

"I love it!" The little girl jumps in excitement.

"I knew you would." Ryland glances up at Doug. "Want to show her the inside?"

"Would love to," Doug says as he gestures to the garage. "As stated before—oh, hello."

Fuck.

Caught like a deer in the headlights, I awkwardly stand there, looking at them, unsure what to do or say.

"How convenient. Ryland, this is Gabby, the tenant of the space above the garage."

Ryland takes the little girl's hand in his, then glances in my direction. I can barely feel the air flowing through my chest as I watch his eyes meet mine. For a moment, I feel that he won't recognize me, that maybe he forgot about that night, but then his eyebrows rise in surprise.

Recognition is written all over his face.

Yup, he knows.

I take the rest of the steps down and wave briefly. "Hi, nice to meet you."

"Gabby, Ryland will be the property's new owner, pending closure, but everything is looking very good so far."

I can feel his eyes boring into me as questions race through his mind.

"Uncle Ry Ry, can I go stand under that tree? Chewy Charles wants to stare at the branches."

Ryland takes in the large oak in the backyard, assesses the space, and then nods. "Don't go past the tree."

The little girl giddy-ups to the backyard, leaving me alone with Ryland and Doug.

"I'm going to go open the house," Doug says. "I'll let you two get to know each other."

He takes off as well, leaving just the two of us.

I stick my hands in the pockets of my jean shorts as I try to figure out what to say. This is not what I expected. Not even in the slightest. I thought the first time I saw him again would be at school, and we'd just have a bit of a laugh about it all. I was hoping he'd find the whole situation funny, but seeing his reaction now, I can genuinely assess that he doesn't find this amusing at all.

Not even a little.

"Um . . . hi," I say.

"What are you doing here?" he asks, his voice laced with an edge.

"I live here." I gesture to the building behind me. "Nice place, actually. Glad I found it." Stay calm. Maybe if I keep my cool, he won't fly off the deep end.

"I thought you traveled for a living."

Oh shit, right . . . I forgot I told him that.

Yikes.

What do I say now? I lied, and in fact, I will be teaching at your school, and oh wait, we aren't just co-workers and living on the same property as each other, but also . . . we're coaching together. Doesn't that sound like fun?

49

From the crinkle between his eyes, I'm going to guess he wouldn't think that's fun at all. More like a living nightmare.

"Um, so yeah, got a new job, and it happened to land me here in Almond Bay. Imagine that." Not a lie.

I toe the ground as we hear the little girl in the back galloping with her horse stuffie.

When he doesn't say anything and just stares, I can feel the pressure mounting between us, so I continue, "You, uh . . . you bought the house?"

"We're under contract," he answers.

"Cool, yeah, great choice. Looks like your, uh . . . your . . ."

"Niece," he says.

"Yeah, your niece seems like she likes it."

His eyes leave mine for a moment as he focuses on her. And the crease in his brow lessens as he follows her. I glance over my shoulder and catch her rolling around in the grass, tossing her horse in the air.

When we both find each other's gazes again, he says, "Seems that way."

Not really knowing what to say, I add, "So I guess that means you'll be my landlord. Exciting. I'll have you know, I plan on paying my rent on time and don't intend on causing a ruckus, so no need to worry about me throwing any wild parties."

He rubs the back of his neck. "Do you think it's a good idea that you live in the apartment above the garage?"

What does he mean by that?

Do I think it's a good idea?

Uh, yeah.

It's a great idea.

The apartment is close to town, cheap, and updated. There is no way I could find anything better. This apartment is like Monica Geller's apartment, a diamond in the rough, and I will rot in it until someone scoops me out and throws me to the curb.

"Not that it's really any of your business," I say, "but yeah, I think it's a great idea that I live in the apartment above the garage. It's a real snag. Not sure if you noticed, but the cost of living around here is pretty damaging to the bank account. So when I came upon this gem, it was a no-brainer. One of my best decisions, actually."

"I mean," he says in a dark tone, taking a step forward. "Do you think it's smart living in the apartment after we fucked?"

Oh, okay . . . *ahem*.

So he's just going to say it like that?

Got to appreciate a man for not beating around the bush.

"I don't see why that's an issue," I say.

"You don't?" He raises a brow.

I cross my arms at my chest. "Yeah, I don't see what the problem is. So we did it. It was fine—"

"Fine?" His eyebrows fly up so fast, I swear it blows his hair back. "You're calling that night . . . fine?"

Well, it was more than fine. He rocked my freaking world.

Being with Ryland fulfilled so many sexual fantasies that I always wondered about.

He made me crave things I never thought I wanted.

The groaning.

The moaning.

The spanking.

The dirty talk.

It was freaking incredible and, hands down, the best sexual experience of my life.

But besides the applause I want to hand over to him for a job well done, I don't like the way he's treating this entire interaction. It's almost like he's alluding that he thinks I'm in the wrong and should move.

It's kind of comical.

Because over my dead body will I leave that apartment. I have a contract, a lease, so there is no way I'll back down from it.

"Yeah, it was fine," I say.

His eyes darken, and he takes one step closer, bringing us almost toe-to-toe.

"It was more than fine, and you know it."

I look him in the eyes, arms still crossed. "Seems like you're getting pretty defensive."

"I'm not getting defensive, but I'm also not going to stand here and let you lie to my face. You and I both know that night was more than fine."

Gulp.

Yeah, it was unbelievable.

Sometimes I can still feel him between my legs.

I look down at my nails, pretending they're more important than the irritated man in front of me. "Either way, how people felt that night doesn't matter."

"Sure as fuck does," he says.

"How? Please tell me how it matters? We're grown-ups. It's not like because I see you all of a sudden, I'm going to have this uncontrollable urge to just . . . to just . . . fuck my landlord. I'm able to abide by boundaries."

"And you think you can maintain those boundaries?"

This guy . . . he has no freaking clue about my level of self-control.

"Because I have a little girl I need to take care of, and I don't need . . ." His jaw clenches as he leans forward, his face close to mine as he whispers, "I don't need the fucking distraction."

Something about the way his breath caught in his throat when he said that, like he's truly worried, like this conversation actually means something to him, and it's not some alpha dipshit way to get me to move out.

He truly means it . . . he doesn't want to be distracted.

I pull away from him just enough to look him in the eyes. They're such a beautiful green color. A mixture of seafoam and moss. Stunning despite the sadness I see in them.

"I won't be a distraction," I say as guilt starts to swarm me.

Does he know about the assistant coach job? He probably doesn't given that he hasn't mentioned it.

Is it something that I should mention?

Right now?

I hear his niece in the background, galloping away, and I

realize it's probably not the time. He's already angry about this, so there's no need to double down.

He takes a step back and nods. "Okay." He glances over my shoulder again. "And I'd appreciate it if you didn't mention that night we spent together . . . to anyone." That makes me frown with annoyance. When he says it like that, he makes it seem like he's ashamed. "I was drunk . . . and well, let's just keep it between us."

Wow.

Okay.

I press my lips together and nod. "Sure, not a problem." Feeling my irritation ramp up, I say, "Is that all?"

"Yeah," he answers.

"Good." I move past him, my shoulder brushing against his. "Looking forward to being neighbors."

# Chapter Six

## RYLAND

"When is closing?" Abel asks as he tosses the ball to me.

We're out on the baseball field, fucking around after about three hours of intense landscaping and grooming. The school doesn't have the budget for professional landscapers for the field —well, at least not the budget I need to hire the type of experts I want—so I tend to spend a great deal of time keeping the field in pristine condition myself. Today, I roped Abel into helping on his day off.

I'm rewarding him with a toss.

"In about two hours," I say. "I can still back out."

It's been a whirlwind since I saw Gabby at the house a week ago. I've been gnawing on that information every night since, considering over and over again if I want to go through with the house purchase.

"Can you, though?" Abel asks as he catches the ball. "Mac is in love with the place. Didn't you have to go to the backyard yesterday and watch her play under the big tree?"

"For an hour," I grumble as Abel throws me the ball, the thud of leather hitting leather one of the best sounds ever. "She didn't want to leave. I had to bribe her with horsey rides at the farm."

"And what does that entail?"

"Me forcing Wyatt to get on his hands and knees so she can ride on his back."

"And why weren't you the horsey?" he asks with a brow raised.

"I was making a shitty dinner for everyone."

"Ah, that checks." He catches the ball and starts walking toward me. "Remind me why you want to back out? Because you never really got into that."

Because I don't want to get into it. Words cannot explain how utterly shocked . . . *and angry* . . . I was when I saw her again. There, in front of the house I was buying. How, I don't know or understand.

What are the goddamn chances of the tenant above the garage being *her*? The sexy siren/angel I had a one-night stand with?

Slim.

Yet here we are.

The moment I saw her, I was filled with dread and excitement all at once. Because that night . . . fuck, that night is one I haven't forgotten. I think about it all the goddamn time. I think about the way she listened so fucking well, the way she felt, the way she sounded . . . smelled. It was intoxicating being with her, and when those eyes of hers met mine, for a brief second, I thought about walking up to her, tipping her chin up, and tasting those lips all over again.

Then I was reminded about real life.

A life where I'm the guardian to a four-year-old girl who lost both of her parents.

A life where I'm not the kind of person who would give in to temptation.

A life where I have three things I need to direct all my attention to: Mac, baseball, and school.

There isn't room for anything else.

And with that in mind, dread filled me because I knew I had to have that conversation with her.

What we had could go nowhere.

Absolutely nowhere.

And I made that known despite how I actually felt.

It seemed like she was fine with that . . . so why am I over here ready to back out of a contract to a house that I know Mac loves, that I know she deserves, and that I know she needs in her life?

"You going to answer me?" Abel says as he tosses me the ball, and we both head to the dugout that I power washed yesterday.

"Why do I want to back out of the contract?" We both take a seat on top of the bench and lean against the painted cinderblock wall. I let out a sigh. "Remember that one-night stand I had about a month ago?"

"Yeah."

"Well, that's the tenant who'll be living in the apartment above the garage."

I feel Abel turn toward me. "You're fucking kidding."

I shake my head. "Nope."

"I thought she was an out-of-towner."

"So did I, but now she's very much an *in* towner."

"Don't like the term in towner, so don't use it again." Normally, I'd chuckle, but I'm feeling so defeated that I barely crack a smile. "Correct me if I'm wrong, but didn't you have a great time with her? I'm pretty sure you were walking on clouds for a week."

"I wasn't walking on clouds," I scoff. My penis felt like it was being carried around by a cloud, there's a difference. "But yeah, it was a great night."

"So explain to me how this is a problem?"

"Because I can't have the distraction," I reply while slouching against the wall. "Mac needs all my attention, and I can't have some woman I spent one night with turning my head the other way. Not to mention, I'm going to have a tough season this year, and I'm moving Mac out of her house. The house where she spent all four years of her life and has memories of her mom in."

"Don't start with that. You and your siblings have said she's been happier since the thought of moving. She watched her mom die in that house. Man, you know this move is for the best."

I tug on the brim of my baseball hat. "I know, but that doesn't mean there won't be growing pains or that she isn't going to possibly revert to wanting to be at the old house. I have to tread carefully, and I fear if Gabby distracts me, I might lose out on the promise I made to Cassidy before she passed."

Abel is silent for a moment, staring out at the green grass of the field with a pensive look in his eyes. "You realize you're allowed to be a person outside of the responsibilities you hold for Mac. Cassidy wouldn't want you to set aside your life to take care of her daughter. She'd still want you to live."

"I know. She would say that exact thing to me," I say. "The problem is, I don't know how to do both. I don't know how to have a life while watching over my niece. I barely know how to take care of Mac. I swear to God, and I'm not just saying this to fucking say it, but every day I'm reminded of how shitty a job I'm doing."

"Shitty a job? Dude, you don't really mean that, do you?"

I look Abel in the eyes. "I sent her to school yesterday in a pajama shirt . . . on their end of the summer picture day."

"Oh, who fucking cares. I'm sure you can't even tell."

Deadpanned, I say, "It said 'time for bed' in big letters across the front."

Abel snorts but tries to hide it. He fails miserably. "Not the end of the world, but I see what you're saying. For the record, that's not failing, that's just some funny shit. What you need to focus on is Mac's well-being. If she's being fed, if she's happy and protected. You're doing all those things. To me, that's a win. The small things will come in time. You haven't even been her guardian for a year yet, man. It's only been a few months. You need to give yourself some credit."

"I'll give myself credit when I'm living up to the same standards as Cassidy."

"You can't chase her, Ryland. That will end poorly. She wouldn't want that either. Keep Cassidy in Mac's memory, that's what you can do, but you have to develop your own way of parenting, or you'll kill yourself in the process. Which brings me back to this Gabby girl. Maybe it's a good thing that she's close. Maybe she can be an outlet for you. You know, someone who can help you blow off some steam."

I shake my head. "No, I can feel this snowballing on me."

"Why? Because you liked her?"

"Yeah," I answer truthfully. "I liked her. I liked that night we had. I liked everything about it. And I know if I give myself an inch, I'll take a mile. Mac will end up suffering in the long run."

"Or maybe she'll thrive because you're thriving. Ever think of that?"

I glance at my friend. "You're fucking irritating me."

"Because I'm right. Admit it."

"No, because you have a comeback for everything. Jesus. Can't you just shut up for a second and let me wallow in my situation?"

"Now, what kind of promise would I keep to Cassidy if I let that happen? You were directed to take care of Mac. And me? She told me to take care of you. Therefore, if you had fun fucking the neighbor tenant, I say do it again . . . and again . . . and again."

―――

"Look at me, Uncle Ry Ry," Mac says, carrying a box labeled "The Chewys."

Not that they needed to be packed in a box, but Mac demanded that The Chewys, as in Chewy Chondra and Chewy Charles, got their own special box that she, and no one else, was allowed to haul around. We even put holes in the box so they could "breathe."

"Glad we got The Chewys in the new house," I say as the movers drop what few belongings we have into the living room, one small box at a time.

Aubree and Wyatt have been so helpful the past few weeks with packing and taking care of Mac while I went to different appointments for the house closing. Now that we're here, moving into a new place, just me and Mac, I feel . . . fuck, I feel nervous.

I feel like puking.

A huge weight rests on my shoulders because, before all of this, Aubree was living in the guest house at the old place and would come over for dinner, play with Mac, and help her get ready for bed. But now, we're on our own. We've become a duo. And that scares me.

What if I forget something?

What if I'm not good at this on my own?

Fuck . . . what if Mac doesn't like living with just me?

"Why do you look green?" Aubree asks as she walks by me with a side table in tow.

I reach for it, taking it out of her hands, carrying it to the massive living room. How the hell am I going to fill this space?

"What are you talking about? I'm not green," I say.

"Your face, you look all pukey. Hattie," she calls out to our sister. "Doesn't Ryland look like he's going to puke?"

Hattie comes up to me in her classic bike shorts and oversized Hayes Farrow shirt and examines me—making a whole scene about it of course.

She leans in close, scans me up and down . . . even fucking sniffs me.

"You know what, he does look pukey. Hayes, look at Ryland."

Hayes Farrow—one of the biggest voices in music and my sister's boyfriend—walks up to us, loops his arm over Hattie's shoulders, and looks me up and down. "You know, now that you say it, he does look green."

Deadpanned, I say, "I expect more from you."

He shrugs. "Spending too much time with your sister."

"It's showing."

"What's showing?" Wyatt says, joining us now, wearing a rainbow wig and unicorn horn. Not sure how he became the designated dress-up partner for Mac, but I swear I see him more in costume than anything else now.

"Hattie's influence on Hayes," Aubree says as she moves close to Wyatt. I watch him place a kiss on the top of her head, and if I wasn't so happy for both of my sisters, I'd feel an ounce of jealousy. But how could I when they've been through so fucking much? I just want them to be happy. *They* deserve that. And more.

"Oh yeah, he's a completely different man," Wyatt replies.

"Says the man in the rainbow wig," Hayes counters.

Wyatt adjusts his hair. "You know, it takes quite the personality to pull this off. I have no shame. I know neither of you would wear it."

"I've worn that damn thing at least a dozen times this month," I say to Wyatt.

"Is that why it smells?"

"Fuck . . . off," I reply. "It doesn't smell. If anything, it smells like the lavender body spray Hattie gave Mac. She practically soaks the wig in that."

Wyatt snaps his fingers and points. "That's what I've been smelling. I thought it was some secret flower that I wasn't seeing. Makes more sense now."

I stare at him for a few seconds. "You're supposed to be a bestselling author."

"Yeah, well, we can't live on the pedestal we're propped up on forever. We have our human moments."

"Clearly." I let out a sigh. "Hattie, think you can order us some pizza and drinks—"

"Hold on, why are you looking green? You're not just going to skip over that."

"I'm not looking green."

"It's four against one," Aubree says, circling her finger to the group. "So it's best that you—"

"Uh, excuse me," a voice comes from the door.

Together, we all turn toward the door, where Gabby stands in a pair of bike shorts and a crop top, her curves on full display. She has her hair tied up into a long ponytail, and she's wearing tennis shoes, which leads me to believe that maybe she's about to go work out.

"Hey . . . Gabby," I say, trying not to show the four pairs of eyes watching this interaction that I'm the least bit fazed by her.

"Hey. Uh, someone's car is blocking mine, and I was looking to take off."

"Oh sure, yeah, uh . . ." I grab the back of my neck. "What does it look like?"

"A Rivian?" she says.

"That's me," Hayes says with a lift of his hand. "I'll move it for you. Sorry about that."

"Not a problem," Gabby says, giving Hayes a quick double take. You can see her response written all over her face . . . *is that . . . is that Hayes Farrow?*

In fact, it is.

To her credit, she didn't squeal or carry on. She shakes her head a bit as she starts to turn away from the group. But not before Hattie calls out, "Hold on, you must be the new neighbor. Have you guys introduced yourselves?" Hattie points between me and Gabby.

Oh Hattie, we have more than introduced ourselves.

I've seen her naked.

I've felt her body wrapped around me.

I know what she sounds like when she comes.

"Yeah, we know each other," I say awkwardly as I stick my hands in my shorts pockets.

"You know each other?" she asks.

"I mean . . . we've met," I correct, not wanting to go deeper with my sister eyeing me. The last thing I need is for them to pry into that side of my life that I'm trying to shut down.

"When Ryland and his niece came to check out the house," Gabby adds.

"Oh, cool," Hattie says and then turns to me. "You never told us you met your tenant."

"I don't need to tell you every aspect of my life," I reply.

"Might be nice. We're invested after all," Aubree says with her arms crossed over her chest.

"Not something we need to talk about with Gabby here—"

"Hey, you're the girl we saw the other day," Mac says, running right up to Gabby. "I heard Uncle Ry Ry saying bad words about you."

Jesus.

Fucking.

Christ.

"Bad words?" Gabby says, staring me down with a raised brow.

"Why would you say bad words about her? She seems pleasant," Hattie says.

"And she's your tenant. I feel like that's not a great thing to do," Aubree adds.

"Not to mention, you shouldn't be saying bad words in front of Mac," Wyatt continues.

Why are they making this into a nightmare?

Is that their intention?

Because they're doing a good job at it.

Truth be told, I *was* saying bad words about Gabby. But to *my* credit, I muttered them under my breath with no knowledge of my niece possessing the hearing of an owl.

And if we really need to go there, it wasn't necessarily bad words about her. I was more . . . irritated about my situation.

"Can everyone just fuuhh . . . uh freaking chill? I was muttering bad words because I feel out of my element having to be a landlord." That's quick thinking on my feet. Proud of myself. "Not because of Gabby. It wasn't something I thought too much about until, well, it was too late, so yeah."

"Well, you have nothing to worry about," Gabby says. "I'm incredibly low maintenance. I won't be requiring anything from you."

"Good to know," I say. "But if you need something, don't hesitate to ask." I try to tack on a smile, but I know it seems strained.

"Okay, but I won't need anything."

"But if you do," I counter.

"But I won't."

I nod. "Gotcha, but know that I'm here."

"I think she gets it," Wyatt cuts in.

I give him a look, and when I go back to Gabby, she's already taking off without saying another word.

"Dude, that was embarrassing to watch," Wyatt says.

"Once again, this coming from the guy in the rainbow wig."

Wyatt pulls the wig off his head as Hattie says, "She seems really nice."

"Uncle Ry Ry likes looking at her."

"What? No, I don't," I protest. Is this new house giving Mac some super sense?

"Yes, you do."

I turn to my niece, trying to remain calm as I say, "No . . . I . . . don't."

Mac's lips turn down as she points at me. "You do."

Christ.

"He does, does he?" Aubree asks with a smirk.

A large sigh falls past my lips because Jesus, can we not?

"I don't. I've seen her once," I say even though that's a big fat lie. "Please don't make a big deal about this."

"Who's making a big deal?" Hattie asks. "We're not." The way she bats her eyelashes tells me she's not innocent at all.

"Just drop it, okay? There's nothing to see here. I will barely see this woman, possibly only in passing. Like she said, she won't require anything from me. Not a single fucking thing."

# Chapter Seven

## GABBY

"I'm jealous that you get to work out on the beach," Bower says through FaceTime as I fill up my water bottle with more water.

"You should be. It's amazing. Seriously, you need to move here. We can share the apartment, really cut down on rent costs, and we can live out our *Golden Girls* era."

"We are thirty. I'm not ready to shack up with my friend for life yet."

"Then don't live with me. Just come live here. We can work out together on the beach. While I'm at school teaching, you can do what you do, and then at night, we can meet up and troll the streets, looking for the next hot ticket."

"Hot ticket?"

"You know, penis to ride."

She lets out a heap of a laugh. "Are you really that horny?"

"I'm always that horny," I say. "You know that. I have an appetite for orgasms." Well, I have since Ryland Rowley showed me that they were more than a fairy tale. *Certainly never found them when I was with . . . him.*

*God, don't think about him, Gabby. Those days are over.*

"If that's the case, just wander next door."

I give her a look as I remove my makeup with a wipe. "That's not going to happen. We already discussed this."

"I know, but how great would it be if it did happen?"

"We're not even going to talk about it because it's not going to happen."

"Fine," she groans.

"But you can still move here, you know?"

"Let's see how it goes first when you tell your landlord that you're his assistant coach as well. Because chances are high that you might not have a job after that conversation."

"He can't fire me."

Can he?

"Maybe not, but he can make your life miserable."

I scoff at her as I toss my makeup wipe in the trash. "Please, my entire life has been miserable. Do you think I'm going to let some coach take me down? Never."

"He isn't just some coach. He's the man who made you sing to the angels while he was deep inside you."

"Dear God. Can you not phrase it like that?"

She chuckles. "I kind of liked it."

"Either way, orgasm or not, I can handle him."

"You know, you're scrappy, one of the many things I like about you. You could take him."

"Thank you."

"Also, if he does give you grief, you can always let Bennett give him a talking-to."

I shake my head. "I take care of Bennett. Bennett doesn't take care of me."

"That seems rather . . . one-sided. What happens when he goes up to the big leagues and he's making millions a year? Are you going to let him take care of you then, or are you going to continue to live in squalor?"

"I wouldn't call this squalor," I say as I move to the shower and turn it on. "This is a nice place."

I say that as the pipes behind the wall rumble.

The faucet to the tub rattles.

And when no water appears, I question the very sentence I just spoke.

"Why do you have that look on your face?" Bower asks.

"I turned on the shower, and nothing's happening." I turn it off and make sure the plug that you pull up to get the water to come out of the showerhead is down.

I try again, this time waiting for the water to come out of the tub faucet, but when it rattles and rumbles all over, fear creeps up the back of my neck.

Uh-oh.

"You know, from where I'm sitting, it seems like you're not too happy about what's happening."

"No water is coming out."

"Is there water coming out of the sink?" she asks.

I turn the knob for the sink, and water drips out, just enough to wash my hands and brush my teeth, but it's not a steady flow.

"Uh, a little."

"What about the toilet? When you flush it, does water move?"

When did Bower become a plumber?

I flush the toilet and watch it refill.

"Yeah, that's working."

"What about the kitchen?"

I head out of the bathroom and straight to the kitchen, where I turn on the water and watch it flow slowly.

"Yeah, that's working. So what does that mean?"

She shrugs. "How the hell should I know? I'm not a plumber."

"Jesus, Bower. I thought you knew what you were doing."

"Nope, just interested if there is water coming out of places. Which makes me wonder, can you see water coming out of any walls?"

Hell, I didn't even think about that. I look around in a quick panic. When everything comes up dry, I let out a deep breath and shake my head. "No."

"Fascinating. Well, good luck with that. I'm sure you smell great after that long workout immersed in the briny salt air."

"Bower, you can't just check out."

"Why not? This isn't my problem. I can't do anything from afar other than annoy you with suggestions as to what you might smell like right now."

She's right about the annoying part.

"You need to help me problem solve."

"Okay," she says. "How about this? You walk over to your landlord, tell him your shower isn't working, and make him fix it."

"I can't do that," I say as I lean against my kitchen counter, feeling defeated.

"Um, you realize that's what landlords are for, right? They fix things in your place when they're broken."

"He just moved in today, Bower. Also . . . I sort of told him that I wasn't going to need him for anything."

"Well, that was dumb."

I roll my eyes. "How did I know the shower wasn't going to work?" It was of course working fine before I spouted off about not ever needing Ryland . . . for anything.

"That's what they call karma. You say you don't need him, then bam, you now have to go up to Daddy Landlord and ask him for help."

"Do not call him that."

"Sorry . . . Daddy Coach? Or Coach Daddy?"

"No daddy!" I shout, then drag my hand over my face. "You were right. You are not the person to be talking to right now."

"Told you."

"I'm hanging up."

"Go talk to him—" She's able to get those words out before I disconnect.

I set my phone on the counter and glance at the bathroom. Come on, I'm a smart, independent woman who has been on my own forever. I can figure this out.

I just need a better look.

Heading back into the bathroom, I cinch my robe tighter and throw my hair up into a clip. I get down on my knees to lean over the tub and inspect the shower faucet.

I study it for a few seconds, taking in the workings to make sure I'm not missing anything. You know, sometimes there's a secret button to make the shower work that not all showers have, just the annoying ones where people thought they would be different with the type of faucet system they chose.

Here's what I think: if I ever became president, I would make it mandatory for all showers to be the same. None of these pull ups and pull downs and press the button and swivel the toggle. No, they would all work the same so we don't have issues like this.

After examining it for a few more seconds, I turn the shower back on and wait for the water to come out . . .

The pipes groan.

They moan.

They act like they're on the brink of orgasm ready to squirt . . .

But nothing happens.

Maybe the pipes need some . . . stimulation.

I knock on the white tiled wall above the faucet to see if that helps.

But nothing.

I knock a little harder . . . because maybe this bitch likes it hard like I do.

But nothing happens.

I sit back on my heels, growing infinitely more frustrated. With one last effort, I slam my fist against the wall, only for the faucet to groan so loud that I fear it might blow right off.

That's not good.

The last thing I need is for the faucet to pop off and for water to flood the apartment because then what would happen? Can't live in a watery, mildewy apartment.

I quickly turn off the water and then lean against the tub.

Fuck.

Maybe . . . maybe I can take a bath in the sink?

I lift from the floor and stare at the minuscule sink in front of me.

I don't even think my arm could get a good rinse. Nor would I be able to wash my hair.

Mother . . . fucker.

I look up at the mirror, staring at my reflection. What are my options?

Well . . . I saw a hose out back. That's one way to make my nipples freeze off. Not to mention, if Daddy Landlord—don't tell Bower I used that term—saw me hosing down, he might evict me.

I could go stay at the inn, but that place is pricey. Very pricey.

There is a truck stop about forty-five minutes away that I know has showers because I saw them once and thought, what an unpleasant place to shower given how grubby it was.

There's always the opportunity of sneaking into the school locker rooms and showering there. Then again, if someone caught me, that might not be a good look. Nor do I think a naked teacher in the high school locker rooms is a smart idea.

Can't afford a gym membership right now, hence the beach workouts.

Ughhhh . . . fuck.

That leaves me with one option—talking to Ryland.

I groan even louder, then reluctantly head to my front door, where my shoes and sandals are lined up.

"Of all the freaking days the shower has to stop working. It was working fine before, but then he goes and moves in, and now I need to ask him for something. Why . . . why me?"

I slip my sandals on, fling my door open, then stomp down my stairs, hating every second of this.

I'm not going to need anything . . . *why did I say that?* It's like when someone says there isn't a cloud in the sky, and then out of nowhere, it pours.

Stopping in the driveway, I study which door I should use. I could knock on the back door that leads to the kitchen—I know this because I secretly peeked through the windows before he moved in, you know, just to assess.

Then there's the front door, which is far more formal.

If we were friends, I'd go to the back door, but since he's my landlord, it looks like I'll be going to the front.

Thankfully, the streets are quiet as I walk around the house. I keep my arms pinned down to my side because I know I don't smell like roses as I head up the porch steps to the dark purple door. I take a deep breath, then knock three times.

I shift on my feet, looking anywhere but at the door, and when no one answers after a few moments, I question if I should ring the doorbell. It's late, though. What if his niece—Mac, right?—is sleeping? I don't want to wake her up.

Anxiety prickles at the nape of my neck as I try to figure out what to do. Maybe . . . maybe I should knock again.

So I do. I knock again, a touch louder this time, and then I wait.

And wait.

And wait.

Nothing.

Dammit.

Do I have his phone number? I don't think I do. Maybe it's on some paperwork that I stuffed away in a drawer.

Resolving that he won't answer, I head back down the porch steps toward the garage. As I ascend the stairs, I glance over my shoulder at the kitchen just in time to see him move by the window.

Okay, so he's in there.

Did he just not hear my knock?

Only one way to find out. I head over to the back door and knock again, really making sure it's noticeable this time. I wait a few seconds, and when there is still no answer, I grow extremely irritated.

What the hell is going on?

Is he ignoring me on purpose?

I know I said I wouldn't need anything from him, but he's

taking this to an extreme. And with how ripe I feel right now, in need of a shower, I'm going to make sure he knows I need him.

Taking a chance, I twist the doorknob, and to my surprise, it opens. Full of courage, ire, and stink, I push the door open just in time for him to look up from where he's doing the dishes.

The look of shock and fear greets me right before he throws a plastic plate right at my head.

I scream and duck, letting it hit the door behind me.

"Jesus fuck, what are you doing?" he says as he pulls out his earbuds, and I rise back up and look him in the eyes.

"You threw a plate at my head." I grip my heaving chest, trying to catch my breath from the onslaught of tableware.

"Because I thought you were an intruder. Just be happy it wasn't the knife in my hand." He sets down the cutlery and dries off his hands. "What the hell are you doing?"

"I was knocking, and you didn't hear me."

"I was listening to a podcast." He lets out a deep breath. "Jesus, my heart is racing."

"You're not the one who almost got nailed in the head by a plate." I pick it up and toss it on the counter before shutting the door.

"Why were you knocking?"

"Because I need help."

He lifts a brow. "I thought you weren't going to need anything from me."

How did I know he was going to say that?

He would be the kind of man with so much pride that he would use my words against me.

"Trust me, it's painful to even be here, but I don't have an option."

"I can see the pain in your face, like you're melting on the spot by just being near me."

"I don't need the play-by-play. I'm feeling it, thank you."

The slightest of smirks crosses his face before he says, "What do you need?"

"My shower, it's not working. And I tried everything I could, but it seems like my plumbing skills are as terrible as I thought they would be."

"Was your shower working before?"

"Yes," I answer. "And if I wasn't in such dire need to bathe, I wouldn't be here right now."

His nose crinkles. "You trying to tell me you stink?"

I clutch at my robe. "That's a little personal, don't you think?"

"For someone who has licked your pussy, I would say nothing is too personal at this point."

And just like that, my cheeks heat.

He nods toward the door. "Let's go check it out."

"Want me to stay here . . . because of your niece?"

He shakes his head and holds up his phone. "I have a monitor app on my phone."

"You have a monitor in her room?" I ask. I thought those were just for babies.

"Yeah, I like to make sure she's okay at all times. Got a problem with that?"

"No," I say, shaking my head. Wow, the playfulness in his voice immediately escaped. I don't think I've ever seen someone change that quickly. Note to self: he takes his guardianship very seriously.

"Then let's go to your apartment." We head out of the house and then up the stairs to my apartment. He walks in first, and from behind, I catch him taking in the space I've made my own. All the furniture is in place, centered by a rug in the living area. Curtains are hung as well as pictures. Fake plants are scattered throughout, offering some greenery without the responsibility, and a bookcase full of my favorite books sits in the corner next to my reading chair and lamp.

But he moves past all of that and heads straight to the bathroom, where I see my discarded red thong in the middle of the floor.

Jesus, Gabby.

"Uh, sorry about that," I say, snagging my clothes and tossing them outside in the bedroom.

"Not a problem," he says as he examines the faucet. He reaches to turn it on, and I swear to the plumbing gods if water comes out, I'm going to wish hemorrhoids on all plumbers. Because that would just be my luck.

*Oh dear Daddy Landlord, my water isn't working, please come help me.*

Flicks water on.

It works.

I will freaking scream!

Thankfully, as I wait on bated breath with my ass clenched, nothing happens. No water. He feels around and pulls on a few things . . . again, no water.

That's right, you be a droughting motherfucker.

He does a few more things, checks the toilet and the sink like I did, and then stands up and scratches the top of his head. "This was working before?"

"Yeah. I showered this morning."

"Did you do anything weird to it?"

"Like what?" I ask.

He shrugs. "I don't know . . . shove something up there?"

I purse my lips together as he turns toward me. "Do you really think I would shove something up there and then play dumb as to not knowing why the water isn't working? Don't you think I would have retrieved the thing I supposedly shoved up there?"

Another shrug. "Could have done it for attention."

My eyes narrow. "Do you think that's the kind of person I am?"

"I don't really know you at all. I'm just trying to check all of the boxes here."

"Well, check the box of *nothing was shoved up the faucet.*"

He slowly nods. "Then I think I need to call a plumber."

"Yeah, I could have told you that." I fold my arms across my chest.

"Janet, the plumber, won't be able to come over until tomorrow if we're lucky," he says.

"Tomorrow?" I ask. "She doesn't make emergency calls?"

"No, and this is not an emergency. This is you being unable to shower."

"Not that you need to know this, but I worked out like a beast right before this. I need a shower . . . bad. What am I supposed to do?"

He thinks about it for a second. "Have you ever showered in a sink?"

"You can't be serious."

He scratches the back of his neck. "Yeah, didn't think that was going to be the solution." He glances around. "Well, I guess you could use the downstairs shower in my house for now."

"Your shower? You don't think that's going to be awkward?"

"Once again, I've gone down on you. Nothing is awkward at this point."

"Everything is awkward because you keep bringing up that night," I counter.

"Because you're acting like we're strangers."

"We are strangers." I hold up my finger. "Tell me one thing you know about me."

"You like your nipples played with," he says with a know-it-all lift of his chin.

"Oh my God!" I shout. "Something that's not sexual."

"Okay, fine." He pauses for a moment. "You used to do travel work and now you don't."

"Is that factoid supposed to prove a point?"

"I don't know." He sighs heavily. "Fuck, I don't know how to navigate this situation, okay? The last thing I expected to see when I was showing Mac the house I put an offer on was you, and I've been . . . I've been trying to navigate how to handle this from that moment."

"There's nothing to handle," I say.

I can see him warring with himself because I might say there's nothing to handle, but oh my God, there is so much to

74

handle. Especially when he finds out that I'm his new assistant coach.

"If there's nothing to handle, then why do you think it's going to be awkward to take a shower in my house?" he asks.

Good point.

Got you there, Gabby.

Not wanting him to best me, I hold my chin high and say, "You're right, it won't be awkward . . . after all, you did go down on me, and if anything, oral satisfaction speaks for something."

"I guess it does." His eyes travel the length of my body, the heat coming off him immediately palpable.

I wet my lips.

His eyes fall to them.

I shift on my feet.

His hands clench at his sides.

"What?" I ask.

"Nothing," he says, but his voice betrays him as it's laced with unspoken words.

"Why are you looking at me like that?"

"Like what?" he asks.

I roll my teeth over the corner of my mouth, and he immediately attaches his gaze to it.

"Like . . . like you want to do something to me."

"And what would that be, Gabby?" His eyes meet mine now, and the intensity of green nearly splits me in half. He went from frustrated to intense in a few short seconds. He takes a step forward and adds, "What do I want to do to you?"

God.

I can practically feel his lips on me even though there's distance between us.

I can feel his body between my legs.

I can sense the tension in his shoulders as his orgasm takes over.

That night, it's not even close to a distant memory. No, it sits in my head daily. I'm constantly reminded about the way he owned me that night, the way he gave me everything I wanted, everything I needed. And now that I'm in a room with him, so close to his body, I can practically taste it.

"I . . . I don't think we should be talking about this." I start to move past him, but his hand grips mine, keeping my shoulder up against his. He's so close that I can smell the distinct scent of his cologne. The same cologne that imprinted in my mind as he drove into me, thrust after thrust that one night.

When my eyes meet his, he says, "And this is why I can't have you here . . . you're a fucking distraction."

I swallow the saliva building up in my mouth before saying, "Well, you're going to have to find a way to deal with it because I'm not going anywhere."

He wets his lips. "And what's your suggestion for how to deal with it?"

Fuck me.

Again.

And again.

And again until it's out of our systems.

Take me up against the wall.

Bend me over the couch.

Make me scream your name until my voice is hoarse.

Give me everything you did to me that night until you have nothing left to give.

I clear my throat and say, "Act like an adult." And with that, I pull away and add, "If you don't mind, I need to grab a few things, and then I'll be over to shower."

He steps back, irritation written all over his face, but also understanding. He sticks his hands in his pockets and slowly nods. "Sure. You can just walk in. No need to knock."

And with that, he heads out of my apartment, leaving me hot and bothered, and my body begging him to come back.

It's for the best.

That was the right thing to do despite the hunger in his eyes.

And the itchiness in my body to have him close.

It's one of the things I hate about being a sexually charged individual.

I love sex. I love fucking. I love everything about the rapturous feel of being brought to the apex of pleasure and then having it ripple through your body.

And sure, getting off on my own is fine. It fulfills a need.

But God, getting off with someone else, especially Ryland Rowley, that's an experience I crave.

Sighing heavily, I move around my bathroom and grab my toiletries. Hands full, I go to the kitchen where I snag a large Tupperware bin and place everything inside, using it as a temporary shower caddy. With my towel draped over my shoulder, I walk out of my apartment and down the stairs again to Ryland's back door. I walk right in, body tingling and aware when I see him at the kitchen sink, washing dishes again.

His corded back muscles tug against the fabric of his shirt as his large hands rinse the plates and stack them in the dishwasher.

I find the entire thing overtly sexy, and I know it's because I'm horny and I want him. And now that he gave me that one look, that is all I'll think about.

But I will not give in.

Clearing my throat, I ask, "Where's the bathroom?"

"Right over here," he says while turning off the faucet. He turns to face me, and once again, he gives me a slow once-over, taking in every inch of my body.

He pushes off the counter, and my stomach shivers from the thought of him removing my clothes.

But instead of touching me, bringing me up against the wall, and pressing his strong, hard-as-a-rock body up against mine, he leads me down a short hallway.

"We don't plan on using this shower since we have bathrooms upstairs, so feel free to leave your stuff until the shower is fixed."

"No need to worry about that. The shower will be fixed tomorrow." I smile and open the shower curtain, which is just a plain white sheet. I stare at the faucet. "Do you know how this works?"

"Not really," he replies. He turns on the water, and unlike my shower, this water is flowing. Then he tugs on a toggle, and it shuts the drain. Not the right thing. He undoes that and then looks under the faucet and pulls on a ring. The showerhead fires up and starts raining down on the tub.

"Hate to admit it, but I never would have figured that out." I try to lighten the tension between us, but it does absolutely nothing.

"Let me know if you need anything else," he says in a gruff tone. "Use the shower as much as you want."

I can see that he's mad at himself, more subdued than the man who almost threw me up against the couch and took what he wanted.

I think that realization has set in, and now he's possibly regretting what he said.

And oddly, I don't want him to regret it. Because I'm apparently deranged and like this slow form of torture. I enjoy the idea of him wanting me but denying himself.

But despite all of that, I have to admit, given our circumstances, Ryland Rowley is a nice guy. To offer me access to his shower is actually pretty kind. But I need to remember that he doesn't have the full picture here, and I'm in no rush for him to know it. So . . .

"No need," I reply. "The shower will be fixed tomorrow."

# Chapter Eight

RYLAND

"Two weeks?" I shout while Janet packs up her tools.

"Yes, that's when I can get the part, but then there's installation and fixing the tiling. Might be about two to three weeks, depending."

"Jesus," I say as I tug on my hair in frustration. "You can't just go and find one at the local store?"

She shakes her head. "Supplies are low from the housing boom. Everyone's struggling to find parts at the moment. It's two to three weeks for everything." Janet pats my arm. "Sucks to be a landlord, doesn't it?"

Yeah, I'm figuring that out more and more with each passing day.

"I'll bill you and be in touch about the part when it comes in. Have a good one."

And with that, she takes off, leaving me with some pretty shitty information. There's something wrong with the pipes behind the tiled wall. Since Janet had to tear the wall open to figure it out, not only does she have to change out the part—she explained what it was, but I blacked out—but she also has to fix the wall after that. This is not what I anticipated.

I thought it might be an easy fix, a little poke here, a little poke there—shows how much I know about plumbing—and then Gabby would be using her shower tonight. Fuck, was I wrong.

Also, really fucking annoying this wasn't picked up during the inspection before we closed. That's just my luck, though.

I straighten up Gabby's bathroom since Janet moved some things around. Then I head into her living room, pausing for a moment as I take in the cozy space.

This starkly contrasts what I have going on at the house. Sure, we just moved in, but I know it won't look like this when I'm done putting things away. We have very few pieces of furniture. I sure as hell don't have a rug, nor do I have curtains. We don't have any decorations, and any pictures we might have are small ones that go on a mantel rather than a wall.

Mac deserves a space like this, something cozy and comfy, that reminds her of her mom's love.

I look toward the door, checking to see if Gabby has returned. She said she was heading out when Janet stopped by, so I feel like I have a little time. Therefore, I pull out my phone, open up the camera, and take a few pictures of her place as inspiration. There's no way I could remember this, but with a little bit of—

"What are you doing?"

Startled out of my goddamn shorts, I fumble my phone only for it to tumble out of my hands and straight to the floor, where it crashes with a crack, breaking the screen.

I grip my chest as I bend down to pick it up and stare back at her.

Wearing a pair of jean shorts and a tank top with her hair coming out the back of a hat, she stares at me, hand propped on her hip, looking none too pleased.

Fuck, she's hot, even when she looks irritated.

Trying to return to a normal heart rhythm, I say, "I was, uh . . . I was trying—"

"You were creeping on me."

I feel my brows turn down in a frown. "I was not creeping on you."

"Then what were you doing?"

Yeah, Ryland, what were you doing?

"Checking a text message," I say, not even believing the words as they come out of my mouth.

"Really? You check a text message like that, holding your phone high, your fingers making it look like you're taking pictures of my place."

Well, when she puts it like that.

"It's a position I use for neck pain," I say.

She walks farther into the apartment, right up to me, and says, "Hand me your phone."

My height overpowers hers, but the attitude in her hip pop screams "try me."

"Why?" I ask.

"I want to see if you took pictures."

"Can't you just trust me?"

"No."

I shake my head in disappointment. "That's hurtful."

"Just give me your phone," she says while snagging it out of my hands. She briefly studies my phone. "Your screen is cracked."

"Uh, yeah, from you scaring me."

"Karma."

She flashes the phone at my face to unlock it, then pulls up the pictures. Her mouth falls open, and her eyes sear into me. "You did take pictures of my place. Why? What are you going to do with them?"

I grab my phone and slip it in my pocket. "Nothing."

"Uh, lies. What were you going to do? Is this some sort of creepy, perverted thing? Like take pictures of the places that belong to the women you've banged?"

My face falls flat with derision. "Yes, Gabby. I have an entire collection of random living rooms in my phone."

She nods, then pokes my chest. "I knew it. That's some sick stuff, Ryland. Do you stare at night and reminisce?"

"You realize how ridiculous you sound?"

She points at her chest. "I'm not the ridiculous one in this scenario. That would be you. Taking pictures of random girls' living rooms. That's real sick."

I roll my eyes. "I wasn't being a creep."

"Then what were you doing?"

Seeing as though she's not going to drop this, I just go with the truth. "Use them as an example."

Her face contorts to the side. "An example for what?"

"For . . . for decorating," I say, feeling all kinds of embarrassed.

"Decorating?" Her nose scrunches up in confusion.

I shrug, trying to pass this conversation off as anything but embarrassing. "You did a nice job, and I figured I could sort of use it as inspiration to give Mac a better place to live."

Her expression softens, and her defensive position eases. "Oh . . . well . . . that's nice of you. Thank you."

"Sure," I reply as I stick my hands in my pockets. "I can delete them, though, if it makes you uncomfortable."

"No, it's fine. Use them as an example."

"You sure?"

"Yeah," she says, looking just as awkward as I feel.

"Thanks," I say, then clear my throat.

"Yeah." She toes the floor as silence settles between us.

When she lifts her eyes, I can't help but stare at the two different colors and the way they sparkle in the sunlight. I can remember those eyes staring up at me when I drove into her, seeing the pleasure cross over her from my touch.

A lump of frustration forms in my throat, but I quickly swallow it away. What I wouldn't give for another moment with her, but I know that can't happen, so I need to tuck that away.

"Uh, about the shower," I say, tugging on my hair.

"Is it fixed?" she asks, looking unfortunately hopeful.

"Not so much," I say, causing her shoulders to droop.

"Really?"

"Yeah, sorry. Janet had to open up the wall and order a part, so it's kind of a disaster in there. I tried to make it as clean as possible so you could still use the sink and toilet—which she checked on and that is all good to go—but the shower will be about two to three weeks."

"What?" she shouts. "Two to three weeks?"

"Trust me, I'm not happy about it either. But yeah, it will take time for the part to get in, then it will take time to patch and tile the hole. It's a lengthy process."

Defeated, she sits on the arm of the couch. "So I'll be without a shower for two to three weeks."

"No, I mean you can use my shower. I know that it's not ideal, but it's there and available." Reaching into my back pocket, I pull out a key to the house and set it on the coffee table for her. "Here's a key. You can come and go as you please. I'm really sorry. I wish I had better news."

"So do I." She sighs. "That sucks."

"Yeah, I know."

She looks up at me. "Well, I guess just expect me to pop in at night. I won't bother you in the morning. I'm sure it's a race to get out the door with your niece."

"Mac," I say. "Or MacKenzie."

"Right, sorry. But yeah, I'll be there at night."

"Sounds good. I'll be sure to stay out of your way."

"Thanks."

And then we stare again.

The tension between us is thick as her eyes float to my mouth, and my eyes check out her full lips.

I can still feel them all over me, and it's been weeks.

Fucking weeks and the kisses she spread over my body feel like a sharp branding, a feeling I'm not sure I'll ever shake.

I clear my throat, bringing her eyes back to mine.

"Um, is that all?" she asks as she tugs on her hair.

"Yeah," I say as my gaze falls to her lips one last time. "That's all."

"Okay," she replies with uncertainty.

This is exactly why I need to stay away from her.

This reason, right here.

Because I can't seem to get myself to leave. I can't seem to tell myself to stop staring at her. And the only thing holding me back from pushing her up against the wall and mauling her is the smallest hint of will that's telling me I'll regret it.

That it'll open up a tidal wave of bad decisions that I can't handle right now.

The best thing for me to do is get the hell out of here before I do something I regret. Because I can't stop staring into her eyes, or at her lips . . . or repress the urge to pull her into me.

It's time to leave now.

"Well, if you need anything, let me know."

"Sure. Thanks."

Awkwardly, I nod, then scoot past her, trying not to brush up against her while I take off.

<hr>

"You have got to be fucking kidding me, Herbert," I say as I pace my principal's office. The brightly lit room decorated in academic accomplishments is a stark contrast to the maddened mood I'm experiencing.

"Do you think I'd just say things to piss you off?" Herbert asks as he pinches his brow, clearly not in the mood to deal with me right now, but I couldn't give two shits.

I place both hands on my hips as Mac sits in the chair in front of me, playing on an iPad with headphones. "I'm beginning to think that you are."

After the whole shower debacle, I came to the school to get some things set up for the school year when I got a call from Mac's daycare saying that she scraped her knee and wanted to be taken home.

Normally, I would have told the kid to suck it up and deal with it, kind of like what I tell my boys on the baseball team. But this is Mac. She's been through a lot, and I want her to know I'll be there no matter what—even if it's a minor knee scrape. So I picked her up and took her to my classroom, where I hooked her up with an iPad and headphones. I logged into Disney+ so she could watch *Tangled* for the millionth time. Her favorite character is Maximus. Are you even surprised?

"Ryland, please, the school year hasn't even started yet. I can't deal with this headache."

"I'm not the one creating a headache, Herbert. David is. He's the one who hired an assistant without discussing it with us. He's the one who is giving up my fucking office to the new assistant."

"Because the assistant office is attached to the locker room, and well, since she's a female, she can't really be in the locker room while the underage male players change."

I pinch my brow. "I understand that, Herbert. Given the situation, I'm more than understanding, but that doesn't mean she should take my office. Give her a fucking coat closet to sit in. Have her sit with the women coaches. Why give her my office?"

"I'm working on it, okay?"

"Are you? Because at this rate, she's going to have my job soon, and I worked damn hard for that job."

"I know, Ryland. I know." He exhales and leans back in his chair. "I have to navigate the system, though. It's more than just giving her a different office. I have to please David because what he thinks impacts my job as well."

I lean against the office wall, arms crossed. "Well, maybe David should stop living on some power trip and let the people in the job do their job. This is getting absurd."

"Unfortunately, that's not how school politics work."

"Clearly." I drag my hands down my face, this conversation doing nothing for my mood.

"Can I just ask—in the meantime while I figure out this office thing—that you let her use your space?"

I shake my head in disbelief. "I can't believe this. And when do I get to meet this new assistant of mine? I've been out on the field, working on it all by myself. Does she realize we have fall practice? Does she care to come out and help as well?"

"I can set up a meeting if that's what you'd like," Herbert says.

"I don't know, Herbert, what do you think?"

His face falls flat. "You don't have to be an ass, Rowley."

"Well, help me out here, Herbert. Because . . . fuck."

He tamps me down with his hand as he takes a peek at Mac. I know she can't hear a thing, so I'm not worried. "I know. I know. I'll set up a meeting. We'll get this figured out."

"Good," I huff. "I'd like to at least see her qualifications before the school year starts and maybe introduce her to an infield rake."

Herbert nods and makes a note on a piece of paper. "I'll set something up. How is your Friday looking?"

"Free."

"Then consider it done. Now, can you please attempt to calm down?"

I shake my head. "Not that easy."

# Chapter Nine

## GABBY

**Nathan:** *Haven't heard from you in a while. Heard you moved away. Want to tell me what's going on in your life?*

Do I want to tell my ex, who I've eliminated from my life, what I'm up to now? Yeah, pass.

It's not the first text I've received from him since we broke up, and I'm sure it won't be the last. I just ignore them and move on with my life because that's the healthy thing to do.

Speaking of moving on . . .

This shower is phenomenal. I hate to admit it, but I'm jealous because it's much better than the one in my apartment. The water pressure is significantly better, and I can really feel the water slice the crud off me. It's not that I have a lot of crud on my skin, but you get it.

The showerhead has more holes, so it feels like tiny needles poking me—trust me, it feels good.

And there's more room, a place for me to rest my foot while I shave, and a fan above so all the steam from the shower gets sucked right out of the room.

Kind of wish this was the bathroom in my apartment.

I can't complain, though. Mine is much better than other places I've stayed in before.

I finish drying off and start applying my lotion. When I arrived today for my nightly shower, there wasn't anyone around. The house almost felt . . . eerie. So, instead of looking for Ryland, I helped myself to the bathroom. Is this showering setup in a separate building from my apartment slightly inconvenient? Yeah, but I don't mind the water pressure.

Once I'm done with my lotion, I decide to brush my teeth and do my skin routine. Then I put my things in my bin and slide it in the cabinets under the sink. Since I'll be here for a bit, I might as well make myself comfortable.

With my robe tucked tightly around me and my dirty clothes in hand, I turn off the light and head out of the bathroom. I make my way down the hallway, ready to bolt out of the house, when I'm startled to a stop by the sight of Ryland sitting at the kitchen table, both elbows propped up on the table, hands digging into his hair.

That doesn't look like a pleased position.

For a moment, I think about just leaving and not bothering to ask him if everything is okay, but the small, curious part of me really wants to know what's going on. Maybe see that brooding frown of his that I seem to enjoy so much.

So I clear my throat and say, "Water pressure is great in there."

He lifts up only slightly to take in my silk robe and wet hair. He then brings his attention back to the table. "Glad to hear it."

Ooof, something must be really bothering him.

"Is there something troubling you?" I ask.

"Yes," he answers, surprising me. I half expected him to be like everything is fucking great and encourage me to be on my merry way.

"Oh, uh, want to talk about it? Maybe share a beer?" Not sure where that suggestion came from. What if he says yes? Do I really share a beer?

"I don't drink when I'm in charge of Mac," he grumbles.

"Not even one?"

He leans back in his chair now, and I feel his eyes scan my body before they meet my face. "Not even one." His legs are spread, his forearms casually draped on his thighs in front of him, his chin ever so slightly tilted upward. It's the kind of pose that screams don't fuck with me because he's ready to fight. And I hate that I find it incredibly attractive.

"Okay . . . then do you want to chat about it?"

"Not really," he says as his eyes drop to the slit in my robe.

My body heats up as I feel the intense gaze of those sultry eyes scanning every last inch of my lotioned-up leg.

Swallowing, I ask, "Are you sure? You look distraught."

He pushes away from the table and stands, his eyes remaining on me.

Oh God . . .

"Yeah, I'm sure," he says as he starts walking toward me.

What's he going to do?

My heart hammers in my chest with every step, the tension in his shoulders stiffening his body, giving him the kind of swagger no man should ever have.

But that's how it's been with every interaction.

This push and pull between us.

Right now, it's a whole lot of pull.

"Okay." As he approaches, it's hard not to stare at the way his shirt clings to his broad chest or imagine what the scruff on his jaw would feel like between my legs again. I've felt it before, and I'd love to feel it tonight despite my brain telling me it's a bad idea.

When he reaches me, he pauses and leans close. "You smell fucking amazing." Then he moves past me, his shoulder rubbing against mine as he makes his way into the bathroom and turns off the fan.

I'm humming.

My entire body went from relaxed from the showerhead to now overheated and needy.

It's time to bolt before I do something stupid.

"Well, if you don't want to talk about it, then I guess I should head back."

He leans against the doorway, eyes on me, arms folded. "Yeah, maybe you should."

It's a warning.

I can see it in his eyes.

If I stay, I'm subject to whatever is warring inside him.

Now the question is, what will I choose?

It's an easy answer. Take a few steps toward that door and let your pace propel you out of this house and up those apartment stairs.

I don't want to mess with him.

But then, I look back at him, at that devilish glare, and memories of the night we shared come flooding in. God, he was so good. The best I've ever had. It was addicting, getting that one taste and having to quit him after that. Torture, actually.

And now that he's here, my neighbor, the man whose shower I use when the sun settles, it's hard not to think back to that night and imagine what it would feel like if he took me by my hair, lowered me down, and let me suck him.

Let him bend me over.

Let him fuck me.

"You're not moving," he says.

"I'm . . . I'm thinking."

He pushes off the wall, knowing exactly what he's doing. "What are you thinking about?"

How much I told myself I wasn't going to do this.

How he told me there's no way he'd ever go near me again.

How this moment, right here, our eyes connected, hunger in both, was completely off the table.

"N-nothing," I say, my breath starting to seize in my lungs.

*Leave, Gabby.*

*Just leave.*

He moves forward again, his swagger a drug as he stands right in front of me. "You're thinking, but you're thinking about nothing. Tell me how that makes sense." He tucks a stray piece of wet hair behind my ear, his fingers lingering on my cheek.

"It doesn't," I answer.

"Then why say it?"

"Because . . ."

"Because why?" he presses.

I try to look away, but he grips my chin and forces me to keep eye contact. And with the three seconds that our eyes meet, I know this is a losing battle. There's no way I'm leaving this house without getting fucked.

Not with the mood he's in.

Not with my neediness.

Not with this electricity bouncing between us.

So I say, "I didn't want you to know what I was really thinking about."

"Why not?" He moves an inch closer.

"Because of the conversation we had out in the driveway."

He nods in understanding. "Tell me what you were thinking about."

I shake my head. "You don't want to know."

His hand falls to my hip, right next to the tie in my robe. "I really fucking do."

My mouth goes dry.

My nipples grow hard.

And a dull throb erupts between my legs as I search his beautiful eyes.

This is him giving me the go-ahead.

This is him saying yes.

I wet my lips. "I was thinking about how I'd love to drop to my knees and suck you off," I whisper. *Why can't I breathe?*

His eyes turn dark as his hand grows tighter, his fingers inching up to the knot of my robe.

"Is that all you were thinking about?"

I shake my head. "Not even a little."

He wets his lips as his fingers play with the knot of my robe, loosening it. "I don't want distractions."

"Then you should've told me to leave."

He loosens the strap completely so the robe falls open, exposing the center of my chest and all the way down. He slides his hand along my heated skin, his thick palm connecting with my bare hip.

"I really shouldn't fucking do this," he says as he moves in even closer.

"Then why are you?"

"Because I'm irritated. Because I need something to help me escape for a moment. Because ever since I saw you again, it's all I've fucking thought about." His hand glides up my side and rests at my rib cage. His thumb strokes the underside of my breast, firing off every nerve ending.

It's all I've thought about too.

It's all I want.

My chest heaves, and I want him to move his hand up higher to capture me right where I desire him.

And just as I'm about to say something, his other hand connects with my skin, this one sliding up the front of my stomach, right between my breasts and then all the way up to the base of my neck where he grips me just enough to turn me on more than I could ever imagine.

"Tell me to stop," he whispers, his thumb stroking just below my nipple.

I shake my head. "Never."

"Please, Gabby, tell me you don't want this." He brings his head closer to mine. "Stop me."

"If I did, it would be a lie." I slide my finger through the belt loop of his jeans and tug him closer.

"I need you to stop this."

Instead of listening to him, I undo his jeans and then slide my hand under his briefs, connecting with his stiff length. I shouldn't. I'll be his assistant soon, and he doesn't even know it. But how can I resist this? *It was just so, so good last time.* It's his fault I'm so needy. So desperate. "I want to keep going."

He hisses and bends his head forward as I start stroking him.

"Fuck," he mumbles, taking a deep breath.

"Touch me, Ryland. Play with me. Make me come again."

I squeeze his cock, causing him to growl. He picks me up by the waist and carries me to the bathroom, then shuts the door. Setting me on the counter, he slides the robe off my shoulders so it's resting in the crevice of my elbows and grips my neck again.

Looking me dead in the eyes, he says, "I need you fucking quiet, got it?"

I nod, only for him to drop down, spread my legs over his shoulders, and bring his mouth to my center.

"Oh fuck," I say as his tongue makes a long, languid stroke right up my slit.

He pauses and looks up at me. "I said fucking quiet. Do it again, and we're done."

I seal my lips tight and nod.

Then he disappears between my legs again, and it's the best feeling ever.

The scruff on his jaw rubs against my inner thighs while his tongue laps at me, driving against my clit. He tugs on me, pulling me closer to the edge of the counter, then spreads me wider. He brings his hand up my stomach and right to my breast, his palm brushing against my hard nipple.

"Yes," I whisper. "Play with me."

His dexterous fingers find my nipple, and he starts rolling it. Tugging ever so slightly, he brings me to pleasure so fast that I almost feel embarrassed.

It should not be this easy. I should not get worked up this fast, but oh my God, with what he's doing between my legs and the way he's playing with my breasts, I can't stop myself.

"Fuck," I whisper. "I'm close."

He pulls away for a moment. "Already?"

I nod, feeling my breaths grow heavy.

"Then I need to slow down."

I shake my head. "No, please don't."

But he doesn't listen. He stands and tears off his shirt. I take a moment to appreciate his chest and all the muscular divots.

He's so fit with his bulky arms and thick forearms . . . and those hands. God, I fucking love his hands. Large, thick, and ready to take charge when you give him permission.

Weapons.

Those hands have created chaos in the past.

So goddamn sexy that I want him to create chaos now.

From his back pocket, he takes out his wallet and then snags a condom. Thank God for that. He then pushes his pants and briefs down, revealing his perfect cock.

Yes, perfect.

It has just enough girth not to be too intimidating but to stretch me out and fill me up. His incredible length hits me in a spot no other man has. And it's beautiful. Mouth-watering. So delicious that I find myself sliding off the counter and right beneath him where I cup his balls, then drag my tongue all the way up his length.

He lets out a low, drugged hiss as his hand connects with my face, his thumb passing over my cheek.

"I love your cock," I say right before I take it into my mouth and pump him with my hand. In tandem, I suck and squeeze, working his length all the way down to the bottom and then back up.

I roll his balls in my hand, playing with the seam of his scrotum.

And when I pull off him and look up, I see just how lost he gets in my touch.

It's empowering.

"Fuck, you're so good," he says as he encourages me to take him in mouth again, which I do. I take him all the way to the back of my throat, then gag, so he can feel the way his cock controls me. He lets out a low groan and thrusts to the back of my throat. My eyes water, but I let him do it one more time before I pull away. I flatten my tongue and lick him up to the tip, then down to his balls where I run the tip of my tongue along his seam. I flick at his balls, teasing him, edging him.

"Jesus Christ," he mumbles right before I work my way back

up to his tip. I suck him in, only to the head. I swirl my tongue around and around.

I'm loving the way his chest muscles fire off. How his thighs squeeze tightly. And how his hand sifts through my hair, as if I'm the lifeline he needs.

When I bring him all the way back to my throat again, he stiffens and lets out a garbled sound before stepping away. He backs up against the wall, staring down at me, his eyes full of wonderment and hunger.

"I need that pussy." Then he hands me his condom and I sheath him, only for him to move to the covered toilet. He takes a seat and leans back, then in the sexiest way possible, he beckons me with two fingers. "Get over here."

Drenched and so fucking ready for him, I walk over to him. He spins me around, then gently guides me down to his lap. I reach between us, angle his cock, and let him sink into me as I lower the rest of the way.

"Fuck," he whispers as he presses a kiss against my exposed shoulder. "You're so goddamn perfect. Love this cunt."

I lean back against his chest and swivel my hips as his hands find my breasts. He massages them, using his palms, letting my nipples move across his fingers as he squeezes.

"So wet. So responsive."

"You're huge. God . . . so fucking big," I whisper as I get lost in the way he controls me.

I swivel over him, seeking out my own pleasure, letting him thrust into me, play with me. It's all too good.

So freaking good.

And as I rest against his chest, getting played with by this man, he wets two of his fingers and rubs my clit, heightening the experience. Creating a tingle that moves through my arms and legs.

"Yes," I lightly moan, keeping it quiet as I rock my hips, taking charge of the pace, because now that he's rubbing my clit, I can feel my need for release close in. "Right there, Ryland. Right . . . there."

Adrenaline spikes through me.

Need pummels into my chest.

"Shit, you're close. I can feel it."

"So close," I say.

He then pushes me forward, so far forward that I place my hands on the floor in front of me as he scoots to the edge of the toilet.

He grips my hips tightly, and he moves them up and down at such a rapid pace, letting his cock rub against me in such a delicious way that I turn feral.

I want this release.

I need this release.

I squeeze around him, letting him feel how tight I can be, and it's what he needs as he stands now and starts pounding into me. His pace is relentless, thrusting over and over again.

"That's it, Gabby. Squeeze my cock."

I squeeze again when he slams into me, and he's anything but quiet about it, like he told me. He groans and because I like how unleashed it makes him, I do it again.

And again.

And one more time before I feel my orgasm building to a point of no return.

"Right . . . there," I say right before my orgasm rips through me, the pleasure so intense that my body goes limp. The only reason I'm still standing is because Ryland is holding me up.

It takes him a few more strokes, but as I convulse around him, he stills and then lets out a low groan, coming inside me.

"Fuck," he says sharply as he catches his breath and helps me back up to a standing position.

His hand is wrapped around my stomach, holding me close to his undulating chest. We both stand there for a moment, my vision coming back to me while he slowly starts to regulate his breath.

After a few seconds, he releases me, gets rid of his condom by folding it up in toilet paper and tossing it in the trash, and then he turns to me and helps me adjust my robe so it's back on my shoulders. While I'm cinching it back up, he dresses himself. And when we're both decent, he sticks his hands in his pockets and shyly smiles as if he wasn't just the commanding alpha a few seconds ago.

It's adorable.

Hot.

And is making me think crazy thoughts in my head like . . . maybe I could stay a little longer and we could do this again. But when his eyes shift to the door, I realize that thought is a fleeting one.

*This is a one-time thing, Gabby.*

*Keep it that way.*

I wait for a moment to see if he's going to say something, anything, but as he remains silent, my nerves get the best of me, and before I can stop myself, I say, "Uh, sorry if that was—"

"Don't fucking apologize," he growls, his brows pinched together in irritation that I would even consider apologizing.

"Right." I nod. He's right, I should not apologize. I never apologize about sex, so why start now? "Um, are you feeling better?"

He pushes his hand through his hair. "I mean . . . how could I not?"

That makes my cheeks blush as he reaches for the door, and I lead the way out to the kitchen. Not a child in sight, which is a good thing. We didn't make enough noise to wake her up.

"Is it anything you want to talk about?" I ask. "You know, now that you're more . . . relaxed." God, I can still feel him between my legs.

I can still feel the scrape of his beard.

And I know I have his scent all over me. It's intoxicating me as I attempt to act as casual as possible.

"Just work stuff. I coach baseball, and they hired a new assistant, and well, they're taking a lot of control out of my hands, and I hate that."

I blanch.

God, what was I thinking?

This man is my landlord.

My boss.

And here I am, freely dropping to my knees.

But fuck, it's Ryland Rowley. He's so good. Everything about him.

So good.

"And I don't handle situations well when I don't have control," he continues.

My mouth goes dry, and I don't know what to say when his eyes meet mine.

I really don't.

Because, as Taylor Swift would say, I'm the problem . . . it's me.

"But I don't need to bore you with that shit." He lets out a deep breath. "Anyway, this probably shouldn't happen again."

I nod, feeling like this is some sort of out-of-body experience. "Yeah, probably not."

"It's too risky."

"Right," I say.

"And . . . addictive," he says, his eyes reaching mine.

I swallow, all the worries and the anxiety over the situation taking over. What the hell do I do? Do I report to the school and tell them I can't take the job? When Ryland finds out it's me, he might have a heart attack, especially if they're giving him a hard time.

And God, I just had sex with him again.

He's going to think I'm fucking with him. When, in reality, this is just sort of all a coincidence. I thought I bombed the interview. I didn't think I would get the job, so the one night with Ryland was very appealing. Now that I have the job and he's my landlord and my boss, things are more complicated.

Maybe . . . maybe I just need to go to the school tomorrow and smooth things over with the principal because I don't want them making any special concessions for me.

The last thing I need is for Ryland to be pissed at me. Not only because he holds the key to my shower rights but also because I genuinely don't think he needs the extra layer of stress in his life.

"Okay, well, I'm going to go."

He nods. "Have a good night."

"You too," I answer awkwardly, then bolt out of there as quickly as I can.

I need to make an action plan and make one quick before this all blows up in my face.

# Chapter Ten

### GABBY

I sit in my car, staring at the school in front of me as Bower goes on and on about a piece of chocolate cake she experienced.

Yes, she experienced it, not ate it . . . that she *experienced*.

I've heard that it was life-changing.

That it was orgasmic.

That it was unlike anything she's ever put in her mouth.

And even though I'm happy for my friend that she found a piece of chocolate cake that really suits her needs, I need her to focus on me.

Selfish?

Maybe.

But a piece of chocolate cake does not overtake the situation that I'm currently living.

So while she's describing the sprinkles that were on top of the cake, I cut in, "We had sex."

She pauses.

She pauses long enough that I swear I can hear her thinking from the other side of the phone.

"Umm . . . what?" she asks, popping her lips.

"Ryland and I had sex."

"Yes, I'm aware. Why are you bringing this up again?"

"No, we had sex again."

"Wait, for a second time? Even after he said there would be no distractions allowed?"

"Yup," I say. "It happened last night. He fucked me in the downstairs bathroom." Whispering, I say, "I can still feel the way he gripped my hips."

"Dear God," she sighs. "How did this happen?"

"Well, that's the shitty part. He wasn't himself last night, and I asked him if he wanted to talk about it because, I don't know, he seems like a good guy, and he took pictures of my apartment because he wants to replicate it for his house, and I thought that was cute, and technically, he's a single dad—"

"You're rambling, Gabby."

"I know because I feel shitty, like really shitty, because he was upset about his assistant coach last night. I guess they're making accommodations for me that I never asked for and that I don't even know about, and he feels out of control and—"

"Um, do you not remember how he didn't even pay you the courtesy to show up to the interview? Or have you forgotten that?"

I pause because she's right. I did forget about that.

Still . . .

"I know, but I still feel bad."

"Why?"

"Because he's . . . he's a single dad in a way, and he seems out of his element. I don't know, maybe because he was fucking his assistant coach last night, and he had no idea."

"Yeah, that could be it. Maybe you should tell him, clear your conscience."

"I feel like I need to, but I'm here at the school first because I want to talk to the principal and let him know that I don't want any special concessions. I don't want to step on toes. I'm just happy they hired me. I want to work hard and earn my position."

"You know I love a go-getter, but . . . what kind of concessions because if we're talking you get your own en suite bathroom, I think this is something we should negotiate."

"It's a public school, Bower, there are no such things as en suite bathrooms."

"Uh, I bet they have them in a kindergarten classroom. Take one of those."

"You want me to take a classroom from the kindergartners? What is wrong with you?"

"I'm power hungry," she says. "I'm okay with flapping a dick around and demanding what we want."

"First of all, we're not flapping a dick around. Second, I won't make any friends if I'm stealing classrooms from five-year-olds. I want to go undetected."

"Suit yourself, but don't come crying to me when the annoying, quirky, yet obtuse teacher, Miss Meghan, won't let you pee in peace."

"I'll manage." I get out of my car and lock up before I head toward the brick building.

I will say this, for being a public school, the grounds are very well maintained. And I know this school has been around for decades, given the architecture, but there isn't any paint chipped, or a broken window, or a door hanging off a hinge. It's pristine, well taken care of, without any vandalized spaces in sight.

"You know, I feel like you call me, but you never take my advice. What's that about?"

"You give terrible advice, Bower."

"Then why do you call me?"

"Honestly," I say. "I'm questioning that this very minute."

"Hurtful, Gabby. When you say things like that, it makes me not want to answer the phone when you call."

"Please, you would never not answer. You thrive off the gossip."

She sighs heavily. "You're right. You feed me well with the drama. Let me know what happens with the principal and if he even offers you the kindergarten classroom. If he does, don't turn it down right away. Let's at least take a tour of it before we give him our decision."

"You are deranged, but I love you."

"I'll love you more if you score us an en suite bathroom."

"Us? You don't even live here."

"I might if your classroom has an en suite bathroom."

"Oh my God, goodbye, Bower."

"Bye, love you," she drags out.

Chuckling, I hang up the phone and head into the school entry, where I stop to talk to the admin at the door. I show her my ID and tell her that I'm here to speak with Principal Herbert. She unlocks the door, letting me in, then directs me toward his office.

"He should be out soon."

"Thank you," I say as I sit in one of the chairs outside his office. Most likely, these are the chairs the students sit in when they're in trouble. I never sat in one, but Bennett did. I can still remember the look he gave me when I arrived in the principal's office. He had a black eye and a grin. He wasn't even the slightest bit nervous about what would happen to him.

He got in a fight with a kid at school. The kid was picking on him all week when he found out Bennett was a foster kid. Bennett put him in his place right before he was knocked out by a door that was flung open. He took out the bully, and the door took him out.

He still laughs about it to this day. He thought he was some badass, sticking up for himself, only to be humbled by an entry point. Luckily, he just had to do some community service—trash pickup for four weekends around the school—and all was forgiven.

The door, though? I still think Bennett has a vendetta against it.

I choose a seat directly across from the office so Herbert sees me when he opens the door. I cross one leg over the other and attempt to get comfortable just as the door opens, and Ryland Rowley pops out.

Shit.

It takes about two seconds for him to see me, and when he does, his expression is a mixture of confusion and irritation.

"Oh, Gabby, what perfect timing," Herbert says. "We were just talking about you."

"We were?" Ryland looks between the two of us, clearly searching for answers.

Oh boy.

Here is the moment of truth.

"Yes, this is Gabriel, or Gabby as she likes to be called. She's your new assistant coach."

Ryland's head snaps so quickly that I swear it might tear off. "You?" he asks, pointing at me. "*You* are my new assistant?"

Cue the nervous laughter and terrified wave.

I stand from the chair and clench my hands together. "Um . . . yes."

"Do you remember her?" Herbert asks. "She's Bennett Brinkman's sister."

"Wait, what?" Ryland's head looks like it's about to explode, and I don't blame him. This must be a bit much for him, and I didn't make it easy. I probably should have told him earlier.

"Bennett Brinkman, currently in the farm system, one of the best prospects out there. He was an All-American here," Herbert continues, clearly not reading the room very well.

"I know who Bennett is, but . . ." Ryland studies me. "I don't . . . I don't recall . . ."

"I sat in the outfield most of the time," I say. "I didn't like being around the parents. I think we met a few times, but, you know, nothing that made an impact."

Ryland runs his hand across his forehead. "You have no qualifications. What the fuck makes you think you can coach with me?"

Okay, seems like we're choosing anger.

I don't blame him.

I'm kind of throwing him for a loop at the moment.

"Ryland," Herbert says in a disapproving tone.

"No, Herbert. I want to know. What team has she coached before? What's her résumé?" He's fuming.

He's fuming so much that I actually feel my body start to shake, which means my ability to defend myself becomes smaller and smaller—something I truly hate.

Thankfully, Herbert steps in and says, "She doesn't have experience coaching a team."

"Oh, wonderful. Just the candidate I was looking for," he says sarcastically. "Someone with zero experience."

"Hold on," Herbert says as I try to find my voice. "If you let me finish, I was going to say that she coached Bennett. And Bennett's talent is a wonderful testament to how she can handle coaching. And what David said, under your tutelage, she can understand the mechanics of running a ball club."

"Under my tutelage?" He points at his chest. "So she can steal my job, just like she's stealing my office?"

"I don't want to steal your office," I say, finding my voice.

"Too late, it's already been done."

He starts to move past us when Herbert says, "Ryland, we should really talk this through."

"No, I don't think that's a good idea," he says. "Because if I start talking, you're not going to like what comes out of my mouth."

And with that, he heads out of the office and straight for the exit.

"I'm sorry about that," Herbert says. "He's . . . he's been going through a rough time."

"It's fine," I say. "I actually came here to tell you I don't want you to make any special concessions for me. I don't want his office. I don't want anything from him. I just want to be able to do my job and do it well. I want to earn my spot. I don't want things handed to me."

"Well, that's very commendable of you, Miss Brinkman. Why don't you come into my office, and we can chat some more?"

I nod and let him lead the way. But nothing is taking away

the pain in my gut, knowing how Ryland must be feeling so blindsided. *I did that to him.* And he certainly didn't deserve that.

---

The canned laughter from *The Big Bang Theory* fills my apartment as I lean back on my couch and sip on my water. I skipped the shower tonight and opted for a washcloth-type rinse because, well . . . I was too afraid to go into the lion's den.

With my luck, he's pacing at the door, ready to attack.

Nope, I took my chances with a washcloth and some soap . . . and some good scrubbing.

Tomorrow, I might attempt to take a shower when I see that his truck is no longer in the driveway.

Until then, it's just me and my water and—

*Bang. Bang. Bang.*

A shiver of fear pulses up my spine as I look toward my door.

Oh God.

It's him.

It has to be him.

And he's . . . still seething.

Heart pounding, I swallow the lump of saliva in my throat and call out, "Yes?"

"Let me the fuck in," Ryland says, growling through the door, ready to attack.

Umm, I don't foresee this going well for me, so I shoot off a quick text to Bower.

**Gabby:** *If you don't hear from me by tomorrow morning, Ryland murdered me and disposed of my dead body via garbage disposal.*

"Gabby, now," he says, his voice growing angrier by the second.

Heading toward my doom, I turn off the television and walk to the door. I unlock it and start to open the door, only for him to do it for us both. He charges into the room like a raging bull, then quickly spins around to look at me when he pauses at the kitchenette table.

"Shut the door."

"Are you sure?" I ask. "It would be better for people to hear my screams when you murder me."

"Shut . . . the . . . door," he repeats, and this time, a tiny droplet of spittle flies off his lip.

I do as I'm told because I fear his head will pop off if I don't, creating a mess all over my beautiful, soft area rug. And let me tell you, it's an absolute bitch to clean. The last thing I need are bloodstains on a cream carpet.

He angrily pushes his hand through his hair and turns on me. "What the actual fuck? You knew this whole goddamn time, and you didn't say anything to me?"

Yup, this is going to be way worse than I imagined.

I clench my hands together in front of me. "I did. And honestly, I didn't know what to say. I didn't expect you to be my landlord. I didn't expect you to be so . . . brash at first, and well, I was trying to settle in before everything happened."

He takes a step closer and says in a terse tone, "You fucked me last night. You fucked me knowing that we were going to have to work together. Why?"

I pull on my bottom lip, trying to find an excuse, anything that would make sense, but I come up short. "I don't know, Ryland. I got caught up in the moment, and I . . . I had fun that first night. Not to mention—"

"That first night," he says, standing taller. "Hold on, did you lie to me that first night?"

Oh boy . . .

I take a calming breath. "Listen—"

"Un-fucking-believable," he yells as he heads toward the door.

No, he can't leave, not in the middle like this, not when we have to work together.

"You weren't there," I say before he takes a step outside of the door.

"What?" he asks.

"You weren't at the interview. It was . . . it was insulting. I didn't think I did a good job, and when I ran into you at the bar that night, I thought there was a chance that you would recognize me. And when you didn't, well, I went with it. I always thought you were extremely attractive, and I took a chance on spending one night with you. I had zero inclination that I'd get the job, and I was trying to make a shitty day not be so shitty."

He pauses, his brows slowly lowering. "I wasn't at the interview because I wasn't invited."

"What do you mean?" I ask.

"I mean exactly what I said. I wasn't invited. David, the guy who hired you, kept me out of the hiring process and offered you the job without consulting me. I've been kept in the dark this entire fucking time. So yeah, this is all a big fucking surprise to me."

"Oh," I say, feeling bad now because if I would have known that, I wouldn't have pursued him. I sort of went for it that night out of spite. "I didn't know that."

"So you just used me that night?"

"Uh, hold on." I hold up my hand. "You were an equal participant. We used each other. And I didn't think I'd ever see you again."

"If that were the case, then why did you take the job?"

"Because I needed it," I say in a stern voice. "I need this job, Ryland. I don't have it as easy as you—"

"Easy?" he shouts. "You fucking think my life is easy?"

"You just bought a gigantic house. You're the head coach of one of the most premiere high school baseball teams. You have a family. You have it pretty easy."

He takes a step even closer now, so close that I can smell his woodsy cologne. "My life has been anything but easy. You're just seeing it from the outside. You have no fucking clue what I've been through or what I'm going through."

"Ryland—"

"Do you think I'm just taking care of my niece for the fun of it?"

"I—"

"I'm not," he says, getting so close I can practically taste him. "My sister Cassidy died a few months ago from breast cancer, and she made me promise to take care of Mac. Mac doesn't have a mom or a dad. She lost both of them, and I'm her sole provider, the one person she can fucking count on. And that house? I purchased that house with the money my sister left us and what I saved up when I had to sell my place and uproot my life to take care of my niece. I wanted to get my niece out of the house where she watched her mom slowly die and put a smile back on her face. I needed to pull her out of this funk she's been living in. That was not self-indulgent. That was a last-ditch effort to do the right thing in the honor of my sister's name."

Oh my God.

I . . . I had no idea.

I feel my eyes well up as I say, "I'm . . . I'm so sorry, Ryland."

He takes a step back. "I don't need your pity."

My brows turn down. "I'm not offering you pity. I'm offering you condolences."

"I don't need those either." He pulls on the back of his neck and stares at the wall behind me as silence falls between us.

Because where do we go from here?

I need this job.

I need this apartment.

I need this opportunity to prove myself in the sports field.

And just because things are complicated doesn't mean I need to give that all up.

I clear my throat. "Maybe we can find a way to make this all work."

"Find a way to make it work?" he asks, then shakes his head. "No, there's no way this is going to work."

"You're not even giving it a chance."

"Because this is so fucked up," he shouts. "Jesus Christ, Gabby. Did you really have to fuck me last night? You could have left me alone. You could have walked out of the house. But no, you told me you wanted to suck me off, knowing . . . knowing the situation. Do you know how complicated that makes this?"

"It was a lapse in judgment, Ryland. Okay? We all make mistakes."

"That was a big mistake. Because what the fuck am I supposed to do now?"

"What do you mean?"

"I mean . . ." He looks me up and down. "How the hell am I supposed to coach knowing you're standing next to me?"

"I don't understand."

He tosses his hand to the side. "I fucking like you, Gabby. I don't want to admit it, but I do. I'm attracted to you. I love being inside you. I love hearing the way you moan when you come and the way your tight cunt squeezes my cock . . . it's fucking addictive." He grows closer again. "How the fuck am I supposed to deal with that when you're working so close to me?"

"First of all, that's not my problem," I say. "The way your body reacts to me is your issue, not mine. Second of all, it's not going to be a cakewalk for me either, hence why I couldn't leave your house yesterday. Why I let you undo my robe. And why I dropped down to my knees."

His chest grows heavy as he wets his lips. That same look he gave me last night reappears, the look that says he can lose control and take what he wants in a matter of seconds.

"You can't take the job."

That snaps me right out of the haze I was being sucked into.

I take a step back. "Excuse me?"

"We can't work together. There's history."

"Then learn to deal with it," I say. "I'm taking the job."

"You can't be fucking serious."

"I am serious. And the audacity for you to even mention that I don't take the job . . . because you can't handle it? Well . . . fuck you, Ryland. The world doesn't revolve around you. You're not the only one who hasn't had it easy. I need this job, and I'm not about to give it up because of your inability to control your urges."

"That's not what it's about," he says even though that's what it feels like.

I cross my arms. "Then what is it about?"

"The proximity is too close. You live next to me, and you're going to work next to me. We have to coach together. There's too fucking much. Not to mention, you lied to me, and you don't have any experience."

"I have plenty of experience," I say. "I might not have formal coaching experience like you, but I know everything there is to know about baseball. I trained and coached Bennett from when he was younger to where he is today. Even to this day, he'll send me videos of his at-bats, and I'll tell him what he can adjust. I'm a huge asset to you, and you're too stubborn to even give me a chance."

"Because I don't know you," he yells. "I know nothing about you other than you lied to me about who you are and that you're my tenant with a broken shower."

"Well, maybe you should spend some time getting to know me," I say with a lift of my chin.

He shakes his head and starts moving away. "I have no interest."

"Then this will be a very long season for you, Ryland. Very long."

# Chapter Eleven

## RYLAND

"Thanks for watching her," I say to Aubree.

"Not a problem at all. Wyatt was excited when you asked." She leans in. "I think their bond is getting strong. She might like Wyatt more than me."

Normally, I would chuckle, but I don't have it in me. "Yeah, I don't blame her."

"Hey," Aubree says, mouth agape as she pushes at my chest. "You're rude."

"Just telling it like I see it." I lean against the doorframe of the front door and let out a sigh.

That must clue in Aubree because she tilts her head to the side and asks, "Is everything okay?"

"Not really," I say.

"Okay, what can I do?"

"Exactly what you're doing. Take Mac for the night. I just need to clear my head."

"Are you going to be alone?"

I shake my head just as Abel and Hayes pull up. "No, Abel and Hayes will be here."

She glances over her shoulder and then back at me. "You know, it wouldn't hurt you to invite Wyatt to a guys' night."

"I would have, but Mac insisted on playing with Uncle Wyatt, and I wasn't going to tell her no."

"Fair, but just don't forget about him. He can be sensitive."

I roll my eyes. "You're talking about Wyatt. He writes about murdering people for a living."

Aubree scoffs. "That's fictional, and I bet if you asked him, he'd have marginal remorse about murdering."

"Yeah?" I ask and then call out to Wyatt, who's playing with Mac in the front yard. "Wyatt, do you ever feel bad about the people you unalive in your books?"

He continues to gallop like a goddamn horse, arms up and everything. "I live for it."

I turn back to Aubree with an *I told you so* look.

"Well . . . just keep him in mind next time."

"I will." I then walk down the porch stairs and up to Mac, who is asking Wyatt to canter. "You have fun with Uncle Wyatt and Aunt Aubree tonight, okay? And no negotiating about bedtime, understood?"

"I know," she says in that four-year-old voice that tells me she's over the parenting and knows everything there is to know about the world.

I pick up Chewy Charles and Chewy Chondra—who are friends again—and I say, "Make sure Mac is a good listener."

"I'm always a good listener," she says even though that is the biggest lie of them all.

"Okay. Give me a hug." I kneel, and she launches into my arms, squeezing me tight.

"I love you, Uncle Ry Ry." *This.* This is the only good thing that came from losing Cassidy. *Only this.* Her unconditional, unrestricted love and affection.

I press my head against hers and say, "Love you, too, kiddo."

When I release her, I stand and watch as she takes Wyatt's hand and he brings her over to the car to get buckled up.

Aubree walks by with Mac's overnight bag. "Have fun."

"Thanks. Spoil her."

"Always do." Aubree winks, then she takes off as Hayes and Abel walk up with beer and pizza in hand.

"You look like shit," Hayes says, passing by.

"Real gaunt-like," Abel adds.

"Thanks," I say sarcastically as I follow them into the house.

They pause in the entry, and both look around. They take in the fully packed boxes, the askew furniture that isn't entirely in place, and the empty, barren walls.

"What the hell have you been doing?" Abel asks. "It doesn't even look like anything has changed since you moved in."

"Not true," Hayes says as he points at an empty box that's tipped over and being used as a barn for the Chewys. "That box of blankets is empty."

"I haven't had time or energy to do anything with the house just yet. I have to give it some thought as to what I want to do first."

"Yeah, making yourself a vision board?" Abel asks as we head into the kitchen, where we put the pizza and beer on the table. I grab a roll of paper towels and toss them beside the food as we all take a seat.

Hayes flips open the pizza box and starts handing out giant slices to everyone.

If you had told me a year ago that I would be sitting at a kitchen table with Abel and Hayes, sharing a pizza amicably, I would have told you, you'd lost your goddamn mind. When we were younger, Hayes and I were best friends. Inseparable. Along with Abel, we did everything together.

But when I went off to try my shot at the big leagues, my girlfriend, Samantha, who I left behind, got pregnant. She told me Hayes was the father. And that effectively ended our friendship. It wasn't until a few months ago that I found out the truth. Hayes wasn't the father, but another guy named Nick. Hayes never cleared the air because he thought if I could believe he'd do that to me, then I didn't deserve the truth.

The only reason we're friends now is because he fell in love with my sister Hattie.

But now that he's back in my life, I've never been more grateful for a friend. He's the same guy he was over a decade ago. Loyal, trusting, and passionate about the things he loves, my sister being one of them.

"So . . . are you making a vision board?" Abel asks, really pressing.

"I barely have time to make my own bed, do you think I have time for a vision board?" I ask as I open my beer and take a drink.

Hayes settles for a soda from my fridge, probably acting as the DD for Abel. I know he used to drink a lot—more than he probably cares to admit—but ever since he's been with Hattie, that's changed. He's found his groove again with his music. He's happier, lighter, and fun to be around when he's not jabbing me with playful insults.

"I can get Hattie to make one for you," Hayes says.

I shake my head. "No fucking thank you. You know how she is. The minute you give her any sort of power, she becomes commander in charge, and I don't need her taking control of this house. I want . . . I want to do it myself."

Hayes nods. "I get that. Any plans yet?"

"Nope," I say as I take a large bite of pizza. "Been dealing with some shit."

"Does this have any reason as to why you brought us here tonight?" Abel asks.

"Yeah," I reply as I lean back in my chair. "You know the new assistant who was hired for me?" They both nod their heads. "It's Gabby."

"Who's Gabby?" Hayes asks.

"Are we supposed to know her?" Abel adds.

"My tenant and the one-night stand I had."

Abel sits taller. "Wait, what?"

"Are you serious?" Hayes asks, his eyes widening.

"Why the hell would I joke around about this? Yes, I'm serious. The night that we were together, she was here for her interview. She knew who I was the entire time."

"Oh shit," Hayes mumbles.

"How did you find out?" Abel asks.

"The principal 'introduced' us. Imagine my surprise when I found out she's who I have to work with."

"Jesus." Abel takes a pull of his beer.

"Doesn't help that the other day, when she was using my shower because hers is broken, we fucked again."

Abel nearly spits out his beer but quickly holds it in, letting only a little dribble past his lips. "What? I thought you were against being distracted."

"Yeah, well, I had a shit day, and she was there, fresh from the fucking shower, and I was tempted. I gave in to temptation, and I'm not lying when I say I would probably fucking do it again . . . and again." I wipe my mouth with a napkin.

Hayes sets his piece of pizza on the lid of the box. "I'm confused. So this girl you had a one-night stand with, who is now your tenant, is also your assistant coach and I'm assuming co-worker? And you're mad at her, but you want to fuck her?"

"Yup," I answer simply. "And not just mad. Pissed. She lied to me."

"Yeah, that kind of sucks," Abel says. "But, I mean, can you really do anything about it?"

"No," I answer. "I have zero control over anything, and you know how . . . how out of my mind that makes me feel." I take a deep breath. "I can't stop this itching, nagging feeling that keeps pulsing through me. It's keeping me up at night. I don't know how to fix this. I don't know how to make this right."

"Is there even a way to make it right?" Abel asks. "I mean, it's not like you could have her fired. Not only is that unethical but she also doesn't deserve to lose her job because the circumstances are awkward."

"He's right," Hayes says. "Plus, knowing you, it might temporarily solve an issue, but you would live with that guilt for a

The Path to Loving Him

very long time." Not to mention, I'll be without an assistant coach, something I desperately need. Fuck, this is complicated.

Abel nods in agreement. "You might want to come off as some tough asshole who doesn't give a shit, but we all know that's not the case at all."

"So then what the hell do I do?"

"What's bugging you the most?" Hayes asks. "That she lied? That you have no control? That all you want to do is fuck her again?"

"All of it," I say as I drag my hand over my face in frustration.

They both go silent.

After a few seconds, I say, "Do I just act like everything is fine?"

"Acting like everything is fine has never worked in the history of humankind," Abel says. "I think it's one of those things where you'll have to talk to her."

"Yeah, set aside the anger and talk to her," Hayes agrees.

"That's easier said than done," I mutter just as the back door to the kitchen opens, and she pops in, her robe in hand.

When she notices us all at the table, she pauses. "Uh, I'm sorry. I didn't know you had company. I can shower another time."

"No, it's fine," Abel says. "We're just over here, chatting about you."

I quickly give my friend a murderous glare, and he just shrugs unapologetically.

Taking the bait, she leans against the kitchen counter. "What is he saying?"

Abel doesn't even skip a beat as he says, "That you tricked him, knew who he was all along, and that you lied. He's also struggling with how to handle you since he likes you, so . . . yeah, that about sums it up."

"You forgot the feeling-out-of-control thing," Hayes mutters.

"Oh, right. He feels out of control about the entire situation.

Something you need to know about our friend here is that he doesn't like to feel out of control."

"Abel," I growl.

"It's true. You see, he didn't have the best childhood—"

"That's enough." I turn toward her. "You can go take your shower."

She doesn't move. No, she continues to lean against the counter, holding her robe close to her. "Well, did he tell you that the reason I initially lied to him was because I knew who he was when I saw him at the bar and I was mad because he didn't show up to the interview I had for the job and I thought that he was slighting me? Did he also tell you that I didn't think I would get the job, so I thought a one-night stand would be fine? And did he also tell you that I had no idea he was buying this house, but I took the apartment because I could afford it, and it was better than living in a cardboard box down on the beach?"

Both Abel and Hayes stare at me. "He failed to mention such things."

"Yeah, dude, that's vital information that completes the story," Hayes says. "That's why there are always two sides."

Buying into this insanity, I say, "Well, what she's failing to mention is that the other night we had sex even though she knew that she was going to have to work with me very closely, not only in the same education department but on the field as well. She made it exponentially more uncomfortable."

"Uh." She holds up a finger. "Did you tell them that you were looking all sad and distraught—"

"Because they were giving you my office, and I had no control over it," I shoot back.

"I didn't know that," she defends. "And you were quick to move in close to me when I was talking to you that night. And you were the one who undid my robe. You made the move, and I think we both know at this point that we both find each other extremely attractive. Therefore, keeping our distance takes a lot of willpower that I didn't possess that night, especially when you looked all sad and gloomy."

"He does have a pretty sad and gloomy look," Abel says.

"I think you tried offering him a hand job once when he was sad and gloomy," Hayes says.

"Not fucking helpful," I say as my two best friends laugh together.

"You're right." Abel straightens up. "Being that we have heard both sides, I think the solution is . . . you're both adults, so why not just call it a miscommunication—something everyone hates—and move on from here?"

"I agree," Hayes says as he sips from his soda. "You're both in the wrong."

"How the hell am I in the wrong?" I ask, pointing at my chest.

"By being all butt hurt about the job. Dude, you can't do anything about it, so just move on and find out what her strengths are. You don't even know if she'll be a good asset. You're just over here bitching about how you had no say in it. If she sucks, then you can bring that to the board's attention. At least find out if she's trash before you start complaining."

"Valid," Abel says.

"For the record, I'm not trash," she says.

"And as for the lying, I mean, get over it, dude. She was protecting herself." Hayes shrugs. "We all do it, and she didn't think she would get the job. Also, are you really going to complain about the sex?"

"Yeah, are you?" Abel asks.

"He wasn't complaining when he was thrusting inside me," Gabby mutters, causing both Abel and Hayes to laugh.

I stare them down, letting them know that I don't think it's funny at all.

"Why don't you just go take your shower?" I say, wanting her to leave.

"Sure . . . want to join me?" When I look at her, she wiggles her brows.

I don't find it funny.

Not even in the fucking slightest because . . . yeah, I would love to join her.

I'd love to see the water sluice down her wet tits.

I'd love to press her up against the tile and tease her.

Tease her until she's breathless, then I'd stop.

I'd torture her.

Edge her.

Make her watch me as I stroke myself over and over again until I come all over her beautiful body.

Abel shoves at my shoulder. "Yeah, why don't you join her? We have no problem leaving."

"You're not going anywhere," I say in a murderous tone.

"Ooo, looks like we're in trouble," Abel says to Hayes.

"Yup," Hayes says as he bites into his crust.

"Well, I'll give you guys some privacy, then," Gabby says. "Enjoy the lecture." She takes off into the bathroom.

That's when I turn to my friends, who are wearing smirks that border maniacal. "What the fuck is wrong with you?"

"I knew he was going to open with that question," Hayes says.

"Dude, me too," Abel says, and to my dismay, they offer each other a fist bump.

"I'm going to fucking lose it on you."

Abel rolls his eyes. "Ryland, chill. We're just having fun. Maybe join in."

"How can I join in when—"

"When what?" Hayes asks. "A hot girl is asking for your attention? I know you feel wronged, but I'm having a hard time trying to figure out why this is so bad."

"Same," Abel says.

"She lied and used me," I say, flummoxed that they don't get this.

"It's not like she told you a huge lie. She didn't think she would see you again, so she fabricated a little lie to encourage the one-night stand. And well, I don't blame her for not telling the truth right away about the coaching thing with the way you've been stomping around," Hayes says.

"I agree," Abel kicks in. "She probably didn't want to deal with your grumpy ass."

"I'm not grumpy."

"Right now, you are," Abel counters. "I mean, sure, does it suck that you didn't get to have a say in who was hired as your assistant? Yeah, it does. But you can't do anything about it. The decision was made. Now you have to learn how to deal, and showering with Gabby seems like the perfect way to do it."

"I'm not going to have a fuck fest with my assistant coach," I say. "That's the worst idea. You don't fuck your co-workers."

Hayes shrugs. "I don't know. I fucked my assistant, and it turned out great for me." He smirks when I give him a murderous glare.

"That's my fucking sister you're talking about," I say.

"Yeah, I know." He shoves the rest of his crust in his mouth.

"I think what we're trying to say is that you're making a big deal out of nothing," Abel says. "And for someone who's dealt with blow after blow in his life, why not take advantage of something good?"

"I have a hard time seeing how this will turn out okay," I say. "I can't . . . I can't be distracted. Too much is on the line, and she's a distraction, a huge one. I'm already having a hard time keeping my eyes off her. The last thing I need is to be thinking about her while I'm trying to coach."

"Maybe think about it this way," Abel says, leaning forward on the table. "You don't fuck her every chance you get, you put up a wall and keep her at a distance, never feeding into the urge you have so when you're on the baseball field, attempting to coach with her next to you and one pass of the wind, blowing her perfume up your nose . . . then boom, erection."

"Jesus Christ," I mutter.

"He's right," Hayes points out. "You really don't want a boner on the field. That would be a detriment."

"Yeah, people might think you're smuggling a bat in your pants."

Hayes scoffs at him. "Dude, that's giving him way too much credit. No way does he have a bat-sized dick."

"You're right. My apologies," Abel says.

"Needless to say," Hayes continues, as if he's not annoying me further with the commentary. "I think you go for it with Gabby to avoid all public erections."

I truly can't stand them right now.

"Oh yeah, smart guys, what happens when it doesn't work out? When the fucking ends, and we still have to coach together?"

"Well . . ." Abel pauses. "I guess that's when you erect the wall."

"You're . . . a . . . moron," I say, pointing at him.

"Never claimed to be smart when it comes to women, hence why I'm unattached."

"And I'm not all that better," Hayes adds. "I fell in love with your sister when you and I were not on speaking terms."

"Pretty risky," Abel says and downs his beer.

"You're right. I don't know why I ever asked you two over for advice. I should have invited Wyatt."

"Wyatt?" Hayes scoffs. "You mean the guy who entered into a marriage of convenience with your sister?"

He's right.

Wyatt is *so* not the person to ask.

I scratch the side of my cheek. "Yeah, I need new friends."

"Maybe you can talk to Ethel," Abel says. "You know she'd love to be involved in this little conundrum." Ethel? Christ, I think one of my testicles just shrank into itself.

Ethel O'Donnell-Kerr is the owner of the local inn, Five Six Seven Eight, and the ring leader of the Peach Society, a group of ladies that controls the town's happenings. If something's going on in Almond Bay, Ethel will find out somehow.

"There's no way in fuck I'm talking to Ethel about this, and if she catches wind of it, I'm blaming you two." I motion between my ex-friends—because that's what they are to me now.

"The temptation to let her in on the secret is real," Abel says. Jesus, he's in rare form tonight. "I think we'll keep it between us for now, but if you mess this up, then I will bring it to the society."

"Mess up what? There's nothing to mess up."

"I don't know, she seems pretty chill," Hayes says. "She might be good for you."

"I don't even know her," I say as Abel stands from the table and pats me on the shoulder.

"Then maybe you get to know her." He nods at Hayes and says, "Let's get out of here so they can talk when she's done showering."

"I'm not talking to her," I say. "There's nothing to say."

"Okay, man." He winks, and both of my friends take off, leaving me worse off than when they arrived.

I'm not fucking talking to her.

Nope.

Not happening.

*Then why are you still in the kitchen?*

You could easily slip up the stairs to your room where you haven't even built your own bed yet.

But here you remain, eyes avoiding the bathroom, but also, checking the bathroom every few seconds.

The bathroom door opens, and she slinks out in her purple silk robe, her hair wet and braided, her skin glistening from whatever lotion she applied, a lotion I know smells like cherry and almonds.

I might have smelled it earlier today.

In the bathroom.

Nose to nozzle.

When she sees me sitting at the kitchen table, friendless, she pauses. "Aw, did your friends leave you?"

"Kicked them out," I say casually. She doesn't need to know the truth. She's quite familiar with not telling the truth.

She glances around the kitchen, then saunters to the table and takes a seat. Crossing one leg over the other, she allows the hem of her robe to slide to her upper thigh.

Christ.

I lift my eyes, avoiding the decadent amount of skin exposed, only to be greeted by the part in her robe showing off her cleavage. Those fucking tits. I could play with them all goddamn day. One shift from her would completely expose them. I'm salivating over the possibility.

Fuck.

Me.

"That doesn't seem very nice, Ryland." She flips open the pizza box and plucks a pepperoni off a slice, only to slowly stick it in her mouth. I watch in fascination as she licks her fingers before picking up a paper towel and drying them.

I clear my throat and shift on my seat. "Shouldn't you be going to your apartment?"

She nudges my beer and says, "I think we should get to know each other."

I shake my head. "Not a good idea."

"Not a good idea to get to know your assistant coach and co-worker? School starts in three days."

"Well aware."

She leans forward, her robe draping open. "Don't you think we should chat?"

My eyes fixate on the part in her robe and the delicious cleavage on full display.

"Mm, I see what you're more interested in." She stands from her chair and then, to my surprise, pushes me back and sits on my lap.

I tell myself not to give in.

Not to touch her.

To avoid all physical contact.

But fuck, I can't.

My hands grip her hips, and my tongue wets my lips.

"Is this the only way I'll get you to tolerate me?" she asks, running her hands down my stomach.

"This is not going to help," I say as my thumb rubs against the silky fabric.

"Maybe we can make it a game," she replies. This already feels like a goddamn game, one that I'm sorely losing. "For every question you answer, I'll give you a little something that I know you love." She undoes the tie of her robe and lets the fabric fall open. "You in?"

My head's dazed. Confused. Like I can't think straight as my hands move inside her robe, right to her bare skin.

"This . . . this can't keep happening," I say as I move my hands up her rib cage.

"Then stop touching me."

I wet my lips again. "I can't."

She smiles and shimmies out of her robe, letting it fall to the floor.

"Fuck," I say as I take her in.

Full breasts with dark nipples.

Curves that give me so much to hold on to.

Thighs that squeeze tightly around me.

She shifts on my lap, my joggers doing nothing to hide the way she makes me feel.

"Come on, Ryland. Play with me."

I bite the inside of my cheek, leaning back in my chair. "This can't happen again."

"It can't happen again tonight . . . or after tonight?"

Say tonight.

Set the boundaries.

Tell her no more.

"After tonight," I say, my voice coming out raspy.

She smiles seductively. "Then let's make it a good one and play with me." She trails her fingers down to my shirt and tugs it

125

over my head, leaving me shirtless. The cool air races between us, acting as a stark contrast to my heated skin. "You ask me a question, and I'll answer. When I do, you get to do something to me, anything you want, but also, if I ask you a question and you answer, the favor is returned."

I nod, lust racing through me. Because I want her . . . again. I want to play. I want to be inside her again, feel her clench around me. Hear her moan. See her lose all control.

And not just because it was a long time before her that I had sex, but because I feel alive when I'm inside her. *With her.* Everything about her is like a siren call to me. She's athletic, mouthy, witty—even when I try to ignore those things. Pretty doesn't even touch her beauty.

My body screams *want, want, want.*

Even though my brain says *run, run, run.*

"So you in?" Her fingers dance along my chest.

"Yeah," I say, making her smile.

Fuck, she's so gorgeous.

Why didn't I recognize her?

She's Bennett Brinkman's sister. I know I talked to her a few times. Why didn't I feel this clawing ache that I feel now whenever she's around? Why didn't I notice her before?

And why can I push past my anger and the irritation of the situation for another moment in time with her?

Am I really that easy?

Or am I really that attracted to her?

She shifts on my lap, her teeth pulling on the corner of her mouth . . . yeah, I'm really that attracted to her.

She drags her fingers from my temple to my cheek as she says, "I'll go first. Answer this question, and I get to play with you." She leans forward and says in a whisper, "Favorite movie."

"Favorite movie? That's what you're going to ask me?"

She nods. "There's a lack of communication and knowledge about each other, so we might as well fix that."

"You think knowing each other's favorite movie will help that?" I raise a brow.

"I don't know, Ryland." Her hands claw over my pecs and across my nipples. "You tell me."

I suck in a sharp breath, and because I want her so fucking bad, I decide to play along. "That would be *The Perfect Game* with Kevin Costner."

She pauses and looks me in the eyes. "Really?" It's my turn to nod. "That's mine too."

I lift a brow. "Don't fuck around."

"I'm not," she says as she shifts off my lap and tugs on my hand, pulling me up from the chair. "*Clear the mechanism.* It's what I used to say to Bennett when he'd go up to bat." She brings me to the living room and turns toward me. "I'm assuming since you were drinking, Mac's not here."

"She's not."

"Good." She then slips her hands under the waistband of my joggers and briefs and drags them down, my hard-on springing forward. I step out of my clothes, and she pushes me back onto the couch. "Now, for my reward." She lowers to her knees, but I stop her.

When she glances at me, worry in her eyes, I say, "That's truly your favorite movie?"

"Yes," she says. "I'm not going to lie, Ryland."

"You have before."

I can see the hurt in her eyes when I say that, but I'm not sorry because it's true. She's lied before, so how can I trust what she says is the truth?

"It's different now," she says. "You have my word that I won't lie again."

For some reason, I believe her because of the way she's looking at me and the truth coming from her expression.

"Okay," I say with a nod.

"Okay," she repeats and then lowers her body between my legs. She spreads my knees and starts kissing her way up my thigh, right between my legs. Her breath is heavy on my erection, her touch fucking teasing. She lowers her mouth just above the head and flicks her tongue out, licking the under part . . . only once, and she pulls away.

"Fuck," I mutter as she smooths her hands over my thighs.

"Your turn." She smirks.

Is that how this is going to be?

When she waits for me to ask a question, I realize it is, which means this is going to be really fucking painful.

"Favorite food," I ask.

"Besides your dick?" She leans forward and licks up my length, causing a hiss to erupt out of me.

"Fuck . . . yes, besides that."

She smirks and says, "Pancakes."

I take her by the hand and pull her back up to my lap where she sits, her arousal coming very close to my cock that's stretched up my stomach at the moment.

"Stay here," I say as I lightly drag my fingers up her chest and then circle them around her breasts. "Banana pancakes?" I ask as I make figure eights with my fingers, never coming close to her nipples.

Her head tilts back as she says, "Any kind."

When she sighs, I pull away, returning the same kind of torture.

She smirks down at me and then asks, "Favorite position."

"Sex or baseball?"

She smiles. "Baseball."

"Any position," I answer. "Love them all. They all are important in their own way."

"Mm, love that answer," she says as she reaches between us and grips my cock, then drags her other hand up my chest and starts playing with my nipple, flicking it and plucking at it.

It feels fucking phenomenal.

So good that my cock pulses against her grip.

"Yes," I say as my head falls back and my hips lift, looking for friction, but she doesn't reward me with any. "Uhhhhh, fuck. More."

She releases me and says, "Your turn."

My body spikes with need as I try to gather myself and think of something quick that I can ask her so she can return to what she was doing.

"Favorite . . . uh . . ."

She smirks. "Is your mind really blanking?"

"All the blood in my body is pooling in one area at the moment. I have very little brainpower."

She chuckles and leans forward, pressing kisses against my throat as her nipples rub against my chest.

"Not . . . fucking . . . helping," I say as I tilt my head to the side.

"Fight through it. Ask me a question."

As she drags her tongue down to my chest, I quickly think of something. "Favorite color."

She laughs against my skin and answers, "Purple."

"Cool, now ask me."

"Uh no," she says as she pulls away. "I want my reward."

"Fuck, right." I drag my thumb over my tongue before pressing my thumb to her clit.

"Ohhhh yes," she says as her hips swivel against my thumb.

I then grip one of her breasts and play with her nipple.

Her entire body moves, rocks, uses the very few seconds I'm playing with her to her advantage.

When I pull away, the look in her eyes is even more heated.

"Favorite food," she asks in a daze.

"That was my question."

"Doesn't matter, just fucking answer it," she says, dancing her fingers down my abs.

"Cupcakes."

That makes her pause and look me in the eyes. "Really?"

"Fucking love them."

"That's . . . that's really cute." And then her hand is on my cock, squeezing it so damn hard that my pelvis lifts off the couch.

"Ohhhh fuck. Uhhhhh, yes, more."

She licks my nipple, laps at it, and tugs on it with her teeth, giving me just enough pleasure without any pain.

"Jesus Christ."

I don't wait for her to stop because I don't want her to. "Favorite band."

She keeps a tight grip on me as she pulls away just enough to say, "Does Noah Kahan count?"

"Yes," I answer and then press my thumb to her clit.

"God, Ryland. Inside me. I want your fingers inside me."

I keep my thumb on her clit, then slide my fingers inside her. She bites down on my chest at the same time, and it's the most erotic feeling of my life. She then rides my hand, forgetting the questions as she swivels and thrusts over my fingers.

Her hand on my cock starts pumping while her other hand slides to the back of my neck, and she looks into my eyes.

It takes two seconds before her mouth is on mine.

Shit, I forgot how amazing she kisses. Last time we were together, we didn't kiss, we just fucked, but this . . . this is different.

This feels almost feral.

Like we're both clawing at each other.

Needing more and more.

Her mouth parts open and her tongue dances across mine. So delicious. So fucking good.

I meet her strokes as a whirlwind of pleasure rides through me, from her hand to her mouth. I feel out of control, but in a good way, like all these senses are firing off but also coming together at the same time.

Her grip on my neck grows tighter while her hips move faster. She pulls away from my mouth to moan as her head falls back.

"Fuck, I'm close. So close."

And that's my sign. I remove my hand, grab her by the waist, and move her to the side of the couch where she lies there in shock, a protest on the edge of her lips.

## Chapter Twelve

RYLAND

"What are you doing?" she asks as I stand from the couch.

"Giving you what you want," I say as I grip her jaw. "Open so I can fuck your pretty mouth."

Her eyes go wild as she opens her mouth, and I rub my dick along her tongue. It feels so fucking good.

Addictive.

I don't think I'm ever going to stop craving this.

I slide my length into her mouth and to the back of her throat. She takes me, most of me, as much as she can fit, and when I pull out, she lets her teeth barely scrape along the sensitive flesh, adding to the experience.

"You take my cock so well," I say as I pump into her again and pull out. "Such a good girl, opening wide. Letting me fuck . . . you. Jesus."

She swallows when I hit the back of her throat, and it sends me into a tailspin of needing more. I lean forward farther and grip the back of the couch as I thrust harder into her mouth, watching her the whole time to make sure she can take it, and she can, so I ride her wet, hot mouth until my balls start to tighten and my legs start to go numb.

That's when I pull out and stand there, my quads firing off, my dick pulsing, my chest heaving.

Her eyes are watery when she sits up on her elbows and says, "You need to come."

"Badly," I say as I itch for release. "But you need to ask me a question."

She sits up and brings her heels up to the edge of the couch. She spreads her legs and shows off her wet pussy to me before bringing two fingers to her clit where she starts massaging herself.

Eyes hungry, she asks, "Best fuck of your life."

"You," I answer, not even needing to think about it. "Without a doubt . . . you."

She smirks and then leans back against the sofa, pleasuring herself.

"I want your dick, Ryland. I want you deep inside me."

"Then lie back," I say as I move toward the couch and wait for her to lie down lengthwise. Once she's comfortable, I hoist one of her legs over my shoulder and then slip inside her within seconds.

"Fuck," she cries out and then moans loud enough for the entire neighborhood to hear. "Why is it so good?"

"Fucking incredible." I pulse in and out of her. "Fuck, you're so tight, you're so . . . Fuck," I shout. "Condom."

I go to pull out when she stops me. "I'm on birth control . . . but pull out before you come."

I nod.

"I want you coming on my tits, claiming them."

Well, fuck, she doesn't have to ask me twice.

I play with her tits, making her nipples hard as I start to slowly pump into her. Riding her bare is unlike anything I've ever felt before. This is . . . hell, this is my first time ever going bare, and she's ruining every other woman for me. Because nothing will beat this feeling.

Her walls are so tight, so warm, so wet. I can't get enough of it. I want this to last forever. I want to live here, worship her, and never leave.

"Faster," she says as she brings her hand to her clit. "Fucking faster."

"You close?" I ask. She nods, so I decide to slow down my thrusts, really dragging it out.

"No, Ryland. Please. Fuck me. Fuck me hard. Fill me with your cock."

"Patience," I say as I fall into a glacial pace. And I hold on to that pace. I savor it despite the sweat creeping up the back of my neck and the way my dick begs for more.

"Ryland. Fuck," she shouts. "Please, I'm . . . I'm desperate."

I spread her other leg wider and thrust in, pushing my cock all the way to the hilt, causing her to cry out. Her skin goes red, an acute sweat breaks out over her body, and her inner walls start to tense.

"That's it, baby. Use that cunt to squeeze my cock."

She squeezes again, creating a magical friction that seizes me, that makes me want to submit to her and let her know she is making me bow down to her like she's the goddamn queen as I feverishly pump into her.

Because no longer can I go slow.

No longer can I hold out.

I need her coming.

I want her dripping all over my length.

"Come for me, Gabby. Scream my name."

Her head thrashes to the side, she grips her breast, and her mouth parts open as her pussy clenches around my cock, throbbing, tugging, pulling me in. I thrust harder and harder as she yells out my name.

"Ryland, oh my God!" Her orgasm sends her into a state of bliss just as I pull out of her, lean forward, and use her arousal to lubricate my hand. I pump and pump, and as my cock swells, I groan, my head falling forward as I bust all over her beautiful tits.

"Fucking hell," I yell, spurt after spurt hitting her until nothing's left inside me. "Jesus Christ," I mutter as I fall onto the couch and attempt to regain my breath.

I glance over at her, loving the way I decorated her beautiful body. I watch in fascination as she rubs her finger over my cum and then brings it to her lips.

"Delicious," she says, making me want her all over again.

But before I can pull her to my lap and ask for round two, she's up and off the couch and headed to the bathroom. That's when I lean back on the couch and stare at the blank wall in front of me.

What the fuck am I going to do?

Being with her, being inside her, it's . . . life-changing. It's an escape. Nothing else around me matters. I can't even think of anything but the feeling she gives me when I'm thrusting so goddamn deep, and that's . . . that's a problem.

I black out when I'm with her.

Everything around me fades away.

And all I'm focused on is chasing the feeling I got the first night I was with her. And every time I am . . . that feeling reappears.

It's not good. It's not healthy.

I shouldn't be this attached to a fucking person without barely even knowing them.

I've never felt this carnal . . . feral feeling I get when I'm near her. And I don't know how to stop it.

Because I need to.

Before this started, I said this was the last time, so I need to shake this feeling from my brain.

This euphoric state I'm in.

I drag my hand over my forehead, smelling her on my fingers. It only reminds me of how she tastes and how she reacts to me when I touch her. She's so open sexually, so willing, which makes this so much harder because I want to explore, I want to—

"What's with the pained expression?" she asks as she walks up to me, her robe now on and a wet washcloth in her hand.

She drops in front of me and starts cleaning my dick off.

"Keep doing that, and you're going to make me hard again."

She smirks. "Can't have that." She finishes and takes the washcloth back to the bathroom. I reluctantly follow and slip my joggers on just as she returns to the kitchen.

"So what was the pained expression for?"

"Just thinking," I say, keeping my distance.

"Thinking how you're going to handle this moving forward since I'm your assistant coach, colleague, and tenant?"

"To name a few things."

"Simple," she says with a shrug. "We become friends."

I lift a brow. "Yeah, I don't see how that will help."

"Well, I'm a mystery to you at the moment. You know very few things about me, which is enticing. All you know is that the sex is amazing."

"Yeah . . ."

"Well, maybe if you knew more about me, then you would be more willing to hate me, which then decreases the appeal to have sex with me."

I scratch the side of my cheek. "Doubtful. Hate sex is a real thing."

"Would it help if I told you that I like to eat cheese and ketchup sandwiches?"

"What?" I ask, finding that slightly appalling.

"Yeah, ketchup and cheese on two pieces of bread." She does the chef's kiss motion. "Delicious."

"That's disgusting."

"Add some Doritos in the sandwich as well, and you have my favorite thing to eat for lunch."

"Jesus." I cringe.

"And I like to wash it down with grapefruit juice."

I shake my head. "No, no, you fucking don't."

"I do," she says. "It's a fantastic combination."

"I thought you said you wouldn't lie to me."

"I'm not lying. Dead serious. I love it."

I feel my gag reflex activate. "Why the fuck would you come up with that combination?"

"It's all that was available, all we could afford. So I became accustomed to it."

I pause for a second, my mind remembering something. "Wait, you were Bennett's guardian, weren't you?"

She slowly nods.

"You were . . . foster kids, right?"

I can see the wheels in her mind start turning. "Where are you going with this?"

"Well, if that's all you could afford, that makes me feel—"

"Nope," she says, shaking her finger at me. "Do not even think about it. I'm grossing you out. I'm not making you think anything else about me."

"Gabby."

"Remember when I knew who you were and I didn't tell you? Instead, I used your dick for my own pleasure. Remember how mad you were about that? Go back to that, Ryland."

That gives me pause as I wrestle with my feelings. "This is all fucking confusing."

"How about this . . . who do you think the best catcher in the league is right now?"

I lift a brow at her. "Are you going to say a different name just to argue with me?"

"No, I have a name set in my mind."

"How do I know you won't change it if I say the same person?"

"Fine, how about we write it down? That way, I can't change my answer."

I study her for a second. "From the look in your eye, I'm guessing you'll name someone controversial."

"No, I'm going to be right. And hey, now you can get a glimpse of my knowledge."

She might be right about that.

I take baseball trivia very seriously. The vile ketchup sandwich might have created pity, but if she tries to tell me that someone is a better catcher than the one in my head, that could create a real division, which in return would probably cool the temperament and need between us. Can't fuck someone who is wrong about baseball.

I rip off a piece of the pizza box top, and I hand it to her along with a marker from Mac's marker bin. "Write it down, and then I'll tell you who the best catcher is."

She takes the marker from me, uncaps it, and writes a name down. When she's done, she caps the marker and tosses it on the table, holding her cardboard close to her chest.

"Okay, who is it, Rowley?"

Rowley? Why do I find that so hot?

Clearing my throat and reminding myself what I'm trying to do, I say, "Whatever you wrote down, it's not correct unless you said Asher Peppers."

She smirks and flips her cardboard over. I read, "Jason Orson."

I roll my eyes dramatically. "You have lost your goddamn mind. You're only saying that because he's charismatic."

"Uh, excuse me?" she says. "Do you really think I'm that dense?"

"If you're saying that you think Jason Orson from the Rebels is better than Asher Peppers from the Bombers, then you have lost your goddamn mind."

"Explain," she says, crossing her arms over her chest.

"No." I shake my head. "I want *you* to explain."

"Easy." She takes a seat at the kitchen table, so I do as well. "Jason Orson has two championship titles under his name. Peppers doesn't."

"That's your reasoning? You realize it's a team event, right?"

"And within those two titles," she continues, "Orson averaged a .356 batting average, allowed only two stolen bases, and had a pop time of under two seconds, under pressure. Outside of the postseason, he's maintained a slugging percentage of just over four hundred and has easily one of the quickest, most accurate arms in the league."

I shake my head. "Orson used to be the best. Your question is who is the best now? And I would have said Orson maybe last season, but this season, it's all about Peppers. His pop time is a solid 1.5 seconds. He's had over three hundred and fifty putouts so far this season, his fielding percentage is just over nine hundred, and he's allowed three passed balls all season, as opposed to Jason's five."

"The Bombers pitching staff has more accuracy this year, making it easier on Peppers," she counters. "Not to mention, the Rebels have a tougher schedule than the Bombers."

"The schedule is not that different," I say.

"If you seriously believe that, then you're the delusional one." She folds her arms. "Bennett and I have been over this, how the Bombers skate by every year with an easy schedule."

"If it was so easy, then why aren't they winning?" I ask.

"Great question. Maybe because the team isn't that great."

"Which in return would make Peppers's job harder."

"Or," she counters, "it would make him more shiny to people like you since he's mixed into a talent pool of crap."

"Wow." I laugh sardonically. "You seriously have no leg to stand on. Just admit it, you like Jason Orson because he claims he has the best butt in baseball and is now selling potato salad to the masses."

"I couldn't care less about his potato salad."

"Did you hear that?" I say, holding a hand up to my ear. "That was Orson just squealing from the insult."

"I hope he did squeal." She sets her cardboard down and continues, "Well, this was helpful. Because after this conversation, I have a very small opinion of you."

"Says the person who'll be working for me."

"Oh, good luck firing me." She crosses her fingers and holds them out to me. "Me and David are like this."

That causes my eyes to narrow. "What the hell does that mean?"

"It means that he likes me, he's on my side, and you would be hard-pressed to figure out a way to get rid of me. So . . . good luck."

I give her a quick once-over. "You know what? You're right, this was a good conversation because now I know exactly what I'm going to do with you."

"Oh, you do, do you?"

"Uh, yeah," I say like a child.

"What are you going to do? Try to make my life hell?"

"As a matter of fact, I am," I say.

"Well, good luck to you because I had to army crawl, walk, skip, and jog through the depths of Satan's asshole to get to where I am right now. Nothing you throw my way will scare me."

"We'll see about that," I say, then gesture to the door. "Thanks for the quick fuck, but I'm done with you."

"Thanks for your sticky cum on my chest . . . I'm surprised it wasn't more."

I don't know why that grates on my nerves, but it does. "I fucking unloaded on you."

"I've seen more," she says with a shrug as she moves toward the door.

"I thought you said you weren't going to lie."

She looks over her shoulder and says, "I wasn't lying."

With that, she exits the house and shuts the door behind her.

*Bullshit, that was a lot of fucking cum.*

No way another man shot out more.

I grab a container to put the pizza in as my mind whirls.

No fucking way . . .

⸻

"Are you ready?" I ask Mac as I look at her in my rearview mirror all buckled up, looking fucking adorable with her pigtails.

"Yeah," she says softly as she looks out the window.

"Doesn't seem like you're ready. It seems like you're sad," I say.

"Because I am sad."

I put the truck in park and turn around to look at her. "Why are you sad?"

"Because I am."

Classic response.

"Do you want to talk about it?"

She shakes her head. "I just want to be sad."

"Okay," I say as I turn back around. "You're allowed to be sad, but you know, if you want to talk about it, I'm here for you."

She nods and clutches Chewy Charles close to her chest.

I pull out of the driveway, my chest feeling heavy because I don't like that look on her face.

I spent the weekend with Mac, finishing up the final touches to her room and making sure it's as perfect as can be. She has a horse mural, horse curtains, and horse bedding. Everything horses. And she loves it so much. Her smile last night as I tucked her into bed made all the hard work worth it. Thankfully, Aubree and Hattie helped a lot with decorating, or else it would still look like my room—a mattress on the floor with boxes everywhere.

"Are you nervous about the first day of school?" I ask.

She shakes her head. "No."

"Okay, because it's just like preschool last year. Same friends and everything."

"I know," she says, still looking out the window.

Okay, this is not about school.

"Uh, are you sad that I had a hard time doing a braid in your hair? I'm still learning, but I promise I'll get better."

She shakes her head, her pigtails whipping against her face.

"Are the Chewys in a fight again?"

"No. That's not what I'm sad about."

I sigh because fuck this is hard. "Well, I don't want you to be sad, MacKenzie. And if it's something that I can fix, I'd like to know. But if you don't want to tell me, that's okay, I'll drop it."

She's quiet for a moment and then she says, "Are you going to forget about me?"

Uh . . . what?

"Forget about you? How could I possibly forget about you? You're my top priority."

"What is prio-titity?" she asks.

"I mean you are what I care about most, I could never forget about you."

"But you've forgotten about Mommy?"

Uhhhhh . . .

"What do you mean?" I ask. "I haven't forgotten about your mommy."

"Yes, you have. There are no pictures of her anywhere in the purple house."

Shit.

I drag my hand over my face.

"That's because I haven't finished unpacking yet. Trust me, once I finish unpacking, I will be sure to hang pictures of Mommy everywhere. Okay?"

"Promise?" she asks.

"I promise."

"Okay." She's silent for a moment as guilt consumes me. I need to do something about the house. I thought it would be easy to move, but it's turning out to be way harder than I thought. In my spare time, I play with Mac, so by the time I put her to sleep, I'm exhausted or thinking about the upcoming season. Unpacking has been the last thing on my mind. Now that school is starting, it's going to get harder and harder. I make a mental note to tackle some unpacking this weekend, maybe make a thing of it with Mac.

"I'm sorry that I haven't unpacked," I say. "I've been having a hard time getting everything done."

"'Cause you're fixing that girl's shower?"

"Gabby's shower?" I ask. "No, I hired someone to do that, but it hasn't helped."

"I saw her when I was outside yesterday. She waved at me. She seems really nice."

That's one way to put it.

"Think she would want to play with me?"

Christ, why do kids ask questions like this? I want to answer Mac and say you need to stay far away from that Orson-loving wench, but she wouldn't understand why. I don't want to say she wouldn't play with Mac because that might hurt Mac's feelings. So I go with a simple answer.

"I don't know, maybe."

"Maybe you can ask her if we can have a playdate."

All I need is another playdate with Gabby, although this would be very G-rated.

"Yeah." I swallow. "I can ask her."

"Do you think she likes horses?"

"Who doesn't like horses?"

"Some people."

"Well, they clearly don't have good taste because we are horse people over here."

"You hear that, Chewy Charles?" Mac says and makes the horse neigh. "We are fucking horse people."

My eyes widen, and I look into the mirror. "Hey, we don't say that word."

"Aunt Aubree said it a lot when I was at her house."

I grip the steering wheel tighter. "Well, Aunt Aubree needs to learn that we don't say that word. Don't repeat anything that she says."

"She also said shit."

I nod. "Yup, another word we should not be saying, okay?"

"Okay." She glances out the window. "Mommy used to say crap. Can I say crap?"

I press my lips together, oddly wanting to keep that connection between Cassidy and Mac.

"Yes, but only at the house. You can't say it at school."

That brings a smile to her face. "Can I say it in the truck?"

"Yes." I sigh.

"Cool. Hey Uncle Ry Ry, look at that crap over there." She points at a garbage can.

I tiredly nod. "Yup, Mac, look at that crap."

**Ryland:** *Do you have any free time this weekend? I need help with the house. You know how painful it is for me to ask.*

**Hattie:** *I thought you'd never ask. I'll get all of the things together.*

**Aubree:** *It was looking rather . . . terrible the other day, I wondered when you would get it together.*

**Ryland:** *Wow, was looking for a little love from the both of you.*

**Hattie:** *Hence why we're willing to come over.*

**Aubree:** *It's called tough love, bro. It's what you've done with us. We learned from the best.*

**Ryland:** *I don't know if I should be proud or not.*

**Aubree:** *Hold your opinion until you see what we do on Saturday.*

**Hattie:** *Do you need me to get anything at the store? You know I'd be more than willing to purchase all the things to decorate.*

**Ryland:** *I think I just need to focus on unpacking at the moment, getting some photos up, and putting furniture where it should go. That stuff that we ordered online should be delivered by the weekend. We're going to have to put it all together.*

**Aubree:** *I can do that while Wyatt plays with Mac. I'm sure he'll do a good job distracting her.*

**Hattie:** *Do you need me to paint? I can paint.*

**Ryland:** *I need you to chill and tell me where to put things in the kitchen.*

**Hattie:** *God, that's boring.*

**Ryland:** *That's me . . . boring.*

**Hattie:** *According to Hayes and what he saw the other night, your life is anything but boring.*

**Aubree:** *Uh . . . what did he see? This is exactly why Wyatt needs to go to these bro-nights. I need to know what's going on. And why didn't you tell me, Hattie?*

**Hattie:** *Sorry, I was preoccupied all weekend. We went to a little bed-and-breakfast up north, and I thought Hayes was going to propose. Shock alert, he didn't.*

**Ryland:** *You think he's going to propose when you're clipping your toenails?*

**Hattie:** *I have to be prepared at all costs!*

**Aubree:** *I think the more you talk about him proposing, the more he pushes it out. You need to just let him do his thing.*

**Hattie:** *His thing is taking too long, and I don't appreciate it.*

**Aubree:** *Enough about the inevitable proposal, I want to know why Ryland's life is interesting.*

**Ryland:** *Not necessary to share. Everything is fine and normal.*

**Hattie:** *According to Hayes, the new tenant is also the new assistant coach and she's the girl Ryland had a one-night stand with and also seems to really like.*

**Ryland:** *I said it wasn't necessary to share.*

**Aubree:** *UHHHH WHAT? *Blinks eyes* And you didn't share this with me?*

**Hattie:** *Like I said, I was getting a manicure, preparing to say yes. Clearly a waste of time.*

**Aubree:** *So you like this girl?*

**Ryland:** *No.*

**Hattie:** *He does. He likes her so much that he did her in the bathroom.*

**Ryland:** *Hattie, you realize you're my sister, right? You saying I did someone in the bathroom is really weird.*

**Hattie:** *I don't care . . . he totally did it in the bathroom.*

**Aubree:** *My God! Ryland, this is information we need to know.*

**Ryland:** *Why?*

**Aubree:** *Uh, isn't it obvious?*

**Ryland:** *No.*

**Hattie:** *Because we have the right to meddle!*

**Ryland:** *Says who?*

**Hattie:** *The law! Now . . . tell us how you feel about this woman.*

**Aubree:** *And how you are going to navigate your proximity and professionalism.*

**Ryland:** *Yeah . . . I'm not going to do that. I'm out.*

**Hattie:** *Wait no, come back, we won't pester.*

**Aubree:** *He knows you're lying.*

**Hattie:** *I know, thought I'd at least try.*

# Chapter Thirteen

## GABBY

**Nathan:** *Come on, Gab. We should talk. I miss you.*

That's a hard pass.

Ignoring the pestering ex, I focus on what's in front of me.

This is weird.

Really weird.

I always thought I'd be a good teacher, but having the students love me right off the bat? Now that's new.

The first few days were a bit of an adjustment, especially with the schedule and figuring out exactly what I wanted to do and how I wanted to do it. Not to mention, how I set up my classroom, but after being in it for a couple of days, I realized I didn't like how I set it up, so I spent all night after school rearranging again.

But I think I have it the way I want it now.

Now it's time to make friends, especially since the one person I know won't even look at me.

For the past three days, Ryland has avoided me. I've received one email from him: a list of tasks he expects me to complete this week for the baseball team. Since I have no idea where all these things are, nor do I have access to the facilities, there is a slight problem with me completing them. And since it's Thursday and he's refused to talk to me like a petulant child, I will have to take matters into my own hands.

I have a plan.

One that I know will piss him off.

But listen, we need to get on the same page because we start sixth-period baseball next week.

What is that precisely? Well, for all the athletes on varsity, their sixth period is their sport. Instead of having PE, they go straight to their team facilities for their workouts. My assumption is that this is when the team will weightlift and condition. At least that's what I remember when Bennett went here.

Either way, I need to figure this all out and find a way to be more prepared than Ryland.

With my water bottle in hand, I head to the teachers' lounge, where I plan on making some friends. Always a scary task as an adult, but if Ryland doesn't want to be friends and work harmoniously together, then I can make friends on my own.

I push through the door and immediately find the entire lounge intimidating.

One of the things I love about Almond Bay High is that almost all the facilities are up to date. The classrooms are freshly painted, our desks are modern, the hallways are not dark and dingy, the landscaping is pristine, and unlike other high schools around the country, this is an outside high school, meaning it's not one giant building. It's a bunch of small buildings, so to get around, you walk outside.

You get your vitamin D, you're not trapped inside all the time, and it doesn't feel like a jail. I love it.

But this huge lounge has leather couches and high-top dining room tables. It also has two fridges, three coffee makers, and a snack bar.

A freaking snack bar.

Where does the budget come from?

A few teachers are milling about already, so I decide to make myself known and join a table. I walk up to the first one I see. A man's back is toward me, so I say, "Is this seat taken?"

He turns toward me and . . . good God, is he attractive.

Gorgeous blue eyes, so dark that they almost look like a midnight blue. His blond hair styled into a faux hawk effortlessly falls right into his trimmed beard. His cheeks are rosy, his lips are full, and he looks like he stepped off a magazine cover rather than came from teaching a few classes to some high schoolers.

"Not at all. Take a seat," he says and holds out his hand. "I'm Christian."

I take his hand in mine. "Christian, it's nice to meet you. I'm Gabby Brinkman, the new math teacher."

"Oh yes, I saw Herbert's email about you joining the staff. How do you like it so far?"

"So far, it's been great. I'm still getting into the swing of things. This is only my second teaching job, so I'm still trying to find my voice."

He nods. "I understand that. I remember I was so nervous when I was first starting, but now that I'm five years in, it feels like second nature."

"That's where I'm hoping to get. When I was student teaching, there was a level of comfort there, but now that I'm on my own . . . yikes."

He chuckles as I take out the yogurt, granola, and berries I brought for lunch. "High schoolers can be humbling."

"They can be, but I think I'm handling them pretty okay at the moment. They seem to like me, not to toot my own horn, and they've waved to me outside the classroom."

"They have?" he asks, raising his brow. "Wow, you must be doing a really good job. I consider myself one of the cooler teachers, and even I don't get waves."

I smirk. "Maybe you need to reassess your approach."

He laughs. "Maybe. I might have to observe you in your classroom and take some pointers."

I wink at him. "Observe all you want."

That causes him to raise a brow and turn away, slowly nodding.

Jesus, am I flirting?

I shouldn't be flirting.

Because . . . well . . . I have a, uh . . . what do I have?

A Ryland.

Uh, pretty sure that's nothing.

So, why shouldn't I be flirting?

The first thing that comes to mind is Ryland. But that's stupid because it's not like we're dating or anything. The man hasn't even spoken to me in a few days. When I go to take a shower, he's nowhere in sight. So why would I even think about him?

No, this is not about Ryland. I shouldn't be flirting because, well, this is my first week. I can't be making the moves on a co-worker in the first week.

"Where are you from?" Christian asks, thankfully cutting through the awkwardness that my wink brought upon us both.

I mix my granola and berries into my yogurt and say, "A small town north of here."

"Still in California or in Oregon?"

"California," I answer. "About an hour south of Oregon."

"Nice."

"What about you?" I ask.

"San Diego," he answers. "Born and raised."

"San Diego is gorgeous. How could you leave?"

"Still wondering that myself." He takes a drink of what seems to be a protein drink. It makes sense, given how shapely his shoulders look under his T-shirt. "But I like Almond Bay. It's kind of fun living in a town that feels like Stars Hollow."

"Did you just make a *Gilmore Girls* reference?"

"Yup, you okay with that?"

I turn toward him just as the door to the lounge opens, and in pops Ryland, looking broody. From the corner of my eye, I catch him pause in his path and do a double take at me, but I ignore him and continue my conversation with Christian.

"I'm more than okay with that. Before I nerd out, have you watched the show?"

"Would I have made a reference if I hadn't?"

"True." I take a deep breath and look him in the eyes and ask, "Okay, Team Jess, Team Logan, or Team Dean?"

"How did I know you were going to ask?" He turns toward me as well, and as I look him in the eyes, I can feel Ryland's gaze on us both, but I ignore him.

"Am I predictable already?"

"Maybe," he answers and then leans against the table. "Hmm, well, Dean is an obvious out. Does anyone even like him?"

I shake my head. "I don't think so."

"So the real question is Jess or Logan. Jess seems to know her better, but Logan, he's . . . he's the Christopher."

"Oh my God, did you read that article about Amy Sherman-Palladino saying that?"

He nods. "Of course, but only because my sister sent me the article, not because I searched it out or anything."

I chuckle. "Sure, of course. So you're Team Logan."

"I think I am."

I lean forward and whisper, "So am I."

"Why are you whispering that?"

"Because I think we're supposed to say we're Team Jess."

"Ah, yes, I know what you're talking about. I was just about to—"

"Can I join you?" Ryland asks as he takes a seat, not even waiting for us to answer.

"Of course," Christian says. "How's it going, man? Good start to the school year?"

He glances at me but then brings his attention to Christian. "Doing okay. Working out some kinks, but so far, so good. What about you?"

"Same," he says. "Oh shit, where are my manners? Have you met Gabby?"

Ryland glances at me. "Yup, she's my new assistant coach. Isn't that right, Gabby?"

So now he's going to speak to me . . . when I'm speaking to another man. How convenient.

"Oh, that's right," Christian says. "I think I heard that there was a female hire for the baseball team. Pretty cool, man."

"Oh, he had nothing to do with it," I say, unable to stop myself. "He wasn't even in the interview."

I can feel Ryland's eyes like lasers, trying to blow me up.

"I wasn't invited to participate in the interviews," he says. "But I think they made a great choice."

Sure, like he really believes that.

"Not invited to the interviews . . . let me guess, David?" Christian raises a brow.

"The one and only," Ryland says as he opens up a sandwich loaded with steak. Sheesh, that's a lot of protein.

"At least he didn't mess up the hire."

"I lucked out," Ryland says with all the charm of a . . . uh, of a bracelet.

Where has this guy been?

Because I don't think I've seen him before. Looks like he's a pretty good actor.

"Which reminds me, I'd like to chat after school," he says. "Meet me in my office?"

Oh, he wants to chat now? Hmm, wonder why.

"Sure," I say. "Sounds great."

"Great," he says with a smile and then takes a bite of his sandwich.

⸺

I'm hustling.

I'm hustling so fast that if a teacher saw me right now, they'd yell at me to slow down and tell me no running in the hallway, but I have a point to prove. If Ryland's going to play games, so am I.

My bag clutched to my chest, my legs burn with exertion as I make my way to the athletics department and straight to the baseball office, an office I have a key to.

*Please don't let him be in here. Please don't let him be in here.*

I walk up to the door, test the handle, and when it's locked, I inwardly shout a *huzzah* because this plan is going to work.

I quickly unlock the door and let myself in.

I flick on the lights, and I'm immediately met with a view of all the school's athletic fields. God, that's a great view. No wonder he's butt hurt over losing this office.

I don't have time to examine the surroundings, though. I quickly make work of setting my things up. Lucky for me, he has nothing personal in here. A blank desk and a shelf full of baseball books, but that's about it. Not even a fake plant or a picture of Mac.

I reach into my bag and start . . . decorating.

A lamp, two fake plants, pen holder, yellow clipboard, a few pictures of me and Bennett, a Rebels pennant, along with a picture of Jason Orson next to it, because . . . well, I might as well dig the hole deeper while I'm at it. And then a few other memorabilia items. I don't have much time to think about where to place everything. I scatter them around on the available surface and then sit in his chair and prop my feet up on his desk just as I hear the sound of keys attempting to unlock a door that's already unlocked.

This is it.

Be strong.

The door opens, and a confused Ryland is on the other side, but he's only confused for a few seconds before he spots me.

"Took you long enough," I say as I lower my legs and place my hands on the mahogany wood of the desk.

"What the fuck do you think you're doing?" he asks as he shuts the door to the office . . . and locks it.

"Well, I assumed when you said meet you in your office, you meant mine. Mistakes will happen. You'll get used to it, though. Next time, we can meet in yours if you want. That would be the broom closet, right?" I shrug. "Eh, this one is bigger. Maybe we should just conduct all business here."

"This is not your office," he says.

I hold up my keys and jingle them. "These tell me differently."

He puffs out an irritated steam through his nostrils. "I'm not going to fuck around with you about this. They're finding you a new office. This is mine, so gather up your shit and get the hell out of my chair."

"Hmm, well, I never heard anything, and until I hear from David, I'm just going to remain put. So"—I gesture to the seat in front of me—"what did you want to talk about?"

He crosses his arms over his barrel of a chest and says, "Is this really what you want to do? Piss me off?"

"Oh please, you've been pissed since we fucked the other night. Hence the list of crap you gave me to do. Or the fact that you haven't introduced me to the team yet. Or how you haven't talked to me in a few days."

"You miss me?" he asks, a smug look on his face.

"Did it look like I missed you when I was talking to Christian?"

Okay, low blow, but fighting fire with fire here.

That makes his eyes narrow as he moves in close and takes a seat on the edge of the desk. "Don't even think about it."

"Think about what?" I ask.

"Think about anything with him."

"Oh." I lean back in my chair, letting the squeak of the hinges filter through the room. "So when did you become the authority over my body?"

"I'm not the authority, but I know what you're doing with him."

"Uh-huh, and what is that exactly?"

"You're trying to irritate me by talking to him."

"You're very full of yourself. That was not my intention at all. I was actually trying to make a new friend since, you know, the one person I do know at the school has been ignoring me."

"Please, Gabby, you were flirting."

"I wasn't, but even if I was, what does it matter to you? We're not dating. You have no claim to me."

His jaw tightens as he leans forward and says, "You're right, I have no claim over you." My breath catches in my chest as he reaches out and tucks a piece of my hair behind my ear. "You're not mine. What we had was fleeting." His finger drags along my cheek, and my eyes close for a moment, causing me to hate myself.

Because I shouldn't have this kind of reaction. I shouldn't want him to lower his hand, to drag his fingers along my collarbone, across my chest, over my breasts, and then farther down . .
.

I push my chair away, making eye contact with him. "Don't," I say.

The corner of his lips turns up as he stands from the desk. "You're right, I don't need to worry about Christian when you clearly still want me."

My nostrils flare from the audacity.

"Once again, so full of yourself."

"It's not being full of myself if it's facts," he says. He nods at me. "Tell me right now, if I were to put you on this desk and bury my head between your legs, would you stop me?"

I bite on the inside of my cheek, preventing me from asking him to follow through with such a claim.

But my silence proves him right.

"That's what I thought."

Huffing, I say, "Is this why you wanted to talk to me? Because you're jealous of Christian?"

"Not jealous," he says.

"You're such a liar. The moment you saw us talking, you needed to be involved."

"Maybe I just wanted to have lunch with my assistant coach."

"We both know that's a lie." I sit taller and pull up a piece of paper. "Now, why don't we try to figure out this co-coaching thing because right now, I have no idea what's going on. You gave me a list of things to do, yet I don't know anything about the facilities."

"You haven't done anything on the list?"

"Uh, no. How could I when you haven't shown me around?" I look him in the eyes. "I know you might not be happy about all this, but we need to be on the same page, Ryland. I know you care about this team, so let me be a part of it."

"You are a part of it."

"Am I? Or are you trying to make my life difficult so I'm no longer a part of it?"

"You're the one making life difficult." He gestures to the office. "Taking my office like this."

"Because you were being a jerk! Treat people the way you want to be treated, Ryland."

He drags his hand over his face. "This is a fucking nightmare." He blows out a heavy breath. "And this is never going to work. You and me coaching together. Never."

"Well, I'm not leaving," I say, keeping my stance on the matter. "I need this job."

"You can find another one," he says. "I'll even give you a recommendation."

"You're really so against me working with you that you want to ship me on my way without even giving me a chance?"

"Gabby," he says, sounding exasperated. "We can't even have a normal conversation without getting irritated with each other. We are never going to make this work. It's too complicated, and the last thing I need is complicated."

"You know, your life isn't the only one that's been upended, Ryland. You're not the only one having a hard time. You're not the only one who doesn't need complicated."

I stand now and look him in the eyes. "Complicated has been my entire life. And I caught a break for the first time in my life."

In some senses, complicated is the least applicable word for how much I've fought for things in my life. Taking on a younger brother when I was only eighteen meant I had to work long hours to keep a roof over our heads and allow time with Bennett.

To support his schooling. Build his baseball skills. Get him into the best school so he had the best advantage. As soon as I saw his talent in baseball, I made it my life's goal to work with him. So I studied the game, studied players, and learned all the stats, the positions, and the requirements to be one of the best.

But *my* personal goal? To work in a sports-focused school. And now I am there, something Ryland can't fully fathom. *And mainly because he was kept in the dark.* Which is not his fault I now know. Perhaps we need more of a truce than anything else. Honesty.

"You might not like David, but he saved me, Ryland. He gave me a teaching opportunity I've been dreaming of and helped me find an affordable place to live. I'm finally in a profession that doesn't require me to ask people if they're ready to order. This job, this position I'm in, it means everything to me, and I'm not about to give it up because of you."

He looks away as he sighs and moves his hand over his mouth. After a few seconds of silence, he says, "Fine."

"Fine, what?"

"Fine, I'll show you around."

He moves toward the door, opens it, and motions for me to follow him.

"Really?" I ask, feeling slightly shocked.

"Really, now come on," he says in a brisk tone.

Not wanting to scare him away . . . or bring him back to a state of irritation, I follow him, and together, we walk down the hallway.

He points at a door and says, "That's the locker room. You're not allowed in it for obvious reasons. That's where the assistant coach's office is, so . . . ."

"I don't need an office," I say, throwing him a concession. "The boys are going to talk to you more, and if they want to chat with me, I'll let them know that I'm available in my classroom or down at the field."

He pauses and glances at me. "Thanks," he says.

And just like that, it's almost as if all the built-up anger and

irritation has fizzled. Maybe . . . maybe my speech was something he needed to hear. Maybe he could relate. Who knows, but
I appreciate him easing up, at least just enough for us both to
breathe. Who knows what will happen later on, but for now . . .
we have some breathing room. *Is this a truce?*

# Chapter Fourteen

## RYLAND

"Do you think Aunt Hattie will like my picture?" Mac asks as we hold hands and head to The Almond Store.

"I think she'll love it, especially how you drew her hair."

Mac smiles up at me as she holds her picture close to her chest.

She had a good first week, and today, she was able to count backwards from twenty, so we're celebrating the small victories. I told her I'd take her to the family store for some of our famous cherry almond cookies.

When Cassidy was still alive, she had a vision. She bought a farm, which we all thought she was somewhat crazy for doing since she had no farming experience. And on top of that, she decided to grow potatoes.

Potatoes.

What the hell was she going to do with potatoes?

She fermented them and turned them into vodka. That vodka was fused with almonds and created The Almond Store's biggest seller, almond extract.

It was an odd business model that has proven to work well.

She opened The Almond Store, playing off the town name, and created a touristy destination. Before she passed, she asked Aubree to run the store until Hattie was able to take over when she was done with college. Now, Aubree looks over the farm with Wyatt. Hattie is in charge of the store, and it's thriving. And I, well, I have Mac.

I open the door to The Almond Store, and I'm immediately hit by the smell of freshly baked cookies and almond. The white oak floors are free of dirt, and the white walls are pristine, showcasing the shelves of products. The subtle blue throughout the store offers a cleaner aesthetic, creating a peaceful shopping experience.

Hattie stands behind the counter, and a large smile spreads across her face when she looks up. "There's my girl. How was school?"

Mac releases my hand and runs up to Hattie, giving her a big hug.

I don't know how Mac does it. Hattie looks just like Cassidy, a spitting image. I wonder if that's why they have a strong bond? Maybe that's why Mac and Wyatt have a strong bond too, because Wyatt is actually the brother of Mac's dad, who passed away in a bus accident.

"I made you a picture."

"You did?" she asks. "Let me see."

Mac holds up the picture, and I carefully watch Hattie's face as she takes it all in.

To describe it to you the best that I can, I would say it looks like Hattie has googly eyes and knives coming out of her head. Several knives.

"Oh . . . wow."

"Do you love it?" Mac asks, looking up at Hattie with those big green eyes.

"Yes, of course. You did such a good job." Mac goes in for a hug while Hattie looks in my direction. She mouths, "What the fuck?"

Which makes me chuckle.

"Guess what, Aunt Hattie? Mac also counted backwards from twenty today."

"She did?" Hattie asks. "Well, I think that's a cause for celebration. How about a cookie?"

"Yes, yes, yes," Mac says, jumping up and down.

"Go grab a juice box, and I'll get you your cookie."

Mac takes off toward the back to the kitchen while Hattie whispers to me, "Should I be concerned that it looks like I'm getting stabbed in the head multiple times?"

I scratch my cheek. "Still trying to figure it out. I want to say that's your curly hair, but . . . it does look a lot like knives."

She shivers. "Horrifying."

"You're not the one living with her," I whisper. "For all I know, the knives could be coming for me."

She chuckles and places a cookie on a napkin just as Mac returns with a juice box in hand. Hattie sets her on the stool in front of the checkout counter and opens the juice while Mac takes a big bite of the cookie.

"Are you going to have one, Uncle Ry Ry?" she asks.

"Yeah, Uncle Ry Ry, are you going to have one?" Hattie asks, loving that Mac calls me Uncle Ry Ry now. It used to be Uncle Ryland, but along the way, it changed. At the beginning, it was annoying, but of course in grand Mac fashion, she's worn me down.

"Sure," I say.

Hattie grabs another cookie from the display case, sets it on the napkin, and hands it to me. "How was your day?"

"Fine," I say, giving her a raised brow. "Why?"

"No reason, just wondering how everything's going. Hayes said he drove by the school today and saw you out on the field with your new coach."

"Hayes needs to worry about himself and figure out when the hell he's going to propose."

Hattie's face falls flat. "That's a sensitive subject, Ryland." She leans closer and whispers, "I asked him about it last night. He got all huffy with me, and we got in a little fight. He told me to leave it alone and that he'll propose when he wants to propose."

"Yikes," I say with a wince before I take a bite of my cookie, grateful for the distraction from having to talk about Gabby.

Just then, the door opens behind me, the bell jingling.

When I turn to see who it is, the momentary reprieve I had from thinking about Gabby is eliminated as she comes into view.

"Oh," she says. "Uh, hi."

"Hello," Hattie says with a huge smile on her face.

"Hi!" Mac shouts with a wave.

Great.

This is not what I need after everything that happened today.

When I walked into the teachers' lounge at lunch, I was ready to grab my sandwich and eat in peace, but that all changed the moment I saw Gabby talking with Christian. Nothing against him, he's an okay guy, a bit of a player, but I didn't fucking like it. I didn't like the way she smiled at him, leaned in close, or even joked. I liked nothing about it, and it flipped a switch inside my head, the one I can't seem to control when I'm around her.

It's the same switch that almost made me strip her down in my office.

I don't know what's gotten into me, but after her speech in my office, I realized I need to get my shit together.

This isn't about me getting my dick wet. This is about taking care of Mac to the best of my ability and finding a way to work with this woman without acting on these fucking urges.

And that's what I'm doing.

That's what I promised myself I was doing when I was showing her around the facilities. She already knew about the field because of Bennett, who she kept talking about. That helped because every time I think about him, I think about how pissed he'd be at me for treating his sister the way I have been.

I just need to shake off the irritation. Start new.

Start fresh.

Erase everything up until earlier when she gave her speech

about struggling in life and play off that. Because if I don't, I'll get caught up in all the wrong things.

"Hey, uh." Gabby glances around, confused, and it hits me that she might not know that Hattie runs the shop.

Putting on my big boy adult pants, I say, "Gabby, you've met Hattie briefly, right?"

"Yes," she says, taking a step forward.

"She owns The Almond Store, and together, she and my other sister Aubree—I think you briefly met her as well, she runs the farm—create the products you see here. Hattie, you remember Gabby? She's the tenant above the garage and my new assistant coach."

Hattie's smile only grows wider. "Yes, I remember. How are you?"

"I'm doing good." Gabby glances at me. "I was told I could find some really good cookies here."

"You sure can. Come on up," Hattie says, waving to Gabby. "I actually have some fresh ones in the back. How many would you like?"

"Do they freeze well?"

Hattie nods. "Yes, they freeze so well."

"Maybe half a dozen, then," Gabby says.

"Sure, be right back."

"I'll help," Mac calls out, leaving me alone with Gabby. Again.

I finish my cookie and wipe my fingers. When the silence is too much to handle, I mutter, "She didn't give me a fresh one."

I can see her lips tilt up from the corner of my eye, and I beg myself not to get lost in that smile.

"For the record," she says. "I didn't follow you here."

"Didn't think you did," I reply.

"Okay, because I feel like that's something you'd think."

"Why do you say that?" I ask, now turning toward her. She does the same.

"After what happened with Christian, I don't know, just setting the record straight."

"No need to. Everything's fine."

"Is it, though?" she asks. "This feels more awkward than ever."

"Yeah, well, it'll be uncomfortable for a while." I let out a deep breath and look her in her beautiful, different colored eyes. "I want you to know that . . ." I look away for a second to gather myself because her gaze is too intense. "I'm sorry about, you know, everything, and I promise I'll be better. I've acted like a buffoon, and if I look back at all our interactions, I'm embarrassed I treated you the way I did. It's not your fault you were hired. If I should be mad at anyone, it should be David."

"Wow, uh, thanks. Wasn't expecting that, but I'm sorry too," she says, seeming very surprised that we're having this heart-to-heart in the middle of The Almond Store. "I should have told you who I was and that I got the job right away. That was shitty of me. I was just . . . I don't know, nervous. You were so angry when you found out I was your tenant that I couldn't imagine how you'd react when you found out I was coaching too."

I slowly nod and toe the floor. "Yeah, because I didn't think I'd see you again. I passed off that night we had as an incredible one-night stand that would live with me for a while. Never did I think that I'd have the opportunity to well . . . you know."

She agrees. "Yeah, I know."

"But I promise I'll do better. I just . . . I need to get over this crazy lust I have for you."

Her eyes meet mine. "I know what you mean. That's why I suggested we do the friend thing."

"I mean, it's something we can try. It's not like anything else has worked."

"It really hasn't," she says.

"Okay, so then, we're working on being friends?"

"I guess so," she replies.

"And to be clear, friends without benefits."

"There can't be any benefits whatsoever. Like . . . none."

"Okay." She tugs on the strap of her purse. "And friends

can't get mad when other friends talk to other people in the teachers' lounge."

"Only if friends don't openly flirt with other people in the teachers' lounge in front of friends."

"I wasn't openly flirting."

"Call it what you want, there was chemistry, and I don't need to fucking see it."

Her cheeks blush as she nods in agreement. "Fair. Also, I think friends need to make sure that shirts are on at all times when friends have to use the shower."

"Are friends attracted to friends with shirts off?"

"If we need to keep this as strictly no benefits, then I think we need to make sure shirts . . . and pants, for that matter, are on at all times."

"That counts for both of us." I point at her. "And no more of those . . . robes. For the love of God, put pajamas on."

She chuckles. "I can do that."

"Anything else?" I ask.

"I think we need to keep this as honest as possible, so if we're doing something that bothers the other person . . . like if one friend feels like the other friend is stepping on their toes when it comes to their special baseball team, then the friend needs to say something and not bottle it up."

"Honesty can work, as long as one friend doesn't try to steal the other friend's office."

"Pretty sure that was already established," she says with a roll of her eyes.

"Hey, if you saw the other closet of an office, you'd understand."

"Maybe sometimes friends can share office space . . . you know, on occasion."

"That can be arranged as long as friends remove all personal effects and try not to mark their territory with their perfume. It smells like you in there."

"Well, it smelled like your cologne when I went in there, so . . . maybe you stop smelling nice."

"Maybe friends forget about nice smells altogether. No perfumes, no colognes, no deodorants."

Her nose curls up. "Veto, I say yes to deodorant."

"Fine, but no perfumes and colognes."

"Deal." She cutely holds out her hand and says, "Should we shake on it?"

"No. Friends should not be touching friends."

Her expression falls. "Okay, but before we go into this full-on friends with no benefits thing, could we possibly just . . . hug it out real quick? One last I'm sorry and we're on the same page now type hug?"

How can I say no to that when she looks up at me with those unusual yet stunning eyes, practically begging?

"Yeah, we can do that," I say, opening my arms. She steps right into my chest, her arms circling me as I do the same.

She squeezes me and says, "Sorry about everything, Ryland."

"Yeah, me too," I say, allowing this peaceful moment to exist for a second longer.

Letting my mind commit the feel of her to memory since it won't be happening again.

I soak in her scent.

I log the feel of her arms around me.

And I memorize the height difference where she's just short enough for me to rest my chin on the top of her head.

And after a second too long, I'm about to let go of her just as Hattie walks out of the kitchen with Mac.

"Why are they hugging?" Mac asks, her question immediately breaking me and Gabby apart, making us look infinitely more guilty than what we actually are.

"I don't know, why are you hugging?" Hattie asks as she sets a box of cookies down on the counter.

"We're friends," Gabby says. "And we had an argument today, so we apologized and hugged."

Mac looks at me. "You had an argument? Did you yell?"

"Uh, no. We didn't yell. We just didn't agree on something. We finally were able to say sorry, so we hugged it out, just like you and I hug it out when we sometimes get in an argument," I answer.

She picks up her cookie on the counter and takes a bite, not saying another word.

To be a fucking kid again.

Hattie smirks and starts ringing up Gabby.

"How much do I owe you?" Gabby asks.

"I got it," I say, pushing her hand back into her purse, which is holding her wallet.

"Oh, I can't let you do that," Gabby says.

"Let's just say I owe you. For everything . . . including the shower inconvenience."

She eyes me for a moment. "Well, it is pretty inconvenient."

"So then the cookies are on me."

"Trust me, it's a fair deal if you have to deal with my brother," Hattie says.

"Then I'll take it." She smiles up at me while she takes the box of cookies. "Thank you."

"You're welcome."

"It was nice seeing you, Hattie."

"Yes, come by again, and if you need some friends, feel free to come hang. Aubree is not as outgoing as I am, but we're pretty chill. And our friend Echo would probably love a girls' night as well."

"Sounds great." Gabby steps up and writes her number down on a piece of paper, then hands it to Hattie. "Text me."

"Perfect. We will. Bye, Gabby."

"Bye." And then she takes off, the door shutting behind her.

Hattie steps around the counter and walks right up next to me, fanning herself with Gabby's number. "Did I score her number before you did?"

I roll my eyes. "It doesn't matter if you did or not. I'm not looking to score any number."

I glance at Mac, who has picked up a pen and started drawing on a notepad, ignoring everything around her.

"I don't know. That hug told me differently."

I take Hattie by the arm and lead her to the new honey display. "Can you not make this a big deal? We're trying to be friends . . . friends with no benefits. We're keeping it strictly platonic, and I don't need you chirping in my ear about her."

"Friends with no benefits? How is that fun?"

"It's not," I say. "But I don't have a choice. If I try to have benefits, I become possessive and angry, and I'm a dick around her, and I don't want that. I need some semblance of control over my emotions, so if that means taking the attraction out of it, that's what I'm going to do."

"Do you really think that's going to work?"

"It has to," I reply. "There isn't another option."

"Uh, there is. There's the option that you give in to your attraction and see where it can go . . . maybe you could love her one day."

"You know I don't do love, Hattie," I say sternly. "I don't know love and want nothing to do with it."

The disappointed look on her face is nothing new to me. I know she wants nothing more than for me to find someone I can spend my life with, like she found Hayes, but that's just not me. That's not going to happen. *Loving someone leads to loss.* And I've lost enough people in my life already. I'm also my father's son. Enough said.

"Maybe you could."

I look her in the eyes. "It's not for me. Don't push it, got it?" She nods even though I can tell she doesn't want to agree with me. "Thank you. Now . . . am I going to have to pay for those cookies?"

Her mouth parts open in shock. "Uh, yeah, this isn't a free ride. I have to make money."

"I'm your brother."

"Yeah, my brother who earns a paycheck, so help me earn mine."

"Brutal," I say as I grab my wallet and head back to the counter.

"Uncle Ry Ry?" Mac calls as I start to shut the door to the bedroom.

"Yeah?" I ask.

"Can we go to the park tomorrow?"

"After I pick you up from school? Sure we can."

"Can I bring the Chewys?"

"If you want," I say. "But if they play on the playground, we have to wash them after. You know the rules."

"They don't like the washing machine."

"Then they should stay in the truck while you play on the playground."

She sighs heavily. "Okay."

"Okay, good night."

"Good night, love you, see you in the morning, sweet dreams."

I smirk as I repeat her little saying. "Good night, love you, see you in the morning, sweet dreams."

I shut her door, grab the laundry basket full of our dirty laundry, and carry it downstairs, careful not to trip over the toys on the stairs or the boxes scattered through the living room that Mac has now turned into forts.

I'm almost through the landmine of toys when I step on what I like to call Satan's building blocks—a.k.a. Lego—and I'm immediately taken down to my knees as pain shoots up my leg.

"Motherfucker," I say as the laundry basket scatters across the floor, and my foot radiates in pain. "Jesus."

"Uncle Ry Ry?" I hear from the top of the stairs. "I heard a big crash."

"Yup," I say on a grunt.

And to my luck, that's when Gabby opens the back door, ready to take her shower.

I'm on the floor, dirty clothes all over, with Mac racing down the stairs only to find me in the same position.

"Did you hurt yourself?" Mac asks, racing toward me.

"Mainly my pride," I say as Gabby comes up to us as well and squats down.

"What happened?"

"Stepped on a Lego piece," I say and sit up. I glance at Mac, and she looks guilty.

"Sorry, Uncle Ryland." Her lips turn down, and she lowers her head.

"Hey, I'm fine." I tug on her arm. "Let's try to remember to pick up our toys before bed so this doesn't happen, okay?"

She nods, and I can see those tears in her eyes start to form, so I pull her into a hug, then stand from the floor, my foot still in pain. I squeeze her tight as she wraps her legs around me.

"It's fine. We just have to remember to work together as a team to keep everything clean, right?"

She nods. "Right."

"We'll try again tomorrow, and I'll remind you."

"Okay."

"Come on, let's get you back up to bed."

I start heading to the stairs as Mac pulls her head away from my shoulder and says, "What is that cookie girl doing here?"

I chuckle because cookie girl is quite the name. "Remember, her name is Gabby, and she lives in the apartment above the garage. Her shower isn't working, so she showers here at night."

"Every night?"

"Yes," I say as I look over at Gabby, who waves at Mac.

"How come I never see or hear her?"

"I'm pretty sneaky," Gabby says. "And your uncle said I'm in big trouble if I wake you up."

"What kind of trouble?" Mac asks. "Like time-out?"

"Yeah, like time-out," I say, loving how innocent her mind is.

"Time-out is not fun."

"Not even a little," Gabby says. "That's why I'm sneaky."

"I'm sneaky too. I can show you." Mac tries to wiggle out of my arms, but I hold her tight.

"You can show her another time. Right now, you need to get

back to bed or else you're going to be cranky. Do the Chewys like a cranky Mac?"

Mac dramatically shakes her head. "No, they don't."

"So we better get you some sleep, then. Say good night to Gabby."

"Good night, love you, see you in the morning, sweet dreams."

Gabby chuckles. "Good night, Mac."

I spend the next few minutes getting Mac back into bed, singing *Twinkle, Twinkle, Little Star* with her, and then tucking her in just the way she likes it. Once I'm done, I turn off the hall light and head back down the stairs only to find the living room straightened up and the clothes put back in the laundry basket. I look around for Gabby, but she's nowhere to be found. When I hear the shower, I realize she's in the bathroom.

Jesus, she works quick.

I carry the laundry over to the laundry room, which is across from the bathroom. I can smell her soap coming from under the door and I mentally tell myself to ignore it.

Sure, it smells like heaven, but that doesn't mean I need to blast the bathroom door down and bend her over.

We've turned a new leaf.

We're friends.

We're cordial.

We're not animalistic barbarians seeking carnal pleasure whenever we so choose.

I focus on the laundry, starting it just as I hear Gabby turn off the shower. Feeling awkward, I take in the kitchen and how I already cleaned it up, but maybe I should wipe those counters down again.

I take out the Earth-friendly cleaner Cassidy was always adamant about using and spray down the counters, then I wipe them up with a microfiber towel. I do the same with the table, and once I'm done with that . . . I wipe down the chairs.

I move from the chairs to the fridge, and once that's done,

I'm about to go to the stove when the bathroom door finally opens, and Gabby pops out.

I turn around to look at her, and to my demise, she's wearing pajamas, just like I asked her.

Dammit, I miss the robe already.

But new leaf.

Friends.

*Focus on what's important, Ryland.*

"Hey." I set the microfiber towel down. "How was your shower?"

"Fine," she says. "How's your foot?"

"Recovered."

"That was quite the sight to see."

"I'm just surprised a slew of curse words didn't fly out of my mouth. If it were Aubree, Mac would still be repeating everything she heard."

"Does she tend to do that?"

"All the time," I say. "By the way, you didn't have to clean up the toys. But thank you."

"I did it for your pride, so you didn't come downstairs and have another accident."

"Well, it's appreciated but not necessary. We can do things over here on our own." I hear the words, and they come off as unappreciative, but I don't know how else to say it. I don't need the help, at least from someone I barely know.

"I'm sure you can, but I just thought I'd lend a hand . . . since we're friends and all."

"Thanks." I shift uncomfortably, unsure of what else to say.

"Well, I'm going to get back to my apartment."

"Cool, yeah. Oh hey, I was thinking, have you heard from Bennett recently?"

She pauses at the door. "I talk to him every day."

"Oh."

"Why?"

I lean against the counter and say, "With the playoffs coming up, I wasn't sure if he had any idea if he was moving up when the MLB teams expand to a forty-man roster."

"He hasn't mentioned anything. Then again, we don't really talk about it because he feels a lot of pressure to move up. He's ready, he just needs the call."

"He was ready when he played for me," I say. "Hopefully, he hears something soon. Would you fly out there for his first game?"

She shrugs. "I don't know. I have a lot of responsibilities here, and I think I'd only go if he was going to start, you know?"

"Yeah, I get it. Keep me updated. I'd love to know since I don't have a lot of time to follow things like I used to."

"I will."

She starts to walk away again, and for some reason, I ask, "What does he think about you coaching his old team?"

She leans against the door and says, "He's proud of me. Excited that I get to work with you since you were one of his favorite coaches. Can't see why since you're a bit of an ass."

That makes me chuckle. "Only when I feel that I'm wronged. I'm a pretty decent guy. You'll find out soon when we move from friends to best friends."

She winces. "Ooo, I don't know. Best friends is a bit of a commitment. I don't think I'm ready for that."

"Yeah, you're right. I don't think I have the time for such a commitment either. If we take the pressure out of becoming best friends, that's going to be best for us both."

"Agreed. Just friends, but never best."

I shake my head. "Never best."

"Works for me." She yawns. "Unless you have any other questions, I'm going to bed."

"I do have one more thing," I say, feeling like a total nimrod. I find a marker and an old receipt and hand it to her. "Can I have your number so I can contact you when need be?"

She smirks but takes the paper from me and writes her number down. "You could have just asked your sister for it."

"And suffer the ridicule of her knowing she scored your

number before me and never letting me live it down? No thanks."

That makes her laugh. "Technically, she did."

"We don't need to get into technicalities. Let's just say we both have it now."

"If that will make you feel better, then fine."

"It will."

"I can see I'm working with a fragile ego over here. Noted."

"Good that you see it now," I say.

She smiles softly, then raises her hand. "Good night."

"Good night."

She takes off toward her apartment, and I watch out the window until she's closed her door. That's when I grab my phone and type her number into a new contact. Then I send her a quick text.

**Ryland:** *It's me, your landlord. Now you have my number as well.*

It takes her a few seconds, but she texts back.

**Gabby:** *That was quick. Here, I thought you were going to gatekeep your number a little longer so I wouldn't have the opportunity to annoy you.*

**Ryland:** *The opportunity is always there, whether you have my number or not.*

**Gabby:** *Wow, and I cleaned up toys for you.*

**Ryland:** *Best you know now that I'm not going to be a super grateful asshole when things are done for me out of the kindness of your heart.*

**Gabby:** *Good to know. By the way . . . I like this side of you better, the side where you're not snarling, just . . . sort of frowning in a way.*

**Ryland:** *My childhood created the perma frown. Get used to it.*

**Gabby:** *It seems like there are some things there to unpack, but being a product of childhood trauma as well, I'm not even going to ask.*

**Ryland:** *That's refreshing.*

**Gabby:** *That's what you can get with me, Ryland . . . a sense of refreshment.*

**Ryland:** *We'll see. There's still a lot to navigate.*

**Gabby:** *All I need is for you to give me a chance. From there, I'll work my magic.*

# Chapter Fifteen

## GABBY

**Gabby:** *When are you coming to visit me?*

**Bower:** *Shouldn't you be teaching right now?*

**Gabby:** *Lunch break.*

**Bower:** *Oh, duh.*

**Gabby:** *Answer the question. When are you coming to visit me?*

**Bower:** *When do you want me to visit you?*

**Gabby:** *I'd say tonight and spend the weekend with me, but I don't have a working shower so you'd have to shower at Ryland's place.*

**Bower:** *A shower never stopped me from hanging out with you.*

**Gabby:** *Wait, so you're saying you will come visit me?*

**Bower:** *I can leave tomorrow morning and spend the weekend with you. Maybe we can have our very own in-house spa day like we used to do, my treat. There are fancy shops there, right? We can try out all the scrubs.*

**Gabby:** *I like that idea. I can go to the general store and grab us a bunch of frozen food like back in the day.*

**Bower:** *When you say frozen food, do you mean pizza bites and frozen pie from Marie Callender's?*

**Gabby:** *Obviously.*

**Bower:** *Don't forget the grape soda, Pringles, and cheese puffs.*

**Gabby:** *Do you think I actually would?*

**Bower:** *No, but it makes me more excited just saying it out loud. Want me to bring the DVD player and . . . the seasons?*

**Gabby:** *I think it's necessary. I don't think we can get through all of them, though, do you?*

**Bower:** *You're underestimating our ability to do nothing in a weekend. We can get through them.*

**Gabby:** *Then bring them all.*

**Bower:** *Excellent! And we're still in agreement that we should skip season five?*

**Gabby:** *If you bring it, I burn it.*

**Bower:** *Noted.*

**Gabby:** *Great! I can't wait to see you.*

**Bower:** *Same.*

**Gabby:** *And when you're here, get ready to be convinced to move.*

**Bower:** *I can feel the heavy guilt and rose-colored glasses already.*

**Gabby:** *Perfect. See you tomorrow!*

---

It's sweltering.

I can actually feel sweat dripping down my back.

And if I wasn't the new teacher on campus with the possibility of one of the students or athletes spotting me, my shirt would be off and tucked into the back of my shorts right now, allowing me to bake in just my bra.

But unfortunately for me, this is a shirt-on establishment at all times.

I bend down and dip my paintbrush in the paint again, wishing this torture would end. Just a few more strokes and I should be done.

During sixth period today, I met the team. It was a little awkward because they were all slightly confused about why a woman would be coaching them, but thankfully, Ryland spoke highly of me and how I helped Bennett get to where he is despite Ryland never seeing me coach.

Now, do I wish my hiring was handled differently? Absolutely.

But am I grateful? Always.

I just believe if David included Ryland, we wouldn't be in this weird limbo where I have to prove myself. Instead, Ryland would have hired me based on my merit. Now it feels like I have to prove myself to him, which doesn't seem fair.

Hence why I'm up on a ladder, on a Friday after school, touching up the paint on the foul pole.

It was one of many things on the list Ryland gave me and told me not to worry about, but I thought maybe if I did some of the things, he'd respect me more and notice my dedication to the team.

Next week, we'll start conditioning with the boys, and Ryland said he expects me to help in all ways. I told him it wasn't a problem, as I work out myself and keep up on my weight training—even if that means working out with rocks rather than actual weights in the gym—so I could help with anything he needed.

After our conversation last night, I feel like we really have started a new chapter. Seeing how he picked up his sweet niece and snuggled her into him was stupefying. *Those muscles of his. How he held her so tenderly.* But also finding him sprawled across the floor, his laundry scattered everywhere and him writhing in pain from an itty-bitty Lego? Well, it showed that he's very human, and that maybe he's not as intimidating as I assumed. Meaning, I think I can make this work.

No, I know I can make this work.

"What are you doing?"

"Jesus Christ," I shout. I'm startled half to death, shaking the ladder beneath me with a jump.

"Careful," he shouts.

But it's too late . . .

The ladder wobbles, I quickly grab the wet pole for stability as my paint tray tips, it totters, and then with a goopy splash of yellow, it falls off the ledge and right onto Ryland Rowley's head.

"Motherfucker," Ryland says as he wipes paint away from his eyes, unable to see.

I wince as I stay glued to the wet foul pole, my legs quivering to keep the ladder in place. But my overcompensating only makes it worse, and before I can stop it, the bitch of a ladder crashes to the ground.

With catlike reflexes coated in desperation to save myself, I wrap my legs around the pole and cling to the wet, sticky surface.

"I'm going to die," I say as I stare down at my impending death.

It's been nice knowing this earth.

I had a rough start, so it's a shame I have to perish just when things start to look bright.

Isn't that just the witch's tit?

"What's going on?" Ryland asks, unable to see from the paint.

"The ladder," I shriek. "It's down."

"Fuck. Really?"

"Nope, just lying to create an unnecessary amount of drama on a perfectly fine Friday afternoon."

"Sarcasm isn't needed," he shouts, wiping at his eyes still, but the paint keeps smearing.

"Idiotic questions aren't needed either."

Huffing, he feels around. "Where are you?"

"Holding on to the pole, staring at my immediate death, where else?"

"I know you're on the pole."

"Then why ask?" I yell as my arms start to sweat around the pole.

"I don't know, I'm stressed."

"You're stressed?" I glance down at the ground. "You're not about to break your spine with one slide down a pole."

"Christ." He moves around. "Let me try to grab the ladder."

"Might be a novel idea."

I hear him bumble around, swear, then bump into a few things. When I glance down to the ground, I see him on all fours,

176

feeling around for the ladder. At that point, I realize there's no way this will work out in my favor.

He's unable to locate a ladder, a giant sixteen-foot ladder. He can find the exact spot inside me that can make me scream out his name, but a ladder? Nope.

Such a freaking man.

"I think . . . I think I'm going to slide down the pole."

"What, no, you're going to hurt yourself," he calls up.

No shit.

"I can't hold on much longer. I'm . . . I'm slipping."

"Just give me a second. Fuck, this paint."

"To the right," I shout. He goes to the left. "No, the other right." He moves forward. "Jesus, Ryland. Your right. Your right. YOUR FUCKING RIGHT!"

He fumbles some more.

I slide.

He curses.

More sweat forms between my arms and the pole.

"Ryland, I can't."

"Fuck," he shouts just as his hand connects with the bottom half of the ladder. "Got it."

But it's too late.

My grip loosens on the pole, allowing the most intense, ear-piercing screech to fill the silent air, the sound of my skin getting raw-dogged right off the bone as I make it all the way down to the ground.

I land with a thump.

A grunt falls out of my lips.

And a fiery pain shoots up my legs.

"Death," I whisper as I flop back on the grass and stare up at the brilliantly blue sky, my inner thighs on fire . . . and not in a good way.

"Fuck, are you okay?" he asks as I take deep breaths.

I don't answer.

Because I'm floating like the clouds above me.

The angels are pulling me into their tunnel of another dimension.

"Gabby." He shakes my arm. "Are you okay?"

On another whisper, I say, "This . . . is . . . death."

"You're not dead," he says.

He's right. If I were dead, I wouldn't be subject to the blistering agony between my legs.

I slightly turn my head to the side to look him in the eyes. Him. He's the one who did this.

"Why would you sneak up on me?"

"I wasn't—"

"Look at us. You're covered in paint, I'm covered in paint, and I'm pretty sure I just removed all skin from my inner thighs by sliding down that pole."

He glances down at my legs, then back up at me. "There's skin still."

"Probably the thinnest layer." I scowl at him. "Why did you scare me?"

"I didn't do it on purpose. Why were you out here alone on a sixteen-foot ladder? That's not smart, Gabby."

"Uh, I was painting, checking things off the list that you gave me. I already cleaned out the visitor's dugout, removed all the gum, and polished the bench. I was tackling this task before heading home." I sit up to get a good look at my legs. As expected, they're beet red.

That's going to be very unpleasant.

Sex was awesome, but I'll probably never experience it ever again because nothing and I mean nothing is pulsing between these legs.

"I told you not to worry about the list." He strips out of his shirt, and then uses the back of it to wipe at his eyes. I attempt to keep my eyes off his chest, but I find it really hard as it ripples under the sun, like a Greek god ready to . . . to . . . I don't know what Greek gods do, but you get the idea.

He's hot—even when he's covered in paint.

When his eyes are finally clear, he blinks a few times and then makes eye contact with me, a stern set in his brow, as if he's about to lecture me.

Repeating himself, he says, "I said don't worry about the list. This was stupid, Gabby."

"Uh, I was doing fine before you showed up." His scowl grows. "Plus, I wanted to show you how dedicated I am to this team, and those things had to be done."

"Yeah, and they're things I would have made the boys do."

"Then maybe you shouldn't have put them on a list for me."

He shakes his head and places his hands on his hips, looking so ridiculous covered in yellow paint. "You're going to be stubborn, aren't you?"

"Not stubborn, just right." I attempt to stand but find it hard as my legs rub together.

"Don't move," Ryland says as he notices my struggle.

"I'm fine."

"You're not." He drops to his knees and then, in a flash, maneuvers between my legs and spreads them wide.

And here I thought I was never having sex again.

"Uh, excuse me," I say as I try to squirm away. "You're kind of invading my privacy."

His eyes meet mine again, giving me a *get real* look. "Gabby, I've been between your legs in a much more intimate way. I just want to see what we're dealing with."

"*We* aren't dealing with anything. I am. So please just leave my inner thighs alone." I attempt to squirm away from him, but he holds me in place.

"Stop, you're going to make it worse."

"Ryland, I can't just stay seated."

"I know, but let me at least look at your legs."

"Why? They're red, nothing else."

He grows angrier. "Stop being difficult." Then he pushes my legs apart again and lowers himself down. Dear God, if anyone saw us, they would think Ryland is getting geared up to . . . well, go down.

"Your legs do not look good. Let me text Abel."

"You don't need to text Abel," I say. "And why would you even text him in the first place?" Thankfully, he lets go of my legs.

"He's a doctor."

Not caring that he's getting paint on his phone, he texts away while I glance around, taking in the chaos. Ryland took the brunt of the paint, but there's some splattered on the grass, some on the fence, and quite a bit on the ladder. What a disaster.

When he's done, I say, "I'm sorry about the mess."

"No need to be sorry," he says, then stands and starts picking everything up.

"I can do that," I say as I go to stand, but he whips around and looks at me with daggers in his eyes.

"Don't even fucking think about it," he says in such a deathly tone that it keeps me seated.

I watch him carry the ladder, paint pan, brush, and paint can over to the dugout, where he sets them down. He must get a text back because he checks his phone. He quickly types something else, then brings his phone to his ear. Turning away, I can hear him talking to someone, but I can't make out what he says. When he hangs up, he sticks his phone back in his pocket and walks toward me with determination in every step.

His pecs bounce with his stride.

His eyes are set on me.

His arms flex as he gets closer, and when he squats down in front of me, only to slip his arms around my shoulders and under my legs, I can't even ask him what he's doing before he picks me up and stands . . . with ease.

He picked me up from the ground and stood as if I weighed nothing.

"What are you doing?" I ask.

"Carrying you to my truck to take you back to your apartment."

"Oh my God, Ryland. It's not that serious. I can drive home."

He shakes his head. "No, I don't want your legs rubbing

together. Abel is bringing over some arnica gel and said he would look at the burns."

"This is getting out of hand. Seriously, it's not that severe." I attempt to wiggle, but when my legs touch, I nearly scream.

Okay, maybe he has a small point.

"Did that hurt?" he asks, clearly to try to prove a point.

"Actually, it felt great."

"Liar." He takes me to his truck, somehow opens the door, and then sets me down.

"I'm going to get paint all over your seats."

"Mac has already put them through hell. It's fine."

He shuts my door, and from my side mirror, I see him grab a towel from the bed of his truck and then walk over to his side, where he opens the cab door to the back seats. He picks up a water bottle and dumps it over his head. My mouth goes dry as I watch the water cascade down his chest, where each muscle stands out like a siren, beckoning me to stare.

Droplet after droplet drips down his tan skin, curving into his contours, highlighting every beautiful inch of him.

Easily, he's the most fit, attractive, and burly man I've ever seen, with a few scars on his ribs and laugh lines in the corners of his eyes.

When he's done with the water, he wipes down his body with the towel, then sets everything in the back of the truck. I realize I've been staring, so I quickly face forward as he joins me in the cab.

"Get a good show?" he asks as he buckles up, and I do the same.

"Don't know what you're talking about," I say as I look out my window.

"Okay," he says, not believing a word I say.

"And that's pretty rich, coming from someone who just gave me a gynecological exam out near right field."

"Gynecological? I barely even had your legs spread a few inches."

"Uh, you had me wide open. You could have fit the entire team between my legs with how wide you were spreading me."

"Wow, exaggerate much?" He roars the truck to life and pulls out of the parking spot. "We can get your car another time."

"It's fine," I say. "My friend Bower is coming to visit this weekend. She can help me get it."

"Okay . . . cool." He's silent for a moment as he makes the short drive from the school to the house. "So your friend is visiting?"

"Best friend," I answer, still looking out the window because I can't trust myself to keep my eyes off him. "I'm trying to convince her to move here."

"Oh yeah? Are you winning?"

"Not at the moment, but I have a fair shot this weekend." I spread my legs a touch farther apart because the burn is real.

"Well, here's hoping you can accomplish it."

"Thank you," I say softly. As we pull down our street, I realize just how quiet it has been. "Hey, are you supposed to get Mac?"

I glance toward him, and I see the frown on his face. "Do you really think I'd forget about my niece?"

Ooof, I can see how that sentence came off.

"I'm sorry, I didn't mean that to be insulting."

"I don't need you checking up on me."

"I wasn't," I say quickly, feeling the tension immediately. "That came out wrong. I'm sure you know where she is at all times."

He clears his throat and turns into the driveway. "I do," he says before he puts the truck in park and hops out. I'm about to do the same when he rounds the front of the truck and opens my door.

He goes to scoop me up, but I stop him. "I can walk."

"No, you can't," he says, more sternly than before.

"Really? You haven't even seen me try."

"Trust me when I say you can't."

"I can," I say, growing irritated with him. "Watch."

I push at his bare chest, ignoring how rock hard it feels against my fingertips, and I shimmy out of the truck, keeping my legs spread as far as they will go. Then, in a crouched position, legs spread, almost freaking walking around like a chimpanzee with their arms out, I wobble over to my apartment stairs . . . stairs that look like they're one hundred flights up.

Oh boy, this is going to hurt.

I attempt the first step and find it incredibly uncomfortable. So I grab the rail and attempt the second, but before I can even plant my foot firmly into the step, I'm lifted off the ground and whisked over to Ryland's house.

"What do you think you're doing?" I ask. "I was doing just fine."

"You looked like a grandma deciding on where she should go to the bathroom."

"No, I did not," I protest as he takes me inside his house. "Uh, my place is that way."

"Yeah, and last time I checked, you didn't have a working shower," he says, once again right. It's incredibly annoying.

But instead of taking me to the downstairs bathroom, he makes his way through the living room and starts heading up the stairs.

"Uh, I recall my shower being downstairs," I say.

"Yeah, and I recall your shower not having a tub, and according to Abel, you should soak."

Dammit, right again.

"Well, I don't have my towel or my soap."

"All things that are not nailed down to the bathroom," he says in a dry tone, clearly annoyed with me.

I don't bother arguing anymore because when he carries me into what I'm assuming is his room, I'm caught off guard with just how . . . not unpacked it is.

There are bed pieces stacked up against the wall off to the right, a mattress on the floor in the middle of the room, and unpacked boxes lined up under the window. But the room itself . . . gorgeous. Three square stained-glass windows are above the bed, offering light and creating a kaleidoscope of color against the opposite white walls. A window seat is the focal point of the room, covered in dark-stained wood but accented with light, creating an ethereal space where if I were the occupant of such room, I'd spend every waking moment there, especially since it looks out toward the large oak tree in the backyard. Just stunning.

Pushing forward, he moves us through a door and right into a large primary bathroom. The first thing I notice are the floors—penny-tiled marble without a stain in the grout, pristine, immaculate. Then there's the rustic vanities with black hardware. The wood has dents and scratches, making it seem purposeful like the vanities have been passed on from generations.

Absolutely gorgeous.

He sets me down on the cool countertop, then walks over to the main piece of the bathroom—the large claw-foot tub.

Dear God.

"Wait here," he says after examining the tub and leaving me alone to look around.

To dream about what it would be like to live in such a house. Never in my life have I ever seen anything like this. I come from very meek dwellings. Nothing so elegant or with so much charm. It's so perfect. So beautiful. Something you'd see in a Pottery Barn magazine but never in real life.

When he comes back into the bathroom, he's holding a bag of Epsom salts. But then he pauses and looks at me. "Do you have any open wounds on your legs?"

I glance down and barely have a second to see before he's spreading my legs again and doing his own personal exam.

"You know, I can look myself."

He just ignores me as his fingers lightly trail over my skin.

"Let's not risk it." He sets the salts down and starts the bath. "We need to clean your legs with some mild soap and then dry them well."

"We?" I ask with a raise of my brow.

"Yeah, we."

I shake my head. "I can do it myself."

"Gabby, I've seen you naked plenty of times. It's not a big deal."

"Says the guy who doesn't have to be naked."

"Do you want me to get naked so you feel more comfortable?"

"No," I say quickly. "That would . . . that would not lead to good things."

His eyes go dark as he says, "Pretty sure it has led to great things."

"You know what I mean." I sigh and hop off the counter. He's quickly taking my arm and helping me over to the tub. "I can do this myself, Ryland."

"Just at least let me help you get in the tub. I won't look. Promise."

"Ryland, that's not—"

"Please, Gabby," he says with more force. "This was my fucking fault, just let me . . . let me fix it." His chest grows heavy as our gazes mix. "Stop arguing, and just let me fix it."

I can see the desperation in his eyes.

The need to be the one who corrects the wrong.

And I can feel that deep in my soul. As the older sibling, the one who's supposed to be the protector, I know what it means to have this undeniable, itching need to make sure everything is okay.

So I let him.

"Okay," I say softly.

"Thank you." He lets go of my hand. "Hold on, let me grab you a towel."

I stay where I am as the tub fills up. He heads out of the bathroom and into the bedroom, where I hear him move some boxes around. When he reappears, he has a tan towel in his hand that looks about thirty years old.

Looking embarrassed, he says, "I, uh, I haven't gotten to cleaning all the towels."

"You can always grab mine from the bathroom," I say. "But that works too."

"Right, yours, that'll be better." He places the towel at the base of the tub and then takes off downstairs.

Wanting to help, I remove my shirt and my shorts. They're decorated in paint, giving me the sneaky suspicion that these will now be my permanent work clothes. I take my time with my shorts because of how sensitive my flesh is, so when Ryland returns to the bathroom, he finds me standing in my underwear.

His body language immediately shifts.

"I thought I'd get started on the undressing," I say, not sure how else to address the fact that I'm in my underwear. "I hope that's okay."

He sets my towel down and nods. "As long as you didn't hurt yourself."

"I didn't."

He nods in approval, then tests the water. Seemingly happy, he turns it off, grabs some soap and a washcloth, then brings it over to the tub. "Uh, I should have grabbed your shampoo while I was down there."

"I can use whatever you have," I say. "As long as you're cool with that."

"Yeah, that's fine."

From his shower, he grabs his shampoo and no conditioner. For a moment, I consider asking him to grab my bottle from my shower, but I have some spray-in conditioner I can use later—at least that's what I tell myself so he doesn't have to go back downstairs again.

"Well, the water is ready," he says.

"Okay." I shift uncomfortably. "So I should just get naked?"

"That's usually how baths work," he replies.

Right.

Wanting some privacy, I turn away from him and remove my bra, letting it join my clothes on the floor. I don't know if it's the slight chilliness in the air or the fact that Ryland is behind me, but my nipples are hard as stones. With one light breeze, a very feral moan might fall past my lips.

I work on my thong next, slowly lowering it and avoiding contact with my legs. When I'm done, I say, "Okay, I'm naked."

He clears his throat behind me, causing me to look over my shoulder. He's staring at the floor, his neck muscles tense. "Give me your hand."

I slide my fingers across his palm, and he lightly clutches my hand as he helps me into the tub, guiding me to sit. When I'm settled, he asks with his eyes closed, "You good?"

"I am, thank you." Then I cover my breasts with one hand and say, "You can open your eyes, Ryland."

"You sure?"

"I'm covered."

He opens his eyes, and I watch in fascination as his Adam's apple bobs while his eyes roam down my body, to my toes, and then all the way back up where my arm is pressed into my breasts. I can see the disappointment in his eyes, but he masks it with a slight lift of the corner of his lips.

"Are you comfortable?" he asks.

"Yes."

"Because I can get you a towel to rest your head on or—"

"I'm fine, Ryland."

"Okay," he says as his hand absentmindedly scratches his chest. I'm not sure why I find that move so incredibly sexy, but I do. "Um, want a drink?"

I almost chuckle at how uncomfortable he looks, but I hold back because there's something else I want to do.

I drag my finger through the water, then look him in the eyes. "I wanted to apologize."

His brow pulls together. "Apologize for what?"

"For asking where Mac was. I don't want you to believe I think you're doing a bad job parenting her or anything like that. That's not my impression of you at all. It was just . . . it was a question. A stupid question at that. Nothing negative behind it."

"Yeah . . ."

"Hey," I say, pulling his attention. "I mean it, Ryland. I can't imagine what it's like to be in your position. You're doing a great job. She's a wonderful kid."

He clears his throat, making it obvious just how uncomfortable he is with the conversation. I'm not sure this man knows how to take a compliment, a serious one. It becomes more obvious that he doesn't when he says, "Well, if you need anything—"

"Wait." I reach out and grab his hand before he can walk away, but I use the hand covering my breasts, causing his eyes to narrow in on me. "Shit, sorry," I say, covering up with my other arm. "I didn't want you to leave just yet."

He wets his lips, looking down at me now like I'm a piece of steak ready to be devoured. "Why not?"

*Yeah, why not, Gabby?*

You should let him leave.

Let him give you your privacy.

But . . . God, I want him around.

I want him near me, with me, talking to me.

I swallow my nerves. "I want to make sure everything's okay between us. That you're not mad."

He looks off to the side, his jaw ticking.

"Ryland," I say softly. "Are you . . . are you mad?"

When his eyes return, he says, "Yes, Gabby, I'm mad."

"Why?"

"Because you got hurt," he replies tersely. "You shouldn't have been painting by yourself. That was incredibly dangerous. I wrote it down because I was just trying to be a dick. I didn't think you'd actually follow through with it."

"If you ask me to do something, Ryland, I'm going to do it."

He drags his hand over his face. "Well, I'm pissed about it, okay?"

Whoa. Okay.

He's not just mad. He's really mad.

I nod. "I'm sorry."

"No, don't apologize. I'm pissed at myself."

"You don't need to be pissed with yourself." I pick up the

washcloth on the side of the tub and wet it. "As we move forward with working together and living next to each other, I need you to know something. I can take care of myself. I'm tough. I don't need someone watching over me, helping me, attempting to take care of me. I've been on my own for a very long time. I can handle anything that comes my way. So please don't tiptoe around me. Please don't think I can't handle a task, a fight, or whatever might present itself in front of me. I'm strong, Ryland. I can handle my own."

"I don't doubt that," he says.

"Then why are you trying to shield me?"

"Because it's in my nature," he says, placing his hands on his hips. "It's just in me to care."

I nod in understanding. "Well, consider me shielded . . . by myself." I squeeze out the washcloth with one hand and try to soap it up, but find it difficult, so I just say fuck it in my head, uncover my breasts, and start soaping up.

When I glance up at him, he's staring anywhere but at me. "I want to say I'll try . . ." Our gazes connect. "But once I consider you a part of my life, there's no way for me to turn off that switch."

"You consider me a part of your life?"

He slowly nods. "I do, which means you're mine to shield."

"Ryland, I—"

But he cuts me off as he kneels next to the tub, takes the washcloth out of my hands, and starts cleansing me. "You might not want to be shielded, but you sure as hell will be shielded by me. Don't fight me on it."

His tone is final.

There's no arguing with him.

There's no questioning.

At this moment, what he says . . . goes.

And I'm so entranced with the way he's cleaning me that I can't muster any words. Because he's so gentle. Because I've never had someone do this to me before. No one's ever cared for me like this.

He's thorough.

He's slow and deliberate.

He's a protector.

I'm transfixed as he moves to the other arm. He washes all the paint off, then rinses the washcloth and adds more soap. When he's done with my arm, he moves the terrycloth fabric over my chest and around my neck. His touch is such an entrancing sensation that when he reaches my breasts, I lift my chest out of the water so he has a better angle.

He clears his throat again, his eyes focused on the task as he circles my breasts a few times. I tamp down my moan, but I can't stop my nipples from growing hard, nor can I stop the dull throb erupting between my legs.

After a few more circles, he dips his hand under the water to wash across my stomach and right below my belly button.

God. Yes.

I gulp a quick breath as he lifts one of my legs and gently washes the paint off, avoiding my inner thighs. The terrycloth fabric caresses over my knee and down my shin to my foot. I bite on my inner cheek as I feel a bolt of lust shoot up my leg from the touch. And when he pays the same attention to my other leg, it only increases the need inside me.

The need that I shouldn't be considering.

That I should be tamping down.

And stuffing away.

Yet when he says, "Spread," I listen to that dark, dangerous voice and spread my legs wide enough for him to bring the washcloth right to my pussy. He runs it along my slit a few times, and when I gasp from the touch, he pauses . . .

His eyes connect with mine.

My mind begs for his fingers to slip inside me.

My teeth pull on my lip while my chest heaves.

I can see it in his expression, the word "fuck" on the tip of his tongue as his heady eyes fall to my lips.

"Do it," I beg.

Touch me.

Break the rules and give us both what we want.

But to my chagrin, he pulls away.

Leaving me in a state of bottled-up yearning.

A bothered state.

One where I'm turned on that will require release.

I want to groan.

Protest.

Beg him to return.

But I can't as he sets the washcloth down, turns on the hand-held sprayer, and wets my hair.

Surprised, I ask, "What are you doing?"

"Washing your hair," he replies as he finishes soaking my long blonde strands.

I should tell him he doesn't need to, but I want to feel his fingers in my hair because I'm so desperate, and he's worked me up so much.

He picks up the shampoo, and I hear him squirt some into his hand. He rubs his palms together and gently massages the soap into my scalp.

And it's the most delicious feeling of my life.

Mmmm, yes.

Thick, strong fingers dig into my head where my neck meets my skull, driving away the tension and the stress I carry there. And I want more. I want him to do this forever, to feel him take control of such a sensitive part of my body and do it with such care, but also with the kind of force making me weak.

It's making me crack.

I find myself leaning into his firm grip.

Moving my head to feel him in certain places.

Attempting to calm my racing heart as he turns on the water again and rinses all the soap out of my hair, gently stroking the strands to help remove the suds.

When he's done, he turns off the water and moves to my side. My eyes flutter open, and I stare up at him. "Want to soak a little longer?" he asks.

I shake my head.

No, that's not what I want.

"You're done?" he asks, and I slowly nod. "Okay." He reaches into the water and unplugs the bathtub, letting the water drain, then he takes my hand and helps me to my feet. He keeps his eyes away, but I don't want him to look away.

I want him to take me in.

All of me.

So I press my finger to his chin and force him to look in my direction.

"Gabby," he says softly. "I . . . I can't."

"I know," I say as I move my hand up his bare chest.

"Then what are you doing?"

I take a deep breath, and on a chance, I say, "Looking for release." Then I turn around and bend over, gripping the tub on one side and popping my ass up in his direction.

"Jesus Christ," he says as his hand lands on my backside, soothing over it. "Gabby . . ."

"Make me come."

"Gabby . . . we said—"

"Just one more time, please, Ryland? Just fuck me one more time."

He wavers behind me, trying to keep our promise while also wanting to give in. The moment he washed between my legs, I was done. I broke.

Snapped.

And now I need to feel him.

"Give me your cock. I need you inside me."

A low rumble falls past his lips as he moves in a step closer, and his hand glides down over my ass. "I don't want to hurt you."

"You'll only hurt me if you don't give me release. Just fuck me."

"Christ," he says as he steps behind me. I hear him rustle around, and when I look over my shoulder, I spot him pushing his shorts and briefs down, freeing his mouth-watering erection.

He's so hard, which is just what I had hoped. He turned himself on while doing the same to me.

"Yes, fill me with your dick. Make me scream."

"Fuck, Gabby," he says right before offering my ass a solid spank.

A surprised sound falls out of my lips before a smile crosses my face. "Yes, Ryland. More. Make me come hard."

He grumbles, then brings the head of his cock to my entrance. And with one solid thrust, he bottoms out, making me cry out his name. My head falls forward and my stomach hollows as he hits me in that spot only he has ever touched.

"You're huge." I squeeze my eyes shut. "So fucking big."

He slaps my ass, and I tense around him. "Shit," he grumbles.

"Again. Spank me again."

He slides his hand up my back, then down, and when he reaches my ass, he spanks me a little harder, causing my inner walls to shake.

"Shit, that feels amazing," he says. He does it again.

And again.

And again.

And one more time until I can feel my arousal start to drip because this is what I need. What I want. Sex with Ryland. It's rough. It's erotic. It's raw. There's no finesse, it's just us trying to make each other come as quickly as we can, and this time, he has me on a short leash.

"I'm close," I say as he spanks me again. "So close."

"Let me get there," he says, and then he starts pumping inside me. I take that opportunity to squeeze every time he pumps inside. The first time I do it, he cries out my name. The second, he goes feral.

"This fucking cunt," he says, gripping my hips and pounding into me. "It will kill me." His fingers dig into my skin, and he rocks me so hard that I focus on holding the tub, not letting him budge me. "Take my fucking cock. Every inch."

I bite down on my lip as my orgasm climbs higher and

higher. The way he's rocking into me, bottoming out with every stroke, hitting me in just the right spot, filling me up so much that the room starts to spin.

The light starts to dim.

And pleasure starts shooting up my legs, down my arms, pooling in the base of my stomach.

"Fuck . . . I'm . . . I'm there," I say.

"Then come, come all over my goddamn cock." He spanks me, letting a large snap to sound through the room. It's all I need as I squeeze around him, and my orgasm races down my spine and right between my legs.

"Oh my God!" I shout. "Ohhhhhhh, yes, Ryland. Yes."

I squeeze his cock, creating such a tight friction that he slows his pace and intensifies his grip on me.

"Uhhhh, fuck," he moans right before I feel him pull out. The sound of his hand riding over his length fills the room right before I feel his hot cum fly over my backside. "Fucking hell," he says softly, his breath heavy as he tries to catch it.

We both remain still for a few seconds before he picks up the washcloth and wipes himself and me.

When I'm cleaned up, he tosses the washcloth to the side, then lifts and turns me around. He lifts my chin, forcing me to look him in the eyes. When I do, there's concern in them.

"Did I hurt you? I fucking forgot about your legs."

I shake my head. "I'm fine."

"Are you sure?"

"Positive."

He lets out a deep breath and then surprisingly, pulls me into a hug. "This wasn't supposed to happen again." His hand lightly caresses my back.

"I know, I'm sorry."

"Me too."

To my surprise, he doesn't let go. He keeps holding me. "This can't happen again."

"It can't," I agree. "This was a one-off."

"Definitely a one-off. No more."

I shake my head against his chest. "Definitely no more because we are friends without benefits."

"Exactly," he says. "And we need to remember that." His hand smooths down my back, just above my ass.

"Yes . . . we do."

He sighs, then releases me. After helping me away from the tub, he wraps me up in my towel, tilts my chin up, and says, "I'm going to shower. But first, dry off."

He moves away from me, and I watch his fine, tight ass trail into his bedroom. If he weren't here, I'd melt to the ground and place my hand to my heart as I try to regain all the feeling back into my body, but unfortunately, I don't have the privilege to do that as he heads back into the bathroom with a shirt in his hand.

"What's that?" I ask.

"It's for you," he answers.

"What do you mean it's for me?"

"To change into. Unless you plan on me carrying you to your apartment in a towel."

"Are you really going to carry me?" I ask.

"Yeah . . . I am." And with that, he sets the shirt on the counter and moves toward the shower before turning toward me. "If you leave this bathroom, you won't like what happens."

And just like when he told me to take his cock . . . I listen.

# Chapter Sixteen

### RYLAND

That felt amazing.

So fucking good.

It's safe to say that I'm addicted to her, and I don't see that ending anytime soon. It's only going to get worse.

But I won't slip up again. This was a special occasion—if that's how you want to phrase it. I felt like I needed that connection after what happened. It was . . . fuck, it was terrifying. I felt my heart racing as I was trying to find the damn ladder, only for her to slide down and fuck up her thighs.

I still hate myself for it.

So fucking her, giving her what she wanted—hell, what I wanted—it was as if I was giving myself permission to make sure she was okay. And that's how I knew how to do it on a deeper level. I didn't want her telling me she was fine—those are just words. I wanted to feel it. I wanted to feel her around me, squeezing me, letting me know she was okay.

And that's exactly what I got.

Another taste.

Another moment with her that I'll have to tuck away and not revisit because we do have to keep this platonic.

I finish up in the shower, and when I step out, Gabby's leaning against the counter in one of my old baseball shirts.

And she looks damn good in it.

I grab my towel from the hook and keep my eyes on hers as I dry off. "Comfortable?"

She nods. "Your shirt smells good."

For some reason, that causes a surge of pride to pump through me. It shouldn't. I should not care in the slightest. But hell, knowing she can smell me on her? Yeah, I fucking like that a lot.

I wrap my towel around my waist and watch as her eyes travel over my body, taking in every inch. I don't blame her. I was doing the same thing when she was in the tub. When I washed her hair, I couldn't take my eyes off her wet tits and hard nipples, the way her chest heaved, moving them in and out of the water. I was entranced.

Leaving her to look, I head into the bedroom and grab a pair of clean shorts. I drop my towel to the ground, showing off my ass, and slip on the shorts. When I turn around, catching her eyes on me, it takes every ounce of willpower not to capture her mouth with mine.

If I touch those lips, I'll be a goner.

I have to remain neutral. I allowed this momentary lapse, but now we're back to friends with no benefits. It will be better, easier.

"You ready?" I ask her as I pick up my phone and check it. I spot a text from Abel saying that he left the arnica gel on her doorstep.

"Ready," she says as she pushes off the counter and takes one step toward me, but I'm quickly at her side and lifting her into my arms. "You realize how ridiculous this is, right? You can't carry me everywhere."

"I can actually," I say, weaving her through my room, down the stairs, and out the back door to my truck.

Luckily, I remembered to grab her things before we left the field. So I snag her purse and carry her up the steps to her apartment, where I set her down. While she digs out her keys, I pick up the gel. When she finds them, I take the keys from her and unlock the door, only to scoop her back up.

"Bedroom or living room?" I ask as I shut the door behind me.

"Living room is fine."

I walk over to the couch and lightly place her on the cushion.

"Can I ask you to do me a favor?"

"Yeah, anything," I say.

"Uh, can you get me a pair of underwear? Not a thong, just a regular pair. From what history has shown us today, you'll insist on applying that gel, and when you go to spread my legs like you do, I'd rather have a barrier between your hands and my . . . lower half."

The corners of my lips tick up as I nod. "Yeah, I can do that. Where's your underwear?"

"Top drawer of my dresser," she answers.

I head back to her bedroom, where my eyes roam the space. Wow. It's beautifully decorated. White bed with green and white bedding, nightstands on either side, a matching white dresser, cream-colored rug, green curtains . . . and a fake tree in the corner. It's put together. It looks like a home in here rather than the jail cell I'm living in.

I need to get my life together.

When I open the top drawer of her dresser, I'm greeted by lace and silk. Bras, thongs, cheeky underwear. She has it all. I sift through the fabric and pull out a pair of black lace underwear. Pleased with my choice, I take it to her in the living room, only for her to stare me down.

"That took you longer than it should have."

"Wanted to make sure I got you the right pair," I say as I move in front of her.

"I can put it on myself," she says as she reaches for it.

"That's okay, I can do it," I say with a smirk as I move the underwear down to her feet. On a sigh, careful of her inner thighs, I slip them up her legs, then help her stand where she pulls it up the rest of the way.

"That was my job," I say.

"I think that's above your pay grade as a friend." She sits back down with my help, then spreads her legs and gestures toward them. "For your inspection."

That makes me chuckle as I squat down and look over her legs. "These are going to bruise bad." I pick up the arnica gel and open the top. I squirt some on my fingers. "I'll be gentle." She sucks in a sharp breath as I start to spread it across her right thigh. "I know, just grin and bear it." While I spread the gel with one hand, I hold her leg with the other and make soothing strokes with my thumb over her skin, letting her know that I'm not here to hurt her. I'm here to take care of her.

It takes a little bit of time, but once I'm done, I lift and wash my hands in the kitchen sink. Once I dry them off, I ask, "Do you want me to get you anything to drink?"

"Could I have some iced tea? There is a pitcher in my fridge. Cups are in the cabinet next to the fridge."

"Sure," I say. I remove the iced tea from the fridge, then pull two cups from the cabinet and fill them up. After returning the iced tea in the fridge, I bring the cups over to the couch and hand her one. When I take a seat next to her, she eyes me.

"What are you doing?"

I grab my phone from my pocket. "How do you feel about sandwiches?"

"Um, what?"

"Sandwiches, do you like them? Figured that would be easy for dinner."

"Are we having dinner together?"

"I'm hungry, and I don't feel like making anything, and you sure as hell are not making anything, so I can either order sandwiches for us both, or you can sit there and watch me eat a sandwich in front of you."

"What a hard decision," she says sarcastically. "Whatever will I choose?"

I hand her my phone, and I watch her scroll through the options. "What are your thoughts on tuna?"

"Well, if you really want to keep this friends with no benefits, that's the way to do it."

She chuckles, then scrolls some more. "You know what? Just a ham and cheese sounds good."

"Yeah?" I say. "That's what I get."

Her brow raises in curiosity. "Are you just saying that?"

"No, of course not. Did you?"

"Do you really think I believe a ham and cheese sandwich is the way to impress a man?"

I shrug. "Times have changed. I don't know what the youth are doing these days."

That makes her chuckle again, and hell, I like the sound. "Are you calling me your youth?"

"Well, you're younger, right?"

"Not that much younger."

I finish the order and ask, "How old are you?"

"Thirty."

I slowly nod my head. "Thirty-five. So . . . not bad."

"We can share the same likes and dislikes of our childhood."

"We could." I drape one arm over the back of the couch and then shift to turn toward her. "What was your favorite show growing up?"

"*Muppet Babies*," she says without giving it much of a thought.

My lip curls. "*Muppet Babies*? Really?"

"Are you judging me?"

"Yes, yes, I am."

She rolls her eyes. "It was a solid show that made me happy. What did you like? Something lame like . . . *Power Rangers*?"

"Uh, *Power Rangers* was great."

She shakes her head. "I can't have this conversation with you because I know that you're just going to believe that you're right and I'm wrong."

"That would be correct."

She chuckles. "And that's exactly why we're not talking about it."

"Then what do you want to talk about?"

"First of all." She reaches for the remote, but I help her and hand it over. "I think we need to turn on the Bombers game."

Christ, a girl after my own heart.

She turns on the TV and doesn't even have to change the channel as she must have been watching the game last night. The game just started, so the score is zero-zero, but the Bombers are up.

I get comfortable and ask, "Have the Bombers always been your favorite team?"

"They're not my favorite," she answers, surprising me.

"Oh wait, you like the Rebels."

She shrugs. "Not really. I just think Jason Orson is really good."

"Then who is your favorite team?"

"If I said the Bobbies, what would you say?"

"Fairweather fan. It's easy to like the Bobbies when they have a high payroll and a shit ton of championships."

"I knew you were going to say that." She sips her drink. "Who's your favorite team?"

"Bombers," I answer. "I grew up here. It's the hometown team."

"Makes sense. I watch the Bombers because Bennett's on their Triple-A team, and I'm hoping their third baseman gets injured so he's called up. I've never wished for so many pulled hamstrings in my life."

I laugh. "That would be fucking awesome if he was called up. Shit, I should have been following him. I didn't know he was with the Bombers minor league system."

"He was traded last year. It was part of a big trade deal. Worked out because he was with the Texas Hot Dogs, and he hated it there."

"Oh, that's right, the Hot Dogs. Fuck, what a terrible draft."

She laughs. "Yeah, it was brutal. It was right when they went through the rebrand too and chose the new name to get fans more involved. They thought the Hot Dogs was just odd enough that it would work." She shakes her head. "It did not."

"No, they have the worst record in baseball, lowest stadium attendance, and they're the laughingstock of the league. Bennett is lucky he was traded."

"Yeah, tell me about it."

All of a sudden my phone rings, and I glance down at it to see it's Hattie.

Fear races up my stomach because the only reason she would be calling is if something happened with Mac.

"Hello?" I answer in a panic. "Everything okay?"

"Yeah," Hattie says. "Sorry about calling, but Mac was missing you, and she wanted to call you."

"Oh," I say, the panic slowly easing. "Okay, put her on."

The phone gets passed from what I can hear and then her little voice comes on. "Uncle Ry Ry."

"Hey, Mac," I say. I catch the soft smile that passes over Gabby's lips. "What's up?"

"I miss you."

Fuck my heart.

"I miss you, too," I say. "Are you not having fun with Aunt Hattie and Uncle Hayes?"

"No, I am, but I still miss you. Don't you want to sleep over here with me?"

"If I sleep over there with you, then I might eat all the pancakes Uncle Hayes said he's going to make you in the morning. Then you won't have any for yourself."

"You can't eat all of those pancakes."

"Oh, I bet I could," I say.

"That wouldn't be very nice, Uncle Ry Ry."

I chuckle. "See, that's why you don't want me to spend the night too. I'm the pancake monster."

She laughs. "No, you're not."

"Okay, fine, if I have to prove it to you, then I will. I'm

packing my bag now, and I'm headed over. Be prepared to eat no pancakes tomorrow morning."

Her cute laugh rings through the phone. "No, no pancake monster invited."

"I don't need an invitation. I'm just going to show up."

"You better not, or Chewy Chondra will bite your toe off."

"Bite my toe off? I don't think Chewy Chondra's teeth are strong enough to bite my toe off."

"She does," Mac says with conviction. "She'll bite it right off, then give it to her spiders."

"No, not the spiders," I say in a scared voice.

"Yes, the spiders."

"Well, sheesh, I guess I better stay here, then. That means no pancakes for the pancake monster."

"Yeah, no pancakes for you."

"Sad," I say. "Tell me this, did you get to swim in the pool?"

"Yes, Uncle Hayes got a new floatie, and it's a horse."

"What? A horse floatie? You have a horse floatie over there, and you're missing me? How is that possible?"

"Because I love you," she says, breaking down every goddamn wall I've ever had up.

I smile softly. "I love you, too."

In the background, I hear Hattie say, "The s'mores are ready."

"S'mores?" I say. "Uh-oh, the s'mores monster is coming over."

"No," Mac shouts into the phone. "You stay there, Uncle Ry Ry. These s'mores are for me."

I sigh heavily. "Fine, eat two for me."

"I will. Love you."

"Love you," I say, but I don't think she hears it because the phone is shuffled around again, and Hattie comes on.

"Pancake monster?"

I chuckle. "I don't know. It was a spur-of-the-moment thing. Seemed to work, though. Is she okay?"

"Yeah, she just got sad out of the blue, kind of weird but also good."

"Good?" I ask.

"Yeah, because she's attached, and that's a good thing, Ryland. A very good thing."

I swallow hard, feeling overwhelmed by the responsibility of that sentence. "Okay." I swallow back the tightness in my throat. "Well, let me know if she needs to chat or if she really does need me to come spend the night."

"I'm sure she'll be fine. She's already snuggling up against Hayes outside."

"Okay. Well, thanks. Bring her with you tomorrow when you come over to help out."

"Of course. And just by chance, what are you doing tonight?"

Not wanting to get into it, I say, "Goodbye, Hattie." Then I hang up on her and set my phone down next to me. I look over at Gabby and say, "Sorry about that."

"No need to apologize." Her lips twist to the side, and I can tell she wants to say something she's not saying.

"What?" I ask.

"Nothing."

"What are you not saying?"

She tugs on her still wet hair and says, "It's just cute, hearing you talk to her. You're really sweet with your niece."

"Would you prefer I tell her if she calls me again she's sleeping under the stairs?"

She laughs and shakes her head. "No. I'm just saying it's sweet. You seem to handle it very well, and she's incredibly lucky to have you."

I shift uncomfortably because it isn't easy for me to take compliments. When I was growing up, compliments were not a thing in my household. Our mom died of breast cancer, same as Cassidy, and our dad was an alcoholic. I was left with Cassidy to be the parent of Hattie and Aubree while consequently getting the brunt of our father's abuse. Nothing about our house was loving other than the love Cassidy shed on all of us. I'm pretty sure she's the only reason I'm still here, that, and Hattie and Aubree.

"Thanks," I say softly, looking toward the screen to distract myself.

"I made you uncomfortable," she says. "I'm sorry."

"Can you stop apologizing?" I say. "Jesus, Gabby, there's nothing to be sorry about." My tone is harsher than I anticipated, and I can tell it is by the expression on her face.

"Okay, I'll stop."

She turns toward the TV as well, and I hate myself even more. This is exactly why I don't enter into romantic bullshit because I have fucking issues. I have anger issues. I cannot regulate my emotions, and I don't know how not to be an asshole when I'm stressed or uncomfortable.

I drag my hand over my mouth, and in an annoyed tone—annoyed with myself—I say, "Fuck, now I have to apologize. I didn't mean to snap at you like that."

"It's fine, Ryland."

"It's not," I say. "I'm just . . . I'm not good at taking compliments."

"I can see that." She turns toward me, her eyes like a beating heart, offering me a lifeline with their understanding. "You can be real around me. You realize that, right? If you snap at me, you snap at me. It's not going to change my opinion of you, but I will call you out if I don't approve. I know what it's like to have baggage. I know what it does to you as a human, and it's baggage you never should have been carrying in the first place. I understand you, but know, if I apologize, it's because I mean it."

Guilt consumes me.

An uncomfortable tension rolls through my body.

And my mind is having a hard time comprehending that she has no problem talking about such . . . sensitive topics. Because what did she go through in order to thoroughly understand me?

For me, we've skirted around sensitive topics my whole life.

We've never really gone into detail what our dad did to me . .

. did to our family. And Gabby, she so easily speaks of baggage and what a bad childhood could do to someone. It's perplexing.

I don't know what to say, so I reply with a simple, "Okay."

Thankfully, there is a knock on her door, and our sandwiches have arrived. The reprieve I needed.

---

"So did you play ball?" I ask Gabby as I wipe my mouth and set my napkin down on my finished deli paper.

"I did," she says. "I didn't get to play it like Bennett, though." She pops a cut-up strawberry in her mouth. I grabbed them from her fridge when the sandwiches arrived.

"What do you mean?"

She wipes her fingers on a napkin and says, "Didn't have anyone to take me to practices and games." She shrugs as if it was no big deal. "I practiced, though, with Bennett. We'd watch and read everything we could about baseball, and I made sure Bennett found a way to and from games and practices."

"Wow," I say, not knowing any of that. "So you never really got to play the game?"

"A little here and there, but not like you and Bennett. But I never had to play the game to love it. I enjoy playing catch, hitting the ball off the tee, getting grounders, simple things like that, which practice the skills of baseball."

"What's your favorite part of the game?"

"Defense," she answers. "I love everything about it. Bennett and I would go back and forth between who got grounders. We even had a pitchback at one point, and we'd rotate, one right after the other, throwing the ball and catching it from the pitchback. There's something about not knowing where the ball will end up, only for you to find it in your glove from the effort you put behind in retrieving it. I love it."

I slowly nod my head. "I, uh, I love offense."

"Really?" she asks.

"Yeah, I love the intricacies of it. How one minor glitch in your swing could cause a month-long slump. I love problem-solving and adjusting the swing to get out of that slump. And I love that the swing isn't the same for everyone. What might work for some doesn't work for others. Plus, the sound of the ball hitting the bat is probably the best sound ever."

She smiles. "Not better than the ball hitting the glove."

"Looks like we might need to test that out at some point, play some catch and hit some balls."

"Are you suggesting that we play baseball together?"

I gesture to her legs and say, "When your legs are better of course."

"Of course." She leans back on the couch and looks over at me. "You realize we make a pretty good match on the field. You with offense, me with defense. Not that I'm going to suggest anything because you're the head coach, but that can work to our advantage."

I clear my throat. "Yeah, I thought of that."

"And did you know that David actually asked me that question in my interview? He asked what I liked coaching best, and I said defense. Maybe he knew you were an offense coach and thought we would make a great pair."

I give her a *don't fuck with me* look, which makes her laugh. "Do not give that man credit."

"I mean, you have to give him a little bit of credit." She shifts to turn toward me more, and I can tell it's uncomfortable for her. "You have gotten off a few times since he made such a solid choice in picking your coaching staff."

"Pretty sure his intention in picking you wasn't so I could get off."

"Just a supreme benefit."

"That we're not partaking in anymore," I remind her.

"Of course. Never again. It was fun creating orgasms with you while it lasted, but from here on out, no more extremely satisfying and mind-blowing pleasure."

My mouth goes dry as I catch the grin on her lips. "If you're trying to make this . . . hard, keep talking like that."

Her grin grows. "Trust me, I know how to make it hard. I don't need advice."

My eyes narrow, and she laughs.

"Come on, we need to be able to joke about it, or else this is just going to be torture."

"It's already torture."

"You suffering over there, Rowley?"

I don't know why, but I like her using my last name like that in a teasing tone.

"Yeah, aren't you?"

"Well, my inner thighs are in need of some soothing." She wiggles her brows, and I find it far too adorable.

"You're being annoying," I say even though I don't feel that way. I kind of wish she'd do more, maybe even allow me to drag her over to my side where I could just casually slip my hand under her shirt and play with her while we watch the game.

"Seems like you like annoying." She wiggles her finger at my smile.

"Just humoring you."

"You're a liar, Ryland Rowley. But that's okay." She's silent for a second. "But seriously, you're the best sex I've ever had."

I press my lips together and stare at the TV for a few seconds. Then, I loll my head to the side and say, "Sex will never be the same after you."

That brings a huge smile to her face, and that's all I can ask for.

# Chapter Seventeen

## GABBY

"Mother . . . fucker . . ." I say as I roll to my side and sit up, letting my legs dangle off the edge of the bed. I stare down at my inner thighs, which are now an ugly shade of black and blue. It looks like I tried to fuck a cannon and failed.

Slowly, I get out of bed and waddle over to my bathroom, where I brush my teeth, pee, wash my face, and fix my hair by pulling it up into a high messy bun. I tug a few strands to frame my face, then call it a day, not even bothering with a coat of mascara. Bower's coming today, and she couldn't care less about my appearance.

Not wanting to change just yet, I keep Ryland's shirt on—the same shirt I shamelessly went to bed smelling—and move to my kitchen at a snail's pace to make some coffee. Just then, there's a knock on the door.

Is Bower here already?

"Coming," I call out. "Very slowly but coming."

"Gabby, it's me," Ryland says. "I have a key so I can let myself in."

"Please do," I say as I lean against the kitchen counter.

He unlocks and opens the door wide, only to pick up two cups of coffee and a bag from the ground. When his eyes meet mine, he must see my pain because he quickly rushes over, depositing the bag and drinks on the table. "Shit, are you okay?"

"Umm, I want to say yes so you don't have this need to take care of me, but in reality . . . ouch."

He lightly chuckles. "Okay, let me help you get to the couch."

And just like yesterday, he effortlessly scoops me up and carries me to the couch, where he sets me down.

"Let me see—holy shit!" he says, his eyes going wide when he takes a look at my thighs. "Fuck, Gabby." He kneels in front of me. "That looks terrible."

"Feels just as terrible," I say as I lean against one of my throw pillows. "And I don't say that so you feel obligated to help me. It's the freaking truth."

"Let me grab that gel. I can put some more on."

"I can put it on, Ryland," I say as he finds it on the coffee table.

"It's fine. I got it." He uncaps the medicine, and I stop him by placing my hand on his chest.

His eyes lift to mine as I say, "You touch my inner thighs and turn me on this morning without relief, and we're going to have a problem, especially when you smell so freaking good."

The lightest smirk appears at the corner of his lips. "I smell good?"

I nod, my mouth watering at the sight of him. "Really good."

"Okay, yeah. You're right."

"Thank you," I say as I apply the gel myself. "While I do this, why don't you bring me that coffee over here that I assume is for me?"

"It is," he says as he moves toward the kitchen. I catch him wetting a rag, probably for my hand, and then he grabs the bag and the coffee.

When he returns to the living room, he sits on the coffee table next to me and helps me wipe my hand free of the gel.

"Here." He gives me a cup of coffee. "There's milk and sugar. I'm not sure what you liked, but I took a guess."

"This works great, thank you. You didn't have to."

"Didn't think you'd be getting around easily this morning, so I wanted to help."

"You know, for someone who was pissed to see me a couple of weeks ago, you're actually very nice."

"You have to break through the tough exterior to get to the nice." He smirks.

"Are you saying I broke down your barriers?"

He takes a sip of his coffee and looks me in the eyes. "The first squeeze of your wet pussy over my cock broke down my walls."

My cheeks go red, and I can't hold back the smile. "That's not a very *friends with no benefits* thing to say."

"Hey, you said we should joke about it."

"Was that a joke? Because to me, your giant cock is nothing to laugh about."

His lips twitch as he blows out a breath. "Okay, change of subject."

I chuckle, then nod at the bag next to him. "Please tell me there's something to eat in there."

"There is." He sets his coffee down and picks up the bag. He pulls out a muffin and says, "These are from the bakery here in town, and they're amazing. Aubree is feral for them."

"They smell delicious." I take a large whiff. Apple, maple, and cinnamon all filter through my senses, making my stomach gurgle. If Ryland wasn't currently present, I'd bury my head into this muffin, but I maintain control and break off a piece instead. When the flavors, warmth, and fluffiness hit my mouth, I know this won't be the last time I eat one of these.

"I can see why Aubree's feral over them."

He chuckles. "I actually got some for her too because she's coming over today."

"She is? What do you have planned?"

He breaks off a piece of his muffin and tosses it in his mouth.

"The family is coming over to help me with my house. I have to finish unpacking and get it all set up. I think Mac wants some normalcy, and boxes everywhere is not normalcy." He pauses, and if I didn't know him better, I'd say he was embarrassed. But I see remorse in his expression.

"What is it?"

"She asked me whether I had forgotten her mom. Cassidy." He looks so forlorn that I know *forgetting* his sister will always be an impossibility.

"You wouldn't, Ryland. Even I know that," I say, hoping he hears the sincerity and honesty in my voice. He smiles one of his reticent smiles.

"Yeah, of course, I won't. But Mac asked if I'd forgotten her because we hadn't put any pictures of her on the walls. Fuck, I felt awful when she asked that."

"Hence your sisters coming to help."

"Hence the sisters coming to help. It will be good to get things set up and make it look more like her home. More normal. Homey."

"I know that feeling, which is why I spent a good amount of time making sure I was comfortable in this apartment. If I wasn't in a bad spot with my legs, I'd offer to help."

He waves me off. "It's fine. We got it handled."

I tilt my head to the side. "If I wasn't hurt, would you have let me help?"

"Probably not," he answers.

"Why not?"

"Because my family would be annoying. You saw what happened the other night with Abel and Hayes. Imagine that times ten with my sisters involved."

"Do they meddle?"

"They didn't used to," he says. "But ever since they found loving relationships, they think I need the same thing."

"You don't think you do?" I ask, surprised.

He shakes his head. "Not for me."

Huh.

Interesting.

I mean, not that I'm looking for anything from him, but it's good to know where he stands. Maybe that's why he's been so hot and cold.

"So you don't ever see yourself in a relationship . . . getting married, nothing like that?"

"No," he answers matter-of-factly. "I wouldn't be a good partner. I know that for certain. And I need to give my attention to Mac and make sure she's taken care of."

"And who takes care of you?" I ask.

"Myself," he says. "Like you, I don't need someone taking care of me. I've done it all my life."

"I can understand that," I say even though it hurts me because I know how lonely it is to take care of yourself and everyone else around you. "I never considered I'd ever be in a relationship either."

"You haven't?" he asks, seeming surprised by that.

"Nope. I've been so set on ensuring Bennett gets what he needs that I haven't thought about it before." Not to mention the abuse I suffered through from my one and only boyfriend. "But I guess if I found someone who changed my mind, I'd consider it. Until then, I'm good just fucking."

His brow rises. "Just fucking, huh? You going to continue to scratch that itch?"

I smirk. "I don't know, maybe. Would you be irritated if I brought another man back here?"

"No," he says with a tense jaw.

I chuckle. "You are such a liar."

"You're not mine, so I can't tell you what to do, and . . . we're friends without benefits."

"Yeah, but if we weren't, you'd be the one fucking me, right?"

His eyes match mine with a steely, hungry gaze. "I'd make sure you woke up every morning still feeling me between your legs."

I wet my lips and look away. "Good thing we're just friends

then. I'm not sure I could handle feeling you between my legs every morning. I might become addicted, and as we both just established, you don't do relationships."

"Right," he says as if I'm using his logic against him.

"So it's a good thing this is all just hypothetical, and we're just two friends enjoying muffins. Although I kind of wish you were enjoying my muffin . . ."

"Christ," he says while standing, making me laugh.

"Sit back down."

"Nope." He shakes his head. "Too dangerous."

"Remember, we can joke about it."

"Not when I'm already feeling horny as shit."

"How on earth are you horny after last night?"

"Because," he says, looking me in the eyes, "it's you."

And with that, he heads toward the kitchen, making me feel all kinds of giddy.

"When is your friend getting here?" he asks.

"This morning," I say.

"Then I can assume I can leave you now, and you'll be okay?" I find him near the door, looking desperate to leave.

"Yeah, I'll be fine. Thank you for breakfast and the help."

"You're welcome," he says. "You have my number. Call or text if you need anything."

"I will." I wink at him, and he sighs with a shake of his head before leaving the apartment.

I rest my head back and stare up at the ceiling. That man keeps confirming what I already knew about him. He's so . . . steadfast, wholesome, and good. He's a provider. Mac and his sisters are so lucky to have him in their corner.

*And of course, he has a dirty mouth that I'd love to experience every day.*

He'd become an addiction, so it's wise we stay just friends. But I'm starting to see that if there were a man I'd want in *my* corner, to love every day, to go through life's ups and downs, Ryland Rowley would be a strong contender.

If only things were different . . .

"I don't understand why I'm here," Bower says from the couch. "He has a big penis, incredible hands, and a body to die for. He's protective, sweet, and loves baseball. Why isn't he over here, on top of you at the moment?"

Can you tell that I filled Bower in on all things Ryland?

She barely even made it through the apartment before I made her sit, and I went over everything with her—from last night to this morning and everything in between. There is a bit of a stunned look in her eyes, and she slowly started to form an opinion . . . hence where we are now.

"Because, I told you, we're friends with no benefits."

"That is the stupidest thing I've ever heard. Sounds like the worst movie title. A good way to take a positively erect penis and deflate it with one poke. Terrible conclusion of a wild few weeks. And if this were a romance, in a romance book, I'd chastise the author for even thinking she could fool the readers into believing that friends without benefits is a real thing. If you want to fuck, just fuck!"

I let out an exasperated sigh. "It's not that easy, Bower. If it was just him and me, and we were neighbors? Sure, I'd tell him to come over, kick you out, and let him do whatever he wants to me, but there are complications."

"You said his penis was perfect. That's the only complication I can think of."

How can I keep forgetting how unhelpful Bower is?

"We have to work together, coach together, he has his niece, and from what he told me today, he has no desire to ever be in a relationship . . . ever. Like it's not in the cards for him."

"He said that to you?" she asks.

"Yes. To my face. Not happening for him. Not that I want to be in a relationship with the man. I'm still on the fence about any sort of romance in my life, but I don't want there to be a moment when I possibly want more, and he's not open to that. I don't think I could handle the rejection, so I think we just have to keep it how it is as friends without benefits."

She crosses her arms and leans back on the couch. "That's stupid. He sounds like a great candidate to sweep you off your feet and carry you into the sunset."

I study my friend for a moment. "What have you been doing recently?"

"What do you mean?" she asks.

I wiggle my finger at her, motioning up and down her body. "You're different. More romantic. More . . . more into this whole love thing. What have you been doing since I've been gone?"

Chin held high, she says, "Not that it's any of your business, but I've been dabbling in some reading lately, and I've just grown to appreciate the possibility of finding one's soulmate. We all deserve love in our life, even the ones who want to push it away."

"When have you ever read books?"

"Ugh," Bower complains. "You sound like my mother. If you must know, I was scrolling through social media, and there was a girl doing her makeup and talking about how she met a man on the side of the street and how he asked her to pretend to be his fiancée and baby mama. I was so invested in her story that when she announced it was a book at the end, I was fooled. But of course, I had to find out what book because a spin-off of *Pretty Woman* really got my gobbler gobbling."

"Ew, don't say gobbler gobbling."

"Anywho, found the book, read it in a day, and it's been a downhill spiral into romancelandia from there." She leans forward, placing her hand on my shin. "And do you know what I've learned?" She holds up three fingers. "Three things. One, love is for everyone, and we can find it, need it, explore it, and savor it in different ways. Two, books can make you laugh and cry at the same time. And three, there is such a thing as a bloody hand job."

She leans back, almost as if she's metaphorically dropping a mic.

I should have never left her.

"Uh, what is a bloody hand job?"

"I'm glad you asked," she says. "You see, they slice the palm of the person giving the hand job, and then they use the blood as the lubricant. The guy gets off on not only seeing the blood all over his penis, but also . . . obvious friction."

I blink a few times.

"Umm . . . Bower—"

"Before you start judging." She holds up her hand. "I was semi into it. Also, romance is a judgment-free zone. If you float to the kinky side of things, then who are we to judge how people get their jollies? Let the people do their bloody hand jobs without feeling criticized."

"You know, I think we're getting a little off topic."

"Possibly, but God, I had to talk to someone about it. I'm glad I got it off my chest. Also, I was sort of into it. Would I ever do it? Absolutely not. I'm a weenie when I get a papercut, let alone getting my hand sliced. But that's what's great about romance. You can live through the fantasy of it all."

"True." I'm unsure of how we got to this point in the conversation. Unsure of where to go, I say, "Are there things you've read that you want to try?"

"Absolutely. And I think that's also one of the reasons I'm a solid no on the friends-with-no-benefits thing because you have no idea the kinds of activities you could be doing with that man. He seems like an A+ alpha, and when you have one of those in your life, you take advantage."

"He is very alpha, isn't he?"

"From the sound of it, yeah. And it's such a sad thing that you don't get to take advantage of it."

"I know," I sigh heavily. "But I think putting up that boundary is smart. The last thing I need is to lust after the man when I'm hitting groundballs to a bunch of high school boys."

"I don't know, maybe they'd cheer you on?"

"Once again, this isn't some romantic comedy. This is real life, and those boys would not cheer us on. They'd probably judge the female coach for lusting after the head coach right away. You know what, Bower?" I look her in the eyes.

"What?" she asks.

"This is all of your fault."

"My fault." She points at her chest. "How is this my fault?"

"Because if it wasn't for you encouraging me to have a one-night stand with Ryland, I never would have known how amazing in bed he is or how delicious his kisses are, how . . . how undeniably . . . full he makes me feel."

She cracks a smile. "You know what? I'm not going to apologize. If anything, I'd like to find a time machine and go back in time where I'd encourage you to stay a few more days and spend more time with him."

"That is not helpful."

"Pretty sure your vagina would thank me."

I chuckle. "See, this is what I need, you here all the time. Can't you move already?"

"I'm not moving unless I see what this town has to offer."

"Sure, why don't I just take you around, show you the town," I say sarcastically.

"You know, humping a foul pole has really ruined this weekend."

"I was not humping it," I say. "I was sliding down it."

"You should have slid down Mr. Hunky—"

*Knock. Knock.*

We both still, then look toward the door.

Whispering, I say, "Oh God, that must be him." A large smile spreads across Bower's face. "Don't embarrass me. I swear I'll never be your friend again."

"Oh, I wouldn't embarrass you," she says. I don't believe a word.

She pushes off the couch and heads to the door, where she opens it.

"Hey, you must be Gabby's friend," I hear Ryland say. I glance over my shoulder to find him standing in the doorway wearing black athletic shorts and a gray T-shirt. He's wearing a baseball hat and didn't shave this morning, so he's looking all kinds of hot.

"Dear God." Bower presses her hand to her chest. She then turns to me and says, "This is the man you're going to practice friends with no benefits with?" She shakes her head in disappointment. "I honestly don't think we can talk anymore. You've clearly lost your mind."

And here I told her not to embarrass me.

"Bower," I say through my clenched teeth.

She rolls her eyes and then turns back to Ryland. "I've been told not to embarrass her, so here is my attempt. Hi, I'm Bower, I'm Gabby's friend and I think you are both fools for playing this game of not pressing privates together."

Ryland lightly chuckles. "Well, Bower, it's nice to meet you and I appreciate your honesty."

"If anything, I'll tell you how I see it." She pauses and studies him for a moment. "You realize you're incredibly attractive, right?"

"Bower, can you not harass him?"

"I'm not harassing him. I'm pointing out the obvious. I think it's a compliment."

"He doesn't like compliments," I say.

"Oh, if that's the case." She looks him up and down some more. "I think your shorts should be shorter, as those are too long. Man thigh is in now, millennial."

"Oh my God," I say as I start to get off the couch, but Ryland is in the apartment and walking over to me before I can even attempt to get up.

"Don't fucking move," he says, holding his hand out. "She's fine."

"She's offensive," I whisper.

"Not anything worse than what my sisters would say."

"Oh my God, look at you two." Bower holds her hands together. "Adorable."

I roll my eyes and whisper, "I'm sorry."

"It's fine. I came over because well, Hayes is grilling and told me to come up here and ask if you wanted to join us for lunch."

"Oh that's—"

"We'd love to," Bower says. "We were just saying how we're starving. Now, we don't want to come empty-handed." She taps her chin and then gestures to my legs. "Can we offer you a bruise or two?"

Ryland gives off that playful smirk that he's so good at. "We'll take the bruises."

"Great, I can also offer you dessert. What's between the bruises."

"Oh my God, Bower!" I shout this time, making Ryland laugh harder.

"That kind of dessert shouldn't be shared around the table." He winks. "I personally like that to myself."

"Oh dear heavens." Bower places her hand on her chest and rocks into the wall. "Straight from a novel. You, my guy, are straight from a novel."

"What?" Ryland asks.

"Ignore her. We'll come down."

"I can come get you when you're ready . . . unless you want to keep wearing that shirt."

"I don't . . . I mean, I do, I like it, but I don't want to wear it down there because you know what's under . . . uh, never mind. I'll change and walk downstairs myself. There will be no carrying of me."

"Gabby."

"I'm serious, Ryland. I will not have you carrying me around in front of your family. I can manage. Okay?"

I can see that it's painful for him to acquiesce, but he does. "Okay. Food will be ready in about ten minutes. No need to rush."

"Don't worry, we'll be down there in time," Bower says. "Oh, but before you leave, maybe you can rub some more of that arnica gel on her. I'd do it, but I'm just not into arnica, you know?"

"What does that even mean?" I ask.

"Some people like the arnica, some people don't. Count me in the dislike column."

I turn to Ryland and say, "I can rub it on myself."

"You sure?"

"Yes." I shoo him away. "Now go."

"Is that how you treat our host?" Bower asks. "Thank you, Ryland, for the invite. I'll be sure to bring the bruises . . . and if you're up for the dessert, you just let me know, I can shimmy and waddle her into any position."

"Bower . . . one more word and you're going home."

"Can you believe this girl?" she asks Ryland while motioning to me with her thumb. "And she wants me to move here."

"Not anymore."

Ryland chuckles. "Okay, see you down there. My offer still stands if you need help."

"Thank you," I say, and then he's out the door and down the stairs.

I turn to my friend and point a scary finger at her. "Unless you want me to tell everyone down there that you once farted in your trainer's face at the gym and made him dry heave, then you better be on your best behavior."

Her expression flattens. "I told you that in confidence."

"And it will remain in confidence unless you act like you just did . . . down there."

# Chapter Eighteen

## RYLAND

"Do you think Bower's single?" Abel asks as he stares over at Bower and Gabby sitting under the large oak tree, both eating hot dogs and chatting with Aubree and Hattie.

"Dude, she's way too much for you," I say. "From the brief interaction I've had with her, I'd say it's a no."

Hayes shuts the lid of the grill and whispers, "She reminds me of Maggie, Hattie's best friend. Not a filter in sight and has zero embarrassment. Ryland's right. Not for you, man." Hayes pats Abel's shoulder.

"Yeah, you're probably right."

"Are you interested in dating?" Hayes asks. "Always got the impression that you weren't really into it."

He shrugs. "Now that Ryland has a . . . has a Gabby—"

"I don't have a Gabby," I say, annoyed.

"I just feel like I need something in my life. Maybe not a woman. Could be a pet. Maybe I need a dog."

"You realize that a woman and a dog are not the same thing, right?" I ask.

"Well aware. Just feeling out my options is all."

222

The girls all laugh, and I hate to admit it because I'm not that guy who'd even consider a girlfriend, but Gabby seems to fit in well.

"Uncle Ry Ry," Mac says as she approaches us, ketchup smeared across her face. "Uncle Wyatt wants another burger, and I'd like more chips."

"Did you eat your fruits and veggies?" I ask her.

She glances toward her plate, which I can see from here. She and Wyatt are having a picnic out in the grass with the Chewys. No one else was invited. And from what I can see, cucumbers are still on her plate.

"Not all of them."

"Well, you need to eat them all. Then you can have more chips."

"Fine," she says in a deflated tone.

"And tell Uncle Wyatt he's not getting another burger until you eat all of your cucumbers."

An evil grin spreads across her face. "He's not going to like that."

"Those are the rules."

"Uncle Wyatt!" Mac shouts as she runs up to him to tell him the news.

I stare off at them, and the bond that they share makes me feel . . . slightly left out.

And I know I shouldn't feel that way. I should feel happy that she has Wyatt in her life, but hell, their bond is just different.

"What's that look for?" Hayes asks.

I clear my head and avoid looking at Mac. "What look?"

"The look of sadness, like you're doing something wrong."

"Nothing," I say.

"Nope, there's a sad look there," Abel points out. "What is it? And don't tell us nothing. We know you well enough to know that it's something."

He's right.

I tug on the back of my neck. "I don't know. Sometimes I think that Cassidy made the wrong decision."

"What are you talking about?" Abel asks.

"With MacKenzie. She clearly has a special bond with Wyatt. Maybe Cassidy should have given custody to Wyatt and Aubree."

"Wyatt wasn't even in the picture when Cassidy was sick," Abel says. "How would she have known he'd be coming back into our lives, let alone marry your sister?"

"Not to mention," Hayes says, "Mac found a picture of you in our house last night, and she carried it around all night, holding it close to her chest. She also slept with it, making both Hattie and I say good night to you. She might have a special bond with Wyatt, but her bond with you is stronger. Cassidy made the right decision."

"He's right," Abel says. "Cassidy always said that you were the reason she, Hattie, and Aubree turned out as normal as they did. You gave them a place of safety."

I shake my head. "That was Cassidy."

"Cassidy learned from you," Abel counters, and fuck, this conversation's too heavy for a backyard grill party—if that's what you want to call it.

I clear my throat. "Let's, uh, let's not get into that."

"No, maybe not," Hayes says. "Maybe we talk about Gabby and what you did last night."

"Or," I counter, getting sick of the inquisition from my family members, "we talk about when the hell you plan on proposing to my sister. She's a ticking time bomb, and you need to do it soon."

Hayes glances over his shoulder and then back at us. He whispers, "I started mapping things out, but you can't fucking say anything, not even to Wyatt. He's a loudmouth."

"You didn't ask me for permission," I say.

Hayes rolls his eyes. "Don't need it. But I want to make it something special, so I'll need help. I need to finalize the details first. I want it to be a total surprise."

"When are you planning on doing this?" I ask.

"A few weeks. The ring should be done by then."

"Shit, you got a ring?" Abel asks.

"Yes, custom."

"Fancy," Abel says.

"Well, keep us updated, and don't tell Aubree or Wyatt until the last moment. Or Mac. Christ, don't tell Mac," I say.

"I'm not a moron, man. But you two are the only ones I'm telling, so if word gets out, your necks are on the line."

"I won't say shit," I say.

Abel brings his drink to his mouth and says, "You can trust me not to say anything. I like my neck."

Just then, Aubree walks over with her plate. She leans in, and I already know that look on her face. "I like her."

Aubree was the impenetrable one in our family. She doesn't like emotions. She doesn't like touchy-feely things. She's very much the rock and always has been.

But ever since she's been with Wyatt, she's changed. She's softer. And I don't like it, especially when she comes at me with that look that says she's going to say something annoying to me.

"Good," I say. "She could use more friends."

Aubree juts out a hip in annoyance. "No, I like her for you."

"Can we not, please? You made me invite her. I did it to be nice, but please don't start with this shit, okay?"

"But . . . her friend Bower was telling us how you've been taking care of her . . . carrying her upstairs to her apartment?"

"You carried her?" Abel asks. "You didn't tell us that."

I tug on the brim of my hat. "She could barely walk, so what the hell was I supposed to do, just watch her suffer?"

"She was wearing his shirt this morning," Aubree whispers.

Hayes and Abel turn to me with a raised brow.

"She was wearing your shirt?" Hayes asks.

"Did you swap? Did you wear hers last night?"

Hayes and Aubree laugh. "God, I'd love to see that," Hayes says.

"Does that mean you spent the night together?" Aubree presses.

"No," I answer.

"How did she end up in your shirt?" Abel asks. "Did she fall into it?"

"Did she just so happen to trip, tumble, and stumble into one of your unpacked boxes and come out wearing your shirt?" Aubree asks.

I look up at all of them. Their gleeful faces are really fucking annoying. "You know, I don't need this." And with that, I walk right past them toward . . . hell, right toward Gabby.

The three of them chuckle behind me, but I ignore them. Instead, I focus on Gabby while my mind thinks about her in my shirt last night and how I loved seeing her in it.

How I loved seeing her in it this morning.

And seeing her in it this afternoon.

When Gabby spots me approaching, she smiles sweetly. "Thank you for inviting us. The hot dogs were amazing."

"Yes, thank you," Bower says. "And the pasta salad was the best I've ever had."

"That would be me," Hattie says with the raise of her hand. "I'm not very good at cooking. I'm better at baking actually, but I can make a mean pasta salad."

"Delicious. Actually, maybe you can describe the way you made it to me right over there," Bower says, not sounding coy at all.

It takes Hattie a second, but she nods and smiles. "Yes, I'd love to tell you all about it right over there."

Together, they take off, and I just shake my head and take a seat next to Gabby. "Do you need anything else? Want another hot dog? Another drink? Maybe a new friend? Because I'm looking for some new family members."

"I'm good," she says with a laugh, patting her stomach. "Seriously full over here."

"You sure? Not even room for dessert?" I tease.

"What kind of dessert are we talking about?"

I smirk. "Gummy worms. It's all I have."

"Hmm, shame."

I look back at our group of friends staring at us, but when they see me stare back, they turn their attention away. "They're irritating."

"At least you don't have to spend the night with them. Bower is going to go on and on about this all night. I'm not going to get any sleep. She's going to repeatedly tell me how stupid she thinks I am and how I'm making a bad choice by doing the friends-with-no-benefits thing."

"Yeah, join the club," I say while smoothing my hand over my jaw.

"Are we being stupid?" she asks softly.

"Maybe," I say. "But next week will prove that we're right. When we start working with the boys in strength and conditioning and basic drills. It will be different, and we'll be happy for the separation."

"That's what I keep saying to myself. But seriously, I don't want to talk about it anymore. I'm pretty sick of discussing it. It's like we're living in some reality show, and the main plot everyone is following is our sex life."

"For real," I say as I lean back in my chair. "I think our friends and family need to get a life."

"I could not agree more. Maybe we should start meddling with them."

"Ooo, that's a good idea. I already have some intel."

"You do?" she asks, looking excited. "Do tell."

"Well, when I was over there with Hayes and Abel, Abel asked me if Bower was single."

"Shut up," Gabby says, sitting up on a wince.

"Hey, careful." I hold out my hand to help her up. She takes it and settles in closer to me.

"He wants to know if Bower's single?"

"Yeah, he was curious. I told him she's not for him, but now I think we could have some fun since they seem to be torturing us."

"Hold on, why don't you think she's right for him?"

"Because I don't think he could handle her. From what I've seen, she's out of his league, and he'd have a hard time keeping up."

"I don't know," Gabby says, looking over at Abel and Bower,

who are talking with Hayes, Hattie, and Aubree. Or at least they're pretending to. "I think he might be able to tame her."

"You think Abel could tame her?" I shake my head. "Abel is . . . how do I put this? He's not the kind of guy who I think would put himself out there to be changed. I don't know if that makes any sense, but he's pretty quiet about his personal life, so I was surprised when he asked about Bower. Then he mentioned that maybe getting a dog was better."

That makes Gabby turn up her nose. "Bower is way better than a dog."

"But Bower is not the person he's hung up on."

"Who's he hung up on?" she asks. Honestly, I don't know why I brought it up, because now I have to answer her.

"Uh . . . well, he sort of had deep feelings for my sister Cassidy."

Gabby presses her hand to her chest. "Oh God, that's so awful."

"Yeah, I didn't know about it until later, and let's just say I don't think he will ever get over those feelings."

"Yeah, so maybe we don't play with them."

"Maybe," I say, irritated.

"Have any other ideas?"

"Yeah, but I can't tell you because I was sworn to secrecy, and my neck is on the line if the news is spread. I'm one of two who know."

"Hmm, are you saying you don't trust me?"

"I don't trust my luck," I say. "And now that we run in the same-ish circle, I can't chance it."

"Shame, I'm a great secret keeper." She points at her stunning eyes. "See these eyes? They hold all of the secrets. That's why they're different colors."

I smile softly. "I love that they're two colors."

"You do?" she asks, sounding surprised.

"Yeah, they're beautiful."

"What's beautiful?" Mac asks, coming up to us completely unannounced.

"Uh." I sit back and clear my throat. "Miss Gabby's eyes. Don't you think they're beautiful?"

Mac walks up to Gabby and looks at her carefully. "They're different colors."

"They are," Gabby says. "Can you believe that?"

Mac shakes her head. "I wish I had two different colored eyes."

"No, your eyes are so pretty, MacKenzie, I like them just the way they are," Gabby says.

"You can call me Mac. Everyone does," the four-year-old says so casually.

Gabby chuckles and tilts her head to the side. "Would you prefer that?"

"Yeah, because that means we're friends."

"Ah, you want to be friends with me?"

Mac nods her head. "Because I like your bruises." Mac leans forward, inspecting them. "They look very bad."

"They kind of are," Gabby says with a twist of her lips.

"How did you get them?"

"I slid down a pole the wrong way. I wasn't being very smart."

"Can I touch them?" Mac reaches out her hand, but I quickly grab it gently.

"Uh, let's leave Miss Gabby's bruises alone. They're very painful, and we don't want to make her hurt any more than she already is."

"They hurt?" Mac asks, her brows turning down in concern.

Gabby nods. "Yeah, I can barely walk. Trust me, if I could walk, I think I'd be trying out that tree swing over there."

Mac glances at the swing that Hayes and Wyatt just installed today while we were unpacking the house. "My uncles put that up for me."

"Wow, you are so lucky. It looks like so much fun."

Mac holds out her hand. "Come try it."

"Oh, I can't, my legs."

"Just try," Mac says, tugging on Gabby's arm.

"Mac—" I start but Gabby presses her hand to my thigh, nearly making me come out of my skin.

"It's okay." And then she stands. I'm quick to my feet, helping her, but she shoos me away. "I got this."

"Gabby," I say, but she doesn't listen as she takes Mac's hand. They walk slowly toward the tree together.

I stand there, watching them. Watching Mac look up at her, telling Gabby what a good job she's doing. Gabby smiling down at her . . . it . . . it makes my heart beat faster.

It makes my palms sweat.

It makes my ears go hot because . . . because they look cute together.

Like Gabby was supposed to hold her hand all along.

And when they reach the swing and Mac shows Gabby how to get on, Gabby pushes Mac lightly, causing Mac to smile back at her.

"Jesus fuck," I mutter as I stare at them, looking like a goddamn mother-daughter duo, and it hits me hard.

Harder than I expected.

So fucking hard that I have to sit back in my chair that's behind me as Gabby takes her turn on the swing now. I can see the pain in her face as she adjusts, but once she's settled, she kicks her legs out and lets Mac push her.

"Look, Uncle Ry Ry," Mac calls out. "She's doing it."

I swallow the lump in my throat as I nod. "She is." I offer a thumbs-up because I don't know what else to do at this moment as I stare at them.

Smiling.

Laughing.

Having a good time together.

"You okay?" Hayes asks as he takes a seat next to me. I didn't even hear him approach, but I'm not surprised he did.

"Yeah," I say, my voice coming out gravelly.

"You don't look like it."

"Dude, don't make me talk about it, okay?"

I see him nod out of the corner of my eye.

"Sure, we don't have to talk about it." He's silent for a moment but then says, "Coming from someone who never planned on getting married or becoming involved with anyone for that matter, I will say this—meeting your sister and allowing myself to fall in love was the best decision of my life. It was scary but fucking worth it."

He pats me on the back and takes off, leaving me in a state of unease.

Panic.

And confusion.

# Chapter Nineteen

## GABBY

"Are you sure you can do this?" Bower says as we walk—very slowly—down the street toward town.

"Yes, I need to get used to this, or else I'm going to look like a fool teaching tomorrow."

"You do seem to be walking a little better than yesterday. Watching you hobble over to the tree swing with that little girl was painful."

"That little girl's name is MacKenzie, or Mac for short."

"Whatever," Bower says. "It was awkward to witness."

"Glad I could make you uncomfortable."

We turn the corner right onto Almond Avenue, the main strip of Almond Bay, where all the cute shops and delicious restaurants are located. Almond Avenue was one of the main reasons I fell in love with Almond Bay and wished to live here when Bennett attended school. Because Almond Bay is so close to the ocean, it's expensive. We lived outside of town in a more affordable place, so being able to say I live in town now feels like a big accomplishment.

"Do you know who else looked uncomfortable?" Bower asks.

"Can we not? I know what you're going to say, but I'd rather not talk about Ryland right now. That's all this weekend has been, and I'm over it."

"Okay . . ." She pauses for a moment and then continues. "But seriously, you should have seen Ryland watch you and Mac together. He looked enchanted and freaked out at the same time."

"Like I said, we're not talking about it. Okay? We have to have other things we can discuss."

"You're right." She sighs. "How's Bennett?"

"Good," I say, excited for the change in subject. I can easily talk about Bennett. "The forty-man roster expansion is coming up for the majors, and he's hoping he gets called up for playoff season."

"Are the Bombers going to be in the playoffs?"

"They're in the lead for the wild card, so a good chance."

"Surprising, given the cheating scandal they've been going through."

"I'm surprised you even know about that," I say.

"It came across my Instagram. Oh my God, is that a bookstore?" Bower points at Pieces and Pages.

"Yes, want to go in?"

"Uh, yeah, I can get you a romance novel. Maybe it will help you change your stance on this whole friends-without-benefits thing." She takes my arm, and we head into the store.

Keeping my voice low, since the shop is on the narrow side—long but narrow—I say, "The cheating isn't a proven thing. They're just going through allegations now."

"And what if the cheating turns out to be real?"

"Then there will be some big team revamping."

"How does that affect Bennett?" Bower asks as she spots the romance section and makes a beeline for it.

"Honestly, I don't know. I can't think about it because he's worked so hard to get to where he is now that it would be really upsetting if something were to taint that."

"I can understand that," Bower says as she scans the books,

quietly saying *read it, read it, read it* under her breath as her finger scans across the spines.

"Wow, you've really been reading."

"Had to make friends with fictional characters since my best friend left me." She turns to me with a smile. "And up until this weekend, my fictional friends were far more interesting than you, but with this new Ryland—"

"Shhhhh." I look around. Whispering, I say, "You can't say anything too loud around here when it involves other people from the town."

"Why?" she asks.

"They talk, Bower. They talk a lot. Think of the game telephone but on a much larger scale. Please, just stop mentioning him."

"Mentioning who?" I hear a voice pop up, startling both of us.

We turn to find Hattie with a puzzle in hand, looking all adorable in a matching bike short and top set.

"Jesus," I say, bringing my hand to my chest. "You startled me."

"You can't be startled around here, Gabby. You always have to be on your toes. And you're right, you can't talk about anyone in this town in public unless you want someone listening in."

I wince. "Did you hear us?"

"A little." She smirks. "But it's not anything I don't already know." She glances down at my legs, then up at me. "How are you getting around?"

"Better," I say. "Taking it slow."

"Probably smart. You don't want Ryland carrying you around school tomorrow." She winks. "Or maybe you do."

"I think she does," Bower whispers, leaning in.

"Oh my God, both of you," I say, making them laugh. "Change of subject." I glance at Hattie's puzzle. "Is that a pickle puzzle?"

"Yes." Hattie beams. "Word around the street was some new puzzles came in, and one of them was a pickle puzzle. Those are two of my favorite things combined into one. So I had to come down before it was taken."

"I'm glad you secured it," I say just as Hayes walks up to us.

I remember when Hayes Farrow's *Black* album came out, and I was enamored with his voice. Seeing him in person and trying to act all normal, as if I haven't cried to his lyrics, is pretty hard. I had to warn Bower to be as normal as possible. Thankfully, she listened. But still, he's a god.

And the way he's so protective over Hattie? It lowers the wall I have up around the need for a relationship. Just look at him, at the way he always has to touch Hattie, be near her, and see the sparkle in his eyes when he looks down at her. It's hard not to be jealous. He used to be such a playboy and never into relationships at all. But he's so protective of Hattie, which makes me think I'm right. Sometimes it only takes the right person to come along to be *your* person. It makes the idea of a relationship less objectionable.

And he has written songs about her too . . . he has a new album releasing later this year, from what I've been told. He's a swoon-worthy man.

"You found it," he says, staring at the puzzle.

"I did. And look." She shows him the box and points. "It has my favorite pickles on it."

He smiles down at her as if she's the world. "Meant to be."

She lifts and presses a quick kiss to his lips before turning back to us. "Well, we're going to head out. We have a day of puzzling and watching movies. Did you pick out your puzzle?"

He shakes his head. "Stuck between two choices."

"Well, let me decide," Hattie says. "Catch you guys later."

"Bye," we both say, watching them walk away. Hayes has his arm draped over Hattie's shoulders.

"Who would have freaking guessed that the man whose music can make you come with one single strum of the guitar enjoys puzzling on the weekends with his girlfriend?"

"I would have told you, you were crazy," I say.

Bower shakes her head and goes back to the romance books.

"Now I'm going to be searching for a rock star romance. Seeing them together has me all hot and bothered."

I stare at my friend. "You really have grown hornier."

"Not even ashamed. Remind me to share with you my list of vibrators that are absolute must-haves."

———

"This freaking burger," Bower says, mouth full of meat as she stares at the cheeseburger in her hand. "The best thing I've ever had in my mouth, and that includes Danny Frankton's dick."

"Jesus, Bower," I say. "Danny Frankton?"

She swallows. "Gabby, I've never seen a more dignified rod in my life. A perfectly proportioned head, girth, and length all in one, bulging veins, taut skin that made you truly believe you were the one stretching that cock to the limits. Just magnificent."

"You have serious issues."

"Please, do you not sit back and look through your rolodex of cocks and think, wow, that one was just a sight to behold?"

"I haven't known the men long enough to remember."

She eyes me. "That is somewhat true. Nathan had a horrible dick, though, probably to go along with his horrible personality." She grows quiet for a second. "Has he contacted you since that night?"

I shake my head. "Nope." It's a lie because I don't want to worry her. Yes, he's texted me. No, I have not responded. Simple as that. No need to discuss.

"Good," she says. "I saw him a few weeks ago in the grocery store. I didn't say anything because I didn't want to freak you out, but now that you're in a better place, I feel like I can tell you."

I swallow and nod, knowing I could probably handle her information. I've grown. I'm stronger, hence being able to ignore his text messages.

Nathan was my boyfriend of many years. When we first met, something about him was mysterious—fun in a way, a touch on the crazed side but nothing harmful. He was adventurous, and well, being someone who took on the responsibility of raising their brother, I liked the idea of having some adventure in my life.

I grew close with his mom, and I really liked her, almost felt like she could be a wonderful mother figure until . . . she wasn't.

"How did he look?" I ask.

"Terrible," Bower says. "And I'm not just saying that to say it. I mean it. I took a picture because I thought you might want to see it. Get some closure and show you that you made the right decision. Do you want to see?"

I take a sip of my water, thinking it over. After a few seconds, I nod. "Yeah, I want to see."

She sets her burger down, wipes her hands, and picks up her phone. "Last I heard, he lost his job, and well, as you will see in the picture, he's lost pretty much every sparkle and attribute about him that you fell for in the first place."

She turns the screen of her phone toward me. My stomach twitches as a picture of Nathan with greasy, unkempt hair comes into view. His beard is splotchy, his cheeks are discolored, and he looks like he's gained about twenty pounds. He's a very different man to the man I once knew. That I once thought I loved.

In his right hand is a cigarette, and his gaze is fixed on something in the grocery store's parking lot. Gone is the luster I fell for, and a sad, unhappy man is in its place. It almost feels like looking at this picture is like taking off the rose-colored glasses I wore for so long.

"Wow," I say.

"Yeah, he looked terrible."

*"You look like shit. What have you been eating today?" Nathan says, a heavy scowl on his face.*

*"Wh-what?" His eyes sharpen on my face, and I hate the look he's giving me.*

*"I said, what have you been eating today? You look terrible."*

*"Nothing abnormal, Nathan," I whisper.*

*And I hate that I feel the need to whisper around my boyfriend.*

237

*When did that change? When did I fear him? Fear his reactions? His* anger . . .

"Are you okay?" Bower asks.

"I am, actually." I shake out of my reverie. "Thank you for sharing this. I think it helps remind me that I made the right decision."

"It is a great reminder, and I'm proud of you for making that decision," Bower says. "It was tough, but it was right. And I know Bennett feels the same way."

"How do you know that?"

"We talk." Bower shrugs.

"Uh . . . what? You talk to my brother? Like on the phone?"

"God no, who has time for phone calls? We text."

"We talk on the phone," I say.

She tips up my chin. "Because you're more needy." She then goes back to her burger as I try to wade through this revelation.

"How much do you guys text, and what do you text about?"

"Not that much, maybe once a week," she says. "And we talk about you and some random things."

"Random things?"

She shrugs. "Yeah, random things. It's not a big deal."

"You acted like you didn't know what was going on with him," I say.

"Well, we don't talk about baseball or anything like that. It's not a big deal."

"Have you texted him recently?" I ask, feeling really weird about all of this.

"Yeah, I told him that I was visiting you. He asked me to take pictures and send them over, so I did."

"What?" I nearly shout, and when I see that I'm being loud, I lean in and ask, "What kind of pictures did you take?"

"Well, not of the gross bruises, because yikes." She wipes her mouth. "Of the apartment, of the inside of your fridge to prove that you have food. I took one of your broken shower, but then told him that you're showering at the hunky neighbor's house, so I took a picture of the house as well."

"Oh my God, Bower." I hold out my hand. "Let me see your phone."

"Ooof, can't do that, sorry. There's personal stuff in there."

"What do you mean, personal stuff?" I ask, my eyebrows raised. "Are you . . . are you sending dirty texts to my brother?"

"Wow. That's where your mind goes? I mean personal stuff from him about you that I'm supposed to keep confidential, you know, just that he worries and all that crap. I don't want to break that confidence. Therefore, you're not allowed to see my phone. Sorry."

I lean back in my chair. "I can't believe you talk to Bennett."

"Oh yeah, we've been talking for a long time. I'll have to mention that I'm wishing him luck on the expansion thing. He'll probably think I lost my mind since we never chat about baseball, but it might be nice to throw in some encouragement. Oh, I also sent him Nathan's picture. He was very pleased to see he wasn't doing well. I think his exact words were 'I hope Nathan finds hell soon.' I chuckled because I've never seen that side of Bennett before."

She takes another bite of her burger as I try to filter through this information. "Does he tell you things he doesn't tell me? Like is he dating anyone? Does he need more money? Is he hungry?"

"Nothing like that." Bower shakes her head. "I asked him recently about his love life because, you know, the romance novels have me invested in everyone's love life now, and he told me that he's not interested in anyone. I then probed and asked if he was, would he make a move. He said he would."

"He doesn't talk to me about that."

"Do you ask him?" Bower picks up her iced tea. "Or do you just talk to him about baseball?"

"I talk about his life."

"Well, maybe you don't ask about his love life because you don't want him asking about yours."

"Maybe," I say, looking out toward the busy restaurant. "So he's not interested in anyone?"

"Nope, he did say he had a crush, but he wasn't sure it would ever be anything, so he wasn't going to invest time in it."

"A crush?" I ask, my heart pumping faster. "Why doesn't he think it would be anything?"

Bower shrugs. "He didn't get into it. But I told him if he set his mind to it, he could make it happen. Gave him the old Gabby advice, pulled it straight from the book."

"Yeah, that is advice I'd give him." I gingerly cross one leg over the other as I pop a fry into my mouth. "Maybe I should talk to him more about his personal life."

"No, he'd know I talked to you about it, and I don't want him to lose trust in me. Remain cool."

"You realize he's my brother, right? I can talk to him about anything that I want."

"Yup," Bower says with a smile. "But we're friends, and I refuse to break that confidence."

⸻

"Drive safe and let me know when you get back home," I say to Bower as she pulls out of the driveway with her head hanging out the window.

"I will. Love you!"

"Love you," I call out and watch her pull away, her taillights lighting up the barely lit street.

I'm going to miss her.

It was so much fun having her here. I really hope that I was able to convince her to move. If not, maybe I can wear her down over time. After she went on a shopping spree in Pieces and Pages, I feel like I have a pretty good chance because she would not stop talking about how amazing their romance section was.

What I thought was really funny this weekend is that when she found out Wyatt was a bestselling author, she nearly flew out of her shorts to speak to him, but when she found out the genre of books he wrote, she wanted nothing to do with him. I think her exact words were "you can go back to playing horsey with your niece."

She had a minor change of heart when Wyatt brought over a signed copy of *The Virgin Romance Novelist* by Rosie Bloom, which he secured at his book signing this summer. Bower took one of his books out of pity after that—that's what she told me. I think Wyatt could see right through her, but he went with it. My job is to encourage her to read it because if she likes it, then all the more reason for her to move here. There's me, Hayes Farrow, and a bestselling author, plus the adorable town of Almond Bay. What more could she need?

I head toward Ryland's house in need of a shower for tomorrow. I take it slow because my legs still hurt, but I have confidence that with the right outfit, I'll be able to go to school tomorrow and not look like a fool in front of the students.

I check the door first to see if it's locked, and when it's not, I help myself inside, only to find Ryland at the kitchen table with a bowl of ice cream in front of him.

When his eyes meet mine, he smiles, and that smile . . . twists my stomach up in knots. He's so handsome, and now that he's wearing his hat backward, looking all relaxed in his plain T-shirt and shorts . . . no socks, God, I'm tempted to just go over there and sit on his lap.

"How are the legs?"

"Okay," I say as I shut the door. "How's the ice cream?"

He looks down at his bowl, then back up at me. "Cold."

"Great. Well, I'm going to take a shower."

"Let me see them."

"Huh?" I ask.

"Your bruises, let me see them."

"I'm wearing spandex shorts."

"I can see that. Take them off."

"Ryland, I'm not going to just take my shorts off for you, that's . . . that's weird."

"What's weird is that you think that's weird. I've seen everything. I've seen your pussy glisten."

"Oh my God, Ryland."

He chuckles. "I just want to know how your bruises are doing."

"Can't you take my word for it?"

He shakes his head. "No, I can't."

"Ryland—"

"I was thinking about practice and what we're going to do this week, and I want to see if you can handle it. I'm not going to take your word for it because I know you'd lie, so let me see."

Irritated, I walk up right in front of him, slip my hands into my shorts, and push them down to the floor. To my surprise, he moves his bowl of ice cream to the side and sets me on the table.

With hands on both knees, he spreads my legs and looks up at me.

"Um . . . sir?"

"Yeah?" he asks.

"Is this really how you're going to examine me?"

"Are you complaining?"

"I'm wondering what your intention is."

He smooths his hands up my thighs, causing my nerve endings to jump and knot. "To make sure you're able to help me this week." He then takes in the bruises, looking over them care-fully. "Have you been applying the gel?"

"I have," I say. Abel even had a quick look on Saturday and said the arnica was doing exactly what it was meant to do.

He gently passes his hand over one. "Does that hurt?"

"Not really," I say. "If you pressed down, then I'd say yes."

"And how was walking today?"

"Better than yesterday . . . Doctor."

He smirks up at me, then leans back and lifts his hat, only to replace it on his head. "Good."

I sit there, staring down at him, unsure of what to do. "Are we done here?"

He picks up his ice cream bowl and scoops up some ice cream. "If you want to be."

"What does that mean?" I ask.

"Anything you want it to."

I lean back, pressing my hands to the table. "You're acting weird."

"How so?"

"I don't know. You're being all evasive, and you're eating that ice cream suggestively?"

"How am I eating suggestively? I'm just putting it in my mouth." He scoops up some ice cream and then brings the spoon right in front of his mouth. "If I were being suggestive, I'd do this." He rapidly flicks his tongue over the ice cream, causing my entire body to heat.

He then opens his mouth and chews on the ice cream before swallowing.

"That would be suggestive."

I wet my lips as I stare down at him, my legs opening some more. He notices, and the grin that spreads across his face is dangerous.

Very dangerous.

"You want my tongue, don't you?"

*I want so much more than your tongue.*

*I want your mouth, your lips all over my body.*

I want you driving your cock in and out of me, making my back arch and my body yearn.

I want his cum all over me, marking me, claiming me.

"I can't even remember what your tongue feels like in order to want it."

"Maybe you need a reminder," he says as he smooths his hand up my thigh, grips my underwear, and tugs on it.

God, I'm so easy.

Because I can't even stop myself from lifting and letting him take it off. To my surprise, he lifts my shirt as well, dragging it over my head, leaving me in just a bra, spread over his kitchen table.

"I thought we weren't doing this anymore."

"I already fucked you this weekend," he says. "Might as well round it out." He presses my knees farther apart and brings ice cream between my legs. "I've been craving this cunt ever since it was offered up for dessert."

He drips some of the melted ice cream across my slit, then sets the bowl down. The cold liquid shocks me, only for his warm tongue to lap it up and create such a different sensation that I groan in pleasure.

He pauses and looks up at me from between my legs. "Fucking quiet, Gabby. Mac is sleeping upstairs."

"S-sorry," I say.

He scoops up some more ice cream, holds it on his tongue, swallows, and then goes back to flicking his tongue across my clit. The coldness of his tongue lights me up and causes the burning need I have for him to grow even stronger.

My head falls back as I allow this man to pleasure me. I commit this feeling to memory, the way he so easily possesses me because I know there will never be anyone else like him. No one will be able to make my stomach coil like him. No one will ever be able to make my heart stutter and pound the way he does. And no one will ever be able to give me the kind of pleasure that one single flick of his tongue gives me.

"You taste fucking phenomenal," he says as he brings two fingers to my entrance and slowly pushes them in. "This pussy is so greedy, I can feel you sucking me in. You wanted this."

"All weekend," I say, desperation in my voice.

"Should have asked for it."

"Rules, Ryland."

He pauses for a moment and looks up at me from between my legs. "Well, fuck rules right now." And then he lowers his mouth back down, and with his lips, he sucks on my clit, causing my hips to buck.

"Fuck," I whisper. "Yes, Ryland, right there. Oh my God, yes."

He curls his fingers up inside me, pumping in and out of me so hard that I start to build faster and stronger than ever.

"Christ," I say, my head falling back again. "I'm going to come hard."

"Good," he says as he goes back to flicking his tongue in fast, rapid strokes, working harder than any vibrator I could ever use.

He builds me up, driving so much heat into the pool of my stomach that my legs start to tremble.

Everything around us fades away, and the pleasure gathers at the base of my spine, ready to tip, ready to burst.

"Fuck, oh God, Ryland . . . fuck, right . . . there," I whisper just as his fingers curve up and hit me in the right spot, tipping me over the edge.

A flood of warmth spreads through me as warm liquid drips down my center.

"God," I say as I open my eyes, slowly floating down from the high he just sent me on. That's when I feel him lapping at my legs. When he's done and he looks me in the eyes, he looks positively feral. "What?"

"You fucking squirted, and it was the sexiest fucking thing I've ever seen," he says as he stands and pulls his dick out of his shorts. With his hand covered in my arousal, he uses it as lube as he tugs on his incredibly hard cock. "Play with your tits."

Still trying to comprehend what he said, I sit up and undo my bra, letting it fall down my stomach before tossing it to the side.

"Best fucking dessert," he says right before licking his lips and pressing one hand to my knee as he leans forward. "Play with your tits, Gabby. Don't make me ask again."

My hands smooth over my hard nipples, and I palm my breasts, pressing them together. Watching Ryland the entire time, I love how the veins in his neck tighten, how his eyes stay fixated on me, and how even though his shirt is still on, I can see his chest muscles flex as he squeezes his length.

"Pinch your nipples, Gabby." I do as I'm told and roll my nipples between my fingers, pinching them and tugging on them just enough to make him go crazy.

"Want inside me?" I ask, spreading my legs for him.

He shakes his head. "I'll hurt your legs. But I'm coming on that cunt." He brings two fingers between my legs, swipes at my arousal, and sucks them into his mouth. His eyes roll in the back of his head as he pumps his length even harder. "Lean back."

I lean my hands behind me, tilt my chest up for him, and then observe.

I watch as his body stiffens.

As his balls grow tight beneath his frantic hand.

The ripples of sinew firing off in his forearm.

And then the drop of his jaw as he stills and then comes all over me with a low moan falling past his lips.

He decorates me, one pearl-sized drop at a time, until he's completely done. He leans both hands on the table, catching his breath.

After a few seconds, he looks up at me with a satisfied smile. "Okay, that was the last time."

I chuckle and shake my head. "So you say."

"Has to be." He straightens up and tucks his penis back into his shorts. He lends me a hand and helps me to my feet, only to pick me up in his arms.

"Shame you didn't fuck me. That would have been a great way to end it."

He walks me to the bathroom and says, "Need help in the shower?"

"Only if you plan on bending me over."

"Is there any other way to take a shower?"

# Chapter Twenty

RYLAND

It's a new week.

I'm not going to think about Gabby in a sexual way. She's my tenant, my assistant coach, my co-worker.

I'm not going to imagine how she looked last night in the shower, bent over, begging for my cock.

I'm not going to remember the muffled sounds she made as I drove into her over and over again, slamming my rock-hard cock inside that addicting pussy.

And I'm sure as fuck going to eliminate the feeling of her pussy squeezing me as she comes from my memory.

None of that matters. Because like I said last night when she was leaving my house, that was it. Not again.

No more.

So why, as I sit at my desk in my classroom, staring at the clock, ready for the bell to ring for lunch, am I hoping that I see her in the teachers' lounge?

Because I'm a fucking pathetic mess.

Because something weird happened to me this weekend.

Something that still scares me and should scare me so much that I want nothing to do with her.

What scared me? It was what I saw.

I saw . . . I saw a brief glimpse of a future. A future I've never thought about before. One I didn't think I wanted or cared for.

For a few seconds, as I watched Mac push Gabby on the tree swing, there was a small part of me that . . . liked it. How they were together.

I liked the way that Mac smiled when pushing her.

I loved hearing her laugh. *So carefree.*

I loved the hug she gave Gabby after.

I loved how Gabby responded to Mac.

I loved how she went along with everything Mac wanted even though I could tell, at times, she was in pain. *So kind.*

I loved how Gabby handled Mac so delicately, how she listened with full eye contact. She put Mac first, and that surprised the hell out of me.

Hell, it made me . . . made me like her.

Like her more than I should.

And I spent all day yesterday counting down the damn hours until I knew she was going to take a shower. I waited and waited until the moment she walked through the door. I knew I needed her. One last taste, I told myself.

And I got that last taste. I got my dessert I so desperately wanted.

It was fucking perfect.

Seeing how much I could pleasure her with just my fingers and mouth . . . addictive. I needed more. And even after the shower, when I sent her on her way, I lay in my newly made bed, staring up at the ceiling and wondering what would happen if I texted her and asked her to come over.

See, I'm a goddamn fool.

The bell rings, and the class packs up their workbooks while I knock myself out of my reverie. I shout something about what pages of homework they need to complete for tomorrow and then watch them walk out of the classroom.

Once they're all gone, I slip my phone into my pocket, lock my door, and nearly sprint to the teachers' lounge. On the way, I get a few head nods from some of my players, a few hellos from some students, and one fist bump from a kid I swear I've never seen before in my life.

When I reach the teachers' lounge, it's empty, so I grab my lunch from the fridge and find a table that could accommodate Gabby and a few stragglers if they decide to join. Am I one to eat in the teachers' lounge often? Not really.

I've pretty much stuck to my classroom, but apparently, my mind has changed as to what I do during my lunch break.

A few teachers trickle in. Some that I don't care to speak to, not because I'm an ass, but because they're more into student drama, and that's just not my vibe. And they know it because they sit at the farthest table from me.

I unpack my lunch and take my burger patties to the microwave, where I heat them for a few minutes. When I packed my lunch, I just dipped into the leftovers from the weekend, which makes it super simple. Burgers with no buns, pasta salad, and some cut fruit. Easy.

When my burgers are done, I bring them back to my table, worried that Gabby might not show up, but that's when the door opens, and she walks through laughing.

Something light in my chest floats up when I see her . . . until I see who's behind her, making her laugh.

Fucking Christian.

I swear to fuck, if this man thinks he has any chance at even remotely entertaining Gabby, he's fucking wrong.

When Gabby spots me, she smiles and brings her lunch over to the table, making me feel better, only for that to be squashed when Christian joins us too.

This fucking guy.

"Hey, how was your morning?" Gabby asks, taking a seat and wincing at the same time. She's clearly still in pain.

"Good. How are your legs?" I ask.

"What's wrong with your legs?" Christian cuts in, looking concerned.

*You can put the concerned look away, you fuck. While you were probably ironing your shirt last night, I was tongue deep in Gabby's pussy.*

"Oh, I have some bruises on my thighs."

Christian's brow creases. "Oh, how did you get those?"

"Painting the foul pole," she answers easily. "My ladder slipped, and I had to slide down the pole. Apparently, I forgot how to slide down a pole properly and, well, bruised up my legs pretty good, but they're doing better. I think I'm holding it together in front of the students."

"Ouch, that sounds unpleasant."

"Kind of was. I spent all weekend rubbing cream on the bruises."

*That's not all you did this weekend.*

*I recall some other things . . .*

"Well, I'm glad you're feeling a little better," Christian says like the dweeb that he is.

Okay, to be fair, he's not really a dweeb, but I'm feeling pretty poorly about him at the moment, given how attached he seems to Gabby. Therefore, I'm lashing out.

"Hopefully, you don't have to slide down any poles for a while," he continues.

Fucking idiot. Can't even do banter right. The only pole she'll be sliding down again is mine.

"Yes, let's hope that's the case unless you need me to paint more foul poles, Ryland?"

"Nah, we're good."

"So . . . how is it working with the famous Coach Rowley?" Christian asks. Excuse me, but did I hear a sense of . . . jealousy in his tone? Or is that just me reaching for another reason to hate this guy? Not that I need another reason. He's talking to Gabby, so that's reason enough.

"Well, we haven't done much, but I think we're kicking it up this week, right?"

I nod. "Which reminds me, I actually want to talk to you

about a few things." I look at Christian. "If you'll excuse us, we could use some privacy."

Christian sits back and points at himself. "You want me to leave?"

"That would be great, thanks."

"Oh." He looks at Gabby, who doesn't know what to say, so instead of making a fuss, he stands from the table and says, "Okay, well, I'll see you around, Gabby. I'll stop by later for that recipe."

"Or I can email it."

"Either way." He touches her shoulder, and I nearly reach across the table and snap his wrist in half.

When he's gone, Gabby leans forward and whispers, "That was rude."

"What was rude?" I dig into my burgers, cutting them up with the knife and fork I brought with me.

"Kicking him out like that."

"I don't know. I feel pretty good about it."

"Ryland," she chastises.

"What?"

"I'm being serious."

"So am I," I say as I pop a piece of burger in my mouth, but when I'm met with her unpleased stare, I set my fork and knife down. "He needs to know you're not someone he can talk to."

"Says who? You? Because I hope we're not getting into this again."

"We're not . . . we're here to talk baseball."

"We could have talked baseball in front of Christian."

"And bore him?" I wave her off. "No, that's not being fair to him. This is better, you and me, no distractions."

"Uh-huh, and would you prefer if I sit next to you so we can really talk closely together?"

*I prefer if you sit on my lap and let Christian know he has no goddamn chance.*

"No, across from me is fine," I answer.

She shakes her head and pulls out a salad from her lunch bag.

"What?"

"You're just unbelievable, you know that?"

"Yes, because that's what you said last night."

Her eyes widen, then quickly narrow. "Jesus, Ryland, where is your professionalism?"

Yeah, where is it?

Apparently, it flew out the window the minute I saw her with another man.

"It's still intact," I say even though I fear it's not. "Enough of this bullshit. Let's talk about today."

"Fine," she says definitively. "What about today?"

"Did you get my email about our plan?"

"Yes," she answers.

"Do you have any questions?"

"No."

"Good," I respond and then wait a second. "Glad we got that sorted. What else do you want to talk about?"

"That's all? That's why you kicked Christian away from us?"

"I didn't know if you had more to discuss," I say. "Or if you had questions."

She shakes her head and, to my surprise, stands from her chair. "Unbelievable, Ryland."

She takes her lunch to the table where Christian is sitting and settles beside him.

And the smile that crosses his face makes me want to knock his goddamn teeth right out.

Well, this fucking backfired.

---

**Ryland:** *What do you guys think of Gabby?*

**Hattie:** *OH MY GOD! It's happening, Aubree. I told you. I told you it was going to happen.*

*Aubree:* You know, you did, but I didn't really believe you. But you're right, it's happening.

*Ryland:* What's happening?

*Hattie:* You're falling for her. I could see it in your eyes this past weekend.

*Aubree:* I don't usually go along with her foolishness, but I agree, I saw it this weekend as well.

*Ryland:* I'm not falling for her.

*Hattie:* Then why ask what we thought of her?

*Ryland:* Just general interest. She's . . . different, right?

*Aubree:* I don't understand. Different from what?

*Ryland:* I don't know . . . other people.

*Hattie:* Yes, she's different from other people because she's her own person.

*Aubree:* ^^^ Facts.

*Ryland:* But I mean, you know, different.

*Hattie:* You might have to elaborate because you're not making much sense at the moment.

*Aubree:* Agreed, I'm not following.

*Ryland:* Never mind. Forget I even asked.

*Hattie:* Oh no, we're not forgetting this. This is a moment. A huge moment! The biggest moment, because you're actually showing interest in a girl for the first time since Samantha.

*Aubree:* And that was ages ago. You shut down after she cheated on you, and we didn't think you'd ever open up to another person. But here we are.

*Ryland:* I'm not opening up, okay? I'm just . . . fuck, I feel weird.

*Hattie:* Does your heart pound when you see her?

*Aubree:* Do your palms get sweaty when she's nearby?

*Hattie:* Are you thinking about her all the time?

*Aubree:* Do you have this undeniable, happy feeling that bursts through you when she is around you?

*Ryland:* I'm not answering any of those questions.

*Hattie:* Oh my God, it's because they're true, aren't they? Gah, Aubree! He likes her.

*Aubree:* Looking over the symptoms we just described, I'd conclude that he likes her as well.

*Ryland:* I don't like her. I just . . . she makes me . . . I don't like it when . . . fuck, I don't even know what I'm saying.

*Hattie:* Because you like her. Just admit it, Ryland. You like someone. It's okay. You're not about to explode.

*Aubree:* Maybe if you admit you like her, you won't stumble over your words as much.

*Ryland:* She's just different, okay?

*Hattie:* She is, she's very different, and that's what's so amazing about her. She's independent and strong and doesn't take any shit, but she also knows how to accept help when she needs it and is kind and loving.

*Aubree:* And confident. Can handle her own and, most importantly, knows how to handle you.

*Hattie:* Not to mention she's so great with Mac.

*Aubree:* A definite plus and since we're mentioning things, there's an obvious attraction between you two which only heightens the feelings you're trying to suppress.

*Hattie:* What we're trying to say is that we approve.

*Aubree:* We definitely approve.

*Ryland:* I don't know why you approve, there is nothing to approve of. I wasn't looking for approval. Honestly, just forget this entire conversation.

*Hattie:* No chance in hell will we forget this. I'm actually screenshotting everything as we speak.

*Aubree:* Send me those screenshots and then upload them to the cloud.

*Hattie:* Should I just send the screenshots in this text thread to remind our brother that we approve?

*Aubree:* Probably is best.

*Ryland left the group thread.*

⸻

"Get your butt down," Gabby yells at Johnson, one of the juniors on the team. "If I have to say it again, you're doing poles."

From the dugout, I lean against the fence and stare at the practice Gabby's running.

I'm in fucking awe.

I don't think I've ever seen anything like it.

The outfielders run routes by themselves, weaving through cones, tossing balls to each other, constantly moving like a well-oiled machine.

The infielders are set up in tight formation, standing at short-stop and second with Gabby in the middle, hitting short quick hops to the boys and then tossing the ball to the other line. They're all moving and tossing and putting balls in buckets, and I swear if I didn't watch her explain, I'd have stood here trying to figure it all out.

"Faster feet, outfield," she calls out.

How is she even watching them while hitting balls and tossing balls at the same time?

Fuck.

She's putting me to shame.

And the boys, fuck, do they respect her.

They respected her the minute she came out on the field and started warming up with them.

Throwing with them.

Even getting in the dirt, showing them glove position, where to catch the ball, and the minimal stepping she wants to see from them when they get the ball and go to throw to first.

And with a few minutes left of practice, I know they've exhausted all energy and it's only fall ball. They're going to wonder what the hell they got themselves into, especially after yesterday's conditioning.

"That's it, a few more," she says.

The entire time I've watched her, I've marveled at the way she commands their attention. I've been envious of her innovative ideas. And I've had a hard as hell time keeping my damn eyes off her ass in those spandex pants.

And once I saw her take charge, I just let her have it because I wanted to observe. I wanted to see how she'd run things, and I hate to admit it because I hate David so much, but fuck, she was a good hire.

No, not a good hire, a great hire.

An asset.

Someone who'll better the team.

With her skills and knowledge on defense and my ability to fine-tune a swing, I think we will be unstoppable.

"Okay, bring it in," she calls out, and I watch all the boys pick up the balls and toss them in the buckets before taking a knee in front of her.

Christ, she even has them hustling.

I walk up to them and clap my hands, letting them know they all did a great job today. Gabby turns to me to speak, but I gesture for her to go.

So she takes the stage. "Great first day on defense, boys. I know the drills were a little complicated to learn at first, but I'm impressed with your ability to adapt and listen. A few of you need to work on getting your butts down farther. Johnson, I'm talking to you." He hangs his head. "But that's something we'll work on moving forward, and this fall, we can build your legs so they're stronger, so you can get down farther, right, Coach Rowley?"

I fold my arms across my chest and nod. "Yes, I know this isn't what you expected when you signed up for sixth-period baseball, but this is what we're offering. We want to finesse your skills and build you up so when spring comes, we can be ahead of everyone else. Which means putting in the work every day like you did today. Bring it in." We all put our hands in a circle, and I say, "Almond Bay on three. One. Two. Three."

"Almond Bay," everyone chants. The boys take off, and the seniors dictate who has to pick up the equipment. I remain on the field with Gabby standing next to me.

"How did I do?" she asks, sounding unsure.

I keep my eyes on the boys and their trailing backs.

"Fucking phenomenal," I say. From the corner of my eye, I can see her bright smile.

"Seriously?"

I turn this time to look at her and stick my hands in my

pockets so I don't do something like . . . touch her, hug her, kiss her. "Yeah, Gabby, that was unlike anything I've ever seen. Were you doing that with Bennett?"

"Yeah. Constantly."

"No wonder his goddamn feet are so quick."

She laughs. "Yeah, it was important for me to show him how vital it is at third base to have quick feet, quick reactions. I think that serves all positions."

"Well, you really impressed. And the boys, you could see it in their eyes how much they respected you. I wasn't sure how they were going to accept a female coach, but you didn't even take a second to let them establish an opinion. You were in their face, telling them what to do right off the bat and then sandwiching that in with positive feedback. Hell, I think I could learn a thing or two from you."

"Now you're just reaching."

I shake my head. "I'm not. I mean it."

She fully turns to me, her eyes studying me up and down. "Are you just saying nice things because I'm mad at you?"

"Are you still mad at me?"

"Annoyed is more like it."

I nod, understanding. "Trust me, Gabby. I'm annoyed with myself as well."

"Great, that makes two of us." She starts heading toward the dugout, but I grab her arm to stop her.

When she looks over her shoulder at me, I say, "I wouldn't say shit just to make you happy with me again. I meant every word I said."

"Okay," she says, freeing herself of my grip. "Thank you."

Then with that, she takes off toward the dugout without another word.

# Chapter Twenty-One

GABBY

*Knock. Knock.*

I look up from my desk, where I'm eating lunch today, and see Christian standing in the doorway.

"Is it okay for me to come in?"

"Of course," I say.

He holds up his lunch. "And join you?"

I smile. "You don't even have to ask. Pull up a chair."

With that cute smile, he grabs my spare chair and moves it over to my desk, where he takes a seat and starts unpacking his lunch.

I know what you must be thinking—what are you doing? Ryland would hate this. *Are you doing this on purpose?*

No, I'm doing this because there needs to be separation between me and Ryland. I realized that when we had sex in the shower, and then he got pissed about Christian the next day.

We're not attached. Ryland has no claim over me. He has said he doesn't want a relationship. He doesn't want the distraction, yet we keep falling into a dangerous pattern where I'm going to get hurt in the long run, because I can see myself falling for him.

Falling for him and the feeling being unreciprocated.

And that can't happen. Therefore, there needs to be separation. My shower's currently being fixed and should be ready to use in a few days once the tile and everything are set. I don't eat in the teachers' lounge anymore because I don't want any more instances of jealousy. And when it comes to baseball, well, we talk baseball, and I think he gets it.

Because he hasn't pushed me for more.

He hasn't talked to me when I take showers.

And we've been able to completely separate ourselves, which I truly think is for the best.

This is what it should have been all along.

And now that I've had some breathing room, I can focus on something else . . . possibly someone else.

"I've missed you in the teachers' lounge," Christian says. "I thought that maybe you were avoiding me."

I'm avoiding someone, but not you.

"Gets kind of stuffy in there, and I like the big windows in my classroom," I say. "Not avoiding you at all. I'm actually glad you came into my room. I thought about inviting you to have lunch with me in here, but I didn't want to be too forward."

He smirks. "I would have accepted the invitation instantly."

"Oh yeah?"

"Yeah," he says, his cheeks blushing.

"Good to know, guess I won't make that mistake again."

"I'd prefer if you didn't." He opens up his protein yogurt and starts plopping berries in it.

"Looks like you copied my lunch idea."

"I did actually. When I saw you bring it last week, I told myself what a great idea it was and that I wanted to do the same thing. Only thing is"—he reaches into his lunch bag and pulls out another yogurt—"I need two."

I chuckle. "A growing boy?"

"Trying to bulk up a bit. You know, make myself irresistible."

Now my cheeks blush because he's definitely flirting. "This is where you're supposed to say you're already irresistible, Christian."

"And inflate your ego more than it needs to be?" I shake my head. "I think I'm good."

"Damn." He stirs his yogurt. "You're pretty tough."

"I'm not just going to hand out freebies, Christian. You have to earn it."

"Any suggestions on how I earn compliments?"

"Don't try," I say with a wink, causing him to chuckle.

"Noted." He takes a mouthful of his yogurt, then asks, "How has your day been?"

"Okay," I say. "I felt like my brain wasn't working very well the first two classes. I kept stumbling over my words and couldn't explain the math properly. I had to pause a few times and take a deep breath because I was getting frustrated with myself."

"I've had those days. They suck. You kind of just have to move past them and tell yourself you'll be better next class."

"That's what I'm trying to do." I sip my water. "I'm still getting my footing with this whole teaching thing. I worked hard to get here, and now that I'm here, I feel like I might be trying too hard. I want the kids to like me, which I know they do, but I also don't want to be their friend because that's not what I am. But then I can see myself in a few students, and all I want to do is scoop them up and take them under my wing."

Christian's expression morphs into one of understanding. "I get it. I had the same issue when I first started teaching. Do you know what I ended up doing?"

"What?" I ask, appreciating his advice on this.

"I learned to let them come to me. As much as you want to help, reach out, and be there for the kids, you need to realize that you can't force them. They're just going to resent you, so have the door open for them to walk through, but don't pull them through."

"That's really good advice, Christian."

He smiles, perking up. "And there's my compliment."

"See. Doesn't it feel better that you earned it?"

"It really does," he says with a smirk.

⸻

"Okay, don't think I'm weird or anything," Christian says as he sits at my desk, pulling up a chair *without* asking. "But I made cupcakes last night, and I brought you one."

"You made cupcakes last night? You don't seem like the kind of guy who just makes cupcakes randomly."

"I'm not, but my nephew came over, and his mom dropped off cupcake mix and icing and told us to have fun."

"That was kind of her," I say, a sarcastic lilt in my voice.

"Tell me about it. It was a mess, and the biggest challenge was to tell my five-year-old nephew that the batter goes in the tins, not in his mouth."

"Ooof, did he eat a lot?"

"More than I care to admit, but we made them without eggs. We used applesauce instead, so if anything, he overloaded on sugar, and I just sent him back to his house."

"So really, she was the one hurting in the end."

"I don't know," he says as he pulls out the cupcakes and pats his stomach. "His mom wouldn't take any home besides the ones he touched. Therefore, I have a whole bunch, and I'm going to go into a sugar coma if you don't help me eat them."

I eye the cupcakes through the Tupperware. "Is that Funfetti?"

"Is there really any other box cake mix that's worth our time?"

"There isn't." I smile. "And just to be cautious, your nephew didn't handle these cupcakes?"

He shakes his head. "He had his own muffin tin for that specific reason. No one wants tainted, clammy-hand cupcakes."

"Clammy hands." I shiver.

"This kid, I swear to God, the clammiest hands you'll ever touch. I asked my sister if it's some sort of glandular issue because holding his hand is slippery and wet like holding the fin of a dolphin."

"Oh God." I grimace.

"And guess who's an extreme hand holder?" Christian chuckles. "When he leaves, I spend a solid thirty minutes soaking my hands in scalding water with soap. And I love him, I love him a lot, but God, he needs to air out his hands from time to time."

I laugh. "Yeah, I don't do well with that stuff."

"Neither do I." He pops open the cupcake lid, and I take one. "Do you have any nieces or nephews?"

"No, I'm the oldest, and my brother, Bennett, is currently pursuing his dreams, so he doesn't have time to think about a family."

"Bennett?" he says with a question in his voice. "Wait, is your brother Bennett Brinkman?"

"He is. Was he a student of yours?"

Christian nods. "He was. Pretty quiet but really smart. How's he doing? I'm assuming still playing baseball."

"He's doing great. He's up in Triple A right now for the Bombers. Killing it of course. We're really hoping he'll be called up for the forty-man roster expansion."

"Hell, that would be amazing."

"It would be. But if it doesn't happen this year, that's okay. He'll come back here for a few days to hang, and then he's going to head back to his place. He's renting with a couple of the guys and working on getting better during the off-season."

"I can't imagine how grueling that process is."

"It's pretty tough, but he's always been adamant about making it. There's no doubt in my mind that he'll be called up to the big show. The only question is, when?"

"Amazing," he says. "And your parents, they must be proud."

I wince because it's a simple question that shouldn't cause such deep-rooted anger, but it does.

"They're not in the picture," I say simply, not wanting to make things awkward, but of course it does, because how could it not?

"Shit, I'm sorry." Christian places his hand on mine, his warm palm eclipsing my knuckles. "I should have known better than to assume something like that. I'm sorry, Gabby."

I offer him a smile. It's a small smile, but it's a smile, nonetheless. "It's really okay. No big deal. Didn't know my dad, and Mom couldn't handle us." I shrug. "Built resilience in us, and that's why Bennett will make it to the big show. He's determined to make something of himself. Not sure he'd have such determination if his life was . . . easier."

"Yeah, I can understand that. Still, I'm sorry."

"No need to apologize, Christian. It's really okay."

---

"Sorry I'm late," Christian says as he steps into my classroom with a short, stumpy vase of what looks to be wildflowers. He sets it on my desk, then brings his chair over.

"What are these?" I ask him.

"Those are for you."

"Why?" I ask, feeling my cheeks blush. I'm not sure I've ever received flowers before. *Possibly since Nathan accused me of cheating when I bought myself some flowers for my birthday.*

"For yesterday. I still feel shitty about bringing up your parents."

"Oh my God, Christian. I told you it wasn't a big deal, but this was nice."

And then because I feel guilty that he feels guilty, I walk over to him and hug him.

I feel the relief in him as he wraps his arms around me. *Christian is nowhere as broad as Ryland*, something I shouldn't think about when another man is holding me. *But his hugs were all-encompassing.* "I'm sorry," he says softly.

"It's really okay." When I pull away, I hold his arms and look him in the eyes. "I didn't think twice about it, but these flowers are so sweet."

"I'm glad you like them, which makes me think I can ask

this." With a bout of courage, he swallows and says, "My sister has an art exhibit tonight, and she asked me to go. I didn't know if you might want to go with me."

Oh God, he's asking me out.

What do I do?

What do I say?

I mean, I like him. He's nice and kind and thoughtful and—

"Am I interrupting something?" a deep, dark voice says from the doorway.

As if I'm touching fire, I release Christian's arm. Ryland's standing in the doorway looking none too pleased.

"Umm, not interrupting," I say.

Ryland sticks his hands in his jean pockets, probably attempting to look casual, but the bulge in his pecs and the flex in his forearms are anything but casual.

"Gabby, I was hoping to talk to you about practice tonight."

"Sure," I answer, feeling so incredibly awkward.

But why?

It's not like I'm doing anything wrong.

In fact, I'm doing absolutely nothing wrong. Like I've said before, Ryland has no claim over me. None.

And that dent in his brow and the light snarl in his lip should not be directed toward me or this situation. We're friends without benefits—*which means just friends*—and that gives me the freedom to do whatever I want. Do I miss the sex? Yes, of course. But this is how it's meant to be between us, and I'm good with that.

With that rolling around in my head, I turn to Christian and say, "Um, tonight sounds great. I can text you where to pick me up. Just let me know what time."

"Great," Christian says, a large smile on his face. "I'll text you."

With his lunch in hand, he moves away and nods at Ryland, who barely even acknowledges Christian's presence as he stares me down.

Not this again.

Wanting privacy because I know what's coming next, I walk

past Ryland and shut the door. When I turn around, he's standing right in front of me, crowding my space.

"Ryland," I say with a hand held up to him. "Don't even start with me on whatever is going through that mind of yours. You're here to talk about practice, so let's talk about practice." Before he can even touch me, I move away and take a seat on top of my desk.

It takes him a few seconds, but when he turns around, he asks, "Are you really going out with him tonight?"

And here I thought he was going to listen to me. "What does it matter to you?"

"It doesn't."

"It clearly does if you're asking."

"I'm asking because he's not the kind of guy you should be going on dates with."

I roll my eyes. "And how the hell do you know who I should be going out with?"

"He's a serial dater, Gabby. He's been around the block with every single teacher in this school. He's just asking you out because you're another woman to check off his list."

"Wow, that's incredibly insulting. Maybe he's asking me out because he finds me interesting, attractive, and possibly fun."

"You're fresh meat to him."

I fold my arms across my chest. "Unless you plan on talking baseball with me, just leave. I can't do this runaround with you, Ryland. That's why I've distanced myself from you. And honestly, the past week and a half has been smooth for me. I haven't been in my head, confused about what you want, what I want. I've been able to breathe, and I've enjoyed the distance from you."

He rears back. "Wow, I didn't know I was repressing you so much."

"You haven't been repressing me. You've been messing with my mind, and I don't want to deal with it anymore."

"I'm not doing it on purpose," he says back. "Christ, do you think this has been easy for me too? This is fucking torture,

Gabby. I don't like . . . hell." He pulls on the back of his neck in frustration. "I don't like being this attracted to you."

"Well, I'm sorry for the inconvenience I've bestowed upon you."

"Cut that shit," he says in a stern tone. "You know I'm not blaming you. If anything, I'm blaming myself. I never should have taken that first taste. Now it's like a goddamn spiral that I can't seem to get out of. And I don't know what to do about it."

"That's something you need to figure out on your own and not invite me into your personal hell, because I've found space. I've found a good rhythm to my day. Maybe you should do the same."

His jaw ticks as he stares back at me. "Have you really found a way to deal with it? Or have you run into the arms of someone else?"

My mouth falls open in shock . . . because the audacity of this man.

*"You been sucking someone off on the side, baby? I always knew you were a whore, but I was okay with it because you're my whore."*

*Enough.*

Ryland is not Nathan, but his words come eerily close to Nathan's.

I stand from the desk.

"Fuck you, Ryland. If you really think that's the kind of person I am, then fuck . . . you."

And with that, I move past him and head straight for the teachers' bathroom because if I stay in that room with him any longer, I might cry. And the last thing I want to do is cry in front of him.

I will not be belittled for wanting to spend time with another man.

Refuse. To. Be. Controlled.

Never again.

# Chapter Twenty-Two

## GABBY

"I'm sorry. That was not as fun as I thought it was going to be," Christian says as he drives me back to my apartment.

He's right, that was boring as shit, but I'm not about to tell him that.

"Stop, I thought it was fun."

It was not.

The art was okay—no offense to his sister. The people were stuffy and pretentious. And the food that was passed around was not nearly enough to fill me up for a dinner date, which means when I get home, I'm going to be ripping open any and all food in the pantry, tilting my head back, and letting my chompers do the work.

And if I happen to add a drink . . . or two to that, then so be it. It's a Friday, and I had a rough practice, trying to act like everything was normal even though I could feel Ryland's gaze on me the entire time.

"Was it, though?" Christian asks as he turns down my road. "I think I saw you yawn five times."

It was eight, but he missed three because I was discreet.

"I had a rough night last night," I say even though that's not the case. I slept like a baby because my legs are much better, and I'm no longer in pain while I sleep.

"You sure? You don't have to lie to spare my feelings."

"I wouldn't do that."

I so would.

I'm lying through my teeth.

"Either way, thank you for coming. My sister was glad to have another body in the building. She's always worried that no one's going to show up."

"I can't imagine how nerve-wracking that is. I thought it was a great show, though, and she sold a few paintings, right?"

"She did. She was really excited."

"That's great for her. It was fun to do something different. Thank you for inviting me."

"Thanks for saying yes," he says as he pulls into the driveway. "Wait, is that . . . is that Ryland's truck?"

"Yeah," I say. "He actually owns the house. He's my landlord."

"Oh really? I didn't know that."

"Neither did I when I rented the place," I say, sounding annoyed.

Christian puts the car in park and turns toward me. "Seems like there is some tension between you and Ryland. Everything okay there?"

I unbuckle my seat belt and turn toward him as well. From the corner of my eye, I catch movement, and that's when I see Ryland sitting on the back porch of his house, holding his phone in his hand. What the hell is he doing out there?

"Hey, everything okay?"

"What? Oh yeah, sorry." I let out a sigh. "Everything's fine with Ryland."

"You sure?" he asks. "Because it kind of seems like there's some history there." If he only knew. "And I really don't want to step on any toes or anything like that. I already know Ryland's not a fan of mine."

"Ryland can keep his opinions to himself," I say. "No one wants to hear them."

"Ahh, so he did tell you how he feels about me."

I look Christian in the eyes. "He might have said a few things, but that didn't change my opinion about you."

"I appreciate that." Christian pushes at his hair. "Why would he tell you, though, unless something is going on there?"

"Trust me, nothing's going on," I say.

And maybe that's what's making me snappy. Because nothing is going on, yet he feels like he can approach me as if there's more to us than there actually is.

"Do you wish something was going on?" Christian asks, catching me by surprise.

It takes me a few seconds to answer, but those few seconds are all Christian needs to hear.

"I get it," he says. "I bet you guys have more in common with the whole baseball thing."

"No, Christian, it's not like that. It's . . . it's complicated."

"I know, I can tell." He sighs and looks out the window. "I like you, Gabby, but I don't want to be mixed up with something complicated. I have a hard enough time trying to get along with him at school, and I don't want to make it worse by stepping in on something he thinks is his."

"I'm not his," I say, wanting to make that very clear.

"You might not think that you are, but from the way he's reacted when I'm around you, you are very much his."

"That's not for him to decide."

"I know, and I respect you for that. But I think it's something you need to settle with him before we do anything else, that's if . . . you wanted to go out on a proper date. The offer is there, but I'm not going to push for it."

I lean back in the seat and stare out the windshield. *Do I want to go on another date with Christian?* I'm honestly not sure. There wasn't any . . . spark, if I'm honest. Not when he hugged me and not tonight. Part of why I yawned so much was because we had to try so hard just to make small talk. *But I am not telling him that either.* "God, I'm sorry, Christian. This is really messed up."

"It's fine. I know complicated. I did complicated before. It's not fun. And I know what it means to be interested in someone else when things are complicated. From my experience, the best thing is to figure out the complicated and then move on from there."

I nod even though I don't think this is my problem. It's Ryland's.

Yes, I'm still attracted to him. He's still an incredibly handsome man with enormous sex appeal. When he's not being a jerk, he's great to be around. Smart. His dry wit is awesome. But if living in foster homes taught me anything, it's the ability to detach yourself from feelings. They're often wasted emotions, anyway. *And being rejected by your only biological parent gives you more resilience than anything else.* Yep, that taught me how to disengage.

Ryland keeps making it hard.

"And I want you to know, if you do decide to move on, I want to be the first person to know." That makes me laugh. He takes my hand in his and adds, "And if you don't decide to move on, then just know, no hard feelings. Okay?"

I squeeze his hand, appreciative of how nice he's being. "Thank you, Christian."

Then I lean in and press a chaste kiss to his cheek.

He offers me a sad smile. I do the same, then exit his car, feeling Ryland's eyes on me as I make my way up the stairs to my apartment. I unlock the door, shut it, then let out a deep, irritated sigh just as there's a knock on my door.

I squeeze my eyes shut, my heart and head unable to take another fight with him.

But I should have known this was going to happen.

Turning, I open the door, willing myself to be ready, but then I'm met with the sad, confused expression in Ryland's eyes.

Normally, this man airs out his pride every chance he gets.

He's confident, he's unflappable, and he doesn't show an ounce of weakness, but the man standing in front of me right now is not the man I'm used to.

Hollow eyes.

Bothered eyes.

Sunken eyes.

Depleted.

Restless.

But that doesn't matter to me, because I can't do this runaround anymore. I'm tired. I don't have anything else to say. And I don't have the energy to deal with how he's feeling about me going out with Christian.

"Ryland, I can't—"

"I'm sorry," he says before I can even finish. "I'm really fucking sorry, Gabby."

I lean against the doorway. "Sorry about what, Ryland? About the way you've been acting or the way you've been leading me on?"

"I haven't been leading you on. At least not intentionally. I told you that night it was the last time, and it has been."

"Yeah, and you've been an ass ever since. And the way you stare Christian down, it's just rude."

Maybe I do have the energy to talk about it.

Maybe I'm just so fed up and frustrated that I don't mind letting loose.

"I told you, Gabby, I'm having a hard time dealing with all of this."

"And that's not an excuse. You're a grown-ass man, Ryland. Act like one."

My phone rings in my purse, and I think about ignoring it for a second. However, I need to get out of this conversation, so I pull it out of my purse and answer it. "Hello?"

"Gab." *Bennett?*

I lift the phone away and see his name on the screen.

"Hey, is everything okay?" I ask, recognizing the shake in his voice.

"Gab . . . I . . . I'm." My heart pounds in my chest as I wait.

"What?"

"I'm playing tomorrow . . . in the big leagues. Gab, they called me up."

Everything inside me drains as tears fill my eyes. My legs wobble under me, and I crumple to the ground before I know it.

"What the fuck," Ryland says as he squats down next to me.

"Are you serious?" I ask. "Please don't lie to me."

"Gabby, I swore to you I'd never joke about this. It's happening. Tomorrow, I'm starting at third."

"Oh my God," I say as tears are now streaming down my face. Full-on sobs wrack my body.

"Fuck, is everything okay?" Ryland asks, taking one of my hands.

"Are you with someone?" Bennett asks.

"It's . . . it's Coach Rowley."

I look up at Ryland, and his face is full of concern.

"Put him on speaker," Bennett says.

I pull the phone from my ear and put it on speaker. "Go ahead," I say.

"Coach Rowley?" Bennett says, making Ryland more confused than ever.

"Bennett?" he says.

"Coach . . . I got called up. I'm going to the show tomorrow. Starting."

"What?" Ryland yells and leaps to his feet, stealing the phone from me. He then takes my hand and helps me up as well. "Holy fuck, man. That's incredible. Fuck, I'm proud of you."

"Thanks, Coach. I'm stoked. I'm on my way to San Francisco now. Can I ask you a favor?"

"Sure, anything," Ryland says.

"Can you make sure my sister gets to the game? I have two tickets with her name on them. I need her there, and I know she's going to be a crying mess. I need her there safely."

Ryland looks me in the eyes. "You can count on it, man."

"Thank you," Bennett says and Ryland hands me the phone.

I take it off speaker and walk farther into the apartment. "Bennett, I . . . I'm so proud of you." More tears fall from my eyes. "You did it."

"We did it, Gab," he says softly. "We fucking did it."

I nod even though he can't see me. "You soak in this moment, you hear me?" I say, my voice getting choked up. "You soak in every second when you walk out on that field, and you warm up, but the moment that game starts . . ."

"I clock in."

"Exactly. You show them why you deserve to be there. Got it?"

"Got it," he says.

I wipe my eyes. "Text me the info, and I'll be there, and after, I'm taking you to dinner."

"You better."

"I love you, Bennett. Drive safe. I'm proud of you."

"Thanks, Gabby. I love you too."

And then we both hang up. I set my phone on the counter and then cover my face as I slowly lower to the floor again and cry some more.

I cry for everything we've been through.

I cry for the heartache, the suffering, the unknown.

I cry for the countless hours we spent together on the field.

I cry for the years of him working his way up the system.

I cry for the injuries he sustained, the coaches who didn't believe in him . . . and the coaches who did.

And I cry for the perseverance, the resilience, and the strength he has had through this entire process.

He deserves this more than anyone, and I just hope he can prove it. I hope he can have his moment.

Ryland settles in next to me, a warmth I was missing. He brings his arm around me and pulls me into his chest.

All the anger, the frustration, the countless circles we've been running in, they're all washed away as I bury my head into his chest and let out my tears. I let out my happiness. I cry for what's to come, tears of joy streaming down my cheeks.

And he holds me the entire time, stroking my hair, pressing soft kisses to the top of my head, showing me that I'm not alone at this moment—a moment I've been waiting for, for so long.

After what feels like forever, he lifts my chin with his forefinger and forces me to look him in the eyes. Those green eyes penetrate me harder than ever before. "Congratulations," he says in a soft voice. "You should be really fucking proud of yourselves."

"Thank you," I whisper. "I am."

And then I rest my head against his chest again and let out more tears as I let the relief drain from my body.

He did it.

No . . . like Bennett said, *we* did it.

---

With pajamas in hand, I walk over to Ryland's house feeling elated, nervous, and sort of like I'm going to puke and cry at the same time. It took me a little bit to peel myself off the floor, but once I did, I thanked Ryland and said nothing else. He got the hint and headed toward the house to check on Mac, who was sleeping.

Bennett sent over the details of the game tomorrow when he stopped for some food. It's a night game. His first big league game will be played under the lights, and the fact that the game is driving distance for me makes it seem like everything is aligning.

I walk into the house and glance toward the kitchen, and when I don't see Ryland, I move right into the bathroom.

As I'm soaping up, I keep thinking about how when I get to the stadium, which we're allowed to get there early and watch batting practice, I want to go to the team store and deck myself out in Bombers gear. I don't really have anything because I wasn't sure if he'd stay with the Bombers or move to a different team, but now that I know he's been called up, I need a hat and a shirt and a sweatshirt and bracelets and foam fingers and everything you could possibly imagine.

God, I'm so freaking excited. Once out of the shower, I quickly go through my routine, brush my teeth, and lotion up before putting on my pajamas, hanging my towel, and exiting the bathroom with my dirty clothes. I find Ryland leaning against the counter, clearly waiting for me.

"Hey," he says as his eyes give me a brief once-over.

"Hey," I say awkwardly.

"Talked with Aubree and Wyatt, and they're going to watch Mac for the weekend. They were thinking about taking her up to the Redwoods, one of her favorite places. Hayes also offered us his apartment in the city to stay so we don't have to drive back late at night."

"Oh wow, okay. That's really nice of him. Um, were you planning on spending the night?"

"It's about a three-hour drive, and we're not going to want to do that after the game."

"Right, okay. Looks like I need to pack." I let out a deep breath. "Um, Bennett sent me the info. I can text it to you. We get to watch batting practice."

"Really? That's awesome."

"And I told Bennett I'd take him to dinner after."

"Not a problem. You two can do whatever you want after the game. I can give you the info to Hayes's apartment so you know where to go after."

"Oh, I didn't mean you weren't invited."

He shakes his head. "I'm uninviting myself. You two deserve the time together."

And when he says things like that, it makes me want him all over again. It makes me wish he could get over this thing in his head where he doesn't think he deserves or could handle a relationship.

"Thank you, Ryland."

"And if you want to sit alone at the game, I can hang out on the concourse. I know things are weird between us, and I don't want to encroach on your space. I just ask that I can at least see his first at bat, then I can leave if you want."

"Is that what you want?" I ask him. "To leave me alone?"

"Do you want the truth?"

"I do," I say.

He shifts on his feet and looks me in the eyes, sincerity pouring from him. "The answer is no. I don't want to leave you alone. I want to be there for you. I want to hold your hand. I want to capture the moment of you watching your brother play his first big league game so he can watch it over and over and see how much pride you have for him. I want to make the day special for you because you deserve it. But I also want you to be comfortable, so if that means I step aside, I act as the driver, and that's it, then I'll do that too. I just want you to be happy, taken care of . . . protected."

A lump the size of a golf ball forms in my throat because how can he say such beautiful, wonderful things without messing with my standpoint? How can he expect me not to want him, to run into his arms and beg him to second-guess his stance on relationships? *On me?*

And this is exactly why I was trying to keep my distance. This reason precisely because even though I've tried tirelessly to keep my heart out of this, I've been fighting a losing battle.

He's too wonderful.

Too thoughtful.

Too much of everything I think I've ever wanted, everything I didn't know I wanted. And I hate that. I hate that with one apology, I can let go of all my anger. That I can look him in the eyes and know that deep down we have a connection unlike anyone I've met before. And that despite everything he does, everything he puts me through, the mental game of *does he want me or does he want me to push away*, I still find myself gravitating toward him.

Wanting him.

Because he's a damaged soul, just like me.

I swallow past the lump and softly say, "I want you there, next to me."

"You sure?" he asks.

"Positive," I answer, looking him in the eyes.

"Consider it done." He offers me a curt nod, then pushes off the counter. "See you in the morning, Gabby."

"Yeah, see you in the morning."

# Chapter Twenty-Three

## RYLAND

"You look like hell for someone about to go watch one of his players play their first ever big-league game," Aubree says as she comes up to me in Mac's bedroom, where I'm packing Mac an overnight bag.

"I feel like hell," I say as I throw in a few extra pairs of underwear for Mac because you never fucking know.

"Why?" Aubree asks as she takes a seat on Mac's bed. I glance out the door to see if Mac's around. "She's with Wyatt at the swing."

Knowing she's not in hearing distance, I lean against the dresser, taking a seat on the floor, and let my body relax for one second. "I need to talk to you, Aubree, but I don't need the snarky side of you. Okay? It's serious, and I'm not in the mood to deal with your annoying sister tendencies."

"What a way to open a conversation," she says. "But I get it. I promise I won't be snarky."

"Okay, because this is something I would have talked to Cassidy about, and she's not here . . ."

I see the seriousness cross her face, Aubree knowing exactly what I'm talking about. "I can do that for you. What's going on?"

I drag my hands over my face. "I like her. I like Gabby. I tried to keep my distance. I tried to push her away. I tried to forget about this almost nauseous feeling I get when I see her talk to other men, but I can't fucking shake it. It just keeps growing and growing, and now it's all I can think about."

"She's a great person, Ryland. I'm surprised you lasted this long."

"Lasted is a loose term, more like survived." I lean my head against the dresser, looking up at the glow-in-the-dark stars we stuck to Mac's ceiling and the one she claims is Cassidy, watching over her. As I talk to Aubree, I almost feel like I'm talking to Cassidy at the same time. "I don't want this. I don't want to be sucked into these feelings. I'm already passing off Mac to you guys more than I should."

"What do you mean?" Aubree says. "You're not passing her off. We're a family unit, Ryland. You might have custody, but we're all in charge of her. It's in Cassidy's letters that she left us. She wanted us to help you, to watch over you while you watched over Mac. You're not passing her off. You're letting us be a part of her life."

"I know, but I should be doing more with her. It feels like ever since Gabby came into my life, I'm not spending the kind of time with Mac that I should be."

"That's not true. You spend every evening with her. Just when we arrived, she showed me the fort you made for her with the boxes and how you spent the other night painting the sides so there were vines on the fort. The swing on the tree that she loves was your idea. This room full of horses and stars, that was you. This freaking house, Ryland. This is all you. You're doing what you're supposed to be doing for her. You're going above and beyond. It's okay to want to have some time for yourself and a life of your own. We encourage it."

I shake my head. "Cassidy was better at this."

"Of course she was. She was Cassidy," Aubree says. "And

we've talked about this. You can't compare yourself to her. She was Mac's mom. You are her uncle who's slipping into the parent role, and, if you ask me, you're doing a better fucking job than I think I could have ever done. You cann*ot* feel guilty about liking someone because you think it's distracting."

"It is a distraction. Gabby is a huge distraction, Aubree. Last night, when she found out about Bennett, at first, I didn't know what she was crying about. All I saw were tears and I went into protective mode. Everything else around me went black and all I could focus on was her. What if . . . what if Mac needed me at that moment, I'm not sure I would have responded, I was so focused on Gabby."

"I don't believe that for a second. I think you can care for more than one person. You did it for us when we were growing up. You took care of all of us girls, shielded us from Dad, and took the brunt of his abuse so not one of us had to suffer through it. That was all you."

I run my hand over my mouth. "This feels different, Aubree."

"Because Gabby is different. She could very much be your person. I know that might freak you out, that hearing such a thing might be too soon for you, but there's a strong bond there that all of us saw. There's something different between the two of you, but there is one thing I know for certain. No matter how strong that bond is between you and Gabby, it won't get in the way of you and Mac. Because I know you won't allow it and I know for certain that Gabby won't allow it."

She's right. Gabby would never let anything come between me and Mac, because I know she has the same sort of feelings about her relationship with Bennett.

"I know you're right."

"Then what's holding you up?"

I look Aubree in the eyes and say, "I'm too . . . I'm too damaged. Between Dad and Samantha, I don't think I can open myself up to someone else. I don't think I have it in me. I'm not strong enough and need to save my strength for Mac. But, fuck, I can't seem to let her go."

"Then don't, Ryland. Figure out a way to open up to her. Take baby steps."

"But what if those baby steps don't amount to anything? What am I going to do? Should I just lead her on? That's not fair to her. And then we have to fucking work together? This is so messed up."

Aubree moves down to the ground and sits next to me, shoulder to shoulder. "I get where your head is at. There are a lot of what-ifs rolling around in there. I had the same fear when I started to fall for Wyatt because we were in a different situation. I didn't want to have feelings for a man who planned on leaving after a year, but I couldn't stop them from developing, no matter how hard I tried. When it came to that point, the one when I couldn't take it anymore, I just . . . I jumped. Feet first, with no parachute, and hoped that he was there to catch me at the bottom. I think with Gabby, you have to do the same thing. Trust that she's going to be there to catch you, to hold your hand, to help you. She's a good person, Ryland."

"She's a really good person," I say. "That's why I don't want to hurt her."

"Then don't." Aubree takes my hand in hers. "Take it slow, discuss your fears, and you never know, you might very well be surprised with how she responds."

Take it slow.

Discuss your fears.

Of those two things, the last one is the most terrifying. What if I discuss my fears, and she bolts? Because who would want to take on someone who had a monster as a father . . . who might have his same anger inside him?

I get what Aubree's saying. And I'm thankful again for Wyatt, who has helped my sister be this open. This wise about relationships.

But I'm not ready to explore the what-ifs. Not yet. Not when Bennett deserves all of her attention and focus.

I let out a deep sigh. "Not today. Today is her day with Bennett, but after that, I'll have the conversation with her."

"What are you going to do tonight?"

"What do you mean?"

Aubree wiggles her brows at me. "Hayes only has one bed and a shitshow for a couch in that apartment."

My body grows warm. "I guess that's something we'll have to deal with when the time comes."

"Uh-huh." She smiles and stands to her feet. She takes my hand and helps me up. Then to my surprise, she wraps her arms around me and gives me a hug. Aubree's not the hugging kind, or the touching kind, but it seems as though Wyatt has worn off on her, so I hug her back. "I really hope that you give this a shot. You deserve to be happy. You deserve more than a life of being the uncle who has custody. You're more than that, Ryland, and you can excel at many things. Multiple things. You did when you were younger, so you can now."

"Thank you, Aubree," I say as I squeeze her. "I appreciate the talk and the hug."

She steps away. "Cassidy would have done it."

"Yes . . . yes, she would have."

---

"Picking up tickets under Gabby Brinkman," Gabby says as she shifts on her feet next to the will call office, looking nervous and excited at the same time.

The entire drive from Almond Bay to the stadium was filled with podcasts. Yup, we didn't talk. Not a single word. I saw it the minute she got in the truck—she was not in the talking mood. She's bottled up with nerves, so I put on one of my favorite podcasts, Smartless, and we just listened.

It was probably for the best because I know if I spoke, I would have said something stupid like . . . I like you and I don't know how to deal with the feelings, but I'd like to deal with the feelings with you, and what are your thoughts on the matter?

Really not the time.

So I kept my mouth shut.

"Can I see ID?" the attendant asks.

Gabby digs her ID out of her purse while I take in the gray stone-encased ballpark. One of the prettiest, in my opinion. Right off the bay so you can smell the salt water, and near bars and restaurants where music plays and pre-gaming occurs. There's a rich history within the walls, and you can almost feel the electricity in the air, knowing that the Bombers are close to clinching the wild card slot for the playoffs.

"Great. Here you go, sweetheart."

"Thank you," Gabby says, taking her ID and the tickets from the attendant.

"Enjoy the game."

Gabby waves to her, then stares down at the tickets. "Do you mind if I keep both of these?"

"You can do whatever you want with them," I say, my voice sounding weird, probably because I haven't used it for the past three hours. "Are you sure you want me to go in with you? I know I said I want to see his first at bat, but I can sit in one of the bars across from the stadium and wait."

She shakes her head, and then, to my surprise, she takes my hand. "I need you here, next to me."

A lump builds in my throat because fuck, is that something I wanted to hear. "Sure, anything you need."

Together, hand in hand, we walk up to the large gates and go through the metal detector before showing our tickets to the attendant, who scans them and waves us in. Immediately, we're thrust into the hustle and bustle of the stadium. Since we have early access, we're not swarmed by crowds, but vendors are still setting up their kiosks, carts are being wheeled around, and a few people mill about, deciding what they want to get for food.

"What do you want to do first?"

"I need Bombers gear," she says. "Right away."

"You got it," I say. "Follow me."

Since I've been to the stadium quite a few times, I know exactly where the team store is—right past the main stairs that lead to the higher decks. Thankfully, because of our early access, the store's pretty empty, so we have time to look around. One of the things I love about the Bombers is their untraditional colors. You think baseball, and you think blue, red, and white. A high percentage of the teams have those colors, but not the Bombers. They went with teal for the ocean and yellow for the lighthouses around the bay.

When we reach the store, I take her straight to the women's section, where she starts pawing through the different shirts.

"What are you looking for?" I ask, wanting to help.

"I want something traditional. Nothing like this." She holds up a pink shirt with the Bombers logo in white.

"Yeah, I get you," I say. "Want a jersey like mine?"

I'm wearing the teal jersey with the yellow Bomber logo. It's their best seller and the colors everyone wears during playoff games when the team is home because the entire stadium lights up in teal.

"I think so. I like that a lot."

"Over here," I say and lead her to the jerseys. "What's your size?"

"Medium."

I grab one for her and hold it out. She slides it on over her tank top and buttons it up. The female cut fits her perfectly.

"How does it feel?"

"Great. I think this is the one." She slides it off and then looks at the price tag, her eyes widening. "Or I can get a regular T-shirt."

She goes to hang it back up, but I take it from her. "My treat."

She shakes her head. "No, I can't let you do that."

"You can, and you will." I loop my finger under her chin and have her look me right in the eyes. "I planned on getting you whatever you wanted in here anyway. This is a special moment, so you're doing it right."

I can see her mind wavering, trying to figure out what she should do, but I don't give her a chance to change her mind. I lead her to the hats and ask her which one she wants.

She eyes me, looking like she wants to tell me no, but then she turns back to the hats and picks the classic Bombers hat.

Since it's adjustable, she doesn't need to try it on.

We move through the store, looking through the other shirts, the sweatshirts, and the blankets. I attempt to grab them all, but she pushes my hand away. When she sees a bracelet that she likes, I snag that, and when she finds a foam finger, I grab two of those.

Once we're done, I guide her to the register, where I see some cheap Bombers bead necklaces. I grab those as well.

"Ryland, I can buy—"

"Nothing," I say. "You can buy nothing."

The attendant rings us up, and when he asks if we want a bag, I shake him off, knowing we're ready to put everything on. We move out of the store into a side hallway, and I help remove tags and watch her as she transforms into a diehard Bombers supporter. And fuck does she look good.

She's wearing cut-off jean shorts and a white tank top. She has the jersey on over the tank top but has left it open. Her Bombers hat is secured over her long, curled hair, and her necklaces and bracelets give her the good-time vibe . . . along with the foam finger that I put on as well.

I grab my phone from my pocket. "Follow me." I take her hand again and move her out toward the field. I place her right behind the lower seats leading to home plate and hold up my phone for a picture. "Pose for me so we can send a picture to Bennett."

She holds up her foam finger and does a few poses, smiling large. Then I turn the camera to selfie mode, wrap my arm around her, and say, "Smile."

She leans her head into my shoulder, and we both smile into the camera, capturing a moment I know will live in my mind for a very long time. I like this. It feels so right . . . finally having a woman by my side to enjoy baseball. *Her.*

I send the photos to her so she can send them to Bennett, and then we flash our tickets to the section monitor of our seats.

Somehow, Bennett was able to secure us lower-level tickets, which I know is not where they usually stick first time family members. Hopefully, he didn't pay for them because they'd cost a lot.

And just as we move down toward the netting, the Bombers take the field.

"What number is he?" I ask.

"Twenty-two."

"Why twenty-two?"

She smiles up at me. "June twenty-second, the day that we moved out on our own."

Well . . . fuck.

"Fuck, that's cool," I say, feeling my emotions get the best of me. Maybe it's the day, the meaning behind all of it, seeing someone's dreams come true, but I feel like I'm going to be an emotional wreck the whole goddamn day.

"When he told me, I cried for an hour."

"I can imagine," I say, seeing twenty-two out on the field. "There he is." I point at Bennett, who's currently stretching with his bat in hand.

Gabby follows my hand and immediately bursts into tears when she spots him. "Wooooo," she shouts over her tears. "Go, Bennett!"

And it's the fucking sweetest thing to witness as Bennett turns around after hearing his sister's voice. He scans the crowd, and when he sees us, his face lights up with a huge smile.

"You got this," Gabby shouts, not even caring about everyone else around us or that we're on the biggest stage for baseball.

He nods to us. I offer a wave, and then he gets back to business, concentrating on what he should focus on.

Gabby and I stay silent, watching, entranced with the entire process as batter after batter takes their swings out on the field, and when Bennett steps up to the plate, she takes my hand, holding it tight.

He gets into his relaxed stance that I grew to know so well. His bat taps his back and then he lifts it up just as the pitch is delivered. He loads up on his back leg, and with all the power from his lower half, he drives through the ball, sending it right over the left field fence.

"Holy shit," I quietly say as Gabby stares in awe.

His teammates razz him from behind the portable backstop, but he remains locked in and focused.

Hit after hit, he sends them sailing to the outfield, mainly line drives, exactly what I'd tell him I'd want to see from him. Don't shoot for the fences. Just make solid contact, as solid contact will bring home runs.

When he's done, Gabby claps next to me, the sound muffled by the foam hand, and when he turns toward us, I give him a thumbs-up, and Gabby blows him a kiss.

He holds up his hand, offering her the sign for "love you," and Gabby returns it before he heads out on the field with his glove to get some grounders.

"Wow," I say softly. "He's sharp."

"He looked so good, right? I'm not just in some starry haze. He really looked good?"

"He looked incredible. And that boy has stacked some muscle on him. When did that happen?"

She laughs. "He's focused on putting more and more muscle on his bones every year."

"Yeah, because he was a skinny fuck when he was with me."

She smiles, clearly remembering those days. "When he came home, we'd do pushups together because he knew that he had to keep building muscle, and it was a free way to do that. Clearly, having access to a weight room has leveled him up."

"Big time, but without you doing those pushups with him, I bet he wouldn't have leveled up as quickly."

"Now you're just trying to feed me with compliments."

"Am I? Or am I recognizing one of the reasons that boy is out on the field about to play his first major league game?"

She smirks. "Feeding compliments."

"Okay." I roll my eyes and then drape my arm over her shoulder as we finish watching batting practice. When the visitors take the field, I ask, "Want to grab something to eat before the game?"

"Yes," she says. "I don't think I can eat much because I'm a ball of nerves, but I know if I don't eat something, I might pass out."

"I have the perfect idea," I say. "Follow me."

⸻

"How many pictures did you take of me eating that hot dog?"

I give her the side-eye. "Two, because the first one I took, you looked like you had one eyeball, and your tooth was in carnage mode. Didn't think you'd like it."

She wipes her mouth and then her hands. For someone who couldn't eat because she was too nervous, she devoured that hot dog pretty quickly. I was impressed.

"Okay, because it seemed like you took twenty."

"What the hell am I going to do with twenty pictures of you eating a hot dog?"

She shrugs and sips her Diet Coke. "I don't know what you get your jollies from."

"You're demented."

She laughs and then plucks one of the fries from the shared carton in front of us. Eyes on me, she nudges me with her foot under our high-top table. "Thank you for everything today, Ryland. In case I forget to say it later. Thank you for driving me when I know I would have been a nervous wreck doing it myself. Thank you for setting up a place to sleep tonight so I don't have to shortchange my time with Bennett after the game. Thank you for showing me around the stadium and for my gear, for holding my hand, for feeding me, and for making me laugh."

"You don't have to thank me, Gabby. It's really my pleasure. I'm just grateful I get to be a part of it."

"Bennett loves you. Always has. You were one of the few coaches who had a huge impact on the way he played the sport. He was always good, but he developed under your teaching."

"That means a lot, thank you."

"It's the truth." She picks up another fry. "And I know he probably would have given you the extra ticket."

That makes me laugh. "And that means even more."

She joins me in her laughter, her face alight with so much joy that I feel like I haven't seen in a while, maybe not ever. It makes me wonder how much of our ups and downs have affected her. I hate to think that I might have depressed her or put her in a bad mood in any way because that smile deserves to be seen by the world. It's the type of smile that could make anyone's day better . . . brighter. I know for damn sure it's making mine.

But not wanting to get into any of that, I say, "What's your favorite memory of Bennett playing the game?"

"Besides what we just witnessed?" she asks.

"Yes, besides that, before he called you and told you he was moving up."

She brings her cup up to her mouth, staring out at the field as she thinks about it. "You know, there have been quite a few moments. Some accomplishments like his first home run over the fence, his first time batting for the cycle, his first stolen base, things like that will always sit in my memories. Still, I think one of my most prized moments was when he was in high school and had a terrible game, four errors at third, three strikeouts, just a really poor showing.

"Instead of getting down on himself, getting pissed and throwing his gear or just giving up for the day, he spent that night with a lamp from the living room lighting up the front of the apartment building we were living in, throwing balls against the pitchback, over and over again. Focused. Improving. He wanted to prove that he wasn't the player he was that day and that he was so much better. At that moment, I knew he'd make it because he persevered."

"I remember that game," I say as I turn my cup on the table, reminiscing on a shit game. "I remember the look in his eyes after that game. Normally, any other player would have looked

289

defeated." I shake my head. "Not Bennett. He was determined. He was ready for more."

"He's always been ready for more. He's always been hungry. He wants to prove to everyone around him that he deserves to be where he is because of the hard work he's put in."

"He deserves it for sure."

"I just hope he has a good game. I don't need him to get a hit. I just hope he has contact with the ball. Solid contact."

"Same," I agree. "And if he happens to make a killer play at third, then that would be a bonus."

She chuckles. "Just any play works." She picks up another fry and dips it in the ketchup this time. "Can I ask you a question that might be sensitive?"

"Yeah, ask away."

"Did you ever get called up?"

How did I know that was coming?

I shake my head. "I left before I had the chance."

"What do you mean, you left?"

"I dropped out. I didn't like being away from my family. My sisters were stuck with my dad, and well . . . he was an abusive asshole. He never touched them, but the fear that he might lived with me every day. It made it hard for me to focus. I was constantly calling Cassidy to make sure everyone was okay, and then I just . . . I couldn't take it anymore, and I quit baseball."

"I . . . I had no clue."

"Not a lot of people do, actually. I never made it public. A lot of people just think that I didn't have what it takes to make it, and maybe I didn't because my head wasn't in the game like it should have been. But I couldn't chase a dream, knowing that my sisters were possibly suffering at the hands of my father."

"Ryland," she says, reaching out and taking my hand.

"It's fine. I don't regret it. I was able to get my teaching degree, and now I get to coach. I love my life, even when I feel the challenges of it heavy in my chest. I'd have made the same decision over and over again because my sisters . . . and Mac, for that matter, they're my world."

"I know that feeling," she says. "The sacrifice you make to help your siblings. I truly understand your decision, and I commend it. I'd have done the same thing for Bennett."

"You did something similar, didn't you? You gave up a lot for him to have a better life?"

"Not sure I gave up a lot."

"Did you do all the normal teenager things like go to parties, dances, spend weekends at the mall? Or did you work your ass off?"

"Worked," she answers.

"And in your twenties, did you get to go to college and have that experience, or did you work some more and take night classes to support you and your brother?"

"You know what I did," she says.

"I do, and that means you sacrificed a lot. You gave up experiences that others might have had because their childhood was more stable. But you understood the importance of what getting out of a bad situation is all about. I felt the same way, wanting to get my sisters out of a bad situation."

"I guess that makes us a lot alike."

"It does," I say, looking her in her stunning eyes. "I recognize your hustle, Gabby, and I'm glad I can share the moment when you can see all your hard work pay off. It's an honor."

⊏⊐

"I'm going to puke," Gabby says, sitting next to me as she rubs her hands over her thighs. "He's on deck."

I take a few pictures of Bennett on deck because, at this point, Gabby has done nothing to record the day. She's so immersed in the moment that I've mentally taken on the responsibility of being her photographer. That way, she can look back at these pictures and remember this moment. It's amazing.

"Trust the process," I say. "He knows what he's doing. He needs to go in there, trusting himself and his mechanics. The hit will come."

"Just not a strikeout," she says as the batter before him walks.

"Oh God, he's up." She slides her hand into mine and squeezes my palm tightly as she holds her foam finger high and cheers for him. I snap a picture of her as her mouth is open, her excitement evident on her face.

I have a hard time handling my phone with one hand, but I figure it out as I zoom in on Bennett in the box, his stance relaxed, his body ready to explode.

*Come on, man.*

*Just contact.*

*All we need is contact.*

The first pitch is a ball in the dirt, the runner steals second, and now there's a runner in scoring position with the score zero-zero in the second inning. Fuck, it would be amazing if he's the first one to help put a run up on the board.

At the next pitch, I hear Gabby hold her breath as Bennett swings, and he misses.

"Shit," she whispers under her breath.

"It's okay," I say to her. "He's seen it now. He knows what to expect. He's got this." I squeeze her hand, and we watch together as the pitcher winds up and throws a fastball just outside the strike zone.

Bennett lays off.

"That's it. Keep a good eye on the ball," she says, now sitting on the edge of her seat.

I join her.

She leans forward, and as the next pitch comes in, Bennett swings, but he makes contact this time, sailing the ball just over the second baseman's head and into right field. Gabby and I both fly out of our seats, cheering and jumping, our linked hands up in the air as the runner from second scores and Bennett rounds first.

"Yesssss!" Gabby screams and then lets out a loud sob.

Tears come to my eyes as we watch Bennett take off his elbow guard and hand it to the first base coach, who taps him on the head. The other team tosses the ball that Bennett just hit into the Bombers dugout as a keepsake for Bennett.

Gabby continues to cheer and clap while I do the same. The people around us probably think we've lost our mind, but we don't care. Bennett Brinkman just got his first hit in the big leagues in his first at bat.

This is magic.

The game of baseball is so great because of moments like this.

Moments when you can pause and enjoy the crowd cheering, the stands rocking, the sweet smell of stadium food coming in all different directions, all the while dreams are coming true.

When we both take a seat, I turn toward Gabby who has tears streaming down her face, her eyes filled with so much joy.

"He did it," I say. "RBI single, your boy just got an RBI single."

She nods, her lips trembling. "He did."

And then she leans in, places her hand behind my head, and tugs me down to her lips where she places a gentle, sweet kiss. It's no longer than a second, but it's enough to ignite a flame within me.

When she pulls away, she whispers, "He did it."

"He really did," I say, my heart pounding a mile a minute because I know, at this moment, deep down in my soul, that this is my turning point.

I needed this to push me to what I've been trying to avoid.

She's it.

She's what I want.

And there is no way in hell I can go another day without her knowing.

# Chapter Twenty-Four

## GABBY

"Are you sure you don't want to stay?" I ask as I sip my water, my eyes fixed on the front of the restaurant where we wait for Bennett.

The Bombers wound up winning the game ten to four. Bennett went two for four, with one strikeout and three RBIs. He made two plays at third, one of them gunning down a runner with his torpedo of an arm. It was the most thrilling game of my life to watch.

Since Bennett doesn't have all the fancy privileges the other players have, he texted me and told me to meet him at the restaurant down the street, a local taco joint he heard was good.

That's where we've been waiting since we left the stadium.

"I'm positive. You two need your time together," Ryland says, looking sort of stiff as the server comes by with his food in a bag. He's taking his dinner to the apartment, where he said he'll check in with Aubree and wait for me to join him.

I know I won't have a lot of time with Bennett because he needs to get some sleep, but I'm going to try to soak it up as much as possible.

The door to the restaurant opens, and I hold my breath as I see Bennett walk in, wearing a pair of jeans, a plain T-shirt, and his Bombers minor league hat. No one recognizes him—why would they at this point—as he spots our table.

I hop out of my chair and run up to him, where he catches me in a hug, and I squeeze him tight.

"Oh my God, Bennett, I'm so proud of you."

His arms wrap around me, and he holds me close to his chest. "That game was for you, Gabby."

And here I go, crying all over again. I've been a mess all day. When I pull away, he holds a ball in front of me, and I stare down at it and then back up at him.

"What's that?" I ask.

"The ball of my first ever hit." He turns it over, showing me his signature and the words *To my sister, who made this all happen.* "It's yours, Gabby. I want you to have it."

I take the ball from him, my fingers tingling as I run them over the red stitches, floating over his signature, a signature I remember him practicing one night when he was a senior in high school. It was one of those things we talked about, one of the techniques of putting our goals out in the universe. He needed to practice his signature so people knew who signed the ball but so no one could replicate it.

Looking at that signature now, it's perfect.

Through watery eyes, I say, "Thank you. This means everything to me."

"You mean everything to me," he says and pulls me into another hug. "Thank you for everything, Gabby. I fucking mean it. This is just the beginning. It's my turn to take care of you."

I pull away and press my hand to his chest. "You focus on securing a spot on the team next year. That's what you need to do first."

"In the bag, Gabby. I got this."

Some might think it's cocky, but it's not. Bennett truly believes in himself, and that doesn't come naturally. Him having such faith in his abilities comes from constant hours of practicing, day in and day out.

I believe him. This is just the beginning.

"Good." I pull away and say, "I'm sure someone else wants to say hi to you."

Ryland walks up to Bennett and pulls him into a huge hug. I stand there, watching over these two men in my life, appreciating one another as they pat their backs. It's a beautiful thing because I know how much Ryland mattered to Bennett when he was in high school. Bennett relied on Ryland to be a voice in his life other than me. A safe space. A wealth of knowledge, and one of the reasons the scouts came to watch Bennett play.

It was Ryland.

Now that I think about it, I realize that a lot of Bennett's chances came from Ryland. He wrote to scouts and colleges, telling them he had a standout player they needed to see play. Sure, Bennett made a name for himself, but Ryland helped get eyes on him. And I'm just remembering that now.

When they pull away, Ryland says, "You played fucking phenomenal."

"Thank you, Coach Rowley," Bennett says, his cheeks staining pink. "I'm really glad you could come watch me play. Meant a lot to me, and that you drove my sister too. I know she would have been a nervous wreck the entire time."

"Trust me, she was." Ryland chuckles. "I still think she's trying to calm down from the nerves."

"I'll sleep heavily tonight," I say.

"I think we all will," Ryland says and then grabs his to-go bag. "Well, I'll let you two catch up."

Bennett's brow creases. "You're not staying?"

"No, man. I want you to catch up with your sister. This is a special moment for both of you, and I think it's best if I head out. But you owe me a dinner, understood?" Ryland points at Bennett.

"Deal." Bennett holds out his hand, and Ryland shakes it before pulling him into another hug.

"Really proud of you, man. You proved today that the dream can be a reality with determination and putting in the work. You're the ten percent."

"Ten percent?" Bennett asks.

"Ten percent of players who make it. You're now a part of that elite club. Hold on to it, and don't take it for granted."

"I won't. Promise."

"Good." Ryland gently pats Bennett's face, then turns toward me. He grabs my hand for a moment and says, "You have the address?"

"Yes," I say.

"Okay, see you later."

"Bye."

Then he takes off, leaving me alone with my brother. We both take a seat, and I hand him a Diet Coke that I ordered, knowing he'd want one. "Tell me everything—"

"What was that?" Bennett asks, the corner of his lips tilting up.

"What was what?" I ask.

"Uh, that little exchange with Coach Rowley."

"What little exchange?" I ask, the skin at the nape of my neck tingling.

"You guys touched hands, then looked at each other like something's going on there."

"What? Nothing's going on," I say, but even I don't believe it as it's coming out of my mouth.

Bennett's smile grows wider. "Holy shit, something is going on between the two of you."

"No, there's not." I wave him off. "Now tell me about the team. Did they like—"

"Oh no, there's no way you're shaking this off." He crosses his arms over his chest. "I'm not telling you jack shit until you tell me what's going on with Coach Rowley."

"I told you, Bennett. Nothing."

"I don't believe you." He presses his finger to the table. "And on this special day, a day that we should commemorate, you're going to lie to me?"

I roll my eyes. "You know what? You're right; we should commemorate it. We should be celebrating. So why don't we do just that?"

Bennett stubbornly holds his place. "Nope, not happening. Spill the beans and then we can talk baseball."

I groan in frustration because I know there is no way I'm breaking this kid until I give him the truth. "Fine," I say on a huff. "There might be a little thing, but I don't even know what it is."

"I fucking knew it," he says, his hand slapping the table. "I saw it when you two were watching me warm up, and then just now, I was convinced something was going on. So . . . what is it, are you dating?"

"No, not dating."

He lifts a brow. "Are you . . . doing other things?"

I wince because I mean, yeah.

"Oh God." He shudders. "Fuck, maybe I don't want to know."

"It's not like that," I say.

"It's not? Okay, then what is it?"

"I told you, I don't know. It's complicated."

His lips purse for a second. "Complicated? How so?"

"He . . . he's a great guy, but he has different responsibilities than when he was coaching you. His sister passed away this year, and well, she left her daughter in his custody."

"Oh shit, really? How old?"

"I think four. She's so cute. Loves horses, kind of quirky in the best way possible, and he's amazing with her. She's his number one priority, which makes having anything to do with him on a romantic level difficult. He's not in a position to put his attention toward a relationship."

"Do you want a relationship with him?"

"I've thought about it, which is weird because I wasn't really in the market for anything like that. If I was honest, I never really thought I would be, not after everything that happened with Nathan."

Bennett's jaw ticks at the mention of Nathan's name. "Don't let that fuck control your life. He doesn't deserve that kind of space in your head. Fuck no."

"I know. I'm just trying to weed through it all. And yes, I like Ryland a lot, more than I probably should, but like I said, it's complicated. We coach together, and he has his niece. I don't think he has time for a new relationship."

"Have you talked to him about it, or are all of these assumptions?"

I rub my hand over my forehead. "God, I don't want to talk to you about this because . . . I've done things."

He chuckles. "You can tell me, just . . . don't give me details. We're both adults, and you're my best friend. You should be able to talk to me about anything."

"Yeah, I know." I let out a sigh. "When I interviewed for the teaching coaching job, I didn't think I got it. I saw Ryland in the bar that night, and unfortunately for you, I always thought he was incredibly hot." Bennett winces, lightening the mood. "So figuring I'd never see him again, I took a shot, and well, we had a one-night stand."

"Wow, sis." He sips his drink. "I didn't think you had it in you."

"Neither did I, but Bower was the backbone behind it all." From the mention of Bower's name, Bennett's mouth twitches. "Anyway, fast-forward, I found this nice apartment to stay in, and it turns out he's the landlord. Things got a little wild, and well, we did it a few more times."

"Yuck."

I laugh. "And then we decided that the relationship was getting complicated. We thought it would be best to become friends without benefits, and that was honestly to protect my heart. If I kept fooling around with him, I knew I'd get lost in how I felt. Well, despite trying, I still got lost. He's not in the same space, and that's where we stand now."

"Well . . . he's stupid."

"Come on, Bennett, he has a lot going on."

"Nothing is more important than you."

"His niece?" I raise a brow.

"Maybe her, but other than that, nothing else. And if he fucking liked you, Gabby, he'd find a way to make it work."

"It's easy to say, but he's damaged. There's so much you don't know about him because you just know him as Coach Rowley, but when you peel that back, he's a man with many layers that have shaped and molded him into the person he is today. There are things I even learned about him today that explain so much. Like I said, complicated."

"I get it. I'm sure anyone who comes into our lives will find the same sort of battle. We have some pretty heavy baggage."

"A trunk load, some might say," I joke.

"Yeah, just a bit." He sips from his drink. "Not that you need it, but if you do figure out how to make it work, you have my blessing. I like the thought of you two together."

"You do, do you?"

"Yup. I think you'd balance each other well and, in all honesty, I know the type of guy he is. He looks out for his own, meaning I know he'd take care of you. He'd make sure no one ever hurts you, and as your brother who can't be there to protect you, I like the thought of someone filling that space."

"You know I can take care of myself, right?"

"You have told me that for what feels like my entire life, but guess what, Gabby, you don't have to. You can lean on someone to pull some of the weight, and I think that person very much could be Coach Rowley." *I have a feeling he's right too. Especially after today.* I've never felt so connected to someone before.

I smile sadly at him. "It would be nice, but it won't happen, so please don't hold your breath."

I tightly grip the ball from Bennett in my hands, replaying the videos and pictures Ryland sent me while I was at dinner with Bennett so we could look through them together. Bennett loved the pictures of me eating the stupid hot dog, the one-eyed one especially. He laughed so hard that he nearly cried. Lucky for me, I was able to steal a picture from the server with Bennett, both of us holding the ball together, because that was the only picture missing.

We talked about his hits, his one strikeout, and how he got caught up in the off-speed pitch. It nearly buckled him, it was thrown so well. He marveled at the strength behind his team-mates' bats and how he's determined to put on the same amount of muscle. He then went into how he plans on working on the pitch that buckled him so that doesn't happen again.

It was the best night—something I'm so incredibly grateful for—especially after such an amazing day. And now that my Uber is approaching Hayes's apartment, I have a new set of nerves prickling in the pit of my stomach. Because . . . he was so wonderful today. Ryland not only anticipated my *every* need, but he . . . delighted in making me happy. As if I were part of his world, nothing would have stopped him from looking after me.

His encouragement, his thoughtfulness, his integrity . . . it's like he's made for me. *All the things I like to give others.* A support system I never believed I could or would have.

He was a rock.

He helped me through every step of this process that normally I would've had to do alone. I had him as a guide, as a photographer, as a mental release. And all these feelings throughout the day that have been building up are now coming to a crashing halt because I want to thank him. I want to show him how much I appreciate him, and I know that how I want to portray that gratitude is not something we do anymore.

Therefore, I'm a bottled-up block of tension.

The Uber pulls up to the address, and I know it's the place because Ryland sent me pictures of the entrance and told me exactly what to do.

I thank the driver, who tells me to have a good night, then head into the apartment building and right to the elevator. It takes a few seconds, but as I travel up to the floor, I tell myself over and over again that I'm going to stay calm. I'm going to be cool, and I'm going to keep my distance but be grateful.

And we're not going to think about that kiss we shared after Bennett's first hit.

Not even a little.

When I reach the floor, I follow Ryland's directions and then knock on the door. He opens it almost immediately, surprising me as he stands there in a pair of athletic shorts, and that's it.

Dear God.

I don't have the strength for this.

I tell my eyes to look at his face, but hell is it hard to tear my gaze from his massive chest and the divots and contours that make up his sculpted body.

"You made it," he says, breaking the silence thankfully. "Was it hard to find?"

"No, you made it easy. Thank you."

"You're welcome." He holds the door open wider. "Come in. I have your overnight bag in the bathroom so you can get ready for bed. I'm sure you're exhausted."

Actually, I'm feeling a lot more awake all of a sudden.

"Thank you," I say softly as I shuffle into the apartment. I take my shoes off at the entryway and take in the decently sized apartment. It's typical, nothing too fancy about it. Ryland told me it's a simple place that Hayes stays in when he has to come into the city for meetings or to record.

The kitchen and the living room are all one big room with large windows overlooking the city. There's a tiny couch that . . . has blankets and a pillow on it.

He must see me looking at it because he says, "Oh, that's for me."

"That?" I ask, pointing at the couch. "You think you're going to sleep on that?"

"Yeah, what's the problem?"

302

"Ryland, that thing is barely big enough for your left leg."

He chuckles and shuts the door, locking it behind me. "It's fine."

"It really isn't. I can sleep on it. I'm much smaller than you."

"You're not sleeping on that. The bedroom is yours." He gestures to the bedroom to the left with the large king-sized bed.

"Uh, why do I get the room and you get the couch?"

"Because that's the gentlemanly thing to do."

"Stop it," I say as I walk into the room and grab my bag. "The living room is fine for me."

He stops me, taking my bag from me. "It's not."

"Ryland—"

"You're not sleeping on the couch," he says sternly. "So drop it."

Shocked by his tone, I step back, only to watch the regret fall over his face.

"I'm sorry, I didn't mean for that to be so harsh," he says. "Just let me be the nice guy here, okay? I don't want you sleeping on the couch. It's uncomfortable, it's short, and it's not a place you should be sleeping."

"Then why do you have to sleep there?"

"Because I'm used to sleeping like shit," he answers without even thinking about it.

I tilt my head to the side and say, "What do you mean by that?"

"Nothing we need to get into."

"No, tell me," I say, concern building up inside me.

He looks to the side, clearly uncomfortable, but to my surprise, he says, "I slept on the couch in Cassidy's house for months on end, even after she passed. Sleep has never been a top priority. Comfortable sleep, it's something I'm not used to. So yeah, I sleep like shit, and I'm fine with it."

"Maybe you don't have to sleep like shit." I reach out and take his hand, pulling him toward the bedroom.

"Gabby, I'm not—"

"We can share the bed, Ryland. It's big enough."

"It's really okay, Gabby."

I shake my head. "It's not. Either you share the bed with me or I sleep on the floor."

His brow questions me. "You're really going to play it like that?"

"Yeah, I am," I say with finality. I flip the game ball in my hand to him, then take off with my bag to the bathroom where I get ready for bed. I take a very quick shower. I don't bother washing my hair since I did last night and opt for some dry shampoo for it to soak up the oils overnight, and then brush my teeth and go to the bathroom. I slip on Ryland's shirt that I packed for myself—it's the most comfortable shirt I've ever put on—and then turn off the light and head into the bedroom with my charger and phone in hand. Ryland's on one end of the bed, staring up at the ceiling with his hands behind his head and the sheets only up to his waist, making him look all kinds of yummy.

*Keep yourself together, Gabby.*

Seeing me enter the room, he tilts his head to the side. "I packed the ball carefully into a plastic ball holder. We can get you a glass one, but it's all I could find when I saw that he gave it to you."

"You got a ball case?" I ask, shocked and touched.

"Yeah, I didn't want it to get damaged. That's an important ball. Like I said, we can find you a better case later on, one with UV protection, but this will do for now."

"Ryland, that was very thoughtful. Thank you."

He smiles. "No big deal."

Once my phone's charging, I take a seat on the bed, facing him and tucking my legs to the side.

"It is a big deal. I can't tell you how thankful I am for everything you did for me today."

"Seriously, you don't have to keep thanking me. I was happy to be a part of it all."

God, I want to touch him, reach out to him, let him know just how grateful I am, but I don't want to startle him, make him recoil, and give me the lecture on friends with no benefits. I don't think I could survive it tonight.

"Well, I'm glad that you were."

To my surprise, he holds his arms out. "Come here."

*Uh, don't mind if I do.*

I lie down on the bed, enjoying how his fresh soapy scent seeps into my senses as he gives me a warm, gentle hug.

"Glad you had a great day."

When I let go, he releases me as well, letting his palm travel down my back as he slowly removes his hand. I lift just enough to look him in the eyes, and I can feel the energy between us zapping.

The room shrinking.

The sparks flying.

But I know where this leads every time.

It leads to mind-blowing sex, with a conversation afterward about how we can't do this again.

And I don't think my heart can take it one more time.

So reluctantly, I disengage from the energy flowing between us, and I move to my side of the bed.

"Thanks again for finding us this place," I say as I turn away from him and tuck my head against one of the softest pillows I've ever touched.

"Not a problem." He moves in behind me, but not close so he's touching, just enough to have my skin hyperaware that if he reached out, he could pull me in close to him.

I wet my lips and squeeze my eyes shut as I try to relax my body and find a place of Zen.

"How was your dinner with Bennett?"

"Uh, it was so good. It feels like ages since we've caught up face to face. I've missed him." The bed dips as he adjusts behind me.

"Did you tell him about the foul pole incident?"

I chuckle and turn to my back. *He's really close.* Only inches away. *Keep it together, Gabby.* "I did. He was mad at first because I was stupid for doing it by myself."

"Thank you."

"But then he laughed at the image of me sliding down the pole, clinging on for dear life."

"I'm sad I missed that part since I was blinded by paint." He plucks a piece of hair off my face and tucks it behind my ear.

"Like I said before, if you didn't put it on the list, it never would have happened."

"And like I said, I didn't actually think you'd complete the list."

"Well, look who learned their lesson."

"Yeah, I guess so," he says in a light tone. And then, from under the sheets, he plucks at my shirt. "I see that you're wearing my shirt. I assumed I'd be getting it back."

"Ooo, that's embarrassing for you, as you assumed wrong."

He chuckles as his hand slides over my hip, causing goose-bumps all over my body. "I might just have to steal it back."

"If you want it, you're going to have to tear it off my body."

His fingers slide along the hem, and I know he's going to crack me. I can feel it already as a dull throb starts pulsing between my legs. I'm already aroused. The type of arousal that's never satisfied unless fully taken care of.

"Don't tempt me." He tugs on the hem of the shirt and then slightly slides it up my hip to where, lo and behold, I'm not wearing underwear. Why? Because I didn't account for wearing a pair to bed.

He must notice because I can feel his body grow tense as his fingertips dance across my bare hipbone.

"Gabby," he says softly.

"Yeah?" I ask, looking at him.

"I . . . I need to talk to you."

And here we go.

The friends-without-benefits spiel, but this time, I didn't even get to enjoy the sex beforehand. Now just the lecture. This is what my life has come to, and it's entirely too depressing.

I turn toward him now and say, "It's okay, Ryland, you don't have to say anything. I know, close quarters and all. I wasn't trying to entice you or anything like that with the no underwear. I just forgot, I swear."

His brow comes together. "That's not what I want to talk about."

I pat his chest, his strong, thick, corded chest. "I know, friends without benefits. The kiss today was a spur-of-the-moment thing, and I'm sorry. I know we really haven't kissed since, wow, since a long time. I guess we don't kiss. We just fuck, now that I think about it, and that was intimate. It was just something that happened, and I'm sorry."

"Gabby—"

"Won't happen again. That's why I said I'd sleep on the couch. I know your boundaries, and we can't keep going around in circles. So if you want me to, I'll just go out to the couch—"

Before I can attempt to move, his hand moves around my waist and down to my ass where he cups it and pulls me in closer to his chest.

"Oh," I say in surprise. "What—"

"Can you just be quiet for a second?" he says as his hand travels up my back, taking my shirt with him.

"Umm, sure," I say.

He lets out a determined breath, then looks into my eyes. "I need to talk to you because I have to tell you something that I've been thinking about, something I've been wrestling with."

"What is it?" I press my hand to his chest again, this time in a comforting way.

His hand travels over to my side, right to my rib cage, the shirt practically covering nothing of me at this point as I lie here, nearly exposed to him.

"I . . . I . . ." He pauses again, and whatever he has to say, he's nervous about it, so I rub my thumb over his trimmed chest hair. The gentle touch causes him to lock eyes with me. After a few seconds, he finally says, "I can't stop thinking about you, Gabby."

Okay, I was not expecting that.

"It's all the goddamn time," he continues. "In the morning

when I'm getting Mac ready for school, while I'm in the classroom trying to teach, out on the field, at home making dinner,
when I'm putting Mac to sleep, when I'm waiting to hear you
come in to use the shower. It's all the fucking time, and it's
plaguing me."

"Oh," I say softly.

"And I told myself not to get distracted, not to get lost in your
eyes whenever you're around, but fuck, I can't." His grip on me
grows tighter. "I can't, Gabby."

"I'm sorry. I'm trying, Ryland. I really am. I'm trying to put
the distance there—"

"I don't want the distance," he says, snapping my attention
back to his eyes.

"Y-you don't?"

"No. I don't." He moves in closer and pushes me to my back.
He drags my shirt up and over my head, leaving me bare to him
as his large body hovers over mine. "I don't want the separation.
I want this closeness. *Us*. Not distance. And I swore I'd wait to
say something. I told myself *not today*, so I'm sorry for being a
selfish prick, but I want this. I want you. I want to try to be the
kind of man you deserve."

My mind swirls as I attempt to understand what he's saying
and where this is all coming from.

"I . . . I'm confused. I thought you didn't want a
relationship."

"So did I," he says softly. "But I can't deny my feelings for
you, Gabby. They're too fucking strong. So I can either continue
to battle them and get eaten alive from the inside every goddamn
time I see you or I can do something about it. I'm choosing to do
something about it." He cups my cheek and strokes my skin with
his thumb. "Will you let me?"

"Let you try?"

He nods. "Let me try to be the man you deserve?"

Doesn't he realize he's already that man? He's everything I've
been looking for, and the only thing that's currently holding me

back is the uncertainty in his eyes. Almost like he's scared, fearful of what's to come.

"I . . . I don't want to get hurt, Ryland. I know this isn't something you wanted, and I don't want to be the guinea pig, the one you test it out on."

His thumb continues to rub my cheek. "You're not the guinea pig, Gabby. I'd never do that to you. If I was a stronger man, I wouldn't even approach you about this. I'd bottle it up and keep it to myself, sticking to my convictions." He shakes his head. "But I fucking can't. Every time I look into your eyes, a combination of the dark and light parts of the ocean, I get lost. I feel overcome by something more powerful than I ever thought possible, and all I want to do is be near you, hold you, and cherish you. I've attempted to stay away, but it's not working. So if you'll have me, if you'll forgive me for being selfish, for putting myself first, I ask if you'd give me a chance? If you'll be my girl?"

How on earth could I possibly say no to that?

I've been developing feelings for this man for weeks. He certainly made me come out of this fog of not wanting to be in a relationship. He showed me the kindness a man can give. He displayed love for his family, for his niece. He's anything but selfish, and I know I'd never be able to deny myself of him if he gave me the opportunity to take what I want.

So on a shaky breath, I loop my hand behind his neck and pull him down, where I lightly press my lips to his. He sighs into the touch, melts against my body, and then molds our mouths together, deepening the kiss. *Fuck, I'd forgotten how unbelievable his kisses are.*

"Fuck," he whispers, peppering my jaw with kisses. "Tell me this is real. Tell me you said yes."

"It's real," I say as he cups my breast. I wrap my leg around his leg, pulling his brief-covered pelvis close to mine.

His mouth finds mine again, and this time, he parts my lips, and his tongue dances across my tongue, tangling and mixing, causing a swirl of excitement to pass through me. His kisses level up the intensity, bringing it from somber to excited in seconds where I'm clawing at him and pushing his briefs down with my foot. His cock springs against my leg, and I'm enamored with the feeling of how hard he is already.

He helps me take off his briefs and throws them to the side before bringing all the attention back to my mouth. I can't remember kissing him this much, at least not as much as that one night with him.

"I fucking love your mouth. You drug me," he says before pressing his tongue against mine again. His fingers play with my nipple at the same time, all the while he slowly pulses his cock against my leg.

And I love it.

I love it so much.

"You're so hard," I say as he kisses my neck. "I want you inside me."

"We'll get there."

"No . . . now," I say, pushing his chest so he's on his back.

When I glance at him, a sly smile passes over his lips, making me want that mouth all over again.

I slide on top of his body, his arms encircling me as I capture his mouth. My hands hold his face so I can relish in his kisses and explore every inch of them. His hands fall to my ass, where he cups me and slowly rocks me against his erection.

The movement is simple, but for some reason, it feels more intimate, naughtier than anything else we've ever done. *Erotic.*

While our mouths explore, he spreads my legs over him, then sinks his finger inside me.

I pull away and exhale as I stare down at him, but he doesn't give me much time. He captures my lips again, keeping us locked together with his other hand on the back of my head.

Slowly, he works his fingers in and out of me as I rock my pelvis over him, rubbing up against him, my arousal spreading over the lower half of his stomach, the friction creating a warm, billowing emotion in me, the early starts of my orgasm.

"Inside me," I say.

"I am inside you."

"Your cock, Ryland. I want your cock."

He smiles against my lips, then releases my head, allowing me to push up. I sit up on my knees and grab his length, giving him a few pumps as he stares at me, one hand behind his head now, looking all kinds of happy and relaxed as he sucks his fingers past his lips.

The fingers that were just inside me.

"You going to ride me?"

"I'm going to use you." I turn away from him, straddle his lap, then position him at my entrance.

"Fuck, yes," he says just as I sink down on top of him, riding him backward, his cock rubbing against me in a different way that has every nerve ending on fire.

"Jesus," I whisper as I place my hands on his shins and start moving my hips, feeling his length all the way to my freaking stomach as I bounce on top of him.

"Take this cock. Fuck it," he says, sending a thrill up my spine.

Yes, this . . . this position's everything.

With his girth and his length, this is what I need.

"Ryland, I . . . fuck, I'm going to come fast."

"Good, squeeze my cock, baby."

His hands find my ass as I rock over him, and with one spank to my sensitive skin, my orgasm rips through me, surprising me in the best way ever. I ride him, rocking over and over, taking every ounce of pleasure I can get while I let the best feeling ever float through my body.

"God, yes," I say as my hips slow down, only to be flipped off him and to my back. I look up as Ryland hovers over me, cock in hand, pumping feverishly.

"Squeeze those tits together so I can come all over your perfect nipples." I bring my breasts together for him, then watch as this extraordinary man pleasures himself over me.

The ripple in his chest.

The flex in his forearms.

The strain in his neck.

The grip of his large hands over his length.

So erotic.

So fucking delicious.

"Ahhhh fuck," he calls out just before he starts coming on my breasts, his hand moving toward the tip of his cock where he pulses, squeezing out his orgasm until he's completely sated and moves down on the bed next to me. "Jesus Christ," he says.

We both lie there, staring up at the ceiling. His hand finds mine, and he links our fingers together. He kisses my knuckles before getting off the bed and moving around it.

He scoops me up and walks us both to the bathroom, where he turns on the shower. I eye him, and he laughs. "No funny business. Just want to clean you."

And then his mouth captures mine again, our kisses so much deeper and more meaningful than any kiss I've ever experienced in my life. *Is this what it feels like to be with the right person?*

Is this what it feels like to start the path to . . . to loving someone?

# Chapter Twenty-Five

## RYLAND

"You comfortable?" I ask Gabby as she settles against my chest, her leg draped over mine, her bare body plastered against my side.

"Very comfortable, are you? Because I can still go sleep on the couch."

"Funny," I say as I drag my hand through her hair, loving how the soft strands filter through my fingers.

"Are you sure? Because I can really give you space." She starts to get up, and I close my arm around her, keeping her where she is and making her giggle.

"Don't fucking go anywhere."

Her fingers dance across my chest. "Just what I like to hear." She lifts up and presses a kiss to my jaw, the gesture making me feel so goddamn warm inside that I honestly don't know what to do with the sensation.

I had one long-term relationship with a girl named Samantha. I thought she was the one who was supposed to be with me until I found out she got pregnant with someone else's baby. From there, I haven't bothered with a relationship or gotten close to a woman. I've kept my distance and fucked to fulfill a need, but that's been the extent of it.

With Gabby, my life feels like it's been flipped upside down, but in the best way possible. I kiss the top of her head and continue to sift my fingers through her hair. "I'm sorry for everything I put you through these past few weeks as I tried to figure my shit out."

"You don't need to apologize. I get it, Ryland. I really do. I think I was sifting through some past baggage as well."

"You were?" I ask, surprised to hear that. "What kind of baggage . . . did someone . . . did someone hurt you?"

"Yeah." She pauses for a moment, the mood shifting from playful to serious. "His name was Nathan, and for a while there, I thought he was the one thing that I needed in my life to make me forget about everything negative that happened to me in the past. And sure, he was great for a while until he wasn't."

"What do you mean, he wasn't?" I ask, growing tense but trying not to show my anger at the thought of anyone hurting her.

"The last thing I want to talk about right now is my ex," she says, but even I can hear how damaged she sounds.

"What happened?" I ask, gearing up for something I'm sure I'm not going to like. "Did he hurt you? Touch you?"

"Once," she says softly.

And all it takes is that one singular word to set off a combustible war inside my chest. He fucking touched her? He hurt her? He better hope he never runs into me because guaranteed, it won't end well for him.

Keeping my composure the best I can, I say, "How?"

She sits up on her elbow to look me in the eyes. "I'm okay now."

"I know you are." I press my hand to her cheek. "You're so strong, Gabby. But I want to know what he did to you. I need to know."

With her hand still on my chest, she works her jaw to the side. "He was going through a rough time, not that that's an excuse, but when he was down about his self-worth, he took that out on the people close to him. Me being that person. He was mean. He couldn't stand anyone being happy around him. Bennett had a good game, and I came back home—we were living together at the time—and was excited to tell Nathan about it." My muscles grow tenser by the second as she continues her story. "I tried to talk to him, but he wouldn't listen, and I knew not to push him to talk, so I went to the kitchen where I grew upset because I could feel him slipping away. He'd been emotionally abusive up to that point, and I thought that maybe there was a chance I could help him, if only he would let me."

"They won't accept help unless they actually want it," I say, knowing damn well the pattern from my dad.

"I found that out quickly when he came into the kitchen with an empty bottle of whiskey in his hand, wobbling from side to side." She takes a second. I can see the pain in her eyes, so I smooth my hand over her back, letting her know that I'm here for her. "He asked me where his whiskey was, and I told him that he drank it all. He called me a liar and said I was hiding it from him. He threw the empty bottle and nailed me in the head, sending me down to the floor, with the bottle crashing around me."

"The fuck?" I say, sitting up now. "Where?" I search her head, and as she pulls her hair back in the moonlit room, I can see the faint mark of a scar. "Jesus Christ." I scoop her up into my arms, cradling her in my lap, so much anger vibrating through me that I'm losing control of all rational thought. "I'm so sorry, Gabby. Fuck . . . I'm sorry."

"Don't apologize for him," she says, pulling back to look me in the eyes, but I lean in and kiss her scar, so many emotions rolling through me, making me so goddamn sick because the thought of her, lying there on her kitchen floor, bleeding from her head . . . "Ryland." She pats my chest. "I need you to calm down. I can feel you growing really tense. Your heart is beating a mile a minute."

"Sorry," I say as I hold her tight. "The thought of you getting hurt . . . it doesn't sit well with me." I let out a shaky breath. "What happened after that?"

"I blacked out and suffered a concussion. Bennett was the one who found me—"

"Found you? You mean that fucker just left you there to bleed?"

"Yes. He was scared—not that I'm making an excuse for him because what he did was wrong—but he didn't know what to do, so he sent a text to Bennett that I needed help. Bennett rushed over from his friend's house, and that's where he found me. Luckily, Nathan was gone, or else I think Bennett would have lost his mind, which could have affected his entire baseball career. I was stitched up in a few places because of the glass, and that next day, Bennett and his friends helped us move out."

"Where did you go?"

"I lived in my car for about a week or so. Bennett stayed with a friend, and then I was able to find a very cheap place for a bit."

"Jesus Christ." I pull on my hair, unable to comprehend how unfair her life has been, but look at her now. Look how far she's come. It's, it's fucking special. She's special. She's unlike anyone I've ever met, and to see her thriving, to see her and Bennett thriving, it's beautiful. And to think I almost shut an important door to her career in her face. It makes me livid. *I* almost contributed to more pain in her life out of self-preservation. *I am so weak.* "You are so goddamn strong, Gabby. Look what you've been able to accomplish, what you've done with your life. You should be proud."

"I am," she says softly, her fingers dragging over my collarbone. "I should say the same thing about you." I start to shake my head, but she stops me. "You've fought adversity. You've fought out of the depths of your childhood and the demons that come with it."

"I haven't. Those demons still control me."

"Do they?" she asks. "Because it seems like you're opening your heart to me right now. It seems like you're giving us a chance, something you swore you wouldn't do. Instead of being the same abusive man your father was, you're the type of man who fights against such behavior."

"Because it's fucking wrong," I say, my voice strong. "No one should ever be tied at the hands of abuse, ever." I cup her cheek. "And I'm so fucking sorry you had to experience it."

"I'm sorry you had to as well." She presses her forehead against mine as her hand slips behind my neck. Her nose rubs against mine, her lips barely graze my mouth, and right as my grip on her grows tighter, she kisses me.

It's not a frantic kiss, nor is it a deep kiss like earlier. This is gentle, soothing . . . loving.

I slowly lower her to the mattress and move on top of her. She spreads her legs for me, creating room for my large body, then she lightly strokes my length, making me grow in her palm.

I run the tip of my finger over her slit, and then along her clit. She moans into my mouth as she grows wet around my finger. It's so fucking addicting, seeing how easily I can turn this woman on. By a touch, a kiss, she's so goddamn ready for me.

Hell, I'm ready for her too as she brings me to her entrance and encourages me to push in. Keeping my mouth on hers, letting our tongues dance together, I slowly enter her, one inch at a time, the feel of her tightening around me electrifying.

I push, loving her reaction to the way I fill her until I bottom out, unable to go any farther.

That's when I lift away from her mouth to look her in the eyes. Arms on either side of her shoulders, I glance down at our connection and watch as I pulse into her, fascinated with the way her stomach contracts with each thrust and the sweet sounds of her moans every time I hit her to the hilt.

"I love how you feel inside me," she says, pulling my attention back to her beautiful face.

"You're perfect." I kiss her and sweat breaks out over my back from the feel of being inside her. It's so damn good. So damn addicting. "You're strong." I pulse into her a touch harder. "You're beautiful." She wraps one leg around my waist, adjusting the angle and causing her chest to rise when I pulse inside her again. "You're everything . . . fucking . . . everything."

I press down on her lower stomach, right above our connection, and her eyes fly open, the weight of my palm adding to the sensations rocking through her.

"Fuck, don't . . . don't stop that."

I keep my hand where it is and I pick up my pace, creating such intense friction that my orgasm starts to build at the base of my spine. A few more strokes will do it.

"I want to come inside you."

Her teeth pull on her bottom lip before she says, "Fill me with your cum, Ryland."

"Jesus Christ." I grip the sheets beneath my hand for better leverage and start pistoning in and out of her, keeping her steady with my hand and owning this moment, showing her I'm in charge, but I'll take care of her. I'll protect her. I *will* be the man she needs.

"Yes, Ryland. Fuck, right there. Yes."

I push harder, faster, loving her sweet sounds, rocking us up until we hit the headboard. She props her hand against it, keeping her head from banging into it as my pace turns frantic, my orgasm right there, tingling through my arms just as I feel her start to tighten around me.

"Yes, yes, yes, Ryland. Fuck, yes!" she yells. Her mouth falls open, her eyes widen, and then she starts coming all over my cock. I continue to rock into her, hitting her in that sweet spot and making her orgasm last, eating up every second of her convulsing around me until my cock swells, I still, and I come so fucking hard into her, my cum filling her.

"Fucking hell," I say as I lower my forehead to hers. My nose rubs against hers, then our lips pass over each other. I kiss her once. Twice. And then part her lips so our tongues can meet for a few moments before pulling away, kissing her on the nose and then on the forehead. "You okay?"

She nods as she sucks in a sharp breath. When her gorgeous eyes meet mine, she says, "I'm so perfect, Ryland. So perfect."

I glance at my phone. It's six in the morning, and Gabby is passed out next to me, clinging to my chest. I have my arm around her, keeping her close, the same position we were in when we finally fell asleep. If I'm honest, last night was the hardest I've ever slept.

Ever.

In my entire life.

There was no tossing and turning, no nightmares, no waking up and staring at the ceiling as my mind raced. I was content, happy, and at peace. I only woke up because I heard my phone beep with a text from Aubree. Out of fear that something is going on with Mac, I check it.

*Aubree: How was last night? Please tell me you talked with her.*

I glance down at Gabby, still asleep, and text Aubree back.

*Ryland: Not to get too detailed, but she's sleeping on my chest right now. Let's leave it at that.*

*Aubree: You took the leap?*

*Ryland: I did.*

*Aubree: Wow, Ryland. I'm so proud of you. That's huge. How do you feel?*

*Ryland: Oddly at peace.*

I stare down at Gabby, her sweet face buried into my chest, looking like she is in a tranquil state of contentment. I could stay like this all goddamn day. I know I can't because I have responsibilities, but hell, it would be amazing just to have a day like this, a day of me and her, naked, in bed with not a worry tugging us away from each other.

*Aubree: This makes me so happy. I think you two are great together. Hattie's going to lose her mind. Also, if you get married before her, she'll never forgive you.*

*Ryland: Whoa, slow down. We're just taking this one step at a time. Marriage is not a thing at the moment.*

*Aubree: I'm only teasing. Take as much time as you need because the last thing you want to do is rush and mess this up. Make sure you're comfort-*

*able with every step you take. You know Wyatt and I will be here for any dates you might want to go on. We're in this together.*

**Ryland:** *Thank you. I really appreciate it.*

**Aubree:** *Happy for you. Now, can I tell Hattie?*

**Ryland:** *Yes, let her get the squealing out with you so when she sees me she's not as hyper.*

**Aubree:** *Wishful thinking, big brother.*

**Ryland:** *Yeah, I know.*

I set my phone back down on the nightstand and let out a deep breath as I close my eyes, letting my mind drift away and back to sleep because if anything, at least I can have this morning to be lazy. I can be responsible after that, but this morning, this is for us.

---

*Jesus Christ, that feels good.*

*That's it, baby, right there.*

*Fucking suck me hard.*

I groan. A hand slides up my stomach and then back down, right to my cock where it starts pumping . . . and pumping . . . and . . .

My eyes fall open, and I glance down between my legs, where Gabby grips my cock, jacking me off as her tongue swipes along my balls.

"Fuuuuuuuck," I groan, my head falling back to the pillow. "Gabby . . . Christ."

Her lips find my balls, kissing along them until she opens her mouth and pulls them in.

"Fuck!" I yell as I sit on my elbows and spread my legs wider for her. "Yes, baby, suck on them. Fuck, that's it, such a dirty fucking mouth." I glance at my cock and the way she's pumping it, her grip so goddamn tight, pre-cum already on the tip. "That's it. Keep going, baby. Fuck, I'm getting close."

Her tongue slides up the seam to the root of my cock, and then all the way to the tip right before she pulls me into her mouth, where she swirls her tongue around the tip for a few moments before taking me all the way back to her throat and swallowing. The entire time, her eyes are on me.

"Yes, right there. Right fucking there." I lace my hand behind her head and gently move her forward, hearing the sound of her gagging and then letting her catch a breath. "Gag on me, baby." She dips back again and lets me hit the back of her throat twice in a row before gagging and pulling away for a breath. "Jesus, so close, so fucking close."

Her hand moves under my balls and then behind them, where she presses on my perineum. And that's all it takes. My balls tighten, my cock swells, and I'm busting all over her goddamn tongue.

"Motherfucker," I yell as I fall to the bed and drape my arm over my eyes. "Jesus, Gabby."

She cleans me up like the goddamn good girl she is and then smooths up my stomach, where she presses kisses to my neck. I wrap my arms around her. "Give me a second, then you can sit on my face."

"I already got off."

I pause and lift my arm to look at her. "Excuse me?"

"When you were sleeping, I woke up from a sex dream I had of us. I was far too horny, and well, I got off."

"Without me?" I sit up now, causing her to chuckle.

"No, not without you. You were hard as a stone, so I watched your cock twitch as I got off. Then I got you off." She shrugs as if it's no big deal.

But it's a big deal to me.

"What hand did you use?"

"What do you mean?" she asks.

"What hand did you use to make yourself come?"

She holds up her right, and I bring it right to my mouth where I can taste her. When I pull it away, I shake my head and say, "Unacceptable, you wake me, you find me, you wait for me if you're horny. You deprived me of seeing you unravel."

Her hand smooths over my chest, her lips turned up at the

sides. "I'm sorry, I didn't know you were going to be so possessive."

"You didn't know?" I raise my brow. "Uh, I'm pretty sure the way I spanked you last night until you came on my cock shows how possessive I am."

"No, that shows that you like to spank."

"Gabby," I say sternly.

"What?" she asks with a devilish smile.

"Not fucking again. You need to get off, you find my tongue, my dick, my fingers, anything. I have the right to pleasure you now. Don't take that away from me."

She rolls her eyes but kisses my chest. "Fine, but just so you know, I found it so incredibly hot, and I came really fast. Like there was probably no chance to even wake you up."

"Moan louder next time."

She chuckles. "Okay." And then, to my displeasure, she hops out of bed.

"Where are you going?"

"I ordered breakfast for us." She slips my shirt on over her head and moves to the entryway.

Groaning because I want to spend longer snuggling—something I never thought I'd want—I check my phone for messages and see it's just past eight now. After breakfast, we need to head back so I can spend some time with Mac.

I slip on my shorts and make my way into the kitchen, where Gabby's removing to-go boxes from a bag. I walk up behind her, scratching my chest. "What did you get?"

"Pancakes of course," she answers while I kiss her neck. "None of that. We need to replenish, and I'm sure you need to get back to MacKenzie."

"I do." I sigh as my hands fall to her waist. "How about we do this? I eat breakfast off you, so we have fun *and* replenish."

"Why do you think I sucked your balls into my mouth?"

Jesus, she's just going to say it like that?

"Uh, why?"

"So that you could have fun and then replenish. Now if

you're going to be greedy, then I'll remember that for next time and won't suck your balls into my mouth."

"Christ, we can't have that," I say as I float my hand under her shirt to her bare stomach.

"Ryland," she says as she leans against me, and I start playing with her breast. "We can't."

"Mm, I know," I say, working my lips up her neck to behind her ear, loving the way her skin breaks out in goosebumps. "But fuck, just let me taste a little bit. I need a fucking appetizer." I lower my hand and slide my finger over her wet clit. "Gabby." I breathe out heavily. "You can't be this wet and not let me do anything about it."

"Then do something."

She doesn't have to say it twice. I pick her up, place her on the counter, bring her feet up to the edge, and then spread her right before I start lapping her up.

"Oh my God," she says, her hands falling to my head. "I fucking love your mouth. God, you're so good at this. So fucking good."

The encouragement is all I need to flatten my tongue and slowly drag it over her clit, watching her flex and heave above me.

"No teasing. Make it fast. I want it fast." She brings her hands to her breasts, lifting her shirt in the process, and starts playing with her nipples, twisting and tugging on them, making her wetter and wetter.

"I want you coming all over my face," I say as I point my tongue and start making rapid flicks over her clit.

"Oh God, yes, yes . . . right there, oh my God, ahhhhh." Her moan is wild as I move faster, harder, ensuring she feels the vibration of my tongue as I hum against her.

She claws at my head.

Pulls on my hair.

Cries out in ecstasy as she tips over the edge, shaking against me as her orgasm rides through her fast and hard.

I lap her up, enjoying my fucking feast, and when I lift and let her legs relax, I lick my lips. "Thanks for the appetizer, babe. Now feed me."

———

"If you keep looking at me, we're going to get in an accident," Gabby says as she curls into my chest. She's sitting in the middle seat of my truck because the passenger seat was way too fucking far for my liking.

Apparently, once I go in, I'm all in. Something within me has snapped, and my need to keep this woman close, to have my hands on her at all times, is damn near impossible to shake off.

"How do you know I'm looking at you?" I ask.

"I can feel it. Now focus on the road."

I heavily sigh. "I am. You know I wouldn't put you in harm."

"I know," she answers. "But still, focus."

I chuckle and kiss the top of her head. After breakfast, which she made me eat in the living room while she ate at the dining room table, we both took a shower. This, naturally, consisted of me bending her over and fucking her until I felt like I couldn't breathe. After that, I called Mac, told her I was on my way home, and asked her what she wanted to do when I got home.

Play outside.

Push her on the swing.

And build a fort.

I told her all the things we could do.

And now that we're headed home, I feel an ache inside me, knowing that spending time with Gabby is going to be hard, but I missed Mac and I'm excited to see her.

"I need to talk to you about something," Gabby says.

"Why does it sound like it's something bad?" I ask, picking up on her tone of voice.

"No, it's nothing bad, but I do think we need to seriously set some ground rules if we're going to make this work."

"Yeah, you're probably right."

"I want you to go first," she says. "What is your comfort level with Mac? Do you want her to know we're together? Do you want her to be oblivious? Do you want me to keep my distance until we figure out where this is going? That way, she doesn't become attached?"

"Huh," I say, giving it some thought. "I haven't considered your role with her."

"That's okay, you don't have to answer now. I won't be offended if you want me to keep my distance. I understand there are sensitivities to account for, and with Mac losing both of her parents, you might want to play it safe."

"Yeah, maybe. Let me talk with my sisters and see what they say."

"That's totally fair, and like I said, you can take your time on this. I want to be sensitive to the situation."

"I appreciate that."

"That leads me to school and baseball." She lifts off me and takes my hand in hers. "I don't want you to be offended by this, but I'd prefer that we keep things very professional at school and baseball. Meaning no affection whatsoever."

I hate that rule.

I hate that rule tremendously because the thought of locking her classroom door at lunch and spreading her across her desk is very appealing.

"From your silence, I can tell you're not a fan of the rule but let me explain." She squeezes my hand. "I'm new and still trying to prove myself to not just the teaching staff but also the school board and the boys on the team. The last thing I need is for them to find out that I'm seeing the head coach. It just wouldn't look good."

"Yeah." I sigh. "I get that and respect it."

"So can you promise me right now that you can keep your hands and your dirty talking to yourself?"

"Even dirty talking?" I ask. "Come on."

"Ryland, I don't need someone overhearing that you want to fill me with your cum."

I chuckle. "Why not? It's a compliment. There isn't anyone else on this earth who I'd want to fill up with my cum."

From the corner of my eye, I see her clasp her chest as she says, "As honored as I am to know that I'm a vessel for your cum, I don't need other people hearing it."

"Vessel for my cum, huh? Maybe I should change your name to cum vessel in my phone."

"Do that, and this little relationship is over."

I chuckle some more. "Noted. Okay, so no funny business at school or at baseball. I think I can do that. What about texting? Can I at least text you dirty things?"

"If you think you can handle that and receive responses from me without getting turned on, then by all means, text away."

"Hmm, I didn't consider the responses."

"Afraid your cum vessel might turn you on in the middle of school?"

"Jesus." I laugh. "Okay, we're not referring to you as that anymore."

"You started it."

"I know, and I'm ending it." I kiss her knuckles. "Okay, I'll get back to you on the dirty texting. From the way I react to you, I'm going to guess that won't be happening either. So that leaves after school and baseball, and when Mac is in bed. Can I count on you to come to my house?"

"Now *that* you can count on," she says. "I'd also prefer to have a date here and there but want to be respectful of your time with Mac, so don't feel like you need to take me out every week. It's important to me that you put her first, which I know you will, but I need you to know that I'm not going to be that jealous girl who begs for your time. When you can give me your time, I'll take it."

"Thank you," I say, growing serious. "I appreciate the thought you've put into this, making it easy on me."

"I like you, Ryland, a lot," she admits, sending a burst of pride and warmth through my chest. "I know why you didn't want to have a relationship in the first place, so I want to tread carefully, make sure you're comfortable. All I ask is that you're open with me, honest, constantly talking to me about how you feel. I can't have you hiding your feelings on me because that's when things implode."

I nod. "I'm not great at that. I've been taught to repress feelings rather than talk about them. The only reason I can semi talk about them is because Cassidy used to pull it out of me, and now, apparently, Aubree and Hattie. But I can work on it for you . . . and well, for Mac."

"Thank you. Now, one last thing I need to talk to you about."

"Yeah? Just one?" I tease.

"Yes, one. You're not going to like it, though."

"Lay it on me. Maybe I'll surprise you."

"It's about Christian."

"Oh, nope, not going to like it."

She lightly laughs. "I told you."

"What do you have to possibly talk about where he's concerned?"

"You need to be nice to him."

"I am nice to him."

Gabby scoffs. "Oh my God, you are so not nice to him, and he's noticed."

"He's noticed? You mean to tell me that he's talked to you about this? Like he's looking for sympathy?"

"He was not looking for sympathy. It just came up, and he mentioned that you aren't very nice to him."

"Because he's a douche."

"Ryland, he's not a douche. He's really nice actually."

"I'm sure he is," I say, gripping my steering wheel tighter.

"I can see that you're growing angry—"

"Not angry, irritated," I say. "See, sharing my feelings with you. I don't see how mentioning him has anything to do with us."

"It does have something to do with us because he asked me out—"

"He what?"

She sighs and rubs her hand over my thigh. "Deep breaths,

Ryland. I'm telling you this because it's important, so please just listen."

Realizing that I'm acting like a possessive dick, I give her a moment to explain even though whatever she might say about Christian is only going to make me hate him more. "Sorry. Go ahead."

"Thank you," she says while leaning in and placing a kiss on my cheek. I'll admit, the kiss settles me . . . a little. "What I was trying to say is that he noticed there seemed to be something between us."

"And he still asked you out?" There goes that anger, skyrocketing all over again.

"In a way," she says. "He said if nothing was going on, he'd love to take me out. Either way, the asking out doesn't matter because what matters is that he said he was going to give me some space to figure out what I wanted."

"What a gentleman."

"Ryland . . ."

"Sorry." I zip my lips shut.

"The thing is, if I don't go out with him, he'll assume that maybe I decided to give us a chance, but I don't want him knowing about us and then somehow spreading that around the school."

"Okay, so . . . what are you trying to say? If it's that you want to go out with him for a night and then let him down after, that's not going to fly with me."

"How else am I supposed to keep us a secret?"

"Wait." I glance over at her. "Are you serious right now? You were really going to go on a date with him?"

"I don't know."

"Gabby, I'm trying not to be the asshole here, but I can tell you right now, you going out with Christian to keep us a secret is not an option. Not even in the vicinity of an option. Think of another way."

"Then help me."

"Uh, how about just telling him no, not even needing a

reason. No is a full sentence. Period. He doesn't need to know your personal life, nor does he need an explanation."

"That seems so harsh."

"It's not," I say. "It's the truth. It's what I'd tell my sisters to do. Hell, it's what I'd tell Mac. No means no, simple as that. Not a single explanation needed. And if he looks for one, then tell him it's none of his goddamn business."

"Okay," she says softly. "I guess I never really thought about it that way. But you're right."

"I know I'm right." My shoulders relax because Christ, that was a stressful minute. I place my hand on her thigh and rub my thumb over her knee, calming my racing pulse.

"You okay over there?" she asks after a few seconds.

"Barely, fucking giving me a heart attack while I'm driving."

She chuckles and leans into my shoulder again. "I'm sorry."

"It's fine, but Jesus, don't ask if you can date another man ever again. That shit made me nearly drive into another car."

Her infectious laughter easily lightens up the mood.

"Got it. Ryland doesn't want me dating other men. Glad I clarified that."

"Christ . . . me too."

# Chapter Twenty-Six

## GABBY

"Hello, this is Bower, how may I help you?"

"Why do you answer the phone like that? You know it's me," I say as I put my phone on speaker and start to lotion my legs. My shower works, and even though I would have loved to have taken a shower in Ryland's house to spend even more time together, I'm giving him a touch of space and time to get ready for the week ahead.

"I do it because it annoys you, and how am I keeping you on your toes if I'm not annoying you?"

"Maybe just by checking in?"

"Not as fun. Anyway, this is Bower. Who might I be speaking to?"

"You're ridiculous."

She laughs. "Okay, okay, tell me everything about this week-end. I shot Bennett a text congratulating him on his game, and he might have dished a little bit of tea about you, but I will let you tell me, and yes, I am saying this up front because I don't feel like acting surprised and shocked when you do mention what really happened this weekend."

"First of all, the fact that you talk to Bennett, that's danger-ous. I don't like the cross pollination."

"It's for your benefit, so we can keep a close eye on you and make sure you're okay. We've been doing it for years. You'll be fine, suck it up."

"So loving." *Years? How have I not known this? Years . . .* "Second of all, what did he tell you?"

I lotion my arms as Bower says, "Just that there was some-thing brewing between you and the coach and that you said you had feelings but weren't sure how things would go. You left us on a cliffhanger. Now you need to tell us how everything went."

"If I tell you, are you going to tell Bennett?"

"Absolutely," she says, not even pretending to be on my side.

I sigh heavily. "Fine . . . we're seeing each other."

"What?" she yells into the phone. "You're just going to come out with the information like that. You're not going to ease me in? Add some foreplay . . . at least swat at my nipples before you drive it home?"

"Nope, giving it to you hard."

"Well, let me catch my breath for a second. Golly!"

"Golly?" I ask, never in my life hearing my friend say such a thing. It almost feels like a swear word coming out of her mouth.

"Yeah, golly." She clears her throat. "Now that I've adjusted to the girth you just shoved into me, tell me how it happened."

Chuckling, I say, "Well, I got back to the place we were staying at, and there was one bed—"

"Naturally, a romance author's dream place to make the sparks fly. One-bed trope is the epitome of all tropes. Did he pretend he was cold and needed to snuggle? Or were you like . . . *Oh Ryland, I have so much adrenaline, I need you to hold me to calm me down* and then when he held you, he slipped his hand under your shirt and started teasing your tits? Ooof, I love a good swipe of a finger over a breast. Nothing will make me hornier."

"You know . . . you need to stop reading those books."

"Never! Those books give me life."

Shaking my head, I cap off my lotion. "Nothing like that happened, well, sort of nothing. Honestly, it's all a blur."

"So he did swipe the boob."

"Umm, perhaps, it was more of me taking my shirt off and moving over him."

"Dear God in heaven," she whispers. "That sounds fantastic."

"It really was. It was after he confessed how he felt for me and that he couldn't stop thinking about me. Honestly, it was pretty magical. So yeah, we're seeing each other now."

"Well, this is the best news ever. Are you excited? Apprehensive? Nervous? Just so horny that you don't care about the rest of the feelings?"

"Clearly not as horny as you." Bower laughs. "Yes, about being nervous and a little apprehensive. I want to make sure we do this right. He is pretty wary about being in any sort of relationship but is dedicated to making it work with me. But we have to think about his niece and her feelings. I want to be as respectful as possible. So a lot of navigating."

"I get it, still . . . look at you thriving. New job, new place, new beau. I'm proud of you, Gabby."

"It's not a big deal."

"No, it is." Bower grows serious. "This is a huge deal. After Nathan, I honestly didn't think there'd be anyone who could enter your life and help you out of the darkness. What I didn't expect was you helping yourself out of that darkness. You were the one who made the change and that's something to be proud of. And then finding Ryland, who so far seems like a great guy—I wasn't expecting you to open up your heart the way you have toward him."

I sit on my bed and cross my legs. "In all honesty, it was hard not to open up, as I see my pain inside him. Like a mirror, reflecting right back, so I knew that I wouldn't be embarrassed when talking to him about my past, that he wouldn't judge me. I felt very comfortable, which made it easier to open up." I think about the past twenty-four hours and just how comfortable I was.

"I told him about Nathan, and everything that happened with him."

"Please tell me he got all ragey and ready to break wrists."

"Wrists, faces . . . I think he was ready to break all the things."

"We love an overprotective hero. Obsessed." I hear her sigh. "I need to find myself one of those."

"Abel's still single."

"No, I think I'm too much for him. I could already feel the vibe that he'd get annoyed with me but not think it's cute. I need someone who can understand me when I say a one-bed trope is all I need in my life."

"Not sure many would understand."

"Which will make him a unicorn, and I'm willing to wait for a unicorn. Unicorns come glitter. What more does a girl need?"

"Jesus," I mutter as I lie back on my bed. "Remind me why we're friends again?"

"Honestly, I couldn't tell you at this point."

"Figured as much."

———

*Gabby:* Headed to The Almond Store for more of those cookies. Do you want me to grab you anything?

*Ryland:* Is that why you bolted out of practice once it ended?

*Gabby:* That, and I really had to pee.

*Ryland:* And here I thought you were avoiding me.

*Gabby:* Why would you think that?

*Ryland:* You didn't come over last night, didn't say hi to me in the hall today. Barely looked at me during conditioning. You're not playing it cool, Gabby.

*Gabby:* I'm working on it, okay? Sometimes I forget how hot you actually are until I see you, and when I saw you, I got all shy and weird. And yesterday, I didn't come over because I thought you needed the time to reset.

*Ryland:* I'll let you know if I need to reset.

*Gabby:* Okay. Also, if you could stop being so hot, that would be great too.

*Ryland:* I'll try, not making any promises. But back to the cookies, grab one for me and come over tonight when Mac is in bed so we can have a cookie together.

*Gabby:* That I can do.

*Ryland:* And don't wear underwear.

*Gabby:* Ooof, sorry, that's a no can do.

*Ryland:* And why not?

*Gabby:* I got my period today, hence the cookies.

*Ryland:* Maybe I should be the one getting the cookies then.

*Gabby:* I got them, but I wouldn't mind a snuggle when I see you.

*Ryland:* These arms are yours. See you in a bit.

Smile stretched across my face, I get out of my car and head toward The Almond Store, one of my favorite places in town.

When I open the door and the bell rings above me, I'm immediately sucked into the almondy goodness of the fresh, spotlessly clean store. Seriously, it's like a comfort place for me being in here.

I spot Hattie at the counter talking to a woman with red hair, wearing a silky Kaftan, and head toward her.

"Hey, Gabby," Hattie says with a wave of her hand.

"Ooo, Gabby," the redhead says. "You must be the new teacher in town."

"Um, yes." I wave shyly. "Hi."

The lady holds her hand out. "I'm Ethel, the owner of Five Six Seven Eight."

"Oh wow, it's so nice to meet you." I take her hand and give it a gentle shake. "I love your inn. I stayed there when I came here for my interview. It's so charming, and one of the best sleeps I've ever had." She doesn't need to know it's because I slept in a pair of arms that I can't wait to get to later tonight.

"Oh, you've stayed there? How lovely. Did you enjoy the breakfast in the morning?"

"Yes, the fluffiest eggs I've ever had."

She leans in and says, "The chef puts cottage cheese in them."

"Ooo, really? It's a terrific touch."

"I'll give my compliments to the chef." She winks. "How are you liking Almond Bay?"

"I absolutely love it," I say, leaning gently against the counter. There's nothing like some small-town talk to make this *Gilmore Girls*-like dream even more of a reality. I got the grump, the cute town, and now the friendly chatter.

"Here for some cookies?" Hattie asks.

"Half a dozen please."

"On it."

I turn my attention back to Ethel. "My brother, Bennett, went to school here the last few years of high school, but we lived on the outskirts, so being able to actually live in Almond Bay is truly a dream. I love everything about this town."

"It is a great place to call home," Ethel says. "Now, Bennett, is that Bennett Brinkman?"

"Yes," I say brightly.

"Did I hear that he had his first major league start this past weekend?"

Wow, news really does travel fast.

"He did," I say. "I went to the game. He's worked so hard to get there and seeing him on the big stage was everything I could have hoped for."

"That is so wonderful. Not to be nosy, but can I assume your parents are no longer with us?"

Not to be nosy? Something tells me she is the definition of nosy.

"They're no longer in the picture. Just me and Bennett at this point."

"Well, what an accomplishment for you two. You must be over the moon."

"We are. Thank you."

"The whole town is rooting for him. Maybe after the season,

we can have a party for our very own baseball star here. I love throwing parties and events for the town."

"That she does," Hattie says as she sets the bag of cookies on the counter. "You should have seen what she did for Aubree's proposal."

"You helped with it?" I ask Ethel.

"Oh yes, dear." She leans her elbow against the counter. "It was quite the spectacle. We had dancers and a band, and I sang while Rodney drove his train around. Unlike anything you've ever seen."

"Wow, I'll have to ask Aubree to see pictures."

"There are plenty," Ethel says, pushing off from the counter. "Well, I best be getting back to the inn. I'm supposed to meet the Peach Society for a meeting about this year's holiday festivities. I'll be sure to talk to them about a homecoming for our very own Bennett Brinkman." She presses her hand to my arm. "Take care, dears." And then she walks off, the bell above the door announcing her departure.

Hattie looks at me when she's gone and says, "If you want to keep anything a secret in this town, keep it away from her."

I chuckle. "I could sense that."

"Love the lady, but man, does she go fishing for information."

"Thanks for playing it cool then about Ryland and me. I mean . . . you didn't say anything, right?"

"God no, Ryland would murder me. I won't be the one who lets that cat out of the bag." She leans in and whispers, "But I will say I'm so freaking giddy about you and him. Thank you for giving him a chance. I love seeing my brother happy. He deserves it."

That warms my heart because the bond Ryland has with his sisters is the same kind of bond I have with Bennett—it's one of the many things I like about him.

"No need to thank me." I can't hold back my smile. "I really like the man, and I'm just glad he's giving me a chance. I know how difficult it was for him to open up."

"You have no idea, but I won't get into that because it's his business to tell, not mine. I'm just very happy for the both of you, and trust me when I say your secret is safe with me."

Just then, the door opens, and a girl in overalls and a straw hat walks in, carrying a wooden box full of jars.

"Echo," Hattie says. "Have you come with the honey?"

"I have," the girl says as she walks up to the counter and places the box down. She turns to me and smiles. "Hi, I'm Echo. I work with Aubree over at Rowley Farm. You must be Gabby."

I take her hand and shake it as I glance at Hattie. How on earth does this girl know me?

Hattie waves off my questioning brow. "Everyone is going to know who you are at this point."

I laugh. "Good to know. Yes, I'm Gabby. Nice to meet you, Echo."

"I heard we're going to have a girls' night soon. Is that true?" Echo asks.

"That's what I'm planning," Hattie says. "Maybe Friday next week. I was thinking about having everyone over to the house, kicking Hayes out, and then complaining to all of you about how my super-hot, beautifully talented, and sweet boyfriend hasn't proposed yet."

"What did he say? Keep mentioning it, and he'll prolong the wait?" Echo says in a lecturing tone.

"He can't hear me now."

"How do you know? Maybe he bugged the place," Echo challenges.

Hattie looks around the store, eyeing the corners, and then dips her head under the counter to give a good look. "Well, if he did bug the place, then he's going to have a rude awakening when I find the microphone. No sex for a month." She leans toward the counter. "You hear that, Hayes? No sex."

I let out a low rumble of a laugh, loving Hattie. She reminds me a lot of Bower, which is comforting since I miss my best friend so much.

"You know." She stands taller. "Maybe that's what my

problem is. Maybe he's not proposing because I'm giving away the milk for free. Maybe I need to hold out on him."

"Yeah, good luck with that," Echo says and then picks up a few jars to restock the shelves.

Hattie rings me up, and I give her my card to pay. "What do you think?" Hattie asks. "Think he will ever propose?"

"I don't know him well enough to decide, but I will say this. If he takes much longer, he's a fool because you're an absolute delight."

She clutches her chest. "Ugh, that's what I tell him every day."

We laugh together, and I grab my cookies and card from her, telling myself I don't need to eat one of these cookies when I get into the car, but I know I'll fail at self-control.

"I'm serious about next Friday, though. Let me know if you're interested. We'd love to have you. I think my friend Maggie might be coming up to visit as well."

"That would be great," I answer. "Count me in."

"Wonderful." Hattie smiles. "See you next Friday."

━━━

It didn't occur to me until I walked over to Ryland's house that maybe I should have talked to him about hanging out with his sister before accepting the invitation. I'm trying to take this slow for him, and I don't want to overstep my boundaries. Maybe he's not comfortable with me hanging out with his sisters. Not yet at least.

I walk up the steps to his back door and consider knocking for a moment, but then realize that might be weird since I used to just walk in, so I open the door myself and walk into his quiet house. My eyes immediately fall to the table in the kitchen where he usually waits, and when I don't find him there, I glance around the kitchen but come up short.

Confused, I shut the door behind me, cookie bag in hand,

and I peek around to the living room where I find him walking down the stairs.

The moment he sees me, he pauses and then blows out a heavy breath. "Jesus fuck," he whispers, making his way all the way down. "I didn't hear you come in."

"Sorry." I chuckle. "Did I startle you?"

"Yeah, you did," he says walking up to me and wrapping his arm around my waist, pulling me into him and tilting my head back so he can mold our lips together.

And it's so delicious.

God, it's been a day and a half, yet it feels like it's been a week since I've kissed him. Going undetected at school and practice was a challenge to say the least.

When he pulls away, he presses his forehead to mine and whispers, "Fuck, I missed these lips."

Butterflies erupt in my stomach because I'm not sure anyone has ever really said anything like that to me. Not even in my happiest stages of a relationship.

"Go sit down on the couch while I get us drinks. Iced tea okay?"

"That would be perfect," I say as I go to the couch and set the cookies on the coffee table. Since I'm assuming Mac is just falling asleep, I don't say anything to him and just wait. Thankfully he doesn't take very long and saunters over, looking so freaking fine in a simple Almond Bay baseball T-shirt and athletic shorts. He doesn't have to do much, just shorts and a T-shirt and he has me practically drooling.

He sits beside me, places our drinks on the coffee table, and then tugs on my hand. I move over his lap to lean my back against a pillow propped up against the couch arm and drape my legs over his.

"How are you feeling?" he asks.

"Okay," I say as his hand falls to my thigh. "Better now."

"Same." He smiles at me.

I smile back.

And God, I feel like a teenager, getting to hang out with my crush, attempting to be quiet so his parents don't hear us. But instead of parents, it's his niece.

"What did you and Mac do tonight?"

"Well, she was in the mood for quiche."

"Oh really? I wouldn't expect a four-year-old to know what quiche is."

"She learned about it from a book she read in school. Apparently, some mouse is really good at making quiche. I don't know, but she was determined to have one tonight. And I thought *how hard could it be* to make?"

I wince. "How did it go?"

"Let's just say I almost ruined the oven by overfilling the pie crust. Thankfully I was able to save the egg from splashing into the scalding oven. The crust burnt, and I feel like we added too much spinach, but I was nervous there wasn't enough, so I added extra, but then it felt like we were just chewing through spinach. You could imagine how a four-year-old did with that."

"I'm assuming not well."

"Yeah, not well at all. When I asked her what she thought, she gave me a solid thumbs down and said she never wanted quiche again. So I ruined that for her."

I chuckle. "I bet it wasn't that bad."

"When you came in, I wasn't tucking Mac in bed. I was flossing because I got spinach stuck everywhere."

"Oh gosh." I cover my mouth in laughter. "I'm sorry, I don't mean to laugh, but I'm just imagining the entire encounter. Maybe when we open up to Mac about our relationship, I can help her make a quiche that isn't full of spinach. Change her mind a bit."

"Are you good at making quiche?"

I nod. "It was one of the easiest and cheapest things I'd make for me and Bennett. It was great for him because it was filled with protein, and I'd be able to shop at the dollar store for some of the ingredients, making it a very cheap meal."

"I might need a lesson, then."

"I think I can arrange that." I lean over and grab the cookie bag and pull out the cookies, one for him, one for me. I'm the first to take a bite, and the moment the cherry almond flavors hit my tongue, I internally wish I got a dozen instead of a half. "These are so freaking good."

"I can get you the recipe," he says.

"And ruin the magic?" I shake my head. "No way. I will forever and always need these from your sister. I'd never be able to replicate it. I'm more of a cook than a baker."

"I'm neither and very grateful for an air fryer."

He's so adorable. "What would you say is the best thing that you cook?"

"Right now, hmm, I've been winning with the homemade pizza. I've been using a cauliflower crust that Mac seems to love. She gets veggies in her meal, and she likes it." He shyly shrugs. "It's the little wins. I always try to think about Cassidy and what she'd try to do. She never let Mac challenge her with food. She always ate what was on her plate, so I try to replicate that."

"Seems like you're doing a good job in all aspects. From what I've seen, she's happy and healthy, and that's all that really matters, right?"

"Yeah, I think so."

I finish off my cookie. "How's she adjusting to the new house? I know you were worried there for a bit."

"I think putting things away and getting furniture in place has helped a lot, but I still want to try to make this place look more like a home."

I look around at the plain walls and the bare floors. "I think a few small touches would make a difference. Like an area rug for the living room, something large that Mac can play on. You can get a shelf right there with cubby drawers for her toys. Some curtains would look good, and then a few framed pictures. Maybe have Mac draw something for the walls."

"That's a really good idea. I think she'd like to do that. She loves drawing and painting."

"Yeah, and you can get frames from somewhere like IKEA so they look professional. It might make her feel more special."

He finishes his cookie and rubs his hand over my thigh. "You're really smart."

"Not really, just thinking of some simple things to do inexpensively. You learn where to shop and how to be thrifty when counting every penny, that's for sure."

"But they're the type of things that will make a difference, so thank you."

"Of course. I can't imagine what it's like to be in your shoes. If Bennett had a kid that he left with me, I think I'd have a hard time getting up every day to take care of the child because they'd just be a stark reminder of how I lost my brother."

"That's how it was for a while," he says softly as he reaches over me for his drink, which I help him grab. He offers me a sip even though I have my own, and I take it. "But Aubree was really helpful during those days. We were living in the farmhouse. She was in the guest house, and it was like we were both trying to take care of Mac at the same time. We did dinner every night together. She helped with pickup and drop-off at school, and at night, she'd go off to the guest house, and I'd sleep on the couch."

I nod in understanding. "I know the feeling. Was there not enough room for you?"

"Couldn't stomach sleeping in Cassidy's room, so I took up the couch. What about you?"

"One-bedroom apartment when Bennett was a teenager. I knew it was best if I gave him the room for his own privacy, plus I worked late, so I took the couch. It worked. Sometimes you make the sacrifices for others."

"You do," he says softly. "Tell me something about your childhood that you liked. I feel like we always talk about the bad. Do you happen to have a happy memory?"

"I do." I snuggle in close to his chest as he sets down his drink on the side table. His arm wraps around my back, and I've never felt more comfortable. This, right here, this is where I want to be. For someone who has always been at the helm of protection, it feels so amazing to be protected for a moment. "Bennett, I think, was in middle school, and we were headed to get some ice cream down the street. We were walking down the sidewalk when, out of complete luck, Bennett stumbled across a twenty-dollar bill on the ground. He was in awe. We looked around to see if anyone dropped it, but when we found no one, we decided to use it."

"What did you use it for?"

"There was this sundae at the ice cream store that we always dreamed about getting but never had the money for because it was eighteen dollars. It was the extreme of all extreme sundaes. Twelve scoops of ice cream, five toppings, two sauces, whipped cream, and a dozen cherries." I smile, remembering the look on Bennett's face when I sat down at the picnic table with the large dish. "We ate the entire thing and then laid out on the baseball field, staring up at the sky, talking about all the good things. It was as though having that one good thing helped us focus on other positives. It was nice. Much needed. Of course, we had the worst stomachache of our entire lives, but it was so worth it."

He strokes my hair. "I love that story."

"So do I." I lift my chin and press a kiss to his lips. It's quick and sweet and just what I need at the moment. "What about you? What's one of your favorite moments?"

"Easy, my dad wanted us out of the house because we were bugging him. He was feeling particularly gracious that day and gave me one hundred dollars. Told me not to come home until he passed out. Which usually on a weekend was around six at night."

"I hate that."

"Knowing it was six at night was a relief for all of us. Sometimes, when I see that it's six, I still feel that sense of relief, even as a thirty-five-year-old man."

My expression softens as I cup his cheek. "I also hate that."

"Me too." This time, he kisses me. When he pulls away, he cups my cheek for a second and then continues his story. "One hundred dollars got us pretty far that day. The first thing we did was drive to the arcade down the road, and we each got ten dollars to use. Then we all bought huge ice cream cones. We went mini golfing, and since Cassidy was friends with the owner's daughter and they knew about our situation, they gave us unlimited games and free rides on the go-carts. We spent the rest of our money on food and soda. We laughed so much that day. I kind of felt like Richie Rich, going around and spending money without thinking about it."

"What a great day."

"It really was. Interesting how money was a central theme around one of our best days growing up."

"When you're deprived of it, you unfortunately miss out on opportunities, no matter how many times you attempt to make your own."

"It's very true. We did pretty well without any money at our disposal, but hell, when we had moments when we could spare a few bucks, we made sure to make the most of it."

"Same." I smile. "You know, I've never met anyone else with such a similar and complicated life experience as me. Makes me feel not so alone."

He strokes my hair gently. "I feel the same way, babe."

I sigh into his chest, unsure of how I was able to be this lucky. Life has been . . . hard. But right now, sitting with a man who *gets* what it's like to struggle, to grieve with what life has given you, it's truly unbelievable. His comments don't show pity but comprehension, and that's both sobering and reassuring.

*We're both survivors.*

And if this does go well, we could be survivors together.

# Chapter Twenty-Seven

### RYLAND

Why am I nervous?

This is stupid.

There is no reason for me to be nervous at all.

Yet as I stand in front of Gabby's door, ready to knock, I can feel the shake in my legs.

Mac is with Hayes and Hattie right now, swimming and having the time of her life. They sent me a picture of her on the horse float, wearing sunglasses and drinking a lemonade. I immediately made it the wallpaper on my phone because the picture is pure joy, and I know Cassidy would do the same thing.

I lift my hand to the door and knock on it a few times before sticking my hands in my pockets. I wait for a few seconds and the door opens, revealing my beautiful girl, standing there in a pair of leggings, a tight crop top, and a backward hat with her hair down.

Fuck she looks so good.

"Hey." She smiles up at me. "Everything okay?"

"Yeah. You free right now?"

Confused, she nods. "I'm free." She then looks around. "Are you?"

"Mac is with Hattie and Hayes. I was hoping to steal you for a date."

"Really?" she asks, looking hopeful.

"Yeah, but it's sort of a selfish date."

"Any date I'm happy with. What's on your mind?"

I take her hand in mine and stare at the connection. "I was kind of hoping that you could go to a home goods store and help me pick out a few things for my place? Then I could take you to dinner."

When my eyes meet hers, I see them light up with enthusiasm. "Really?"

"Yeah, you interested?"

"More than interested. I'm honored." She brings our connection to her lips and presses a quick kiss to my knuckles. "Let me change."

I tug on her so she's pulled right into my chest. "Nah, I like you like this."

"Ryland, I'm in no way ready for a date with you."

"Babe, it doesn't matter what you wear. I just want you with me. Plus, you look hot." I pull away to scan her, my tongue wetting my lips. "Really fucking hot."

She glances down at herself and then back up at me. "The things that turn men on these days." She shakes her head. "Let me grab my bag and phone. One sec."

She goes back into her apartment, and my eyes fixate on her round rear as she collects a fanny pack and her purse. She drapes the fanny pack over her shoulder like a cross bag and locks up.

"You're wearing that wrong, you know," I say as she turns to me and takes my hand where we walk down the stairs together.

"My belt bag?"

"Belt bag?" I ask on a laugh. "Gabby, that's a fanny pack."

"Not according to the youth. This is a belt bag."

"The youth are wrong," I say as I open the passenger side door to my truck for her. She slides to the middle seat like the good girl she is. "That's a fanny pack and it will always be a fanny pack."

"Look at the old man grump, unable to change his ways."

I grab her seat belt and buckle her up before gripping her chin and saying, "Deal with it." I press a quick kiss to her lips and then round the front of the truck and get in on my side.

I start the truck, buckle up, and rest my hand on her thigh as I back out of the driveway and onto the road.

"Where are we headed?" she asks as she leans into me.

"There's a discount home goods store—"

"Jackson's Home Goods?" she asks.

"Yes. I thought it would be a good place to at least start. And if we have to go somewhere else, we can."

"Jackson's is a great place. Good quality items that are affordable. I got a few things there when Bennett and I first moved to the area."

"So good choice?" I ask with insecurity.

"Great choice," she says as she places her hand on mine for reassurance. "Now, what exactly are you looking for?"

"I don't really know. I was kind of hoping you'd guide me. I think I want to focus on the living room and make it more homey, since that's where we spend a lot of our time. Mac's room is fully decorated, so no need to worry about that."

"And what about your room?"

"That doesn't need anything special, just a place to sleep."

"You know," she says, rubbing her thumb over the back of my hand, "sometimes we have to treat our bedrooms as a place of sanctuary, especially if we have problems finding our best sleep."

"Are you trying to allude to something?" I ask.

"I'm just saying, you don't always have to focus all your energy on everyone else. You can focus that energy on yourself, too. You can create a space for yourself that allows you to sleep better. I know you struggle with it."

"I don't need decorations in my room to sleep better."

"Then what do you need?" she asks.

I pull out onto the main road and head north toward Jackson's, which is outside of town. "It's not anything you can buy at a store," I answer.

"What is it?"

"Nothing you need to worry about."

"Ryland," she says as I can feel her eyes on me. "Tell me."

Feeling ridiculous, I say, "The best sleep I've had in a long while was the night we spent in San Francisco. So it seems to me what I need in my bedroom . . . is you."

"Oh," she says, growing silent.

I glance in her direction and spot the blush on her cheeks, which makes me smile. She might be confident and strong and can put me in my place when she wants to, but the moment I toss her a compliment or the truth in her direction, those cute cheeks of hers turn pink.

"So unless you know where I can buy one of you in the store, I think it's a lost cause."

"Hmm," she says. "Maybe I can google it."

I chuckle. "Good luck with that. Pretty sure the one and only is sitting right next to me."

"This coming from the guy who didn't want to be in a relationship."

I shrug. "What can I say? I'm a changed man."

"I guess you are, but I still would like to make your room into something more."

"I have decorations packed away. When I was at the farmhouse, sleeping on the couch, Hattie actually redid Cassidy's room, took care of all of her stuff and turned the room into something for me, so I have all those things she did packed away. Just need to put it together."

"Then let me help you," Gabby says. "Because I promise, once you get things set up, you might find that you sleep better because you're more comfortable."

"Or you can lend yourself to me, and that will make me sleep better."

She chuckles. "Or that."

I squeeze her thigh. "If you want to help me with my bedroom, then I guess we can put it together, but I do have one request."

"Let me guess, you want me to decorate your place naked?"

I laugh because I didn't expect her to say that. "Not what I was going to say, but now that you suggested it . . ."

"I'm not walking around your house naked."

"Says the girl who spread her legs on my dining room table."

"You were the one who spread me."

"Ehh, I remember it differently."

"Of course you do." I can practically hear her eye roll. "All clothes will remain on because we have a task to do."

"Shame, I was willing to decorate with the willy out."

Her laughter fills the cab of the truck. "Willy out? Seriously?"

"Yeah, might even dance for you."

"You'd never," she scoffs. "The day you dance naked for me is the day . . . hell, I don't even know because it would never happen."

"Why do you say that?" I ask. "I'd dance naked."

"You are such a liar."

She snuggles in close, and I'll be fucking honest, I'm not the kind of guy who would dance naked, but if it made Gabby smile, if it made her laugh, hell, I'd do it.

"Might do it for the right smile," I say.

She squeezes my arm. "Well, I'll keep that in mind. But back to your request with your bedroom. What is it?"

"Oh right, your perfume. I want you to spray my room with your perfume."

"Seriously?" she asks.

"Yeah, seriously. If I can't have you in my room, I at least want to smell you."

"My, my, my. Look at you, Rowley. It almost seems like you're really into this relationship thing."

"When it's with you, I am."

349

"I think we got too much," I say as I stare down at a porcelain horse in my hand that I just unwrapped from its protective tissue paper.

Gabby comes up behind me, places her arm around me, and chuckles. "You're the one who got the horse. That was not on me."

I point at the embroidered horse throw pillows on the couch. "And those, whose idea were those?"

"Those might have been me, but they look so cute in here, and Mac is going to love them."

I let out a sigh and place the porcelain horse—that I got for seventy percent off probably because no one else wanted it—on the coffee table. "If you had told me ten years ago I'd be decorating my purple house with horse decor to appease a four-year-old, I would have told you, you lost your mind."

She laughs. "But it's adorable, and there are not many horse things, only a few." Gabby pulls out a throw blanket with mini horses on it, causing me to raise my brow at her. "Really, there's not that much?"

"Okay." I chuckle and then unload the rest of the bags, putting everything on the coffee table. "At least the area rug is horse-less."

"Which I'm still upset about because I really was in love with that green area rug with the mini brown horses all over it. It would have been so cute."

"It would have been absurd," I reply. "I can get on board with the throw pillows and the blanket, and even the porcelain horse, but the rug is where I put my foot down."

"Such a shame. It could have been a real eye pleaser."

"That rug was not an eye pleaser." I pick up a plant and hold it out, unsure what to do with it.

Gabby takes it from me and places it on a side table along with the modern lamp that she picked out that I actually liked. "What do you think?"

"I think I'm grateful that you're here because I never would have picked half of this stuff."

"I'm glad you asked. I love doing this."

"Well, I feel useless."

"Why don't you move that toy shelf over between the windows and start filling the cubes with Mac's toys."

"Now that I can do," I say, loving the simple task because placing plants and hanging pictures with Command Strips that Gabby insisted I get does not seem like something I'd be good at.

"Is Mac spending the night at Hattie and Hayes's house?"

I shake my head. "Hayes has to head to San Francisco early in the morning, and Hattie's going with him. They're going to drop Mac off around eight."

Gabby takes a look at the time on her phone. "Oh, we'll be done with time to spare. That's if we don't get distracted."

"And how would we get distracted?" I ask with a grin.

"You know exactly how and it's not going to happen. We're putting this living room together so when your niece comes home, she's greeted with a great surprise, which you'll have to record for me because I'm going to want to see her reaction."

"That I can do."

Gabby starts working on hanging some pictures, laying them on the ground before she puts them on the wall. I grab the iron and ironing board and start releasing the wrinkles from the curtains.

"What do you do in your spare time?" I ask, wanting to know more about Gabby.

She applies Command Strips to the back of the frames and answers, "Watch baseball, read about baseball, talk to Bennett about baseball."

"A girl after my own heart. I don't meet many people with such a passion for the sport. I usually see that kind of enthusiasm for football."

"Same," she says as she hangs her first picture, one of Cassidy and Mac together. It's my favorite picture of them out on the farm before Cassidy got sick. "It kind of annoys me because baseball was America's pastime and it almost seems like it's a dying sport now, which makes me sad."

"I agree. Do you think the new rule changes will help bring more people into the sport?"

She shrugs and hangs another picture, which is of Mac and me in the Redwoods. We took it a month or so ago. She's on my shoulders, and we're both looking up at the tree. "I mean, it adds a bit of drama with the pitch clock. But I don't know if it will bring more viewers to the game. I just think society has changed. We're more about instant gratification. It's hard for us to just sit still, phones down, and enjoy a game that moves at a slower pace, but still offers the same kind of thrill and excitement that something like football offers."

"I like the pitch clock rule. I remember watching baseball with my dad—when he was sober—and listening to him bitch and complain about the batters and how they'd step out of the box, readjust the straps of their batting gloves every single time, tug on their helmet, and take all the goddamn time in the world before they stepped back into the batter's box. Drove him nuts, and I remember thinking it was one of the very few things my dad and I agreed on."

"Ugh, I hated that too. I understand the importance of establishing a routine to trigger your muscle memory before going up to the plate, but adjusting your batting gloves every time is not the way to do it. There was this one season, I think when Bennett was a freshman, and he was still trying to establish himself, and he started the whole batting glove thing. I told him to stop it immediately. The way your gloves feel will not get you a hit. It's the mechanics. So that's what he focused on."

"You're very smart, you know that?"

"It's why David hired me," she says with a wink.

I chuckle and then set my second-to-last curtain panel over the couch. "You know, the more I think about that situation, the more I wonder if I would have hired you."

"I think you would have," she says with confidence as she takes a step back to observe her work. The third and final picture is all of us at Aubree and Wyatt's wedding, in front of the barn and staggered on hay bales. "You're a smart man. You would have grilled me on my knowledge, found out what an asset I'd be to you, and you would have hired me."

I rest the iron on the wrinkled fabric, moving it up and down. "I think you're right. I'd have hired you and then hated every second of it because I wouldn't have been able to keep my eyes off you, nor would I have ever found out what you tasted like."

She pauses and turns toward me. With a finger pointed in my direction, she says, "None of that. We're not getting distracted. We have a task at hand, and your sweet-talking can't throw it off."

"It's the truth though," I say.

Her expression softens. "I guess we have David to thank, then."

"No, we're not going that far."

She laughs again, and my entire body relaxes as the sound fills my living room. My decorated living room. A room that will reflect joy and happiness, and family. A place I know Mac will love, and a place where she can feel at home, where she can feel her mother surround her, and where she can spend her childhood years growing up.

———

Rain pelts the windows as I break down the last cardboard box for recycling. Gabby just finished vacuuming, and we're about ten minutes out from Mac arriving. Hayes and Hattie had to carefully buckle her up while she was passed out, the Chewys having to be dragged out of her shirt so her car seat fit properly.

Gabby places the vacuum in the hall closet and then walks up to me, wrapping her arms around my waist. "It looks so good."

"Amazing," I say, taking in the living space. Because Gabby works fast, not only were we able to fix up the living room, but she also adjusted some things in the kitchen, added a potted plant to the dining room table, and hung more pictures in the stairwell leading to Mac's bedroom. She marveled at how much Mac looked like Cassidy while I marveled at the woman who spent her evening helping me make my house into a home.

We didn't have time for my bedroom, but I told her it was fine, and we could plan to do it another time. At least I have a bed off the floor and working nightstands. The rest can be put together when there is time. She did slip back to her house for a moment to grab her perfume and spray my bedroom. I'll be enjoying that later tonight.

"Thank you so much for everything you did tonight."

"Of course. It was so much fun. I really hope Mac loves it."

"I know she will," I say as I look out the window. "It's pouring. Let me walk you to your apartment before Hattie and Hayes arrive."

"You don't have to do that. I don't want you getting wet."

"And I'm not going to be an asshole and let you walk back to your place unaccompanied."

"It's like thirty feet away."

"Doesn't matter," I say, taking her hand in mine.

"You're being ridiculous," she says as I bring her out into the rain, the drops careening down from the sky at such a high speed that the water pelting the blacktop sounds more like a roar than a simple rainstorm. "Seriously, Ryland."

But I don't listen. I bring her out into the rain with one tug, and instead of rushing to her apartment, I wrap my arm around her waist and start dancing.

"What are you doing?" She laughs as we both get drenched in seconds.

"Dancing . . . be happy it's not naked."

She presses her hand to my chest. "What a show that would be for the neighbors."

"Pretty sure I'd be fired since some students live on this street."

"And here you are, dancing with me in public, in the rain."

"Because . . . why not? Rain is often looked upon as an inconvenience. No one wants it to rain when they're outside, but

I don't know. Sometimes I think the best things happen when it rains."

She wipes away the water from her eyes, then returns her hand to my chest. "Like what?"

"Growth," I answer. "Not just in a natural sense, but think about it, it helps us grow patience, and understanding, and makes us slow down. It's Mother Nature's way of telling us to sit back and enjoy for a moment. So that's what we're doing, we're enjoying."

"I love that," she says as we sway under the pelting rain.

The smell of wet asphalt surrounds us as pools of water form around our feet, and the sound of water rushes around us.

It's peaceful.

And we do just as I say, we slow down.

We relish in the moment, letting our senses take over as we simply sway back and forth under the rain.

It isn't until I catch some headlights coming down the road that I realize Hattie and Hayes are almost here.

"They're pulling up," I say to her.

Gabby lifts her head and smiles up at me. "Thank you for the dance."

"Thank you for the night."

I tip her chin up, then kiss her in the rain, my heart beating a mile a minute as she grips onto me, holding me so tight, as if she never wants this moment to end.

Trust me, if I had it my way, I'd dance with her, in the rain, all night. *She feels so good in my arms.* "Let me know how Mac likes it in the morning."

"I will," I say. "Come over tomorrow night?"

"I thought you'd never ask." She kisses me once more and then takes off up the steps to her apartment just as Hayes and Hattie pull up.

But rather than keeping my eyes on the car in front of me, I'm focused on Gabby and her retreating body, slipping into her apartment.

I think I might be in a whole lot of trouble where she's concerned.

⸻

"No, no, Uncle Ry Ry, it goes around your waist. Not your leg," Mac says, tugging on the tutu skirt she wants me to wear.

"Yeah, I'm aware, but it won't fit around my waist. I'm too big."

Hands on her hips, she stares at me. "It looks weird."

"I don't know, I think I make it look good."

She shakes her head and heads back into the house. "Where are you going?"

"Stay there," she calls out.

Sure, not a problem. I love standing out in the backyard, wearing a tutu around my calf, a crown on my head, and an obscene amount of Cassidy's lipstick on my lips.

Mind you, Mac's wearing a Batman mask, a cape around her neck, and a foam sword sticking out of the top back of her shirt. There's nothing wrong with the role reversal, I actually welcome it, but she could have at least stayed in the lines of my lips when applying the lipstick. I just look foolish with unlined lips.

I will admit, though, that this neighborhood was the right choice. It's quiet, doesn't have much traffic besides residents, and there isn't one vacation rental on the street, leading to a peaceful space. I only wished we had more kids Mac's age for her to play with.

And the house, well, let's just say Mac was ecstatic a few days ago when she woke up and saw the living room decorated with horses, but surprisingly, that was not what made her the happiest. It was the pictures of Cassidy hung on the wall. She laid the new horse throw blanket down on the floor in front of the picture and played with the Chewys, and every once in a while, she stared up at the picture and smiled at her mom.

Fucking gutted me.

But also, I couldn't have been happier because I knew Mac was happy.

The sound of a car slows down, and when I look toward the shared driveway, I see Gabby's car pull up. My heart flutters as I see her get out of her car, still wearing her baseball cap that she wore at practice, a pair of spandex shorts, and an Almond Bay baseball shirt that I gave her—not one of mine because that would be obvious since it would be very big on her.

She pulls out her water bottle and her bag and then heads toward the stairs but pauses when she sees me standing in the grass under the oak tree. She tilts her head to the side, taking me all in, a smile tugging on the corner of her lips.

"Do not laugh," I say to her.

"I'd never," she replies, her cheeks twitching.

"You're such a liar."

The back door opens and closes, and Mac comes storming out with her entire bag of dress up.

"I brought all the skirts." She dumps them on the grass, and when she sees Gabby, she says, "Hi, do you want to play with us?"

"Oh." Gabby glances at me. "That's okay. I don't want to disturb you."

"No, we want you to play," Mac says as she walks up to Gabby and takes her hand. I see the panic in Gabby's eyes when she looks at me. It's been a week and a half since we've officially been together, and in that time, Gabby has kept her distance whenever Mac has been around. But it seems like Mac has other plans.

And you know what, I don't mind. I'm so comfortable at this point that I almost want to see how Mac gets along with Gabby, so I nod, letting Gabby know that it's okay for her to hang, which seems to ease the panic.

"What's your name again?" Mac asks as she forces Gabby to take a seat on the blanket we have laid out.

"Gabby."

"Oh right," Mac says. "Do you like superheroes?"

"Love them."

"Want to be Robin? I'm Batman."

"I'd love to be Robin," Gabby says.

"Great." Mac digs through the clothes and hands Gabby a Spider-Man mask and a tie. "Here you go, you're Robin. Put them on."

Gabby cutely smiles and slips the pre-knotted tie over her head and the mask over her eyes. "And who is your uncle?"

Mac pulls her sword out of the back of her shirt, well, attempts to, but it gets stuck, so Gabby kindly helps her, and once it's released, Mac holds the sword up to me and pokes me in the leg. "This is Godzilla, and she's trying to eat us alive."

"Nooo," Gabby says in shock and then stands, holding her hands out, ready to karate chop me. "How dare she try to eat us. How do we get rid of her?"

"Attack!" Mac screams and then, to my dismay, lunges the sword right into my junk.

Man.

Fucking.

Down.

"Mother of . . . God," I groan as I buckle to my knees and then fall right to the ground face-first.

Ungodly pain surges up my legs and into my stomach as I feel my testicles attempt to crawl inside my body, seeking out protection from the gremlin with the sword.

"Oh God," Gabby says as she drops down to check on me, only for a foot to land directly on my back.

A four-year-old stomp between the shoulders.

With what little energy I have left in me, I glance up toward Mac, who is looking up toward the sky. Her sword is pointed at the clouds, and her one foot presses into me, claiming me as conquered.

"Got her. She's been destroyed," Mac says with pride, only to turn toward me, see that my eyes are open, and then clash the sword down to my neck, where she slits me with the steel foam of death. "Nice try."

To avoid any more pain, I close my eyes and stick my tongue out of my mouth as I attempt to breathe through the radiating pain.

"Now she's destroyed." Mac lets out a cackle that makes my ass shrivel up in fear. The kind of cackle that shouldn't belong to any little girl.

"You stay here with Godzilla while I grab the Chewys. It's time for their feast."

Mac takes off inside the house, and that's when I let out a low, garbled moan.

"Uhhhhhhh, fuck . . . me."

Gabby's hand finds my back, where she rubs me soothingly. "Are you okay?"

"Nope," I say, staying flat on my stomach, because if I roll over, I'm exposed to the evil that is my niece and I can't take another blow to the testicles.

"God, I didn't even see it coming or else I'd have tried to stop her," Gabby whispers.

"No one saw it coming," I croak. "Fuck, I . . . I think she really did slice them off."

"It was quite the stab, she got her hips behind it. Honestly, I think she has some power you can harness, maybe get her involved in baseball. She could have a mighty swing."

"Great, just another way for her to get me in the nuts."

"Now, was it your actual balls or did you get partial penis?"

"Does it matter?" I ask, still holding my junk, afraid if I let go, it might fall off.

"Just genuinely curious."

"Balls, Gabby, she got me in the balls."

"Good to know." She pats my back. "Is there anything I can do for you?"

"Make sure she doesn't attack me again," I say, taking in deep breaths to combat the shrinking I feel between my legs.

Just then, Mac reappears. "Time to eat, Chewys." She moves in beside me, and then both horses start chomping at my fragile body. "Look, Chewy Chondra is eating Uncle Ry Ry's butt!"

"Okay, no butt eating," I say, causing Gabby to snort.

"Why not?" Mac asks.

"Because it's inappropriate to eat butts."

"But Uncle Hayes said he was going to eat Aunt Hattie's butt, and she laughed."

Jesus Christ.

"They shouldn't have said that," I say, making a note to have a conversation with my sister about appropriate language around a four-year-old.

"Then they need to get in trouble," Mac says and then makes Chewy Charles attack my neck.

"Gentle," I remind her as I'm starting to gain feeling back in my legs.

"They said you don't taste good. You're rotten." And then she takes off toward the swing with the Chewys.

"Probably because my balls are now expired, and the rest of my body has turned to rot."

"You realize that your balls don't control your entire body," Gabby whispers.

"Right now, they do," I say as I start to roll over but check for the gremlin first. When she's firmly set in swinging, I sit up and bring my knees to my chest. "Christ."

"Are you going to need me to gently take care of your sensitive bits tonight?"

"That's if I have any left."

Gabby rolls her eyes and stands. "You're being very dramatic."

"You didn't just get a sword plowed between your legs."

She leans down and whispers, "Pretty sure I did over a week ago . . . and I survived." She winks and then takes off toward the swing, where she pushes Mac.

⸻

"Is Gabby home?" Mac asks as she picks up a raspberry and puts it on her finger.

"I don't know," I answer even though I know damn well that she is and that she's cooking some pasta dish for herself, completely naked. She sent a picture, and I nearly came in my goddamn pants.

"I like her," Mac says.

"Oh, you do?"

Mac nods and places another raspberry on her finger, lining them up to look like alien hands. It's how she eats them best. "She's nice and she likes to play with me. Do you think she'll play with me after dinner?"

"Uh . . . not sure. She might be doing her own things."

And this is what I was sort of worried about, Mac getting attached. And it's not like Gabby has been over at all when Mac has been awake. She played with her on Tuesday when I had my world rocked by a sword, and that was it. But ever since then, Mac has been asking about Gabby. Over and over again.

Now that it's Thursday, I think I might have a problem on my hands, and I don't know how to handle it.

"Can you ask her if she wants to play?"

Trying to take a different approach, I say, "Are you getting bored with your uncle? You have to recruit someone else to play with?"

Her brow forms a V. "No," she says loudly. "You're my best friend. I can't get bored of you."

Well, Christ. Way to get me in the fucking feels.

"But I like Gabby."

Well, Mac surely knows how to lift you, only to squash you back down. I'm not sure where Mac is learning all of this. I might need to have another conversation with my sisters.

"Can you ask her to play?"

"I don't want to really bother her, Mac. She might be doing something."

Her cute brow knits together again. "Do you not like Gabby?"

Quite the opposite actually. I like her a lot. I like her so much that I'm trying to navigate me wanting her around all the time and you not growing attached to her in case something happens, like . . . me messing up this entire thing.

"No, I like her."

"It doesn't seem like you like her."

"I like her, Mac."

"Then can you please ask her to come play?" She bats her eyelashes and Christ I'm such a fucking sucker when it comes to this girl.

I'm trying to be tough and set boundaries here, but she is destroying them one eyelash bat at a time.

Grumbling under my breath, I pull my phone from my pocket and say, "Eat your green beans."

"Only if you text her."

I lift a brow. "Nice try, but that's not how this works. Only way she's going to come over is if you eat your—"

Mac fists the green beans on her plate and shoves them all in her mouth at the same time. Cheeks puffed, she chews and smiles at me.

For the love of God.

"Do not choke. Gabby won't come over if you choke."

Mac just keeps chewing, and that's when I open my text messages with Gabby and come face to face with her naked body and her pasta.

Fuck . . . I forgot.

Not that I want to, because hell, I'd keep this picture forever, but with my luck, Mac would look over my shoulder and see it, so I delete the picture from the thread and text her.

**Ryland:** *Think you could put clothes on your gorgeous body and come over here to play with my niece? She's requesting your presence.*

I look over at Mac, who's still chewing and has the rest of her green beans in her hand.

"Why are we not using a fork?" I ask her.

"Godzilla doesn't use forks," she says as I get a text back.

"I thought I was Godzilla."

"You're . . . uh . . . you're Godzilla Plus."

"What's the difference between Godzilla and Godzilla Plus?" I ask, truly curious.

"Godzilla Plus cries when stabbed."

My face falls flat. Well, maybe if Godzilla didn't stab Godzilla Plus in the testicles, Godzilla Plus wouldn't cry.

I glance down at my phone and read Gabby's text.

**Gabby:** *She is? That's cute, but . . . do you want me to come over? I know we're trying to keep the distance.*

**Ryland:** *I wouldn't ask if I didn't think it would be okay.*

Mac shoves the rest of her green beans in her mouth, and I just shake my head at her. I don't think there will ever be any controlling this girl—which I think in the long run will be a good thing. She's going to need her independence and strength to get through life.

**Gabby:** *Are you sure?*

**Ryland:** *Listen, she's relentless. If I don't invite you over, I'm sure she'd find a way to sneak out and knock on your door. Come over . . . dressed, preferably in a turtleneck tucked into a pair of very unflattering pants.*

**Gabby:** *Coming over I can do. The unflattering pants is not an option, sorry.*

Smiling, I set my phone down and say, "Gabby said she can come over and play."

"Really?" Mac says, mouth still full of green beans.

"Really," I say.

And then, she tucks her head and starts shoveling food into her mouth.

"Hey, slow down. It will be a few minutes before she's here. You have time. No choking."

She smiles at me and chews. And that smile right there? I will do anything to keep that smile around, anything to make this little girl happy, because she's the most important thing in my life.

As long as I'm making her happy, that's all that matters, then I'm doing my job, and letting Cassidy's legacy live on.

"Say goodbye to Gabby," I say to Mac who's pouting on the stairs, fresh from her bath that we sped through because Mac wanted Gabby to read her a book before bed.

"Can't she spend the night?" Mac asks.

I mean, I wouldn't mind her spending the night, but I know we're not there yet.

"Where would she sleep?" I ask, not wanting to say no right away.

"With you," Mac says. "Uncle Wyatt sleeps with Aunt Aubree, and Uncle Hayes sleeps with Aunt Hattie. Adults share beds all the time."

I pull on my neck and look at Gabby, who squats down to Mac's eye level and takes her hand in hers. "I had so much fun with you tonight, Mac. You're so good at playing, and I love the pictures we drew, but I have to go back to my place because I have to get ready for school tomorrow."

"You go to school?" she asks.

"I teach at your uncle Ryland's school, and I help him coach the baseball team too."

"You do?" she asks, eyes bright. "Do you play baseball?"

"I do."

"Are you good?"

Gabby smirks at me and whispers, "Better than your uncle Ryland."

Mac gives me a side-eye accompanied with a smirk. "I'm better at baseball than him too."

"Ooo, I bet you are. Maybe next time we hang out, we can throw a ball around."

Mac jumps up and down and nods her head. "Yes. Yes. Yes."

"Sounds perfect, then." Gabby cutely holds her hand out and says, "Shake on it."

They make a deal, and Mac throws her arms around Gabby and gives her a big hug.

I stand there in awe, watching the entire thing unfold like I did when they were playing tonight. Mac's fascinated with Gabby, almost like the same way she's infatuated with Wyatt.

And Gabby, Jesus, the way she spoke to Mac all night, was able to remain in imaginative play for a couple of hours, never breaking, and following Mac around the house, dressed up and ready to defend the Chewys who sat in the middle of the room, vulnerable to Godzilla Plus. Gabby was so good with her that it cracked a hole in my wall, a big hole, a Gabby-shaped hole.

When Gabby pulls away, she says, "Have a good night, Godzilla. Until our next mission."

Mac pats Gabby on the shoulder. "Until next time."

I nod toward the stairs and say, "Get upstairs. I'm going to say bye to Gabby, and you better be in bed when I get to your room."

She doesn't move, and when I fake an attempt to get her, she screams and runs up the stairs, only tripping once.

Gabby laughs as I take her hand and move her toward the kitchen. I push her up against the counter and whisper, "Stay here. Let me say good night to her, and then I'll be back down."

"Why? Is it your turn to play now?" She wiggles her brows.

"Yeah, it is." I tilt her chin up and capture her lips, feeling the kiss all the way down to my goddamn toes before pulling away.

I move toward the stairs and say, "Here I come. You better be in bed."

I hear scrambling come from upstairs, making me laugh as I jog up the stairs and right to her room, where I see her perched under her covers with Chewy Charles on one side and Chewy Chondra on the other.

I take a seat on the side of her bed and push her hair out of her face. "Did you have fun tonight?"

She nods. "I like Gabby."

"Yeah, she's pretty cool, huh?"

"She is, but I like you too, Uncle Ryland."

"I'm glad to hear it, kiddo."

She glances to the side, and I can tell that something is on her mind. "What's going on in your head?"

"I know you said that she's not coming back, but . . . are you sure Mommy's never coming back?"

Fuck.

The question that fucking plagues me. She's only asked it a few times, but every time she does, it feels like a goddamn dagger right to the chest—her hopeful eyes are always dimmed with my answer.

I lean over her and press my hand to her face as I say, "Remember how we talked about Mommy always being with you in your heart?" Mac nods. "Well, she isn't really gone. She's just living with you in a different way." I tap her heart. "Right here."

"But I don't see her there."

"I know, kiddo." My goddamn heart can't take this. "But that's why we have pictures of her, and we talk about her, so she's still with us in a different way."

"So . . . she really isn't coming back?"

"No, MacKenzie. I'm really sorry."

Her little eyes tear up, and my entire life shatters around me as I scoop her up into my arms, and I hug her, squeezing her tight.

"I'm so sorry, Mac. I know you miss her, and if I could, I'd do anything to bring her back, but I can't."

She cries softly onto my chest as I hold her tightly. Squeezing her. Letting her know that her mom might not be around, but I'm here. And I'll be here for her as long as I can be, until my last breath.

I rub her back softly, feeling her relax into me. I pull away to look to see if she's sleeping, and when I see that her eyes are shut, I slowly lower her back to her pillow and cover her with her blanket.

I'm about to stand when Mac says, "Uncle Ryland?"

"Yes?" I ask, wondering why she hasn't been saying Ry Ry.

"Are you . . . are you my dad now?"

Dad.

Am I her dad?

Christ . . . a lump in my throat forms as I attempt to answer this heart-wrenching question as best as I can.

"I'll be anything you want me to be," I say as I take her little hand in mine.

Her lips twist to the side as she thinks about it.

"But I'll tell you this. It's you and me, kid. I'm your main man, the one who will always protect you, always love you, always be there for you. I'll be there for every great thing in your life and every bad thing. And along the way, your aunts and uncles will be there for you too. But this life, this house, it belongs to you and me." I squeeze her hand. "Best friends, kiddo."

She nods, the smallest of smiles passing over her lips. "Best friends."

I lean down and press a kiss to her forehead. "Even when you're Godzilla and I'm Godzilla Plus, always and forever best friends."

"I love you," she says softly.

"I love you, too, MacKenzie."

"You won't leave me?"

I swallow the lump, trying to hold back the emotions that want to pour out.

"Not intentionally," I answer because I can't predict the future. "I'll do everything in my power to always be with you. You're my number one girl."

"You're my number one guy."

"Even over Uncle Wyatt?"

She nods. "Yes, you're . . . you're like my dad, so of course over Uncle Wyatt."

And there it is again, that word. A word I didn't think I'd ever hear directed toward me, yet it's been raised twice tonight.

Wanting her to feel comfortable with whatever she decides despite it making me feel weird, apprehensive, and maybe a bit uneasy, I say, "Yeah, Mac, I'm like your dad."

And for the love of God, that smile that passes over her lips brings a goddamn tear to my eye as she loops her arms around my neck and pulls me into another hug.

"Good night," she whispers. "Dad."

My lip trembles.

My hand shakes.

And my eyes get misty as I say, "Night, kiddo."

And then before she can see me with tears in my eyes, I move away from her bed and turn off her light.

"Good night, love you, see you in the morning, sweet dreams."

"Good night, love you, see you in the morning, sweet dreams," she says just before I shut the door.

And then I move down the stairs to the living room where I spot Gabby in the kitchen, grabbing us both a drink. When her eyes meet mine, she stops and says, "Is everything okay?"

I shake my head. "No." And then I crumple to the couch.

She's at my side in an instant. "What's going on?"

Tears fall down my face as I lean back on the couch and stare up at the ceiling. Gabby's hand falls to my chest.

"Ryland. Is Mac okay? What's happening?"

I take a few deep breaths. Then I look Gabby in the eyes and say, "She . . . she asked if I was her dad."

"Oh God." Gabby's hand goes to her mouth in shock. "What . . . what did you say to her?"

"I told her I'd be whatever she wanted me to be. Then she proceeded to hug me and whisper Dad in my ear."

"Wow." She now takes my hand and rubs her thumb over my knuckle. "How does that make you feel?"

My eyes fixate on a picture of Cassidy that Gabby hung up for me, the one of her and Mac. The smile on her face is the same smile Mac gave me tonight. It's uncanny. And as I stare at my sister in that picture, so happy and carefree, I can't help but feel this weight I've been carrying around slowly start to lift off my chest.

Quietly, I answer, "Makes me feel like I'm doing something right."

# Chapter Twenty-Eight

## GABBY

"Trevor, is that how we field a ball?" I shout to our shortstop, who's being all kinds of lazy today.

"No," he says, looking annoyed.

"Then show me how you field one." I take a ball from my catcher and zip one right to Trevor. He doesn't move his feet but attempts to stab at it, and because he's lazy, the ball takes a weird bounce and goes right past him.

"That's it," Ryland says, stepping in. "Poles, all of you. I'll tell you when to stop."

The team grumbles as they toss their gloves into a pile near the foul pole and start running.

Bat in hand, I walk over to Ryland and line up with him, shoulder to shoulder. "He doesn't respect me."

"No," Ryland says, his arms crossed over his chest. "He doesn't respect the game. He was a cocky punk last year, and I thought that maybe he'd grow up, but nope, still a cocky punk."

"What are you going to do about it?"

I rest the bat against my shoulder as we watch Trevor fall to the last of the line. You'd think that if you were making your entire team run, you'd at least pick up the pace, but Ryland's right. He's a cocky punk.

"What do you suggest?" he asks, truly making me feel like I'm a part of his staff.

When we first started out, I know I felt the need to prove myself, and maybe I did, even though Ryland didn't say I needed to. But he's included me more and more, and now it feels like we're in this together. Not just romantically but in every aspect.

"Honestly, I think Garrett, the sophomore, has more potential and is a workhorse. He lacks a little bit in his lateral, but that can be fixed with some hard work this fall. Plus, he wants to learn, he wants to be here, and he wants to play."

"I agree," Ryland says. "I was thinking Garrett, too, but I wanted to make sure you saw what I saw."

"Why don't you try it out?" I say to him. "Call them in, have Trevor keep running, and put Garrett at short, see what happens."

Ryland smirks and then yells, "Come on in. Trevor, keep running." The boys all grab their gloves while Trevor throws his hands up in frustration. *And that's why you're still running, you punk.* "Garrett, go to short."

Garrett, the quiet one, looks stunned but listens and moves to short where he gets in a ready position.

"Play's at one," I call out and then hit it up the middle. Garrett works hard to get to the ball, dives, and the ball tips off the edge of his glove. Luckily, our second baseman grabs it and then shoots the ball over to first. "That's great hustle, Garrett," I call out. I can already see his potential.

This might work.

We spend the rest of practice working with Garrett, seeing what he has in him, and by the end, the poor kid is sweating, but he's still jogging off the field and helping with the equipment.

Once the boys are gone, Ryland leans against the fence, arms crossed, looking at me with that stare that usually leads to clothes falling off.

I point the bat at him. "Don't look at me like that."

"Like what?" He smirks.

"You know exactly what I'm talking about."

"Can't be quite sure."

"Seriously, Ryland. Stop it."

He chuckles. "Sorry, it's just really hot watching you out here. Hard for me to keep it together."

"If you're trying to get me to go home with you, the answer is no. I told you, I'm going to your sister's house tonight." I'm both excited and nervous. I didn't really do *girly* things when I was a teenager—part of the fun of being into sports. But when I checked with Hattie if last week's invitation was still open, her message made me smile. *"I've been counting the days for this, Gabby. You better be there."* It felt good to be so included. "Playdates" with Mac have been fun, and the nights with Ryland? *Best not to think about that at school while in front of the sexy man.*

"I'm actually giving you a compliment. You're a really good coach, Gabby. Really fucking good. I'm grateful David went behind my back and hired you."

"Wow, never thought I'd hear you say something like that, given how much you hated David at the beginning of the school year."

"Neither did I, but you changed my mind."

"I feel like I changed your mind about a lot of things."

"You did. How the hell did you do that?"

"A magician never tells their secrets," I say, moving past him, letting my arm brush up against his.

He follows me. "I saw you talking to Christian today."

I heavily roll my eyes. "Wow, I'm shocked that it took you this long to mention something."

"Trying to be mature, but now that it's eaten me alive inside and I'm nothing but hollow bones, want to share?"

"You know, I never painted you as the dramatic type," I say as we both head to our cars.

"Gabby, please."

I chuckle. "He was just asking how I was doing. I told him I was good. He asked if I had any thoughts on his proposal, and I told him that I thought he was a great guy, but I think we should just remain friends."

Ryland slowly nods, trying to play it cool, but I see the smile ticking at the corner of his mouth, begging to be released. "That was very respectable of you."

"Oh my God, Ryland, I can see the urge to gloat on your lips."

He smiles large, so freaking large that it takes away the small amount of irritation I have from him bringing it up. "I'm sorry, but that fucker goes and tries to ask you out again?" He shakes his head. "Not my girl. She belongs to me."

"Sometimes your possessive behavior can be a little much," I say.

"Really? You're going to complain about me being happy that my girl claims she's off limits?"

"No, but you don't have to be so cocky about it."

"Where you're concerned . . . I'm very cocky." He wiggles his brows, which just pushes me over the edge.

"God, you're ridiculous."

I open my car door and get in, but before I can shut it, he asks, "Will I see you tonight?"

"I don't know. Not sure how long Hattie's thing will go."

"I don't care if it's late," he says.

"What if you're asleep?"

"Sneak into the house and wake me up the way you did when we were in San Francisco."

"With your dick in my mouth?" I say, causing him to smirk.

"Yeah, babe, with my dick in your mouth."

"Tempting. I'll think about it." I wink and then shut my door. He leans against his truck as I pull away, but I roll down my window and say, "You're looking at me that way again."

"Can't help it," he says softly. "I'm infatuated, Gabby."

My heart flutters. "Same."

"Okay, this is amazing," I say as I take in Hattie's backyard. She went all out.

When she said girls' night, she was serious.

The backyard's breathtaking. An infinity pool is the centerpiece of it all, followed by the view of the ocean, with lights strung everywhere, big bulbed ones that are already lit up, preparing for the sun to set. A firepit is surrounded by chairs and a table is set up for making s'mores. The outdoor dining room table looks like something you'd see in a Pottery Barn magazine, dressed to the nines and ready for the ladies to have dinner. Not to mention the personal chef, a.k.a. Hayes, grilling and looking so comfortable doing something for his girl, that it really reminds me of Ryland.

At each place setting is what seems to be spa baskets full of masks, under-eye moisturizers, foot soaks, and my favorite cookies ever.

And I get to not only be a part of this but I'm being welcomed into a group of women who have seem to have accepted me with open arms all because I'm dating their brother. I remember when I was dating Nathan and met his family for the first time. I was greeted with indifference and sneers. It wasn't a welcoming environment, yet today when I walked into Hattie's house, she gave me a hug and told me how happy she was that I was here.

Just seems too good to be true.

I pull my phone out as I walk toward the edge of the backyard where the rocky cliffs start, and I take a seat on the rocks. I send a quick text to Bennett to wish him luck tonight.

He's been doing a pretty good job since he's been brought up. He's had quite a few hits, some clutch ones, some strikeouts. He's made good plays over at third, and the fans seem to have taken a liking to him, which is important.

**Gabby:** *Good luck tonight. Keep killing it.*

To my surprise, he texts me back right away. He must be in the locker room.

**Bennett:** *Thanks, sis. How are you? How's Coach?*

**Gabby:** *Good and good.*

**Bennett:** *That's all you have for me? Good and good?*

**Gabby:** *I don't know what else to say. Everything feels . . . too good to be true right now. I'm afraid if I move the wrong way or say the wrong thing, it will all come crashing down on me.*

**Bennett:** *Why the hell would you think that?*

**Gabby:** *Because when have good things ever happened for me? It's just been a grind my whole life, and then I get this job, I move to Almond Bay, and now I'm surrounded by a support system, by a man who truly cares about me, believes in me, and you're playing in the big leagues. I feel like something bad is bound to happen.*

**Bennett:** *Or maybe this is your time to stop the grind and just enjoy what you've been able to create for your life. I know you're so used to climbing the ladder. Maybe you're finally at your destination.*

I smile down at my phone, reading his words over and over again as I feel a tightness in my throat and a sting in my eyes.

"What are you doing over here?"

Startled, I look over my shoulder to find Aubree taking a seat right next to me. "Sheesh, you scared me."

"Sorry." She chuckles. "You looked lost in thought. I didn't know how else to break the silence."

"It's okay. I was kind of lost in thought." I dab at my eyes.

"Anything you want to talk about? I'm not much of a talker of feelings, but Wyatt has kind of changed me to believe that if there is something on your chest, you should get it off."

"Wyatt seems like a very smart man."

With a smile, she shrugs and says, "He's okay." Then she nudges me. "What's on your mind?"

"Just how happy I am." And the minute the words come out of my mouth, those tears well up again, but I can't stop them this time. "God, I'm sorry." I dab at them. "I swear I'm not the type to cry when someone asks how they're doing." I let out a deep breath. "Just been an adjustment."

"What's been an adjustment?" Aubree asks in a caring voice.

"All of this," I say. "Bennett, my brother, and I have been on our own for so long and we've been clawing to make something of our lives, and now that I'm here, teaching, coaching . . . in a relationship with your brother, it all feels too good to be true, especially when he comes with a family like yours."

"I can understand that. I know how important family is, how important it is to feel at peace, and to feel like you're finally in a position in your life where everything slows down and you can just enjoy it. It's okay to cry about it. You've worked so hard to get to where you are."

"I have." I wipe at my tears again, hating that I'm crying in front of Aubree.

"Just means you're in the right place if you're this happy, so happy that tears come to your eyes. And we're really happy that you're here. Ryland deserves you in his life. He was, uh . . . he was texting us earlier about his conversation with Mac yesterday, and his sentiments about you, and how you treat Mac. It's a relief, Gabby. When Cassidy passed, our lives were turned upside down. So much responsibility was placed on our shoulders, and all we wanted to do was keep our sister's legacy alive. The pressure of it was insurmountable. Yet slowly but surely, we were able to wade through the darkness and find some light."

"That's what it feels like to me, wading through the darkness and finally seeing the light. I just fear the darkness will come creeping back in."

Aubree shakes her head. "You can't think of it that way. Coming from someone who has suffered a lot of trauma, and has finally found her peace, trust me when I say the light stays as long as you hold on to it."

I stare down at my hands, thinking about the light in my life. How that light is in the form of a six-foot-two man with brown hair and green eyes, who told me just hours ago that he was infatuated with me, a man who had no problem crying in front of me because his niece had called him Dad. He's the light, and I will cling to him as much as I can.

"Come on," Aubree says. "If we don't hit up the appetizers now, Hattie will eat them all. Also, she really wants you to try her favorite pickles."

"Oh?" I ask, curious.

"Yup. It was a special pickle between her and Cassidy, and she offers them to everyone who comes to the house. I kind of think it's her weird way of making sure Cassidy's a part of everyone's life."

"That's kind of sweet."

"In an odd way, right?"

I laugh. "A little bit."

Together, we head toward the firepit where Hattie and Echo are sitting along with a new girl who I've never met. Must be Hattie's friend, Maggie.

"There she is," Hattie says. "Maggie, meet Gabby. This is Ryland's girlfriend, but we aren't telling people outside of this inner circle because, get this, they work together and coach together."

"Ooo, scandal, I love it," Maggie says and then shakes my hand. "I'm Maggie. It's really nice to meet you. I'm glad Ryland found someone. He's a good guy."

"A really good guy," I say, glancing at Aubree, who smiles back at me.

"Okay, now that we're all here. I think we need to start the evening with a celebratory—"

"Maggie," Hayes says, interrupting. "Brody's looking for you."

"Why?" Maggie asks and then turns to me. "Brody's my man, and he's very needy."

"Something about his zipper. I didn't ask," Hayes says.

"Jesus," Maggie grumbles, setting her drink down on the outer ring of the firepit. "Don't start anything without me."

"I thought men weren't invited," Echo says. "Yet Hayes, Brody, and Wyatt are here. What's happening?"

"Aunt Hattie," Mac's little voice rings out as she comes charging toward Hattie and wraps her arms around Hattie's legs. From the sliding glass door, I catch Ryland, hands in his pockets, looking all types of yummy.

"Mac, what are you doing here?"

"Uncle Dad said that Uncle Hayes had food for me."

Uncle Dad, my freaking heart. I can't take it.

Hattie smiles down at her niece. "Was Uncle Dad lazy and didn't want to cook for you tonight?"

"Uh, can I just say the Uncle Dad thing is the cutest sentiment I've ever heard," Echo says.

Same. It's so freaking adorable.

"He said Uncle Hayes had hot dogs."

"He does. Why don't you go get one? Don't forget to load up on the ketchup."

Mac is about to take off when she scans the crowd and spots me. "Gabby." She throws her arms around my legs as well, and I return the hug. The kid gives the best hugs. Each time we've had "playdates," I've been given awesome goodnight hugs. *They're addictive. Like her uncle.* "You're here."

"I am," I say. "I heard there were hot dogs too, and I couldn't pass it up."

"Will you eat with me?" She tugs on my hand, and I start moving in that direction when Ryland calls out to her.

"Mac, grab Aubree too. Uncle Wyatt has a question for her."

"Dear God in heaven," Hattie says in frustration, making me chuckle. "This is why men were not invited. They clearly can't function without us."

Aubree and I head toward the house just as the lights go out, pitching the backyard into darkness.

"What on earth," Hattie calls out. "Hayes, the lights—"

The firepit goes out as well, leaving the sunset across the ocean as the only light, casting an orange pink glow around the backyard.

"What's happening?" I ask Ryland as he keeps his eyes on Hattie.

He nods toward Hattie, and I turn around where I see Hayes playing a guitar and walking toward Hattie, looking like a god with a guitar in hand. Echo moves away, holding her phone up. I assume she is recording the whole thing as Hattie turns to find

Hayes walking toward her. Immediately, her hands go up to her mouth as he sings his new single, *Electric Sunshine*.

We're joined by Maggie and Wyatt, and together, we all watch as Hayes plays to Hattie, sitting down on the bench together that's in front of the fireplace. When he's done, he spins his guitar to his back and then takes a knee in front of Hattie. I can hear her crying from here as my heart hammers out of my chest, watching this perfectly executed moment.

Hayes speaks softly to Hattie, holding her hand, and after a sob escapes her, she nods. Hayes scoops her up and kisses her senseless. Echo and Maggie take pictures. Ryland, Brody, Wyatt, and I all cheer while Mac runs up to them and hugs them.

"Oh my God, did you know this was happening?" I ask Ryland.

He nods. "I was sworn to secrecy. He had it planned this entire time. He was going to go more elaborate but then said he wanted to do it in the same place where he fell for her, during sunset."

"It was beautiful."

Hattie turns toward us and says, "We're engaged . . . finally!"

We all laugh and walk up to the newly engaged couple to offer our congratulations. I let everyone move in first since I'm the newcomer and because I truly love watching Ryland interact with his family. The way he pulls Hattie into a great big bear hug, how he shakes Hayes's hand but then pulls him into a hug, and how he lifts Mac up into his arms so she can high-five everyone.

It's endearing.

And it just solidifies the feelings I have for this man.

He's everything I'm looking for in a partner.

He's kind, has a warm heart, and his family comes first.

He's smart, loves baseball just as much as I do, and cares about the progress of the sport and those in it.

When it comes to me, he's loving, protective, and he's present, something Nathan never was.

"Come here," Ryland says when he notices I'm standing

outside the group. He unabashedly pulls me into his side and wraps his arm around my waist before placing a kiss on the top of my head.

Seriously shocked that he's showing affection, I look up at him, and he just winks. And this exact reason is why I'm falling for this man. He keeps breaking his boundaries. He keeps growing. He keeps putting one foot in front of the other instead of regressing to his past.

He's healthy.

He's happy.

And he's mine.

"They're really cute together," I say to Ryland as I watch Hattie curl into Hayes by the firepit.

Mac's in the house with Wyatt, and they're both watching some horse videos on Wyatt's phone.

Brody and Maggie are snuggled together around the firepit, talking to Hattie and Hayes, laughing and joking, while Aubree's helping Echo clean up after dinner. I offered, but she shooed me away and told me to go sit with Ryland.

She didn't have to tell me twice. So now we're on a large lounge chair together, his arm around me, my head resting against his chest.

"I didn't think so at first," he says softly. "Hell, I fucking hated it. But he showed me that he could take care of my sister, probably better than even myself."

"It looks like it. What about Wyatt? Did you like him?"

"Well, Wyatt, in a way, is our brother-in-law, sort of. His brother was Cassidy's husband, so I already knew Wyatt and when he came around, I was more than happy to have him here, that was until I found out what he was doing."

"What was he doing?"

Ryland chuckles. "Hell, when I tell you, it's going to sound like it's straight out of a book, but I swear it happened."

"Ooo, now I'm intrigued. Tell me."

He tugs on a strand of my hair and twirls it as he talks to me. "Where do I even start, uh . . . well, he owned part of the farmland but didn't want it. He wanted a cabin that his grandpa was leaving the first grandchild who married. He was left at the altar, and well, desperate to inherit the cabin before his cousin, he came to Aubree with an agreement. How did he put it . . ." Ryland pauses for a second, then I feel the rumble of his laughter come out as he says, "Her hand for his land."

"What?" I ask. "A marriage of convenience. That's their love story?"

"Yup. And because Aubree wanted full control over the farm and didn't care about being in a relationship, she was okay with it. Of course she didn't tell any of us because we would have had a fucking fit, but as they moved through their agreement, they fell in love and then just stayed married."

"That's crazy. Yeah, I feel like without the warning, I wouldn't have believed you."

"I'm happy they fell for each other, though, because Aubree needed that love. She was the one I was worried about."

"Why?"

"She was the one who was kind of . . . left behind. Cassidy spent a lot of time focusing on Hattie because she's much younger than us, and I was the one dealing with our dad. Aubree could have used the attention because she was still young, but not as young as Hattie. You're talking about siblings taking care of siblings, so Cassidy's attention could only go so far. As we got older, I could see how jaded Aubree was becoming, and I hated that. I wanted her to find someone who could make her happy and take away her demons. She found that in Wyatt."

I turn toward Ryland and look him in the eyes. "You're such a good big brother, being able to see what everyone needs like that, you're very in tune with your family. I love that about you."

"Yeah? What else do you love?" he asks playfully.

"Hmm, well, I love that you take care of Mac so well, that

even though she's your niece, you treat her like a daughter, and I love that she's calling you Uncle Dad."

"Yeah . . . it's, uh." His jaw ticks. "That was surprising, but I love it."

"And I love that you care about your players but that you won't let them get away with not trying, not hustling. That you instill in them how hard work can take you places."

"Without hard work, you and I wouldn't be where we are today."

"Very true. And I love how you are so tender with me. I know that's sort of a weird thing to say, but I've never had the best track record with men, yet you make me feel seen and special."

"Because you are special." His hand moves up to the back of my head, and he moves me closer until our mouths lock. And for a moment, I forget about where we are, who's around us, and the proposal that happened earlier. Instead, I get lost in his mouth.

I get lost in his touch.

I get lost in this man who I can't seem to shake.

That I don't want to shake.

No, I want to stay glued to him. I want to remain in his life for as long as he will let me because as his mouth parts and our tongues meet, I know for certain my feelings for him grow so much further past like, past lust.

The feelings I have for him are love, and I'm not afraid to admit that to myself despite never thinking I'd ever love someone after Nathan.

But here I am, chest open, heart out, ready to be stolen by this man.

Now, I just need to wait. I need to wait and make sure that my feelings match his. Until then, I will foster this relationship and do everything in my power to make sure Ryland knows that even though he's the protector, someone else can protect him.

Protect him and love him.

# Chapter Twenty-Nine

RYLAND

"Where do you think you're going?" I ask Gabby as she heads toward her apartment while I carry a passed-out Mac to the house.

"Uh, home," she says with a laugh.

I shake my head and then nod toward my house. "Sleep over."

"Are you . . . are you sure? What about Mac?"

"What about her?"

"I don't want to overstep," she says, looking nervous. This is why I'm convinced trying a relationship with Gabby is the right move. She's focused on the little girl in my care and her needs, which says everything I need to know about this amazing woman.

"Would I ask you to spend the night if you were overstepping?"

"No."

"Then sleep over . . . but only if you want to. I don't want to pressure you if you're uncomfortable."

She gives it some thought. "It doesn't make me uncomfortable."

"Then get your ass in my house."

She smiles. "Let me grab my toothbrush and pajamas."

"You won't need pajamas," I say as I move toward the house and let us in.

Mac passed out in the truck after I had to physically put her in myself. For the smallest of moments, I thought about leaving her at Hattie's place, slipping her into the guest room, and then taking off so I didn't have to disturb her. But then I remembered that my sister had just gotten engaged, so there was no way they'd want to take care of a four-year-old the next day.

I carry her upstairs and don't even bother changing her out of her clothes. We slipped her shoes off when we put her in the truck, so all I had to do was place her in bed. I lay her down gently, pull the covers over her, and then place a soft kiss on her forehead. I stare down at her for a moment, my heart feeling really fucking full.

A lot of it has to do with Mac and her acceptance of me but it's also Gabby, too, a person I never knew I needed or wanted in my life.

I sneak out of Mac's bedroom and move downstairs where I wait for Gabby.

Tonight was . . . it was amazing. Seeing my little sister get engaged to the man she loves with her family and friends surrounding her, especially after such a rough year, and then being able to lay back in a lounge chair with Gabby, staring up at the stars . . . I've never felt so completely fulfilled.

This is what happiness is.

After trudging through the trenches year after year and feeling every disappointment, every heartache one person can feel, finding light after the darkness is incredible. I never want to let go of this feeling.

The back door opens, and Gabby walks in wearing the T-shirt I gave her and carrying her toothbrush.

"I thought I told you no pajamas."

She looks up. "Did you want me to walk over here naked and give the neighbors a show?"

"No."

"Then be grateful I'm wearing the shirt." She walks right up to me and presses her hand to my chest before standing on her toes and kissing me.

I melt from the feel of her lips on mine.

Nothing will ever be better.

Groaning, I say, "Upstairs."

I take her hand, and we make our way up to my bedroom, which now actually looks like a bedroom—for the most part. I'm not sleeping on a mattress on the floor. The bed has been put together, and I have nice bedding. Curtains have been hung, boxes have been unpacked, and I even have a few pictures hanging up, thanks to Hattie, who came over one day after work to help me.

Kind of proud to show it off.

I lead her into my bedroom, switch on the light, and await her reaction.

She does not disappoint.

"Ryland, oh my God, it looks . . . wow, it looks amazing in here."

"Yeah?" I ask. "You like it?"

"Yes, look you even hung pictures, and you have nightstands with lamps, and is that . . . is that a fake plant?"

"That was Hattie. She thought I needed it."

"She was right. It adds some nice color. Aw, I love it." She moves into my side. "Do you love it?"

"I do. I love it even more with you in here."

"Look at you putting the moves on and we haven't even brushed our teeth yet."

I chuckle and direct her toward the bathroom. "You're right, what was I even thinking."

We get ready for bed. She leans against the counter while brushing her teeth, and I stare at her legs.

After turning on the shower, I strip down for her and start washing my body. From the counter, she watches. *And wets her lips.* God, I love when she does that.

When I exit, she strips down and steps into the shower, turning on the water.

"Uh, why didn't you join me?" I ask.

She soaps up her body. "Because I don't want to be fucked in the shower. And knowing you, that's what would have happened."

"Depriving me of shower sex. How dare you?" She chuckles, then she wiggles her eyebrows at me. *So fucking cute.*

I watch her carefully when she's out of the shower and dried off, wondering if she's going to put her shirt back on. When she hangs up her towel and moves into the bedroom, I know I'm the luckiest guy around.

She slips into bed, and I follow her closely, turning off all the lights, casting us in the glow of the moonlight. I slide in close to her and rest on my side, and then my hand falls to her bare hip when she turns toward me as well.

"I like this," she says.

"So do I. I like having you here a whole fucking lot." My thumb strokes over her skin. "The night we stayed in San Francisco was the best night's sleep I've ever had, and I've been craving another one."

Her fingers dance over my chest hair. "So have I. I fear after tonight, the craving will only be stronger."

"Same, which means you might be stuck with me."

"I've been in worse situations," she teases. "I think I can handle being attached to you."

"Good, because I have no intention of letting go." I pull her in closer and run my hand up her back. "Did you have fun tonight?"

"I had the most fun. The only thing that would have made it better was if Bennett was there. But maybe after the season, he can come and hang out and meet everyone."

"I'd love to spend more time with him," I say.

"Ethel was saying it might be fun to have some sort of home-coming to Almond Bay for him when the season's over. I know he'd hate it, but I kind of feel like celebrating his accomplishments."

"I think it's a great idea. And we can hang his jersey in the athletics hallway. We always do it for those who have reached the big leagues."

"Really? Oh, that would be so cool. I'll let Ethel know. She said she loves throwing events."

"She lives to throw events," I say. "You should have seen the number she did on Aubree and Wyatt's proposal, which, now that I think about it in the context that it was all for show and that they weren't in love at that point, makes it funnier."

"I keep hearing about this proposal. I'm going to need to see pictures."

"I'll let Aubree know." My hand glides down her back and rounds over her ass. "I'm glad you had a good time tonight. I loved seeing you mesh so well with my family."

"It's hard not to. They make it very easy."

"Feels seamless, doesn't it?"

"It does."

"You know, I was talking to Aubree earlier . . ."

Her fingers pause on my chest. "Let me guess, she told you about a conversation we had out by the rocks."

"Maybe," I say. She nods slowly, so I try to ease the obvious tension growing there. "I need you to know I have the same feeling as you. That this all seems too good to be true."

"You do?" she asks, looking shy.

"Yes, I think about it all the time. It feels like you fell into my lap, and it's hard to comprehend that something so good could happen to me."

"That's exactly how I feel," she says.

"Like something is bound to happen to mess it all up."

"It scares me." Her hand drags down to my stomach. "Because I like you so much, and I don't want anything to ruin that."

"I don't want anything to ruin it either," I say, gliding my palm over her curves and up her side.

"But it does scare you?"

I nod as her finger circles my belly button, immediately making my cock ache as it grows hard from her innocent touching.

"Scares me a whole fucking lot. And I know this seems to be moving fast, that we said we'd give it time and see how Mac feels, but fuck, sometimes I think she likes you more than me."

"Not possible. She loves her Uncle Dad."

I chuckle. "I guess she does." I wet my lips. "I'm glad Aubree told me how you felt, because it made me feel even more connected to you."

"It did?" she asks as her fingers connect with the head of my cock.

I suck in a sharp breath before answering. "Yeah." And then I push her to her back and move over her, letting her gently wrap her hand around my cock as I take her mouth with mine, kissing her over and over because I'll never get enough of this. Of her lips. Of her taste, of her entire body.

I want this forever.

I want *her* forever.

I release her mouth, kiss down her jaw to her neck, and then farther down her body, where I find her supple tits and drag the flat part of my tongue over her nipples.

"Yes," she whispers, knowing she must be quiet. "God, I love your tongue. Will you let me come on it tonight?"

"Planned on it, babe," I say as I move down her body, circle my tongue around her belly button, over her pubic bone, and then place a gentle kiss right on her slit. She opens her legs wider for me, places one hand behind her head, and then watches as I split her with my fingers and press my tongue along her arousal. "Yes, so fucking drenched already. Such a good girl."

She sighs heavily and sinks into the mattress as I work my tongue around her clit. I wipe around, along, and then on top, creating a pattern that seems to make her nuts as her breathing grows heavy and her other hand grips the covers below us.

"Oh my God, Ryland, whatever you're doing . . . don't . . . stop."

I look up at her as I continue to work my tongue over her hardening clit and take in how her skin reddens, the light glisten of sweat over her chest, the slight part of her mouth, almost as if she's in awe from what she's experiencing.

"Play with those nipples, baby," I say, lifting for a second because hell, I love watching her play with herself.

Her hands fall to her breasts, and her hips start rotating as her orgasm builds.

"That's it, Gabby. Fuck, you're so hot."

With my spare hand, I start pumping my cock as I keep my mouth on her, lapping at her clit, loving how goddamn wet she is. From the sounds she's making, watching her play with herself, and her taste on my tongue, my orgasm moves up my spine as well, gearing me up for so much fucking pleasure that it takes everything in me to release my cock and focus on getting her off.

Slipping two fingers inside her, I curl them upward and press into her at just the right spot that makes her fly up to her hands and stare down at me with shock in her eyes.

"Oh my God, Ryland. Fuck . . . oh my God."

She's going to come . . . and hard. I can see it in those eyes of hers. She's right there, teetering on the edge, and because I'm a selfish prick, I don't want her coming just yet, so I pull away.

"No," she says on a gasp. "Ryland. Fuck. What are you doing?"

I sit back and stare at her, the eternal state of unsatisfied washing over her pink skin.

I sit up on my knees and say, "Lie back and open your mouth."

She studies me for a few moments and then listens. I straddle her body and bring my cock to her mouth. "Need to fuck you here." I line her lips with my tip, then I move inside her.

Thankfully, she's ready for me and sucks hard as I enter her mouth.

"Fuck," I say, punching the headboard from how goddamn good that feels. "Jesus Christ, I've thought about this all day. This filthy mouth sucking me off." I slowly pump into her. "This mouth was made for me. That's it, baby, take me deep."

She parts her lips and lets me hit her all the way back to her throat. I pull all the way out and line her lips again with the tip. When I enter, she sucks even harder, making me nearly black out as her cheeks hollow.

"Again," I say, pulling out and moving back in. "Fucking . . . again." Then I pull out and flop back on the bed. My aching, surging cock twitches against my stomach, searching out release.

I breathe heavily, the effects of the edging rocking over my body.

She comes up to me and kisses my neck, then my chest, then my stomach, moving closer to my cock but never going where I need her.

"Torture me. Make me beg," I tell her.

She makes that her own personal mission and spreads my legs before moving between them. She kisses up my inner thigh, then brings her mouth to my balls, where she gently starts flicking them with the tip of her tongue.

"That's it, baby, fucking drive me wild."

She drags her tongue over the seam, then back down while her fingers curl around the base of my cock. She doesn't pump, but she does squeeze tightly, creating a delicious sensation as she hums against my balls, like my own personal vibrator.

"Jesus, fuck," I say as I wiggle under her, looking for friction, anything, but she doesn't give it to me. She just continues to squeeze me, tighter and tighter, while humming against my sack. My legs start to go numb, my cock twitches, and pre-cum seeps from the tip. "Fuck, I need more, baby. Something. Give me that pussy."

I can practically feel her smile against me as she releases my length and moves up my body. She straddles my head and brings her arousal right to my mouth.

I asked for it, and she's delivering.

My dick's so goddamn hard, ready to explode, but I swipe my tongue over her slit and cup her breast, squeezing and running her nipple between my fingers. Her hips rotate over my face, her hand clasping mine, helping me squeeze her breast.

"God, no one makes me come like you," she says. "Yes, right there, Ryland."

She tenses above me, and her mouth parts open, indicating she's right there.

I move her off me and flip her to her back, where I press kisses down her stomach, across her hips, and then I lean back on my heels and grip my cock. It feels so heavy in my hand since I'm so dangerously close to my orgasm.

She stares up at me, looking dazed and confused.

"I'm going to burst," she says.

"Same," I say, unable to control my breathing. I lie back and position my cock upward. "Ride me, baby. Make us come together."

Within seconds, she's on top of me, legs spread, and when she hovers above my cock and presses down, both of us groan loud enough to wake up Mac. But that doesn't stop us because her hands fall to my chest, her fingers digging into my skin, and she pulses over me, creating the most delicious friction of my goddamn life.

"God yes, oh my God, yes, yes," she chants as she moves faster and faster, rubbing her clit over me, her cunt tightening over my cock. "More. More."

I flip her to her back and take charge, driving into her.

"Yes, deeper, Ryland. Fuck me deeper."

Jesus Christ.

A deep, tingling sensation creeps up my back as I pound into her now, rocking the bed to the point that I'm afraid it might fucking snap in half.

"I want your cum . . . deep inside me."

Unable to control myself, I position one hand on the bed, and the other around her neck, lightly gripping her.

"Yes, fuck me, like that," she says.

"Take it, Gabby. Take this fucking cock." I slam into her, making her cry out.

"Ahhhh, yes. Just like that."

"Take . . . this . . . cock," I grunt, moving my hips so fast that I start to lose my breath. The room turns black, my body tenses, and then she calls out . . .

"Fuck, I'm coming." Her cunt tightens around me, contracting and tugging on my cock so hard as she falls apart that I have no choice but to join her.

"Uhhhh, motherfucker," I groan as I spill inside her, my goddamn body floating in ecstasy as I fill her up. I continue to pump a few more times, feeling her continue to contract around me as we both catch our breath.

After a few seconds, I lie on top of her but use my elbows on the mattress to keep my body weight off her.

She sleepily smiles up at me, then wraps her arms around me and kisses me hard. Her tongue parts my lips, and she open-mouth kisses me. When she pulls away, she brushes my hair out of my face and dreamily looks up at me.

"What?" I ask. I want to know what's on her mind.

"Nothing," she says.

"Say it."

She shakes her head.

"Fucking say it, Gabby."

"No." She looks away, but I take her chin in my hand and force her to look at me.

"Don't make me repeat myself."

"I . . . I don't want—"

"You won't regret it. Just fucking say it."

She shifts, and after a few seconds, she finally says, "I'm falling in love with you, Ryland."

Fucking music to my ears.

I press my forehead to hers and whisper, "I'm falling in love with you, too."

Her teeth pull on her bottom lip, and she kisses me again. This time, it's softer, more subtle, and as she lies there with me still inside her, I start to grow again with every gentle swipe of her tongue. Before we know it, I'm starting to move inside her again.

But this time, it's different.

This time . . . we're making love.

---

***Ryland:*** *I love her.*

***Hattie:*** *Ahhhhhhhhhh!!!! I freaking knew it. I saw this coming a mile away.*

***Aubree:*** *Aw, really?*

***Ryland:*** *Yes. I fucking love her so goddamn much. She spent the night last night. She's upstairs sleeping while Mac watches a show and I make pancakes. She's everything. We told each other we're falling in love.*

***Hattie:*** *What a freaking weekend. I get engaged, and you fall in love. Aubree . . . are you pregnant? Maybe round out the trifecta here.*

***Aubree:*** *Definitely not pregnant. Sorry to disappoint, but Wyatt did tell me that he wanted to invest in a new pair of loafers, so maybe that's a new addition to the family.*

***Hattie:*** *No.*

***Ryland:*** *Loafers are essential for a fancy man going on book tours.*

***Aubree:*** *That's what he told me. He then spent an hour shopping online to no avail. So seems like you two had better nights.*

***Hattie:*** *Much better nights. Want me to go into detail?*

***Ryland:*** *For God's sake, no.*

***Aubree:*** *Boundaries, Hattie, have them.*

***Hattie:*** *Just trying to see how close we are.*

***Aubree:*** *Not that close. Share with Maggie.*

***Hattie:*** *Oh, I will, but back to Ryland. This is so exciting. So . . . does this mean I might hear wedding bells for you two?*

***Ryland:*** *It means that I want to take things further, that I want her to* *spend more nights here, see how Mac reacts, and go from there. But yeah . . . I think I can manage this. I think I can have her and still take care of my responsibilities.*

**Aubree:** *I think so too.*

**Hattie:** *I love this for you, Ryland. And I know Cassidy would have loved this as well. Not to get emotional, but she's been on my mind lately, especially with the engagement. I think she'd be proud of all of us.*

**Ryland:** *I think she would too. She would have loved Gabby, and she would have loved the way Gabby treats Mac.*

**Aubree:** *She would have.*

**Hattie:** *So are we going to celebrate your newfound love? Maybe throw a party?*

**Ryland:** *Uh, no, but I was talking to Gabby last night about her brother, Bennett. Ethel wants to throw a coming home party for him when the season's over. Think you guys can keep Ethel in line—the best you can—so we can make the day special for them?*

**Aubree:** *I think we can manage, but if she goes rogue, that's not on us.*

**Hattie:** *You saw what she did for Aubree's engagement.*

**Ryland:** *Exactly, and that's why I'm looking toward you two to help her, keep her reined in.*

**Aubree:** *We can try.*

**Hattie:** *But when she's in party-planning mode, she's difficult to be around.*

**Ryland:** *Have my back, ladies. Make this great for Bennett and Gabby.*

**Hattie:** *Question, why are we in charge? Why can't you speak to Ethel?*

**Aubree:** *Great point. Are you so scared of Ethel that you don't think you can handle her, so you pawn her off on your little sisters?*

**Ryland:** *No. She doesn't respect men. That's the problem. You saw what she did to Wyatt—he was carted around in a kiddie train. She needs to work with her own kind. She'll respect your opinion more.*

**Hattie:** *He has a point.*

**Aubree:** *I'm honestly surprised she didn't make Wyatt blossom from a flower after being carted out in a kiddie train.*

**Hattie:** *Missed opportunity if you ask me.*

**Aubree:** *Could not agree more. Maybe I'll have her make him blossom for the party just for the hell of it.*

**Ryland:** *Please don't.*

**Hattie:** *Please don't? Please DO. I'm over here already researching how to make a grown man blossom.*

**Aubree:** *Let me know what you find. I'd love nothing more than to witness my man grow from a seedling to a flower in front of the whole town.*

**Hattie:** *On it.*

**Ryland:** *I think I might regret this.*

# Chapter Thirty

## GABBY

I stretch out, my body sore in all the right places as I slowly let my eyes adjust to the light coming through the curtains. I turn toward Ryland, reaching for his warm body, but when I come up short, I open my eyes wider and notice that I'm naked and alone in bed.

I sit up, look around, and when I see a note on his pillow, my stomach ties in all kinds of happy knots.

*Making breakfast. Put clothes on before you come down.*

*XXX – R*

Smiling, I set the note down on the nightstand closest to me, where I find a set of clothes, Ryland's to be exact. He thought of everything. I must have been extremely zonked out not to notice him moving around. Then again, he wore me out last night.

After our second time, he cleaned us both up and then wrapped his large body around me, keeping me close as we drifted off to sleep. I was in a heavy slumber when I started feeling him touching me, caressing me, kissing me in the middle of the night. I rolled over, and he moved over me and slowly inserted himself.

I was so turned on that it was a quick but slow fuck if that makes sense. There was no finessing, no foreplay. It was just him driving into me over and over until we both came. And then we went back to sleep.

It almost feels like a fever dream at this point, but I know it happened.

I slip out of bed, take the clothes to the bathroom, and brush my teeth. The whole time, I stare into the mirror, assessing my body and all the places where Ryland left his mark.

His beard grazed all over my chest, up my neck, and around my stomach. His teeth marked along my collarbone and even right above my breasts. My legs and my arms are sore, as well as between my legs.

Yet I'm so freaking satisfied.

Never been happier.

Never felt more content.

Never realized this is what life could be.

I quickly rinse, go to the bathroom, and slip on my clothes. I find my phone on the bathroom counter, so I check it and see a text from Bennett.

**Bennett:** *Did you catch the game last night? I got plunked in the ass, and it's now a GIF.*

And below the text is a GIF of Bennett getting hit in the ass, but as he's getting hit, for some reason, he popped his butt out, so it looks like he's twerking as the ball is hitting him.

I laugh out loud and text him back.

**Gabby:** *Shit, I wish I'd have seen this. I'll be using this GIF for everything now.*

**Bennett:** *How did I know you were going to say that? If you weren't watching me play last night, you better have a good reason.*

**Gabby:** *I do. It was girls' night at Hattie's, which turned into a secret proposal. Hattie and Hayes are engaged. I spent the night with Ryland's family and well . . . spent the night at his house. (Leaving out the rest of the details for your benefit.)*

**Bennett:** *I appreciate it. But wow, sounds like a great night. So things are moving along over there with Coach Rowley?*

**Gabby:** *You know you can call him Ryland. And yeah, they are. We sort of told each other we loved each other last night.*

**Bennett:** *Seriously? Holy shit. That's huge.*

**Gabby:** *It was (and I'm talking about the moment, not what's in his pants, although that's huge too.)*

**Bennett:** *Jesus, Gabby. Please . . . no.*

**Gabby:** *LOL! I have to make you gag a little . . . kind of like how he made me gag.*

**Bennett:** *Okay, I'm done. I love you, please don't talk to me again.*

**Gabby:** *LOLOLOL. Love you too.*

After setting my phone down, I check my hair before I make my way downstairs, where I find Mac sitting on the couch with the Chewys, watching a show.

She's startled at first when she sees me, then she leaps off the couch and runs up to me, giving me a huge hug. "Gabby, you're here."

"I am," I say as I catch Ryland in the kitchen in the same outfit as me, but his fits way better. He glances over his shoulder and offers me a wink before turning back to the griddle.

Ugh . . . I really do love him.

"Why did you spend the night?"

Uh, great question.

"You know, I think that's a question for Uncle Dad."

Taking me by the hand, Mac leads me to the kitchen and says, "Why did Gabby spend the night?"

Ryland puts the last of the pancakes on a cooling rack and turns toward us. He leans against the counter, folds his arms. "Because I like her."

"Oh . . ." Mac looks up at me. "Where did you sleep?"

I turn to Ryland again. "Where did I sleep?"

He chuckles and then takes my hand, pulling me into his chest. "She slept with me last night, Mac."

Mac's eyes flit between the two of us, her little head processing what's going on. "I don't understand."

Ryland squats down to her eye level and places his hands on her hips. "You know how Uncle Hayes and Aunt Hattie are in love?" Mac nods. "And how Aunt Aubree and Uncle Wyatt are in love?" Mac nods again. "Well, Gabby and I are in love." Hearing him say that sends such a warm thrill through me.

"Oh, so you're like married?" Her cute little nose twists to the side.

"Not yet, but we are . . . uh . . . in terms you can understand, boyfriend and girlfriend."

Um, can we pause for a second because did you hear what he said about the married thing?

Not . . . yet.

Cue the girly screams.

She looks back and forth between us again. "Do you kiss?"

Ryland clears his throat and nods. "Yes, we kiss."

She then looks at me with a quirk to her nose. "You like kissing him?"

I don't know why that makes me laugh, but it does. I squat down with Ryland and put my arm over his back. "Yes, I like kissing him."

When she doesn't say anything, Ryland says, "Is this okay?"

Mac shrugs. "I don't care." But the small smile she gives makes me so happy inside.

Ryland chuckles. "Are you sure? Because I'd like to have Gabby around more, but if you don't—"

"Yes, yes, yes." Mac jumps up and down. "She can play with me."

"Yes, she can play with you," Ryland says.

"She's the best player." Mac runs into my arms, nearly tackling me to the ground, but I balance myself and hug her back.

"I don't know, I think you're the best player," I say.

"Uh, am I chopped liver over here? I was pretty confident that I was the best player. No one can top . . . Godzilla Plus," Ryland says in a deep voice and puts his claws out.

Mac screams and runs away. "Come on, Gabby. Godzilla Plus is going to eat us."

"Never," I yell, grabbing a pillow from the couch—a genuinely nice throw pillow—and tossing it at his head. When it hits him, he dramatically spins around, sticks his tongue out, and then falls to the ground with a thump.

I raise my fist in the air and say, "Huh-ha! I got him."

"Her," Mac corrects me. "You got her."

"Right, sorry." I air pump again and say, "I got her!"

"Now we can eat all the pancakes we want."

I lift Mac up into my arms and step over a convulsing Ryland, who is really playing the part.

"Pancakes for the heroes of the day."

---

"You know, I was thinking about something," Ryland says as his finger traces circles over my leg.

We're sitting on the couch. Mac is asleep upstairs, and it's the second night in a row that Ryland has asked me to spend the night. He texted me while I was in my apartment, attempting to think of anything else but him and Mac yet doing a terrible job at it. I gave it a few seconds before I responded, then said I'd love to. Because who was I kidding? I was itching to come over.

This was after I spent a solid two hours on the phone with Bower, giving her a recap of everything. She gushed of course. I gushed. And then we cried.

Because when your friend sees you struggle for so long, and then sees you happy for the first time in a long time, it requires a squeal.

"What were you thinking?" I ask.

"I was looking at tickets for the Bombers game next Friday."

"You were?"

"Yeah. Do you want to go?"

"Those tickets are expensive," I say to Ryland.

"I know a guy who has a suite, and he said he won't be in town that weekend. He asked me if I wanted to take my family since he knows I'm a fan."

I sit up to look him in the eyes to see if he's serious. "You . . . know a guy? Since when have you *known a guy*?"

"I used to mow his lawn for cash, and then he'd let me practice on the freshly mowed lawn. He moved closer to the city for a job, but we always stayed in touch. He was one of the shining lights in a pretty dark childhood."

"What's his name?"

"Patrick Garnett. He owns a dealership in the Bay area and has a suite where he takes executives to schmooze so they'll buy his fleet of cars for their business. But that's beside the point. He can't make it and asked if I want the suite."

This requires my full attention. "You're serious."

"Jesus, Gabby, yes. Why would I joke about this?"

"I don't know. You just . . . you brought it up so casually, and I don't know how to respond because I was just going to watch the game on TV. But now that I can actually go, that seems insane, and I don't know how to react properly other than to ask you if you're serious."

"You're rambling."

"Because this is huge!" I cup his cheeks and lean forward. "This is, this is . . . oh my God, I'm going to fuck you so hard tonight."

He lets out a barrel of a laugh as his hands find my hips. "Well, I thought that was already a given, but okay."

"It was, but this is . . . this is going to be even better. You tell me what you want, and I'm going to deliver. Want a blowie? Consider your dick sucked. Want a vibrator to the ass? Give me a second and I'll grab my toys and lube. Want a—"

"Uh, your what?"

"My toys and lube."

"You have toys?" he asks cutely.

I sit back on his legs. "Ryland, I was alone and horny for a very long time. Do you really think I wouldn't have toys?"

"I mean . . . I guess not. Why haven't we played with them?"

"Well, we're always over here because you have a child, and every time we've done it besides last night, it's been spontaneous. I didn't think holding up my finger and saying, 'hold please while I grab my toys' was very sexy."

"Jesus, I wish you did."

"Yeah?" I pull his shirt up and over his head. "Do you like playing with toys?"

"I find the idea of you getting off in front of me with one of them extremely appealing. Actually, that's what I want tonight. I want you to strip for me, then fuck yourself in front of me."

I smile and stand from his lap. "That can be arranged." I then hold up my finger and say, "Hold please."

"Wait." He grabs my hand, not letting me get away just yet. "Is that a yes to the game?"

"That's a resounding yes."

"Do you want to bring your friend? Fuck, sorry, what's her name again?"

"Bower," I say.

"Yeah, do you want to bring Bower? We can bring Mac and see if anyone else wants to go?"

"I'd love that."

"Then I'll let Patrick know."

I lean down and place a soft kiss on his lips. "Thank you. This means everything to me."

"Anything for you, Gabby." And for once in my life, I actually believe this sentiment. *This man is so damn amazing.*

*And he's mine . . .*

# Chapter Thirty-One

## RYLAND

Mother of fuck.

Gabby slides her robe off her shoulders, revealing a teal strappy lingerie set as I sit in a chair directly across from my bed.

The bra is made of thin ribbons. The cups barely cover her nipples, while the thong sits high on her hips and then another strap across her hips. It's so fucking sexy that my mouth waters and my hands itch to get a piece of her.

On the bed are a few vibrators and some lube. They're all appealing, and I want to play with everything. But the one that seems to suck her clit, that's the one I want to watch her use.

She plays some light music in the background, then walks over to me and places her hand on my shoulder before straddling my lap.

"Fuck, you look hot," I say as she undulates her body against me, letting my face slide over her cleavage a few times. "Jesus."

When she pulls away, she reaches behind her and unclasps her bra. The fabric loosens but doesn't quite fall off, making me yearn for it to go.

"Take it off," I say, my voice husky.

She lowers the straps down her arms, then slowly peels the fabric off her breasts and tosses it to the side.

I cup her breasts, and her head falls back. And as she plays with her hair, she rocks over me. I start circling her nipples, playing with them until they're rock hard. That's when I tug her nipple between my lips.

"Yes, Ryland," she whispers. "Just like that."

My other hand rounds up her back, bringing her in closer as she rocks over my erection. I let my tongue circle her nipple, lap at it, and then I lightly nibble, loving the way she gasps from the gentle touch.

Hell, I love everything about this woman. She's so responsive, so experimental, and wants everything from me, which gives me so much life. I love the freedom. I love how I can be myself with her and not be judged. And I love how amazing she makes me feel.

"God, I'm throbbing," she says as she moves away from me and turns around on my lap so her back is to my chest. She leans back so I can look down her body, and that's when I slide my hand down her stomach and under the small triangle of her thong, feeling just how wet and ready she is.

"Drenched." I lift her and say, "Strip out of that thong, grab the pink toy, and come sit down on me."

She lifts off me, keeps her back toward me, and then slips her thumbs under her thong and slowly pushes the fabric down, bending at the waist and giving me one hell of a show. As she grabs her toy, I strip out of my briefs and let my cock spring forward as she comes back to me. I grip the base and start pumping, giving myself some friction for a moment as I take in her body, the swell of her hips and the roundness of her breasts.

"You're perfect," I say as I pump a few more times. "So fucking perfect. Now sit on me and get yourself off."

"You want to be inside me as I get off?" she asks.

"Do you want me inside you?"

"I want to be full." She straddles my lap and brings my cock to her entrance before sitting all the way down.

"Fuck," I whisper as she leans back, giving me the perfect view.

"Play with my tits. This is going to be fast."

I bring my hands to her breasts while she moves her hand between her legs. She places the toy right at her clit as she spreads her legs and turns it on. The distinct sound of a motor running fills the air as her head leans against my shoulder, and she sighs heavily.

Immediately, I can feel her inner walls start to move around my cock, and it's the best fucking sensation ever.

"Is that sucking your clit?"

"Mm-hmm," she says, her breath starting to grow heavy. "Your cock, though . . . so full, Ryland. This is . . . fuck." She sucks in a sharp breath. "This . . . this is the best . . . fuck."

She shifts, and her walls start contracting.

"Fuck, no," she says as she removes the toy and takes a few deep breaths. "Too much. Not yet."

I pinch her nipples, and she lets out a quiet yelp.

"No, I don't . . . I don't want to come."

I continue to play with her nipples, rolling them and lightly tugging.

"Please, Ryland. I don't . . . oh God."

"Put that fucking toy back and come on my cock."

She sucks in a sharp breath, brings the toy back between her legs, and wraps her feet around mine to use as an anchor.

"Yes, oh God, yes." Her whole body starts to move. "Fuck, I'm . . . I'm so close."

I bring my lips to her ear and say, "Then drench my cock."

She tenses, her body stills, and then a low, guttural sound falls past her lips right before she starts convulsing around me. Her orgasm rips through her, and it's the fucking best thing I've ever seen.

My cock slips inside her, my balls tightening just from watching her fall apart. When she tosses the toy to the side, I bring her to her feet, bend her over at the waist, and pound into her, seeking out my own release.

It takes me seconds before my body's seizing on me, and I'm spilling into her, my cum filling her up until nothing is left inside me.

"Jesus Christ," I quietly say and then help her up. I sit back on the chair, my legs feeling weak. When I look up at her, she's turned around, and I watch as my cum slowly drips down her leg. It's one of the hottest fucking things I've ever seen.

At least that's what I thought until she swipes her finger through it and sucks her finger into her mouth.

"You fucking dirty girl," I say, a smile passing over my face.

She moves over my lap, wraps her arms around my neck, and touches her forehead to mine.

"But I'm all yours."

My hands fall to her ass as I say, "Yeah, you're all fucking mine."

"Bower, it's good to see you," I say as I pull her into a hug.

"I'm excited to be here. I can't remember the last time I got to see Bennett play, nor can I remember the last time I've seen my best friend smile the way she is right now."

We both look over at Gabby. She's decked out in Bombers gear, and Mac sits on her lap with the Chewys as she chats with Hattie.

"You think she's happy?" I ask.

Bower slowly nods her head. "Please. You know damn well she is."

I smirk. "Yeah, I know."

Bower pokes my side. "Look at you being all smug. I didn't know you had it in you."

"Not smug, just . . . happy too."

"Well, I'm glad you were able to get over your initial douchery and give my girl a chance."

"Douchery?" I raise a brow.

"Uh, yeah. You were a total douche at first. Not wanting to cross lines. Think of those weeks when you missed out."

"Didn't really miss out," I say with a wiggle.

"My oh my, look at you coming to life. I think my girl has done a number on you."

"She really has," I say as I look over at Gabby again. "I feel really lucky."

"Do you feel balanced?"

"I do," I say with a nod.

"Gabby was saying Mac took the news well."

"Yeah, better than I expected." I scratch my cheek. "Sometimes I think she's this fragile child who needs to be coddled because of everything she's gone through, but then I realize how resilient she is and the things she needs in life are pretty simple. She wants love, attention, and to be protected. I can deliver on all of those things."

"From what I've heard, you really can."

"Man, all these compliments. I'm not sure what I'm going to do with myself."

"Swallow them, and don't hurt my girl."

"That's the last thing I plan on doing."

"Promise me?" She points her finger at me.

"Promise," I say just as Mac runs up to me.

"Uncle Dad, the game is starting." Mac tugs on my hand and brings me over to the seats where, lo and behold, the Bombers have taken the field. Jesus, I missed all the opening ceremonies. "Watch with me."

"You want to watch?" I ask, surprised. She's never really been into baseball. She's enjoyed running around the bases after games, but that's about it.

"Yeah, Gabby said it's her favorite sport."

I take a seat in one of the chairs in the front row. "You know it's my favorite sport too, right?"

"Yes." She rolls her eyes and takes a seat on my lap.

"But because Gabby likes it, that means you like it?"

"Yup." Wow, no regret, no thought, just a straight-up yes.

"You know . . . I played baseball, right?"

"Gabby plays too."

I smile, shaking my head, because the obsession is real. Hell, it's real for me too. I can't even blame Mac. I have a deep-rooted obsession for Gabby too.

"Who do you think is better at baseball, me or Gabby?" I ask.

"Gabby, of course," Mac answers.

"How can you be so sure?"

"Because I know."

"Ah, okay. Hard evidence."

"Huh?"

"Nothing." I chuckle as she rests her head against my shoulder.

"Where is, uh . . . what's the brother called?"

*The brother.*

I hold back my laughter.

"Gabby's brother's name is Bennett. And he's at third base."

"Where's third?"

I point out at the field. "See that guy right there, close to the base on the far left?"

"Yeah."

"That's him."

"He looks small."

"That's because he's far away from us. Up close, he's tall. Like me."

"You've met him?"

"Yes," I answer. "I used to coach him."

"Really?"

"Yup. Pretty cool, huh?"

"Yeah."

"What's cool?" Gabby asks as she takes a seat next to me. I wrap my arm around her, and she moves in close despite the armrest between us.

"That I used to coach Bennett."

"He did," Gabby confirms. "But I taught Bennett everything he knows." She says it in a teasing tone, but I know she's right.

"Because you're better at baseball than Uncle Dad."

Gabby lightly chuckles. "That is very true, so much better."

I give her a look that just makes her smile before she plants a kiss on my cheek.

And then we all turn our attention to the field, where we watch the Bombers play out the first inning.

Mac is intent on watching.

Gabby is attached to my side, letting me feel her love.

And I sit there, the happiest motherfucker to ever live because the stars have aligned.

For the first time in my life . . . I'm content, I'm happy, and I want time to slow down.

I want to savor these moments, cherish them, keep them so close to my heart that I never let go.

I want this . . . forever.

I can see it.

I can see the future play out. I can see Gabby in a white dress, standing at the back of the aisle, as Mac tosses flower petals to the ground, looking so fucking adorable in a puffy dress with Chewy Charles sticking out the front.

I can feel the love of that day, the lightness, and the presence of Cassidy, as if she had planned this all along. Where she knew I needed to learn to love. It's as though she gave me Mac as a way to break the seal, to open me up and make me realize I'm more than just the stoic asshole I was growing up. More than just the punching bag.

That there *is* worth within me. I have so much more to give than I ever thought possible.

It's as if Cassidy knew that granting me custody of this precious little girl would open me up to someone like Gabby. Someone who brings light to my life and who, in return, makes me feel safe and needed, not discarded.

I know everything will work out as long as I have these two. They will be all I need, nothing else. Us.

Forever.

⊏━⊐

**Hattie:** *Okay, can we just pause for a moment and acknowledge the cuteness of this picture?*

I click on the picture Hattie sent, taking a good look at it. My body melts with happiness.

It's of Mac, Gabby, and me, sitting in the suite, staring out at the field. My arm is around Gabby, and Mac is pointing. We look like the perfect little family, and it's doing a whole bunch of things to my insides. I save the photo and text her back.

**Ryland:** *Did you take this?*

**Hattie:** *I did. I was in love watching you guys today.*

**Aubree:** *So was I. It was great seeing you three together.*

**Ryland:** *I loved it. Thank you for coming today.*

**Hattie:** *I've come in more ways than one.*

**Ryland:** *Jesus, Hattie.*

**Aubree:** *Same.*

**Ryland:** *Both of you, none of that shit.*

**Hattie:** *Are you saying you didn't come in more than one way?*

**Aubree:** *Sad day for you.*

**Ryland:** *If you want to go there . . .*

**Hattie:** *Hmm, do I? \*taps chin\* Doubt he'll say anything. He's such a prude.*

**Aubree:** *I doubt it too, but also, I don't want to read about it. It's Ryland, after all. He's . . . blek.*

**Ryland:** *Uh, excuse me? Blek?*

**Hattie:** *Perfect description. Very blek.*

**Ryland:** *That's not what Gabby thinks. Quite the opposite actually. She thinks I'm hot!*

**Aubree:** *Call the firefighters, Hattie. She thinks he's hot.*

**Hattie:** *\*Cue the sirens\* Weee-ooo, weee-ooo. Someone has to put out the fire that is our hot brother.*

**Aubree:** *He's so hot, he's burning on the spot. Water, stat.*

**Hattie:** *Where's the fire extinguisher?*

**Aubree:** *Grab a blanket, flour . . . anything to put him out.*

**Ryland:** *Are you two nitwits done?*

**Hattie:** *Ooo, nitwit. Look, he's getting flustered.*

**Aubree:** *It's cute.*

**Hattie:** *I agree. I kind of like it.*

**Ryland:** *You're not going to like it when I stop telling you about my life. Then you won't have anything to obsess over.*

**Aubree:** *I'd hardly say we obsess over you.*

**Hattie:** *I barely even think about you. Like . . . last thing on my mind.*

**Ryland:** *Says the girl who took a picture of me with my girls.*

**Aubree:** *\*whispers\* Hattie, he said MY GIRLS.*

**Hattie:** *I know, I saw it. I inwardly squealed.*

**Ryland:** *You realize I can read these texts, right?*

**Aubree:** *It's quite astounding to see the kind of change he's gone through.*

**Ryland:** *Me? What about you, Aubree?*

**Aubree:** *I'm the same human I've always been.*

**Hattie:** *Okay, now you know I like giving Ryland a hard time, but I can't let you just slip on by with a comment like that. Same human? Ma'am, not even close. Wyatt has mellowed you out in the best of ways.*

**Ryland:** *Hattie's right. You're not the same human, and the fact that you think you are is laughable.*

**Aubree:** *Yeah . . . well . . . Hattie's changed too.*

**Hattie:** *Facts, I have, and I'm not afraid to admit it. We all have, and I think . . . in all seriousness . . . Cassidy would be proud of us. I mean, hell, we never had a text thread like this before. Ever. And now I talk to you guys every day.*

**Aubree:** *That's true.*

**Ryland:** *Yeah, I guess we didn't really talk all that much before Cassidy passed, even slightly after.*

**Hattie:** *Makes you sad, doesn't it? That our sister had to leave us for us to come together.*

**Aubree:** *I don't think I'd put it that way.*

**Ryland:** *How do you see it?*

**Aubree:** *I see it more as when Cassidy passed, we were put in a situation where we needed to grow, to learn, and to find our own way. And one of those ways was closer to each other. I don't think we would have just auto-*

*matically come together. Look at how it was before Hattie came back home. We still weren't communicating like we are now.*

**Hattie:** *Maybe we had to find our person to open up to each other.*

**Ryland:** *We were pretty open . . . more hostile.*

**Aubree:** *Maybe we needed to be reminded what love is, so we could love each other again.*

**Hattie:** *See . . . you're wiser. Wyatt really has changed you because that's right on the money. We had to be reminded what love is to love each other.*

**Ryland:** *I hate to admit it, but I think you're right, Aubree. I know that I've always loved you two and I'd do anything for you, but Gabby has opened me up in a way that I never knew was possible. It's as if she lifted my head and said, look, there's a world around you. You don't always have to be go, go, go.*

**Aubree:** *She's right. Wyatt is right. Hayes is right. I think, in a way, Cassidy pulled us together so unexpectedly, but in such a Cassidy manner.*

**Ryland:** *She did.*

**Hattie:** *I miss her so fucking much.*

**Aubree:** *Same. I still ache when I think about her.*

**Ryland:** *She would have been so happy to see me with Gabby and see how Gabby has taken to Mac.*

**Hattie:** *She would have salivated over Hayes and how I was able to win over the brother's ex-best friend.*

**Aubree:** *She would have had a heart attack over the marriage of convenience.*

**Ryland:** *Like me?*

**Hattie:** *Yes, but she also would have had that fairy-tale look in her eyes where she hoped and dreamed it would have turned into something much more. Because she was a lover of love.*

**Aubree:** *And because of that love, look at where we are now.*

**Ryland:** *Yeah . . . look at us.*

**Hattie:** *Some might say at this moment, we made her proud.*

# Chapter Thirty-Two

## GABBY

This is perfect.

Everything about this is perfect.

I'm in the backyard. The crickets are chirping all around, a citronella candle blinks with fire in front of me, and Ryland's in the house, putting Mac to bed so he can come out here and enjoy the night.

The only thing not perfect about it . . . the Bombers must win the next three games if they want to be in contention for the wild card game. It's been a real nail-biter, but at least—despite the Bombers not making the wins happen—Bennett has been performing and had two RBIs the other night. He already has a following with the unruly fans, and I think his future with the team could be very promising. At least I hope it is.

I cross one leg over the other and lean back in my chair as I stare through the branches of the oak tree and right up to the sky, thinking about how far I've come. How I've been able to face adversity and—

*Ding*

I glance down at a text message popping up on the screen. Worried that it's Ryland and he needs help, I open the text message.

**Nathan:** *Gabriel Brinkman, the one and only. Why haven't you texted me back?*

My skin starts to crawl.

And just like every other time, I know what my response will be. Nothing.

So why does he keep texting?

Shouldn't he get a clue?

And because I don't engage in the text messages, I haven't told anyone about them.

Not even Bennett.

Because why? I ignored, I deleted, I let it sink in for a moment that he would text me after so many years, using Bennett as an excuse to message me, and then I moved on.

But he's back . . . again.

*Ding.*

**Nathan:** *After all these years, I congratulate you and your brother on hitting the big leagues, and you can't even take the time to text me a thank you? Is that where we really are, Gabriel?*

Why is he using my real name? He knows I hate it. He knows it's a family name I've always tried to disassociate from. This is him trying to poke me, to instigate, which is classic Nathan.

*Ding.*

**Nathan:** *I thought that maybe after everything we've gone through, you'd show me the decency of responding. Check in on me like I'm checking in on you. Because there's history between us, I thought you'd show me common courtesy to at least see how I'm doing. Guess I was wrong.*

*Ding.*

**Nathan:** *And this just comes back to you being the selfish one. You've always been selfish. It's always about you. About what you need. Never looking to see what others need. The moment you saw that your brother was good at baseball, you used him as your meal ticket. So what now? Are you eating rich while you just ignore the people who got you there?*

The people who got me there?

He can't be serious.

My hand shakes as I hold my phone.

He got me nowhere. He did nothing to help me. If anything, he hindered me. He made me believe that I wasn't meant to love somebody, that falling for someone would never be in the cards after what he put me through.

*Ding.*

**Nathan:** *You realize that I was out there with you, right? Out there on the field, helping Bennett, teaching him. And you don't even have the thoughtfulness to acknowledge that. But that's how it's always been, right? You. You. You. It might get you far, Gabriel, but you're going to be sad and so fucking alone.*

My chest grows heavy as my heart races with anger. With that feeling that Nathan instills in me. *Instability.* Like I'm not good enough, not perfect enough, not lovable enough. I can feel all those dark feelings coming back to me.

And . . . how dare he? Because he wasn't there. Maybe once or twice. And he bitched the entire time. He was pissed that I spent so much time with Bennett.

Hands on my phone, I contemplate texting him back. I want so desperately to tell him he's not right, that he's a liar, but I feel catatonic.

*Ding.*

**Nathan:** *Just remember, Gabriel, when you're living the rich life with your brother, you had to walk over the people who cared about you to get there. You stomped their faces in the dirt, used them, and took what you needed. Enjoy the karma because it's coming for you.*

My lip trembles.

Tears form in my eyes.

And my breath becomes erratic as his words filter into my brain, trying to stick like they did many years ago. I spent so much time ridding myself of his insults, of his barbs, yet here they are, attempting to stick like glue again.

The back door to the house opens, and I barely register Ryland walking up to me with drinks and cookies until he's right in front of me, looking me in the eyes and asking me what's wrong.

"Gabby," he says softly, taking my hand in his. "What's going on?"

I can't hold it back. The tears start to fall, and his concern grows heavier as he cups my cheek and wipes the tears away.

"Baby, tell me. Is it Bennett?" I shake my head, my teeth pulling on the bottom of my lip as I hold up my phone to him.

Ryland takes it and keeps his hand in mine as he reads through the text messages.

I watch as his concerned face slowly morphs into anger. The V in his brow deepens. And then there's the tick in his jaw.

His eyes tear away from the phone as he looks up at me. "Block his number. Right fucking now."

He hands me my phone.

"Right now, Gabby."

With shaky hands, I try to figure out how to do it, but my mind is flying a mile a minute, and instead of doing what I'm supposed to do, I remain still. Unmoving.

"Gabby," he says, softer now. Tears stream down my cheeks, and he pauses for a moment to study me. Then he takes my phone for me. I watch him scroll through the messages, and he pauses again. "Wait, this isn't the first time he contacted you. He . . . he texted you when Bennett was brought up. Why didn't you tell me?"

My mouth's shaking. "I . . . I didn't want to bother you."

"Bother me? Jesus, Gabby, this is not bothering me. This is . . . this is telling me something important. You should have blocked his number then." When I don't say anything, he sets my phone down and forces me to look him in the eyes. "What's going on here? Are there feelings still there?"

"No," I say quickly, my eyes widening as I shake my head. "No. There are zero feelings there."

"Then why are you hanging on to this? Why are you letting him hurt you like this?"

"I . . . I don't know. He just, he has a hold on me and not in a good way."

Ryland calmly stands and then sits down in his chair, pulling me onto his lap. His arm loops around my back as I bring my head to his shoulder, more tears streaming down my face.

"I'm not that person he says I am. I'm not."

"I know," he says softly. "Everyone knows that."

"Then why do I somewhat believe him?"

"You shouldn't. He's fucking with your head because he's pathetic. He knows he fucked up, and he's missing out on the greatest thing that's ever happened to him. He wants to have that hold on you. That's why he's texting. He's trying to take up space in your brain, and you're letting him. You can't, Gabby."

"I know." My voice is quiet, distant, my mind flying away to the days when Nathan was the one who held me. When Nathan was the one who offered me advice when I was sad, yet he wasn't like Ryland. He didn't put his whole heart into consoling me. He didn't love me.

When he said those words, they were empty, but when Ryland says them, they're full of meaning. Full of sincerity and truth.

*"When I look at you, all I see is magnificence. Selflessness. Strength. And hopefully . . . my future."*

No, Ryland would never say things that cut me down or made me feel less.

Ryland rubs my back and kisses my forehead. "I'm sorry," I whisper.

"Don't. Don't fucking apologize. You don't need to be sorry. You did nothing wrong. You . . . you're so much more than those texts. He was not part of your journey with Bennett. You did that on your own, both of you, so don't you dare let him try to take credit for that. You hear me, Gabby? Don't let him into your head."

"Okay." He kisses my forehead again as I fall silent. Unsure of where to go from here because the damage has been done—I read the words—they're settling in, even though I know they're not true. They'll still sit there and fester. They'll make me feel less than I am, less than I've always felt growing up. He struck a nerve. He knew what he was doing, and working through this will take an abundance of strength.

Wounds will heal, but when they're reopened, they take longer and more effort to mend. Even at that, they're never the same.

Nathan knew what he was doing by sending those texts. The question is, how will I rise above this? How will I not let it hurt what I have in my life now?

"Talk to me," Ryland says, breaking through my thoughts. "What are you thinking? What are you feeling? I want you to be open with me. Tell me how I can help you."

"Sad," I say, honestly. "Sad that I'm letting him hurt me like this. That I'm letting these old emotions of feeling less than hurt me like they did years ago. I'm sad that I'm not strong enough to deal with my feelings and you have to coax it out of me."

"Hey." He lifts my chin so I have to look at him. "That's what I'm here for. A relationship is about helping each other, being there for one another, and offering unconditional love, even when sifting through tough things."

"It's a burden."

"The fuck it is," he says. "You are not a burden. This, what we have, is not a burden. Don't ever think that. This is a partnership. This is what real love is about." He lifts my chin again. "You matter so much to me, and whatever might happen to you, I want to be a part of it—the good and the bad. That's love. What that fucker texted you? That's nothing but a sour man trying to take someone down. He's jealous because his life isn't where he wants it to be. Those words are not about you. They're a reflection of him. You, my love, are perfect."

*My love.*

It's two words, but they're words I've never heard before.

Words I've never been called before.

Yet they send a thrill through me.

A happy, gleeful, cheerful thrill.

Because . . . he's right. Everything Ryland's saying is right. I can't let Nathan's words get me down because they're not about me. They're a reflection of him.

I nod. "You're right, they're a reflection of him, not me."

"Keep saying that to yourself over and over again. Anytime you think about what he's said, keep that thought in your mind. It's a reflection of him, not you."

I tip my head back, and I press a soft kiss to his jaw. "Thank you."

"You don't need to thank me, Gabby. This is why I'm here. I'm here to love you, protect you, and make sure no one even comes close to hurting you or anyone close to you." He brings our foreheads together. "You're mine, Gabby. And I plan on keeping it that way. I plan on keeping that mind clear. I plan on making sure every goddamn day that you know you're worth and how special you are."

I'm his.

He's my shield.

He's my strength.

He's the confidence and the reassurance I need in my life that I am the woman I've become on my own.

I cup his cheek, my nose rubbing against his. "I love you, Ryland."

"I love *you*, Gabby."

———

*Gabby: He's it. He's the one I'm marrying.*

*Bower: You're just now figuring that out?*

*Gabby: It was confirmed last night.*

*Bower: Last night, huh? *wiggles eyebrows**

*Gabby: Nothing like that.*

*Bower: What happened?*

*Gabby: Can't tell you because I know you'll tell Bennett, and Bennett doesn't need to know with the Bombers coming up on their last few games that they need to win.*

**Bower:** *I swear I won't tell him.*

**Gabby:** *Promise?*

**Bower:** *Promise.*

**Gabby:** *I'm counting on you.*

**Bower:** *I promise, Gabby. My loyalty belongs to you first and foremost.*

**Gabby:** *Okay . . . well, Nathan texted me last night.*

**Bower:** *WHAT?*

**Gabby:** *It wasn't the first time. He's texted me a few times, but more came through when Bennett was called up. I've just ignored them for obvious reasons. Well, he didn't like that and thought it was me snubbing him. He proceeded to say some awful things. But I don't want to get into that. I'm moving past his words and focusing on what Ryland said to me last night and the love he showed me.*

**Bower:** *Okay, let me take a few deep breaths for a second. Deep breaths. In and out. Okay, settled. Not happy to hear Nathan texted you, but happy that Ryland was there for you.*

**Gabby:** *He was, Bower. And it just solidifies he's the one. I'm all in.*

**Bower:** *Well, I'm glad you're seeing it, because I saw it at the game. You are made for each other.*

**Gabby:** *We are.*

**Bower:** *Can I just ask one thing about Nathan?*

**Gabby:** *Yes.*

**Bower:** *Did you at least block his number?*

**Gabby:** *Yes. Ryland did it for me last night.*

**Bower:** *Good, because you don't need that toxic behavior back in your life.*

**Gabby:** *Ryland said the same thing.*

**Bower:** *He's a smart one.*

**Gabby:** *Very smart. And handsome and loving and so sexy in a baseball hat, with the best forearms ever. And he's sweet and cares about his niece, and . . . I love him so much.*

**Bower:** *Wow, way to make a girl incredibly jealous. If I didn't love you myself, I might hate you LOL.*

**Gabby:** *I wouldn't even be mad at you. I realize how annoying I seem.*

***Bower:*** *Not annoying. You're just in love, and that's something to be celebrated.*

***Gabby:*** *Well . . . we celebrated that love last night.*

***Bower:*** *Hey-o! Tell me more about that. Where did you do it? Did he spank you? Use another toy? Did he call you dirty things while he thrust into you? Possibly choke you?*

***Gabby:*** *You really need to put those books down.*

***Bower:*** *NEVER!*

---

"Come on, come on," I say, hands clutched, watching the game play out in front of me. The Bombers are down by two. It's the bottom of the ninth, they have two outs, and Bennett is on second with the tying run at the plate.

They must win this game to head to the wild card game. If they don't, the season's over.

Ryland rubs his hand over my thigh on the edge of the couch with me while Mac is already upstairs, asleep.

"Just a little poke somewhere. Bennett's fast. We could score," I say as the pitch is thrown, and it's a ball.

"Two and two," Ryland says. "He has to protect."

Bennett takes a big lead off second. No one's covering the bag as the other team doesn't seem to care, so on the next pitch, Bennett takes off toward third, and I hold my breath as the pitch is called a ball, and Bennett is called safe at third after the throw.

I leap off the sofa and silently cheer, not wanting to wake Mac. Ryland joins me in standing, and he puts his arm around me.

"Fuck, that was close. Too close to take as a ball."

"Agreed," I say. "I think everyone's asses were shriveled in the dugout."

The pitcher sets his hands, looks over at Bennett, and then kicks his leg up and throws the ball. The batter, Henson, connects with the ball, sailing it toward left center.

The cameraman tracks the ball, following it toward the fence, and just when I think there's a possibility it might go over the fence, the center fielder leaps out of nowhere, sticks his glove out, and cones the ball with the tip of his glove, ending the game in the blink of an eye.

All hope falls as I stare at the TV, not quite believing it.

"How the fuck did he catch that?" Ryland asks, his hands on his head.

"I can't believe it." I slowly sit down in disbelief. "I for sure thought they were going to score."

Ryland joins me. "Me too."

The camera pans to the Bombers dugout, where Bennett's removing his helmet and sitting on the bench, staring out at the field. A sad look crosses his features, but also a look of determination. I know that look better than anyone.

No way will he let this sit in his memory as the last moment he's on this field.

He's coming back next year, and he's coming back stronger.

That one tick in his jaw, that's all I need to know.

"What is it?" Ryland asks as I feel his eyes on me.

"This isn't over for Bennett. He's going to come back with a vengeance." I lean back on the sofa. "This is just the beginning."

"It is," Ryland says. "This is the start of a very successful career. If I know anyone is going to make it, it will be him."

"He is." I turn to Ryland and say, "Can I ask you a favor?"

"You can ask me anything."

"Please don't feel obligated because Bennett and I can make it work, but do you think I could give Bennett the apartment for the fall, and I could possibly stay—"

"Yes."

"Yes?"

"You're asking to stay with me, right?"

"I am, but I don't want to make you feel uncomfortable. I know I spend a lot of nights here, but—"

"Yes, Gabby. You don't need to explain. The answer is yes."

"You don't mind?"

"Are you kidding me? I attempt to find a reason to get you to stay here every night. Now, I won't need a reason."

"As if you need a reason." I smile up at him. "I think I fell asleep on the couch the other night on purpose, just to have you carry me up to your bed."

He smirks. "I fucking knew it."

That makes me laugh. "You did not know it."

"Oh, I knew it."

I shake my head at him. "You are such a liar. You had no idea I was faking it."

"Yes, I did because the moment I got you in my bed, you were very lively."

"Your erection aroused me from a deep slumber."

He lets out a deep laugh. "Wow, I didn't know my penis had such powers."

"Oh, it does. It has wonderful powers. Orgasm-inducing powers. The kind of powers only found in one in every hundred thousand penises."

"One in one hundred thousand, huh?" He pats his crotch. "Good job, my man."

"Oh my God." I laugh as he tackles me to the sofa and slides his hands up my shirt right to my bare breasts.

I sigh and spread my legs, making room for his large body.

He starts laying down kisses along my neck all the way up to the sensitive part of my ear, a place that he knows will turn me on just as fast as kissing my inner thigh.

"So you're officially moving in with me?" He kisses along my jaw as I start pulling on his shirt to take it off.

"Depends," I say as he helps me take off his shirt, only to remove mine as well. I watch his eyes take in my bare chest, and I swear the look of awe will never get old.

Ever.

"Depends on what?" he asks as he places his hands on my shorts and drags those off me as well, leaving me completely bare to him.

"On how many times you make me come tonight."

His eyebrow quirks up in the cutest way ever. "Is that a goddamn challenge?"

"It is."

"Then consider yourself fucked because you're getting no sleep tonight." He moves his head between my legs, and all I can do is smile as I run my fingers through his hair, knowing I'm about to have the night of my life.

# Chapter Thirty-Three

RYLAND

"I don't think it's too much. Do you think it's too much?" Hattie asks as we stare out at the amusement park in front of us.

Typically, we'd hold a town event in the open space next to the inn, but because Ethel and Hattie joined forces and made this way more than it should have been, they had to move it to the park down the street that's right next to the drive-in movie theater. Now I see why.

A Ferris wheel is the first thing that catches the eye because it towers over the entire space. Next is the movie screen in the background with *Welcome Back, Bennett Brinkman* scrolled across it.

And then filling in the space are other rides like the scrambler and a giant slide. Lots of booths for fair-like games, all themed around baseball. Food trucks and food stands are posted around the perimeter, while picnic tables, blankets, and other seating arrangements are spread throughout.

"Uh, it's a lot." I keep looking around at the bunting and decorations. "Who the hell paid for all of this?"

"Ethel said the Peach Society handled it all." Hattie shrugs.

"I didn't think everything on the wish list was going to be granted. Do you think this will embarrass him?"

I pull on the back of my neck. "Hell, I have no idea. I know that Mac will love it."

"When is she going to be here?" Hattie asks as people start meandering through the gates. There's a charge fee of five dollars a person, which, if you ask me, is a damn bargain given what's going on. "Because I want her to enjoy all the things before they start the movie."

"The movie?" I ask.

"Oh yeah, they're going to be playing *A League of Their Own* on the screen with speakers so everyone can watch, even if they're maybe not watching."

"*A League of Their Own*? Love the movie, but it's about women playing baseball. They know that, right?"

Hattie eyes me. "Are you being a misogynistic douche?"

"Uh, did you not hear me say I love the movie?"

"I did, but what do you have against the movie playing?"

"Just figured something like . . . *The Sandlot* might be more appropriate and family-friendly, especially when Tom Hanks freaking pisses in the locker room for thirty-five goddamn seconds and then shakes it out."

Hattie thinks about it. "Huh, you know, I forgot about that part."

"It's not really an innocent, family-friendly movie. For God's sake, Stillwell Angel gets beamed in the face with a glove in the movie. Is that what we want to teach our kids?"

Hattie lets out a large laugh and buckles at the stomach. "Oh God, Stillwell Angel, such a good scene. Got him right in the head. And Tom Hanks's response after is priceless. I can't wait for that part."

"Okay, so I'm assuming you don't care?"

Hattie waves me off. "It's Ethel's problem, not mine. All I care about is getting a spot on the lawn in front of the screen with a bag of kettle corn on my lap and a burly rock star sitting behind me."

"Glad you have your priorities straight," I answer as I see Wyatt and Aubree walk up with Mac, who looks cute as shit in a pink dress and her hair pulled into a high ponytail. She spent the night with them last night because she said she wanted to dress up Uncle Wyatt in bows and ride him like a horsey. It worked out well because Bennett came back last night, and we were able to have a small dinner, just the four of us, and then spend some personal time with Bennett while Mac went off to play horsey.

I was kind of surprised when Mac didn't take to Bennett like she does to other people, but then again, Bennett looked stiff as fuck and out of place around a little kid. He didn't know how to handle her, which I found comical. But it was good to spend some time with him last night, talking about his experience with the Bombers and his plans moving forward during the off-season. As expected, he has no intention of taking time off. Instead, he wants to lay out a progressive plan with Gabby that will have him ready for strength training.

In bed last night, I suggested to Gabby that he take a second to breathe, even if it's only a week. She agreed with me and plans on working in downtime. But we're going to use him during our school practices and have him help out because he can help instruct the boys. That will also give him access to all the facilities at the school.

"Uncle Dad," Mac says as she runs up to me. I lift her into the air and catch her, loving her little laugh.

"How was playing with Uncle Wyatt last night? Was he a good horsey?"

"No." Mac frowns. "He kept flicking his bows out of his hair."

I eye Wyatt. "You were flicking your bows out of your hair?"

"No," he says with a roll of his eyes. "One was bothering me. I itched it, and it got knocked out. Apparently, that's me flicking *all* the bows out."

"Seems like she's right."

Wyatt scoffs. "Thanks, dude."

I chuckle. "Did Aunt Aubree share her muffins with you this morning?"

"She did. I had two."

"Two muffins?" My eyes pop open as I stare at Aubree.

"Two halves, which make a whole. Trust me, I would not give her two muffins."

"I'd hope not. How would she possibly have room for all the cotton candy Uncle Wyatt will buy her?"

Mac turns toward Wyatt. "You're going to buy me cotton candy?"

"Yeah, who else would? That's my job as the fun uncle." He then takes Mac from me, and they head toward the cotton candy booth.

Her little voice says, "I want to go on the Ferris wheel with Uncle Dad."

"We can arrange that," Wyatt answers her as they move farther away.

More people from town . . . and what seems like people from out of town, start filtering in, and the space on the lawn starts to fill out.

"When's Bennett supposed to get here?" Aubree asks, looking around.

"Soon. Gabby kept him at the house so more people would be here before they showed up. But from the looks of it, it will be full soon."

Aubree tilts her nose up. "Do I smell funnel cake?"

"Yup," Hattie answers. "It's over by the slide."

"Oh, I'll be headed over there for sure."

"Hey, you guys," a voice says, causing us to turn. Bower walks up wearing a red sundress with her hair pulled up into a bun on the top of her head, a few stray pieces framing her face.

"Hey," I say, hugging her. She does the same with Hattie and Aubree.

"Where is everyone?"

"Wyatt and Mac are off to get cotton candy," Hattie answers.

"Hayes is helping Ethel with some speaker issues, and Gabby and Bennett are . . . oh, there they are."

I turn around to see my girl looking so damn good in a pair of white jean shorts and a short navy-blue top that shows about an inch of her midriff. Her hair is half up, and her brilliant eyes are highlighted by mascara.

Consider me fucking infatuated.

When she spots me, a large smile crosses her face, and if I could bottle up that look on her face and keep it forever, I'd consider myself the luckiest man alive.

She walks up to me, places her hand on my chest—*which seems to be her thing, and I love it*—and kisses me on the lips just as she notices Bower.

"Oh my God," she says. "I didn't know you were coming." She gives Bower a hug. When she pulls away, I watch Bower look over Gabby's shoulder, right to Bennett who has his hands in his pockets, his eyes lasered in on Bower.

"This guy was telling me about it last night, and I thought, a spectacle involving Bennett? Well, I have to be there to see his cheeks go bright red." She walks up to Bennett and pulls him into a hug.

Bennett wraps his arms around Bower, bringing her in close. His head tilts into hers, and I swear on my relationship with Gabby, I see him inhale. When she pulls away, his hand glides across her back, lingering before she's fully parted.

"Look at you," Bower says, gripping his arm. "You're all buff and filled out."

He wets his lips and shyly says, "You look good, Bower."

Bower daintily shows off her dress. "Oh, this old thing? Just pulled it out of the closet. But thank you."

And then . . . that motherfucker's eyes scan her up and down, getting his fill.

I seem to be the only one who notices because Gabby's oblivious as she takes my hand while Bower looks around the scene in front of her.

"This is all for you?" she asks, turning toward Bennett again who lifts his eyes.

He tugs on his hair and nods. "Yeah, I had nothing to do with it."

"Shocking," Bower says, looping her arm through his. "This screams like something you would do. The fanfare, your face and name plastered everywhere. I've never seen a more Bennett moment in my life." Her voice is obviously laced with sarcasm as she moves him through the gates and right into the event.

"Did you see that?" I whisper to Gabby.

"See what?" she asks.

"The way your brother looked at Bower."

She pauses our stride, bringing us to a stop. "He didn't look at her."

"Uh, he did, babe."

She shakes her head. "No, there's no way."

"Are you in denial, or do you really believe that? Because I'm pretty sure your brother has a crush on your best friend."

Gabby's eyes float to Bennett and Bower, where Bower is pointing at a picture of Bennett up to bat in his Bombers uniform.

"I'm not in denial. It's . . . it's not true."

"It's not?" I ask.

Her brow crinkles, and it's so cute. "I think so?" She says it more as a question than anything.

I chuckle. "Well, this will be fun to watch play out."

I can feel Gabby thinking next to me as we head toward the Ferris wheel where Wyatt and Mac stand. Mac has a giant thing of sugar on a stick, and I just hope that it makes her pass out later rather than hyper as shit.

Wishful thinking, right?

"Uncle Dad, come on the Ferris wheel," Mac shouts, waving her hand at me.

I turn to Gabby and say, "Got to ride the wheel with my other girl." I kiss her gently on the lips. "Don't get any food without me." I pat my stomach. "I'm starving."

"Promise." She kisses me back just as Ethel walks up.

"We'd love to get Bennett on stage to say a few things."

"Oh, sure. Bennett," Gabby says, calling him over. "This is Ethel O'Donnell-Kerr. She coordinated the event with Hattie. Think you could say a few things up on stage?"

"I have confetti cannons," Ethel cuts in, looking immensely proud of herself.

"Uh, sure, Mrs. O'Donnell-Kerr," Bennett says.

Ethel gushes. "Oh, such beautiful manners on a young man." At that, he blushes.

"I can wait to go on the Ferris wheel," I say, not wanting to miss the speech.

"No, it's cool, Coach," Bennett says and then mutters to me, "The fewer people watching, the better. Go on the damn wheel."

I chuckle and pat him on the back. "Good luck, dude."

I take off toward the Ferris wheel just in time as Wyatt and Mac get in a chair. I take a seat as well, fitting Mac in the middle, and then the lap bar is lowered against us.

"Yay!" Mac says.

"Can I have some of that?" I ask, eyeing her cotton candy.

"Of course." She offers it to me, and I peel off a chunk, not because I want it, but because I don't want her to have all of it.

The Ferris wheel starts moving, and we lift a few feet before another swing is loaded. We see Ethel introduce Bennett on the stage, and a rather large crowd gathers around. Bower, Hattie, Hayes, Aubree, and Gabby are all off to the side while Bennett waves to the crowd. Even from here, I can see that the guy is massively uncomfortable.

The Ferris wheel starts rotating, all the swings full now while Bennett speaks into the microphone. From the wind whipping around us and the subtle sound of the Ferris wheel music, I can't quite place what he's saying, but it seems short and sweet as he waves again and steps away from the mic. Music starts playing, and the crowd cheers for him.

"He seems pretty shy," Wyatt says.

"Yeah, he's not much of a talker. Very focused."

"I get that."

"He doesn't like to play," Mac says. "I gave him Chewy Chondra to play with, and he didn't talk for Chewy Chondra."

I chuckle. "I don't think he knows how to play the way we play."

"He was boring."

"Hey, that's not very nice. I'm sure we can get him to play. We just have to get him warmed up first."

"He's Gabby's boyfriend," Mac says, causing Wyatt to snort.

"No, nope, not boyfriend," I say, correcting her quickly. "Her brother. I'm Gabby's boyfriend."

"Oh. Okay."

Freaking kids.

We spin around a few more times, and as we slow and people start to unload and load back up, I look over the crowd, trying to find Gabby so we can meet up with her.

I spot Hattie and Hayes over by the funnel cake with Aubree.

Bennett is posing in pictures with people from the crowd, Bower being the photographer, taking people's phones and snapping shots, and Gabby, she's . . . hell, where is she?

"Do you see Gabby?" I ask Wyatt.

He plucks a piece of cotton candy from Mac and glances over the crowd. "What's she wearing again?"

"Navy-blue top, white shorts."

We're lowered so we're the third swing to be unloaded. Our view is blocked, but I continue to look.

"Do you see her?"

"Uh, oh, wait . . . is that her? Uh, no, that woman's with a guy."

"Where?" I ask.

Wyatt points, and I follow his hand to behind the funnel cake stand. A man's pushing someone up against the wall.

"Wait, is that her?" Wyatt asks.

I focus on the two people, my heart pounding in my chest as her familiar shirt comes into view.

431

"That is her," I say as my rage spikes to an all-time high. "Who the fuck is touching her?"

"Who's touching who?" Mac asks.

I lift at the bar, but it's locked in, so I try to wiggle out as we move to the second swing to be let out.

"Fuck, help me."

"Uncle Ryland," Mac says. "Don't . . . don't jump out." But her voice is distant as all I see is black, my tunnel vision narrowing in.

"Dude, hold on," Wyatt says.

"I can't fucking hold on." Yelling down to the operator, I say, "Get me the fuck off this thing."

"You're scaring me," Mac says as we start to move to the bottom.

I jam at the lap bar. "Get this off."

"Jeez, man," the operator says as he unlatches the bar, and I leap off the swing, off the Ferris wheel stage, and sprint toward the funnel cake stand. I bump into people telling me to watch it and slow down, but I don't give two shits. I chase down Gabby, turn the corner of the funnel cake stand, and that's where I see Gabby's terrified face, tears streaming down, just as he shakes her shoulders.

At that moment, everything goes red.

My anger, my upbringing, they both take over, and before I know it, I'm tearing this man off her, cocking my fist back, and blowing him right across the damn face, sending him backward at least five steps and right to the ground.

Gabby screams behind me, but I don't stop. I move in on the man, lift him by the shirt, cock my fist back again, and punch him right in the stomach, sending him to the ground.

"Ryland," Gabby yells, pulling at me. "Stop."

But I don't.

I pick him up again, the pathetic man that he is, and I reach back, wanting to hear his skull crack when two strong arms pull me away and hold me back as the man falls to the ground.

"Let me the fuck go," I yell as I attempt to get free, my eyes lasered in on the man whose face is bleeding.

"Stop," Wyatt says into my ear. "Fucking stop. You're scaring her."

That makes me pause. I'm about to ask who I'm scaring when out of the corner of my eye, I see Mac, clinging to Aubree, tears flowing down her cheeks . . . fucking shaking.

*Oh fuck.*

Realization sets in.

She saw that.

She saw all of that.

She saw what I saw as a child, an angry man using his fists rather than his words.

"Mac," I say, moving forward, but she hides away from me, using Aubree's legs to block her.

Immediately, a lump grows in my throat, but I don't have much time to think about it as the man who's kneeling on the floor, holding his bleeding face says, "I'm pressing charges."

"The fuck you are," Bennett says, stepping up. He pulls Gabby into his side.

"Aubree, get Mac out of here," Wyatt says, still holding on to me.

I watch as Aubree lifts Mac into her arms, her cotton candy now on the ground, and they walk away. It's a scene that splits me in half. This was supposed to be fun for her, but she's leaving, crying, and unable to even look me in the eyes.

"What's going on here?" a policeman says, stepping up to the circle around us.

"He attacked me," the man says.

I know I should defend myself.

I know I should say I was protecting my girl, but all I can think about is Mac and the fear in her eyes when she looked at me. I'm devastated. *I* caused that fear.

The same fucking fear that my sisters felt.

The same fear I had to live with day in and day out.

"Ryland, did you attack him?" When I look up and see that

it's Earl, the sheriff, talking to me, I just nod. "Dammit, Ryland," he says, moving behind me.

"Hold on," Gabby says, stepping up to Earl. "He didn't attack him for no reason. He was saving me. That's my ex-boyfriend, and he stalked me." My eyes flash to the man on the ground.

That's Nathan?

That's fucking Nathan?

"I don't know what Nathan would have done if Ryland wasn't there to help me."

Earl glances over at Nathan. "Is that true? Did you touch her without her consent?"

"Yes," Gabby says while Nathan says no.

I just stand there, defeated.

Depleted.

Emotionless because the life has been sucked from my bones and peeled away from my soul.

"He was holding her," Wyatt says, stepping in. "I saw it from the Ferris wheel. That's where we were when Ryland took off to help her."

"I saw it too," a random person says, holding up their hand.

Hands on his hips, Earl turns toward Nathan and says, "Now, you can either tell me the truth and we can make this easy, or you can lie, and this will get a lot uglier for you. Did you touch her?"

Nathan looks away and nods his head.

That's all the confirmation Earl needs. He takes Nathan by the arm, lifts him up, and urges him over to his colleague, who reads him his rights. Earl then steps up to me and Gabby and says, "I'm going to need a statement."

"Of course," Gabby says. "Can you just give us a second?"

"Yes," Earl says, stepping away.

"Gabby," Bennett says, coming up to us now. "Are you okay?"

"Yeah, I'm okay." She pats her brother's chest. "I just need to talk to Ryland for a moment."

Bennett glances at me, then back at Gabby. "Okay." He nods at me. "Thanks, Coach, for taking care of her."

His words don't even register. Nothing does as I stand in this catatonic state.

Once we're alone, Gabby pulls me off to the side, out of earshot of everyone, and takes my hand in hers. I don't return the grip. I can't even fucking look at her.

"Ryland." She shakes me a little. "Ryland, look at me."

When I keep staring straight ahead, she forces me to meet her eyes by taking my head in her hands.

"Ryland, I need you to look at me. I need to know that you're okay."

When I don't answer, she lightly shakes me.

"Ryland, talk to me, please."

I don't.

I can't.

Instead, I reach up, take her hands off my face, and set them down. Without a word, I turn away and grab Earl to give him my statement before I have to get the hell out of here.

⊏⊐

"She wants to stay with me tonight," Aubree says as Mac sits in her SUV with Wyatt in the back, holding her.

Talk about a fucking knife to the gut, watching her curl into someone else, being protected by someone else other than me.

"But I can encourage her that it will be okay to stay at her house."

I shake my head. "Take her, Aubree."

She steps in and whispers, "Ryland, I don't think this is a good thing. I don't want her thinking she can flock to us. She needs to know that you're not a scary human, that you love her, and that you were protecting Gabby."

I shake my head again. "No, it's best she stays with you." I tug on my hair. "I, uh . . . I need to go."

I start to walk away, but Aubree stops me. "Ryland, don't do this."

"Don't do what?" I ask her in a low tone.

435

"Don't bottle this all up inside and turn away from us. I know this look in your eyes. You're disassociating yourself, and that's the last thing she needs."

"Or maybe it's the best thing she needs," I snap.

"What's going on?" Hattie asks, walking up to us as well. "I would have been here sooner, but Earl made me talk to him even though I wasn't involved."

"Nothing's going on. Aubree's taking Mac. It's done."

I start to move away again toward my truck, but both of my sisters stop me.

"What's done? Do you mean she's taking Mac forever?"

"I can have her stuff packed tonight," I say.

"Uh, it doesn't work that way," Aubree says. "You can't just pass her off when the first roadblock comes along."

"Roadblock?" I hiss and then point behind me. "That wasn't a fucking roadblock, Aubree. That was Dad. That was Dad seeping from my skin, controlling my every move. And she bore witness to that. She saw every piece of me turn into a man that I hate. That I despise, that I'm so fucking glad is dead, yet here I am, the reincarnation of him."

"Have you lost your mind?" Hattie says. Not sugarcoating here. "You are not a reincarnation of Dad. Not even close."

"Tell me this, when I found out about you and Hayes, did I shake his hand and offer him best fucking wishes? Or did I try to beat the ever-loving shit out of him?" She goes silent. "And with Wyatt, did I or did I not attack him as well? Say what you want, but it's a lie. I'm dangerous. I have him in my bones, and she shouldn't be anywhere near me. I can't . . ." I get choked up. "I can't ever see that look on her face again."

"Ryland." Hattie reaches for me, but I shake her off.

"Don't. I don't want to hear it. I'll have her stuff packed for you to pick up."

And without another word, I get in my truck and drive off.

# Chapter Thirty-Four

## GABBY

"Are you okay?" Bennett asks once Earl takes off, leaving us by the abandoned stage. The event has continued despite the disturbance. The town seems to be enjoying themselves, which is important because the last thing I'd want to do is disrupt an event that took a lot of time, energy, and money to put together.

"No," I say, still a little shaken from Nathan's ambush. "I didn't even see him coming."

"What happened? I didn't know what was happening until I saw Ryland punching Nathan across the face."

"He must have found out about the event since Ethel posted about it everywhere. Knowing him, he's probably followed us both for a while. And well, I didn't tell you, but he's actually sent me a few texts. Wasn't too thrilled that I didn't text him back."

"He texted you, and you didn't tell me?" Bennett asks, growing angry.

"I didn't want to bother you. It wasn't that big of a deal." I play it down. "You were busy—"

"I'm never too busy for you. This is something you should have told me. Did Ryland know?"

"He found out about the second group of text messages."

"And he didn't tell me either?"

"Because he handled it," I say. "Bennett, please don't get upset about this, okay? I wanted you to focus on baseball."

"Guess what, Gabby? You are more important than baseball. You matter more to me than anything, so not telling me about what's going on in your life hurts me. We have been in this life together, just you and me, so if something's happening with you, I need to know. That's my right as your brother, as the person who has been through it all with you."

He's right.

"I'm sorry," I say softly. "I was trying to protect you."

"I'm a grown-ass man, Gabby. I love you, and I appreciate everything you've done for me, but at some point, you need to realize that I can protect myself. I can compartmentalize my life, and when I'm on the field, I get the job done and don't bring the outside world into that stadium. I know you're trying to shield me, but don't. I don't need it. What I need is for you to tell me the truth about what's going on or else we're not in this together."

"You're right, Bennett. I'm sorry."

"Thank you. Now tell me what that fuck said to you."

I sigh heavily. "In the texts, he said that I was selfish and some other things that I really don't want to get into because I was able to look past them and move on."

"I can understand that. What about today? What happened?"

"It's kind of a blur. I just remember being pulled out of the crowd. He placed his hand that smelled like cigarettes over my mouth and told me not to make a noise or I was going to regret it." Bennett tenses, but I continue. "He was pretty much asking for money. I can't recall everything he said because I could barely hear him over the crowd and music, but it was something along those lines. He didn't get to say much before Ryland tore him off me."

"Thank God he was there." Bennett takes a seat next to me

and puts his arm around me. "I'm sorry I wasn't the one to pull him off."

"You don't need to apologize."

"Hey, I got everyone some water." Bower walks up, looking back and forth between us. "Uh, I can leave these here and step to the side while you two finish up."

"You can stay," Bennett says as he takes the water from Bower. "Thank you."

"You're welcome." She turns toward me. "Also, I wanted to let you know that Ryland left."

"He did?" I ask. "Where did he go?"

"I'm assuming home. I ran into Hattie, and well, they're all pretty shaken." Bower's lips thin. "Mac saw everything, and she's scared. Doesn't want to be near Ryland."

"What? No." My stomach bottoms out, nausea immediately taking over. "She said that?"

Bower nods. "She went home with Aubree and Wyatt, and Ryland, well, he's packing up Mac's stuff."

"What do you mean he's packing up her stuff?"

"I didn't get much from Hattie, as she was really upset. All I know is that Ryland is spiraling, claims he's behaving exactly like his father, and Mac doesn't want to be around him."

"Oh God," I whisper. "This is all my fault."

"How is this your fault?" Bennett asks.

"Because Ryland came to protect me."

"This is not your fault," Bennett says. "Don't even start that way of thinking. This is no one's fault other than Nathan's. No one should be taking the blame other than him. He attacked you, Gabby. Ryland protected you. Plain and simple."

"He's right," Bower says. "And I think the sooner everyone accepts those circumstances, the better because taking the blame is not going to do anything. What needs to be done is you need to go to Ryland and help him. Help him work through whatever demons he's dealing with because my guess is, if he moves Mac out, you're next."

My eyes widen because I didn't even think of that. She's

right. I know Ryland, I know how he can be self-deprecating, how he can claim that he's not good enough, and that he doesn't deserve something in his life. My guess is he's already proclaimed himself as unfit to watch Mac. Next, he'll declare he shouldn't be with me, and I can't let any of that happen.

I stand and say, "I'm sorry, Bennett, but I need to go."

"Don't apologize. Let us know if you need help."

"I will." I give them both hugs and take off.

The house is quiet as I walk inside, not a single sound thrumming through the walls, which makes me temporarily think he's not here, but his truck is in the driveway, and his shoes are kicked off at the door. He's here. The question is . . . where?

I move through the house, looking around, making sure to see he's not sitting in the corner or up against a wall, and when I don't see him, I head up the stairs where I spot Mac's door open. I head there first, and that's where I find him, curled into her bed, a bottle of whiskey unopened on the floor, tears running down his cheeks.

My heart breaks. I can't possibly imagine the pain he's going through, knowing Mac doesn't want to be near him.

Wanting to give him all the love he deserves and needs at this moment, I slip my shoes off at the door and move into the room. When his bloodshot eyes meet mine, he shakes his head.

"No, Gabby. I don't want you here."

I don't listen to him. I move toward the bed and then in behind him.

"I don't . . . I don't want you here," he says, his voice shaky.

I slip my arm around his waist and press a kiss to his shirt and feel the tension in his body slightly decrease, so I do it again.

And again.

And when he finally moves to his back and I slide my body over his chest, he allows me to look him in the eyes. I cup his cheek and wipe his tears away.

"I don't . . . I don't need you," he says weakly.

"I know," I say, still wiping at his tears. "But I'm not leaving. Feel free to make me, but I'm not budging."

He looks away, his eyes focusing on the stars on the ceiling above us. After a few seconds of silence, he says, "I want to be alone, Gabby."

"I'm not going to let you be alone."

He lifts, shifting me to the side, and grabs the bottle of whiskey, uncapping it. He goes to raise it to his lips, but I stop him.

"Don't." I try to take the bottle, but he doesn't let me.

"Gabby, I'm going to get really pissed if you don't stop."

"Then get mad. I don't care," I say. "I'm not going to let you be alone. Not now. Not ever."

Now he stands from the bed and turns toward me, bottle of whiskey at his side. "Fine, you want to do this now, then? I was going to give you a fucking second, but we can do this now."

"Do what?" I ask even though I know exactly what's coming.

"End this." Yup, I knew it. Thankfully, I'm prepared for it and not blindsided.

"You want to end what we have?"

"Yeah," he says, leaning against the wall now.

I take him in—the slouch in his shoulders, his unruly hair, and the deadness in his eyes. This is not the Ryland I know. This is not the same man, and thankfully, I can look at the situation and realize that without getting emotional.

"Why? Why do you want to end this, Ryland? Is it because you don't love me anymore, because from what I saw today, I'd say that's the exact opposite. Is it because you feel like you can't protect me, because that wouldn't be the case either. Or is it because you're spiraling and attempting to eliminate everything good from your life?"

His lips twist to the side, and without emotion, he says, "Because I don't love you anymore."

I feel my stomach turn from his answer, but I know he's lying.

So I step up to him, take the bottle from his hand, and set it on the floor. Then I slide my hand up his chest to the back of his head. "You don't love me anymore? Is that the truth? Or are you lying because you don't think you deserve anything good in your life?"

"It's the truth," he says, looking over my shoulder.

"Then fucking say it to my face, Ryland. Look me in the eyes and tell me you don't love me." I force his eyes to look at me. "Don't be a coward and look away. Look at me. Say those words to me and mean them. Because I'll tell you right now, I love you. I love you more than anything, and I'll be damned if I'm going to stand here and let you ruin what we have."

Tears fill his eyes right before they tip down his cheeks.

"Say it, Ryland. Look me in the eyes and say it to me."

He wets his lips, but he remains silent. So I pull him to the floor with me. He curls against the floor as I lean against the wall. He rests his head on my lap, and he lets out a sob. His body shakes. It quivers. And I remain there, holding him, rubbing his back, and making sure he knows that I will not leave him no matter what happens.

And we stay there for a long time. I'm not sure how long, but long enough to see the sun set, to feel his breathing slow down, and to sense his calm.

I run my fingers through his hair. "I need you to know something," I say quietly. "I'm not sure what would have happened if you hadn't been there to help me with Nathan. Seeing him, feeling him hold me like that, it terrified me, and I went . . . I went still. I couldn't speak, I couldn't yell, I couldn't scream. I went dead inside. If it hadn't been for you at that moment, I'm not sure what would have happened today. And I need you to know that I'm so grateful for you, Ryland. I'm so grateful for you being there for me, protecting me, making sure that I'm taken care of. That's who you are at your core. You're a protector . . . you are not someone who hurts others . . . like your father." I feel him grow stiff beneath me.

I continue to stroke his hair. "You're not him. You'll never be him. You're not even close to being the same man. You've risen above who he was. You stepped up at a young age, taking the brunt of your father's fists so your sisters were never hurt. You worked hard to take care of them. You gave up on your dreams to be there for them. You are selfless. Your father was self*ish*, so don't believe for one second that you are him. You are anything and everything but him. You are the very best of men. In fact, you are the best man I know. And I never want to live my life without you."

My throat grows tight as I continue.

"You're a coach, someone those boys look up to, rely on, and seek out for help. You're a teacher and an educator, impacting every kid in your class. You're a brother, the head of the family, taking over when your dearest Cassidy passed. You're the glue, keeping your sisters close and ensuring your love for each other keeps growing. You're a boyfriend, a lover, a man I respect with everything in me. A man I can trust with my life. A man I will never stop loving, ever. But most importantly, Ryland"—my voice grows tense—"you're Uncle Dad." I hear him sniff, so I continue to run my hands through his hair. "You mean the world to that little girl. You are her best friend, the man she'll look up to for the rest of her life. You stepped up when she lost her dad, you stepped up when she lost her mom, and now, you're the center of her life. You always will be."

His body shakes under my hold, his tears pooling on my legs.

"We can overcome this setback. But first, you need to accept who you are and who you're not. You are the man I just described. You are not the man who held you with his fists, who abused you, who taught you nothing about love but rather everything about hate. You're not that man. You don't even have an ounce of him in you."

I take a chance and encourage him to lift to look me in the eyes. Thankfully, he does, and when he leans against the wall, I straddle his lap and bring my hands to his cheeks.

I lean in and press a very light kiss to his lips. I pause, waiting, and I do it again. This time, he kisses me back.

And then he kisses me again.

And again as his hand loops behind my neck.

When he pulls away, he connects our foreheads and quietly says, "I'm sorry, Gabby. I'm so fucking sorry. I love you. I really fucking love you. So much."

"I know," I say, rubbing my thumb over his cheek. "I know you do."

"I didn't mean it. I didn't fucking mean it."

"I know." I kiss him again. "I know, Ryland."

He lets out a shaky breath as more tears stream down his cheeks. "She . . . she hates me."

"She doesn't," I reply. "I can promise you right now, she does not hate you. She might be scared, but we can fix that. There's no way she hates you. You're Uncle Dad, the love for you will always be there."

He shakes his head. "That look in her eyes . . . it haunts me."

"I'm so sorry. I'm sorry you had to see that, and I'm sorry you were put in a position where you had to help me."

"I lost it," he says quietly. "Seeing a man attack you like that, I lost my goddamn mind. I forgot about Mac and putting her first. I never should have punched Nathan. I should have just pushed him away."

"Ryland." I kiss his forehead and his nose and his lips. "I know not all parents will be perfect throughout their life. There will be mistakes, and there will be moments when you'll have to sit down with your child and apologize for your behavior. But it's having those honest conversations, showing humility, teaching your child how to apologize, those are the teachable moments and that's what this is. This doesn't end anything. This is just the start of that journey of sifting through this world of parenting. You can't give up on that little girl. She lost her parents, don't let her lose you too."

His eyes search mine, and after a few seconds, he nods.

And then he wraps his arms around me and hugs me, squeezing me tight.

"I love you, Gabby. Thank you."

"I love you, too, Ryland."

# Chapter Thirty-Five

## RYLAND

"I don't feel very good," I say as I put the truck in park, Aubree and Wyatt's farmhouse right in front of us.

"I know, but I promise, it will be okay. Just be honest with her."

"Yeah." I push my hand through my hair and stare at the house that once was mine, a house that I moved into when my sister was sick. A house that I watched my sister slowly die in. A house where I had to witness my sister say goodbye to her daughter. And a house I thought Mac would grow up in—that was until her entire life fell apart.

Now, it's a reminder of what she lost, and like Gabby said, she's lost so much. She can't lose me too.

We took the night last night for me to gather myself. I was too fucking emotional, still too raw to talk to Mac like I need to speak to her today. Instead, I spent the evening with Gabby, lying in bed together, in each other's arms. She showed me just how much she loves me by never leaving my side, by wiping my tears when they flowed, and by never once judging me but rather reiterating how she thinks I'm such a good man.

The affirmations took a while to set in and for me to believe, but as the night went on, and the more she repeated herself, the more I took her examples into consideration, the more I realized just how right she was.

I'm not my father.

He was a selfish man. A disgraceful man. An addict. An abuser. He didn't know what love was and had no intention of ever showing any of us what love could be.

I am a selfless man.

I'm a man of honor.

I'm a gentle, understanding man.

I'm a protector.

And I'm a man who can love. Who has love to give and love to receive.

That will never change.

Therefore, I'm nothing like him, and I keep repeating that in my head, over and over again, forcing myself to believe it.

"Come on," Gabby says. "She's waiting in there."

I nod, then unbuckle my seat belt. We get out of the truck, and I meet her at the front. I take her hand in mine, leaning into her for the support that I need to get through this.

We make our way up the porch stairs, and I lead the way into the house where I find Aubree in the kitchen cleaning up breakfast. She glances over her shoulder and turns off the faucet when she sees that it's me.

"Hey." She walks up to me and pulls me into a hug. "You okay?"

I nod. "Yeah."

"You sure?"

"I'm good, Aubree." I offer her a smile, and that's all that needs to be said.

She gets it.

She's been there.

We've all had our breakdowns in this family. What matters is that we keep rising from those breakdowns, and we keep coming back to each other. We keep leaning on each other.

Aubree looks at Gabby and asks, "Are you okay?"

Gabby smiles and nods. "I'm good. How's Mac?"

"She's upstairs with Wyatt, most likely playing horsey."

"How was she last night?" I ask.

"She was okay. We watched a movie and had some ice cream. She asked about you last night."

"She did?" I ask, hope blooming in my chest. "What did she say?"

"She asked if you were okay. If you were alone, because she didn't want you to be alone. I told her that Gabby was with you."

I don't know why, but that chokes me up.

That little girl.

So fucking sweet. And after everything she's been through, she can sit there, in her feels, and worry about me being alone.

I love her. I love that little girl so damn much.

"Can I go see her?"

Aubree nods. "You know where to find her. Send Wyatt down here."

"I will." I turn to Gabby and tilt her chin up. I gently kiss her and whisper, "I love you."

"Love you."

With that, I move up the stairs to the first bedroom door, where I hear Mac's little voice. I pause for a moment, listening in on their conversation. Wyatt is a horse, and Mac's telling him how beautiful his mane is. Wyatt makes a few horse noises, and I chuckle to myself, letting that lightness lead the way as I knock on the door, then push it open.

Wyatt is on all fours, wearing a long black wig while Mac combs his hair.

"Uh . . . hey, man," Wyatt says, looking slightly embarrassed.

"Hey." I smile. "Think I could have a chat with Mac for a moment?"

"Yeah," he says, removing the wig and setting it aside. Wyatt stands and starts to move past me but stops and whispers, "The wig was my idea. Don't let Aubree take the credit."

"Odd thing to be proud of."

He chuckles. "It was a hell of an idea." He pats my shoulder and then shuts the door behind him.

Mac sits on the floor, not looking at me, so I take my time and move to the floor right next to her. "Hey, kiddo," I say. "Can I talk to you for a moment?"

She nods but picks up a horse figurine and starts combing the hair.

"Can I steal your full attention? I really want you to hear what I have to say." She sets down the horse and looks me in the eye. "First, I want to say that I missed you last night."

Her lips curve down as she says, "I missed you too."

"I'm glad to hear that because yesterday was a tough day." She nods, and I take her hand in mine. "I need you to know that I'm sorry about what you saw yesterday. That's something you never should have seen."

"Was that man hurting Gabby?"

"Yes," I answer, wanting to be honest with her. "And I saw him hurting her when we were on the Ferris wheel."

"Why would he want to hurt her?"

"Because he's a bad man," I say. "And I didn't want him hurting her, so I wanted to do something about it. Now, I should never have hurt him like that. That was wrong. And that's what I'm sorry about. I'm not sorry about protecting Gabby, but I am sorry about how I went about it."

"It was scary."

I swallow the lump that forms in my throat. "I know, and I'm sorry you had to see that. I never should have scared you like that. I was very angry, and instead of thinking about my actions, I did what came naturally, and that was wrong. I'm sorry."

She nods and looks away.

"You know I love you, right?"

Her eyes meet mine, and she nods. "I love you, too."

"Yeah?" I ask, that lump forming again.

"Of course, how could I not love you?"

That makes me chuckle. "I really don't know." I open my arms. "Come here."

She stands, then leaps into my arms, squeezing me tight. I wrap my arms around her, my eyes closing as tears form in them again. I'm so grateful for her forgiveness. For her love. For her little self. And I now realize how lost I would have been when Cassidy passed had I *not* had this sweet baby girl. *She* has helped me so much through my own grief, and I honestly don't think I could live without her.

When I came to help Cassidy after her husband passed, I didn't think this is what my life would turn into, but I wouldn't trade it for a thing . . . well, maybe that's not the truth. If I could wish for anything, it would be to have Cassidy back, for her to beat the cancer so she could witness just how amazing her little girl is.

Cassidy not being around to watch MacKenzie grow up will always sit heavily in my chest. With each passing day, there's always something Mac does that I think about how Cassidy would react, how she'd smile . . . laugh . . . steal a picture, take a moment.

This means that I'm now in charge of being that person. And yes, this might have been a minor setback, but it won't be the end. Mac and I have a very long way to go.

When Mac pulls away, I ask, "So . . . do you think I can still be Uncle Dad?"

She nods enthusiastically. "You'll always be Uncle Dad."

I smirk and tip her chin up. "Good, because I have no intention of ever changing that."

"What about . . . what about when you marry Gabby?"

"You think I'm going to marry her?" I tease.

"I think so."

"Do you like her?"

"I do. I do. I do." She cutely jumps up and down.

"So if I did marry her, you would like that?"

"Yes! But . . ." Her nose crinkles. "Does that mean I have to play with her brother?"

I let out a laugh. "He's a fun guy, I promise. Watch, next time you see him, he'll play with you."

"Okay . . ." She thinks for a moment. "But what about when you marry Gabby?"

"What about it?"

"Will your name change?"

"Oh." I chuckle. "No, it won't. I'll always be Uncle Dad."

"Always?"

I tap her nose. "Always."

# Epilogue

## RYLAND

"Have you seen her?" Hattie asks, walking up to me in a beautiful purple gown.

I shake my head, my hands sweating. "No."

Hattie's smile grows wider. "You are in for it. Hope you have tissues." She pats my back and moves over to Hayes, who's wearing a three-piece suit just like me.

"Where's my phone? I want to record this," Aubree says as she moves into the living room portion of the suite we're in.

"Right here," Wyatt says, holding a box of tissues.

"Dude, give me some of those."

"No fucking way," he says. "I want to see the tears flow down you."

"Ass," I say.

"No, I agree. I want to see the tears too," Abel says from the corner, his phone out as well.

Looks like I'll have this moment captured from all different angles.

Instrumental music filters through the windows, setting the mood. It's the perfect day for a wedding with blue skies shining over the bay, the inn decked out in flowers, and chairs out on the lawn, looking toward the ocean.

"You ready?" Hattie asks.

"No," I answer.

But it's too late.

The doors open, the sunlight from the windows behind her filters in, and it takes a second for my eyes to adjust, but when they do, I can feel the sting of tears instantaneously as my girl, my little fucking girl, stands in front of me in a white gown and veil, ready to get married.

"What do you think?" Mac asks as she does a small twirl for me.

"Wow," I say, tears falling down my cheeks, my throat so tight that I can barely get the words out. "You look beautiful, kiddo."

"Doesn't she?" Gabby says as she moves around Mac and right to me. She kisses my jaw. "That's our little girl."

"I can't believe it."

I move closer to Mac, her young life flashing before my eyes —images of her on the swing under the oak tree, laughing as I pushed her as high as she could go. Watching her prance the Chewys around the house. All her drawings and paintings lining the walls. Her first tooth that she donated to the tooth fairy because she felt bad taking money. Her first softball game. The first time she pitched a no-hitter. Her first date with a squid of a boy who I'm so glad lasted one date and that was it. Her prom. Her first heartbreak. The day she accepted a full-ride scholarship to Brentwood University. The day she brought Garrick home to meet me. Her graduation. Her first-ever coaching job. The tears in her eyes when she told me she was engaged.

And now . . . this moment.

"Okay, no tears. I don't want to ruin my makeup," Mac says.

"We're allowed to tear up," Aubree says.

"Yeah," Wyatt says, sniffling off to the side. "With the number of times I allowed you to treat me like a freaking horse, I get to have this moment."

Everyone laughs while Mac rolls her eyes. "You're going to use that for the rest of your life, aren't you?"

"Damn right."

Hayes steps up and presses a kiss to Mac's cheek. "I'm going to get into position. See you down there."

"Thank you, Uncle Hayes."

"I'll let Maggie know we're ready," Abel adds.

Hayes winks at Mac and takes off. He's playing the guitar for the processional. I've purposely listened to him practicing so I could mentally prepare myself and not be a blubbering mess.

"I'm going to go to my seat so I can get comfortable for the cry fest I intend on having," Hattie says.

"I'll join you," Aubree says.

They both walk up to Mac and give her a hug. Hattie cups Mac's face and says, "Your mom would have loved Garrick. He's perfect."

"Thank you," Mac says. Her lips quiver but no tears.

Aubree takes her hand. "Love you, sweetie."

"Love you, too."

And then Hattie and Aubree take off together.

Wyatt is next, still with his tissue box in hand. He gives her a long hug and then whispers something in her ear. I don't know what he says, but she nods and offers him a shaky smile.

When he leaves, the room grows silent.

Gabby turns to me. "I'll let you two have a moment." She slides her hand around my neck and pulls me in for a kiss. I let my lips linger for a moment as I remember the day we got married.

It was out on the farm, a simple, intimate wedding with our closest friends and of course our family present. We spent the night dancing under the stars, watching Mac chase Bennett around with the fake snake he got her as a present—something to show her that he wasn't as boring as he seemed. It was the perfect day . . . just like today will be the perfect day.

Gabby moves away from me and walks up to Mac. "I'm so proud of you," Gabby says. "You're everything I could have hoped for in a daughter and I'm so grateful you allowed me to be in your life."

Mac's eyes start to water, and she quickly fans them. "Stop it," she says with a laugh. "Dammit, I'm not crying."

We all laugh, and Gabby places a kiss on her cheek. "See you down there."

And then that leaves two.

Still fanning her face, Mac points at me. "Don't make me cry."

"I won't," I say.

I hold out my arm to her and allow her to loop it through. Together, we head out of the suite and down the stairs.

I stare down at the bouquet wrapped in satin from Cassidy's wedding dress and try to calm my racing heart. There's no use. This day is monumental. This is the day I step aside and allow another man to take care of my girl. That I have to trust that he will do her right. That he will take care of her. Love her. Cherish her the way I have. And I hope I did a good enough job raising her and that she knows how that's supposed to feel.

We make our way downstairs, where Maggie waits by the back door.

"Oh God, look at you," Maggie says. "MacKenzie, you look stunning."

"Thank you."

"Are you ready?"

"Yes," she answers.

"Okay, let me cue the music."

"Hold on," I say to Maggie. "Give me one second."

Maggie nods her head and steps aside.

"Don't do it," Mac says. "Don't make me cry."

I turn to her, my eyes watery. "Raising you has been the greatest honor of my life, MacKenzie." Her eyes water too. "And being Uncle Dad will go down as my greatest accomplishment. Thank you for letting me be that man for you."

Tears stream down her face. "Dad," she says.

"Huh?"

"Not Uncle Dad, just . . . Dad."

Made in the USA
Coppell, TX
08 January 2025

44140749R00252